ST. MARTIN'S

MINOTAUR

Date: 7/21/11

Be the first to hear the latest mystery book news…

With the St. Martin's Minotaur monthly newsletter,
you'll learn about the hottest new Minotaur books,
receive advance excerpts from newly published works,
read exclusive original material from featured mystery
writers, and be able to enter to win free books!

Sign up for the St. Martin's Minotaur newsletter at:

Outstanding Praise for the
Carlotta Carlyle Mysteries by Linda Barnes

"The most refreshing, creative female character to hit mystery fiction since Sue Grafton's Kinsey Millhone . . . The other first ladies of crime better watch their backs."

—*People*

"Her first-person prose is well-honed, and her touch is sure enough to float her fast-paced narrative while still allowing for sharp development of an intriguing cast of characters . . . Best of all, Barnes can turn a phrase well enough to make even Paretsky and Grafton jealous."

—*Houston Chronicle*

"Like the best of the new detectives, V. I. and Kinsey, [Carlotta Carlyle] is a woman of wit and gravity, compassion and toughness, a heroine worth spending time with . . . [Those of us] who yearn for whodunits with character as well wrought as plot, can only thank Linda Barnes."

—Susan Isaacs

COYOTE

"Linda Barnes is once again brilliant. *Coyote* is damned good."

—Robert B. Parker

"Carlotta Carlyle is better than ever and *Coyote* is the perfect vehicle."

—Sue Grafton

"Linda Barnes has another winner in *Coyote* . . . A great, only-in-Boston climax."

—Jeremiah Healy

MORE . . .

DEEP POCKETS

"[There's] plenty to keep a reader chasing after the delightful Carlyle while she chases after the bad guys."

—Entertainment Weekly

"Barnes weaves an intricate web with a pleasingly poisonous spider at its center . . . Barnes makes superb use of the town-grown tensions . . . The twists and turns in this nail-biter are at once startling without ever becoming absurd."

—Publishers Weekly

"With *Deep Pockets,* Barnes locks in her position as one of the foremost practitioners of middle-of-the-road, character-based mystery . . . I suppose I could have put it down. But I didn't want to."

—Orson Scott Card

THE BIG DIG

"Pure pleasure."

—Kirkus Reviews

"A true page-turner . . . Nobody knows Boston like Linda Barnes's red-haired private investigator Carlotta Carlyle . . . Barnes's knack for crisp, snappy dialogue, and devising a mystery that has both timeless and contemporary appeal is a winner."

—Boston Herald

"Barnes grabs the detective genre by the throat but rarely lets style overtake substance. The plot is thick and original and sure to surprise."

—The Washington Times

ALSO BY LINDA BARNES

HARDWARE

A CARLOTTA CARLYLE MYSTERY

Linda Barnes

St. Martin's Paperbacks

HARDWARE

Copyright © 1995 by Linda Appelblatt Barnes.
Excerpt from *Cold Case* copyright © 1997 by Linda Appelblatt Barnes.

ISBN: 0-312-93265-0
EAN: 9780312-93265-7

Printed in the United States of America

Delacorte Press hardcover edition published 1995
Dell Paperbacks edition / March 1996
St. Martin's Paperbacks edition / September 2005

St. Martin's Paperbacks are published by St. Martin's Press, 175 Fifth Avenue, New York, NY 10010.

10 9 8 7 6 5 4 3 2

In loving memory of my uncle, Hal Weiss

"As a father you shall be to me."
"For a little while."

For their expertise in hardware and software of various types, I wish to recognize and thank Dr. Steven Appelblatt, Richard Barnes, Ann Keating, Olin Sibert, and Dr. Amy L. Sims. The reading committee—Richard Barnes, Emily Grace, Susan Linn, James Morrow, and Julie Sibert—a merciless and gracious group, deserves credit and praise.

The T-shirt crew marches on: Denise DeLongis, Beth King, Lawrence Lopez, John Hummel, and Cynthia Mark-Hummel. Keep those cards and letters coming.

Gina Maccoby continues her valiant efforts on Carlotta's behalf. And Carole Baron surely knows the tall redhead couldn't have done it without her.

BlackNet is in the business of buying, selling, trading, and otherwise dealing with *information* in all its many forms.

Our location in physical space is unimportant. Our location in cyberspace is all that matters. Our primary address is the PGP key location: "BlackNet<nowhere@cyberspace.nil>" and we can be contacted (preferably through a chain of anonymous remailers) by encrypting a message to our public key (contained below) and depositing this message in one of the several locations in cyberspace that we monitor.

BlackNet is nominally nonideological, but considers nation-states, export laws, patent laws, national security considerations, and the like to be relics of the pre-cyberspace era.

—Introduction to BlackNet
Downloaded from the Internet
Tue Feb 15 12:38:44 1994

After such knowledge, what forgiveness?

—"Gerontion"
T. S. Eliot, 1917

HARDWARE

ONE

Drey kenen haltn a sod as tsvey zaynen meysim, my grandmother used to say. Translated from the Yiddish: "Three can keep a secret if two of them are corpses." I'm tempted to print it on my business cards.

Every going concern needs a catchy slogan.

The catch here is "going concern." I'm a private investigator. If people kept their secrets to themselves, I'd be out of a job.

If *I* had a secret, the Green & White Cab Company is definitely not the place I'd choose to dump it. Too many shell-like ears, too many clackety-clack tongues. One thing about cabbies, they talk. Especially after working the graveyard shift.

It's something about night driving; it revs, wires,

gives me a rush. By morning I have tales to tell, of weird traffic and wacko fares.

Bars are locked tight at 7 A.M., so I wind up at G&W with the rest of the graveyard jocks, swilling coffee, listening to bad jokes, bitching about meager tips. All of us on a talking-jag high. Maybe a survival high.

It's a fact: More cabbies than cops get killed in the line of duty.

When I first started driving for G&W, working my way through college, Gloria, dispatcher and co-owner, described her drivers as the Geezers and the Wheezers. To put it bluntly, they were old, the last of the Irish-American career cabbies and proud of it. Held no truck with these new immigrants who could hardly speak the mother tongue, God love 'em.

Four Geezers had a poker game going in a dark corner, *all the better to cheat you in, my dear*.

"Make any dough?" Fred Fergus called in a quavery tenor. "Glad to take it off ya, darlin'."

"You can deal your dirty seconds to somebody else," I said with a grin. Only one of the bunch still cabbed. The others seemed to have taken up residence, smoking and choking, enjoying the clubhouse ambiance.

A guy I knew only as Bear, a diminutive soul with an outsize nickname, was giggling and whispering at a pimply youth, outlining obscene curves with both hands. I'd heard his routine before: Sports and tits, sports and tits, sports and tits. Endless variations on a theme.

Beneath a bare lightbulb, a skinny, underemployed Ph.D. named Jerome Fleckman was earnestly discussing free-market economics and the Marxist social dialectic with "Not My Fault" Ralph. Ralph, in tummy-bulging T-shirt and tight pants, had a miles-away expression on his face. Jerry might as well have been chatting with his refrigerator.

"Looking for Sam?" he asked as soon as he saw me.

Green & White's other proprietor, Sam Gianelli, is also my on-again, off-again lover. In many ways he marks a turning point in my life. If he hadn't dumped me to marry "a suitable girl," who knows? I might never have married Cal on the rebound, never have become a cop. I might be a Mafia wife, instead of a divorcée currently sleeping with her first flame, a man as divorced as a Catholic can get, short of annulment.

Everybody asks about Sam. It's irritating, near-strangers knowing my love life.

I said, "You want to grab Ralph's attention, Jer, ask him how he feels about cab leases."

Ralph began whining his signature tune. "Not my fault," he declared.

"Sweatshops on wheels," Jerry said dismissively. Then he got a panicky look in his eyes. "Sam's not planning to switch to leases, is he?"

Anything bad happens at the garage, Sam's behind it. Anything good, it's Saint Gloria.

I could see her behind the phone console, waving a meaty, beckoning arm. The dispatch area has few distractions—a rusty desk, a few cast-off plastic chairs, the kind you might find in a welfare office or an unsuccessful dentist's waiting room. A wheelchair-bound three-hundred-pound black woman wearing a scarlet dress stuck out.

"Relax," I said to Fleckman. "No leases as far as I know."

"Don't drive another shift," he counseled. "You're tired. Bosses, man, they suck your blood."

I find it hard to regard Gloria as a bloodsucking boss.

"Glad to see you, babe," she said, waving a Hostess Twinkie under my nose. "Want to eat?"

Twinkies don't do it for me. I found a lone doughnut in a wrinkled sack.

"This spoken for?"

"Help yourself. Hardly stale."

The phones lit up. She murmured, "Stick around."

I plunked myself into a chair molded to someone else's contours, rose immediately, and ruefully rubbed my backside. Light filtered through the front window. I walked over and lifted the corner of a broken venetian blind. Its slats were thick with dust.

G&W, where I moonlight to afford such luxuries as Fancy Feast cat food and quarterly tax payments, is wedged behind Cambridge Street on an ugly commercial strip in Boston's Allston-Brighton area. Neither Allston nor Brighton is eager to claim it. Understandably so: the exhaust fumes from the nearby Mass. Pike are less than a draw. A huge rug store dominates a nearby corner. There's a food co-op, a cleaning plant, another rug wholesaler, and a restaurant that advertises itself as the pinnacle of casual dining, which means they keep a squadron of large-screen TVs blaring all hours of the day and night.

"Green and White," Gloria sang over the line. "Where are you now, and where do you wanna go?"

She has one of the world's great voices, a deep Gospel-touched melody that speaks to my Motown roots.

I consider G&W an endearing eyesore, a semi-remodeled warehouse resembling a vandalized Taco Bell. Gloria insists the stucco started out white, but turned grit-gray so quickly there was no point swimming against the tide. Busted wooden garage doors—no excuse from Gloria, just a fact of life—add to the general air of dilapidation.

"You think I'm losing weight?" Gloria, off the phone, smoothed the red tent over her massive contours. "You seen Sam lately?"

"No," I said, "and no. In that order."

Gloria sighed. "Diet place my brothers signed me up for this time does packaged meals. Frozen gunk-in-a-box. Supposed to be healthy."

"Huh?" I said, gazing out the window, wondering if the glass was frosted or filthy.

Gloria ordered a Green & White to 700 Comm. Ave. "Careful 'bout those B.U. kids racing across the street," she admonished the driver. "Dummies run smack into traffic."

"I'm talking diet here," she said to me, sticking the handset back in the cradle. "Healthy food."

Gloria's brothers are concerned about her weight. Someone ought to be.

Gloria works full-time and three quarters. She lives in the back room. A hard worker before the auto accident that left her paralyzed from the waist down at nineteen, a hard worker she remains.

She used her insurance settlement to buy into Sam

Gianelli's latest failing business venture. Together they form an unlikely team—African American and Italian, street-raised and Mafia bred—and run one of the few successful small cab companies in town. Dispatching is Gloria's vocation, but by preference and inclination she is an information trader, and what she doesn't know about city politics and the cab scene in particular is not worth knowing. Sam handles the money side. He rarely hangs out at the garage.

Gloria doesn't miss the company; she substitutes food. Bags of Chee tos, boxes of Mallomars. Cold Pop-Tarts. Nothing remotely nutritious crosses her lips. Junk food is her chosen comfort and solace.

"You mentioned Sam," I said, dropping the blind back into place. "Do *you* know where he is?"

"Nope," Gloria said cagily.

"You eat the diet stuff?" I asked. On her desk, within gobbling distance, an enormous jar of Bacon Bits dwarfed a box of double-cream-filled Oreos and a can of ready-made Betty Crocker chocolate frosting. As I watched, spellbound, she dipped an unresisting Oreo into the frosting, coating it liberally.

"Can hardly choke it down," she said, admiring her creation before engulfing it in a single bite.

"You eat *it*—and *only* it—you ought to lose something," I ventured.

"I'm losing patience is what. Eating cardboard lasagna's bad enough, but I won't listen to another 'motivational' tape, and if I have to go to one more crappy seminar, I'm gonna call the Better Business Bureau, close 'em the hell down. These folks have probably killed half a dozen people. You should taste what they call tuna casserole. Bean sprouts in it."

"You don't follow the diet, you don't listen to the tapes, you don't go to the seminars, why are your brothers doing this?"

"Makes 'em feel useful."

Another Oreo smeared with Betty Crocker's best went down the hatch.

"I bring Tootsie Rolls to class, chew 'em in front of the other fat folks. Counselor's gonna toss me out, give the boys their money back."

You'd have to be a first-class fool to quibble over a refund with Gloria's three enormous brothers.

She motioned me closer, lowered her voice to a whisper. "Lee Cochran called an hour before you drove in."

It took me a moment to place the name. "Head of the Small Taxi Association."

"Seemed real eager to talk to you, asked me if you were any good."

"And you told him . . . ?"

"That I wasn't your secretary, thank you very much. He's planning to drop by in half an hour, if you're interested. You want to make tracks, feel free."

"I'm interested," I said.

"You can use my room." Gloria repeated the cookie maneuver, her fingers plump as sausages. "For privacy."

"Thanks," I said.

Lee Cochran . . . As I inhaled chocolate fumes, I pondered. I'd never warmed to Lee. He wouldn't pay me a special visit to collect dues for the organization he'd run as a personal fiefdom for years. A job, perchance. The morning seemed suddenly brighter. I'd rather poke my nose into other people's business than battle Boston traffic any day.

I racked my brain for information concerning Lee. There was a wife somewhere. Kids. Maybe a runaway. Lot of that going around.

I gave up speculation in favor of a stroll. Two more minutes and I'd be cramming Oreos in my mouth, just to keep them safe from Gloria.

Not a lot of space to stretch your legs at Green & White. It's compact, with enough room to park all eight cabs inside as long as you don't intend to open any doors. The two mechanics' bays were occupied, cabs hoisted side by side on hydraulic lifts. The grease boys were sharing a joke in a language I couldn't identify, much less understand.

The narrow passway near the back wall is lined with twelve battered metal lockers that look like they were stolen from my old high school. Full-timers get to claim one, and fasten it with a combination lock if they so desire. Sometimes I crack the combos for practice.

As a part-timer, I don't rate my own locker. I drive when I need cash. I drive when I can't sleep. Considering my P.I. income, sporadic insomnia's a blessing in disguise.

To get to the toilet, you need to walk through locker central. I make every effort to avoid G&W's rest room, stopping at hotels to use their infinitely more attractive facilities. This morning, nature and coffee had caught me off guard.

I ran the locker gauntlet quickly, nervously. A friend

of mine, a cop at the Dudley Street station, had recently been attacked by a rare-in-these-parts brown recluse spider. The venom had ballooned his foot to twice its normal size, turning it purple and black before a specialist recognized the symptoms. The guy almost lost his foot.

If I were a brown recluse spider, I couldn't think of a cozier nest than G&W's back corridor. Except the bathroom itself.

I knocked on the wooden door, got no response, and entered. It's a unisex cesspool. I normally inspect the corners for cockroaches and mice. This time I surveyed the rafters as well. No webs. After spraying the seat with Lysol, I used the toilet, and exited fast, leaving the light on and the door closed. That's protocol. Scares the roaches out of sight, keeps the mice in one place.

I'd forgotten all about brown recluses till I saw the spider scamper across the floor.

I'm no spider stomper. No spider lover, either. We've got a deal: I leave them alone; they leave me alone. But my friend at Dudley Street had described the little so-and-so who'd caused him so much pain: a small brown three-eighths-inch-long sucker with black markings. Much like the critter who'd just scooted by the lockers.

I had a mop in my hand before I consciously thought about it. I couldn't locate the spider and panicked momentarily, feeling itchy. There. It had moved fast, reeling in line, making for the ceiling.

I thought I'd better wait till it hit a hard surface before I whacked it. I watched it rise through the air, and the more I observed it the more innocuous it seemed. I wasn't sure it had black markings at all. It seemed larger than half an inch. I'd decided to smack it with the mop handle after all, for scaring me half to death, when I noticed something more intriguing.

A tiny microphone hanging from the ceiling, where no microphone should have been.

TWO

Lee Cochran approached so silently I almost jumped. I stared quickly at the floor, pretending to brush doughnut crumbs off my sweater.

"Gloria said there was a room where we could talk," he said by way of greeting.

"For privacy," she'd said. *Privacy*.

I said, "Right this way to the executive suite."

A room behind a garage . . . You're probably thinking patched linoleum, bare bulbs, concrete walls. Scratch that image. Entering Gloria's place is like stepping from one planet to another, arriving in a world of glossy paint, fresh flowers, and framed museum prints. The airy space is soundproofed, so the clatter of the cab company stops dead at the door. Remodeled for wheelchair access by her three brothers, it's equipped with every state-of-the-art device for the handicapped, including a system of bars, ropes, and pulleys she can use to haul herself to the bathroom and into and out of bed. Gloria's not big on home health-care workers.

I eyed the ceiling suspiciously. No dangling microphones met my gaze.

"Wow," Lee murmured. I didn't blame him; it's hard to believe a high-tech wonderland exists behind G&W's squalor.

I've known Lee in a vague sort of way since I first started driving. While he examined Gloria's room, I studied him. His face was thinner than I remembered, his nose beakier, but on the whole he'd aged well, trimming down instead of bloating. His features had sharpened. He looked like he always had—steely gray eyes, thin lips, chin marred by an off-center cleft. He was wearing a grubby chocolate-colored sweater, dark slacks of indeterminate hue.

"Maybe we could take a walk," I said, shaken by my recent discovery.

"A walk?" He stared at me incredulously. "Have you been outside lately? I left my coat on top of the radiator, hoping the damned thing might thaw. Wind cuts right through you."

So much for guaranteed privacy. I led him to an alcove with two chairs, one enormous enough to handle Gloria's bulk, both strategically placed near snack tables that could double as writing desks. I glanced at a floor lamp, took a long look at a potted palm, then waved Lee into the larger chair.

He seemed puzzled by my behavior. And why not?

"Thanks for seeing me on such short notice. This is association business," he said, surprising me with his directness. Typically, my clients approach their problems sideways, like crabs.

Good, I thought. He doesn't want me to catch his wife cheating on him, find out if his current lover has AIDS.

"My lawyer recommended you," he went on. "Hector Gold." The name meant nothing to me. "I checked with a couple cops. And Gloria." He smiled, showing tobacco-stained teeth. "I hope you don't mind."

"Not if I passed," I said softly, hoping he'd lower his voice to match. I didn't want to risk losing a perfectly good client. I couldn't very well suggest that we turn on a little mood music.

"You're a driver; that was a factor as well," he said.

I nodded, waited. I can wait quite a spell, having had considerable practice when I was a cop.

"It's about the number of attacks on Boston cabdrivers in the past two months," Lee said.

"Six," I said.

"Six reported," he corrected sharply. "At least three others were never, uh, mentioned to the police."

I kept quiet; either he'd tell me why or I could spell it out for myself. Some cabdrivers don't like to mess with cops. Various reasons.

"Immigration problems," Lee said.

Parole problems, too, I thought.

"Do you have any other, um, engagements?"

"If I take your case, Lee, I'll give it my full attention, but we ought to get something straight from the start."

"What?"

"You can't hire me to protect a thousand cabbies. The police are better at that kind of thing; they have the personnel. Your best bet would be to work through the Hackney Carriage Bureau, try to set up more safety guidelines, get more cab checkpoints. Convince the cops to use decoy drivers."

"You don't understand," Lee Cochran said, banging a clenched fist against his open palm for emphasis. "Cabbies are getting beaten for a reason."

Cabs get hit 'cause they're out there, I thought. Mountains get climbed; cabbies get robbed.

"I want the city to know. I want the mayor and the police chief and every asshole on the street to know," Lee said, cranking himself up to full podium cry.

I wished I'd thought to fetch a glass of water from Gloria's kitchenette. I could have "accidently" left the water running.

"So why come to me?" I asked. "I'm private. Talk to the mayor. Talk to the police chief. Hold a press conference."

If he spoke much louder he wouldn't need to, I thought.

"I want you to catch him in the act," Lee said.

"How about a drink, Lee? Water?"

"Hell, are you listening to me or what?"

"I hear you," I assured him. "If you know who's responsible, go to the police. They'll listen. They'll give you a medal."

"It's political," Lee said, finally lowering his voice. "It's not random street crime like everybody says."

"Political," I repeated.

"It's about medallions," he said. "This whole business is about medallions, and if it doesn't stop soon, somebody's going to get killed."

"Killed over cab medallions?" I fished a notebook out of my handbag. "Try some facts, Lee."

"History lesson," he said, running a hand through his thinning hair. "The number of cabs, the number of medallions, is fixed by law, by act of the state legislature. The 1934 state legislature."

"1934?"

"Right. In 1934, our forefathers decreed there could be fifteen hundred and twenty-five cabs operating within the city limits. That number was reached—stop me if you've heard this before—in 1945."

"So?"

"There've been no new licenses granted since," Lee said.

"Boston has the same number of cabs it had in 1945?"

"Honest to God. No peeps about it either, until '87, when a guy sued the state for restraint of trade, saying he couldn't earn a livelihood because he was a cabdriver who couldn't afford the going rate for a medallion."

"Which is?"

"Which *was* ninety to a hundred grand. You limit the quantity of a thing, the price climbs. Like with original art, you know? Monet painted only a certain number of water lilies, the city of Boston doles out only a certain number of medallions."

"I understand the basic economics, Lee."

"The Department of Public Utilities gets into the ring with this guy, and all the hotel owners and restaurant owners crowd into his corner. The department caves in and says they'll put five hundred more cabs on the street. In three months' time!"

"That must have made medallion owners happy."

"Overnight the price of medallions slides. Seventy-five, heading for seventy and lower. The DPU's gonna issue the new medallions for a token fee. First, it's gonna be a hundred and forty-five bucks, with the new medallions supposedly nontransferable and preference given to experienced Boston cabbies with good driving records."

I grunted and took notes.

"Then the fee shoots up to three ninety-five. And the medallions can be immediately resold. We protested. Held a huge rally, a Taxi Mourning Week. You remember?"

I remembered the protest week. In '87, when the trouble began, I wasn't driving a hack. I had a full-time job as a cop. Other problems.

Lee went on, his lips easing into a smile as he reminisced. "We filed suit and we won. The only new cabs allowed were forty specially equipped handicapped-accessible vans. A victory for small owners, because you know damn well who would have bought up all those new medallions."

As his voice hit top volume, I faked a coughing fit.

"Hang on, Lee, I need a drink," I said, moving before he could jump up and pat me on the back. "Thirsty?"

"You all right?"

"Allergy," I lied.

"Don't you want to know who?" he demanded.

"In a minute. Water okay?"

"You been taking notes? You got everything I said?"

"Sure." The sink's low, like every other appliance in

the place, geared for someone who sits all the time. I ran the water cold, filled two glasses, left both taps roaring like Niagara. Cochran didn't seem to notice.

"Now," I said, handing over a glass. "Who?"

"Who owns the three biggest fleets in town? Phil Yancey, that's who. He's the guy behind the beatings. And I want you to nab him."

"Whoa, Lee," I said. "I've met Mr. Yancey. He's what . . . seventy, seventy-five years old?"

"I don't mean he's doing it himself. He's hiring thugs. He's trying to take over the industry. I figure he's working both sides of the street. First he's got his goons. Then he's got the hotel and tourist associations fronting for him, demanding more medallions, more cabs on the street. We little guys turned them back in '91, but I don't know if we can pull it off again, what with the business jammed with immigrants like it is. They don't exactly vote union; they're too grateful to have a job."

Lee's certainty about Yancey's guilt seemed unreasonable, over the top.

Unless he knew something he wasn't telling me.

Lee kept talking, his arms moving so expansively I was afraid his water glass would hit the floor. "The hotels and restaurants, they want a line of cabs sitting outside their doors all fucking night—you should excuse me. They don't care the economy sucks and cabbies can't earn enough to pay rent. Long as they got fifteen cabs lined up to ferry some Armani-suit guy from the Ritz-Carlton to the Four Seasons, God forbid he should walk a block in the cold."

"Lee," I said slowly, tapping my pen on my notebook. "I don't get the connection between roughing up drivers and getting hold of more medallions. It's a paradox; it doesn't make sense. If the Hackney Bureau issues new medallions, Yancey can grab them by the carload. So why would he get involved with beating drivers? Why take the risk?"

Cochran said, "If I knew all the answers, I wouldn't have to come to you, am I right?" His voice sank to a murmur. "I know this for a fact: Two of the guys who got beaten up on the q.t., they're STA members. Not the kind of guys who run to the cops, understand? These are single medallion owners, independents. They don't want trouble. They were maybe thinking of retiring in a couple years."

"Yeah," I said, impatient for the punch line.

"Suddenly, they're both gonna sell their medallions, and guess who's the only buyer in the market? Guess who's offering top dollar?"

"Yancey?"

"I want you to nail him."

"Have you tried the police?" I said. "Lodged a complaint?"

"What? Fill out a form and wait a hundred years? The man's got to be stopped."

"There's stuff I can do," I said. "Follow him around, ask questions, see if his daily routine, his habits, have suddenly changed, but if he's hiring outsiders to do the dirty work—"

"I gotta tell you how to do your job? Tap his phone. Steal his mail."

"Both illegal, Lee."

He awarded me a withering glance.

"What if it's not Yancey?" I said. "Have you considered the possibility?"

"It's Yancey," he said.

"Since wiretaps and mail tampering are out," I said, "I could start with the robberies. I'd need the names of your two cabbies, the ones who haven't reported the crimes—"

"Oh, no," he said, waggling a finger at me. "You concentrate on Mr. Philip Yancey."

"You can hire me, Lee," I said. "You can't tell me how to run the show."

"When I pay the piper," he said, "I get to call the tune."

"Wrong," I said. "And we haven't talked money yet."

"I can't give you the names of the drivers. I *can* guarantee that Phil Yancey's the guilty party."

I sipped water. *Don't be stubborn, Carlotta*, I silently pleaded with myself. *Take it, say you'll do what he wants, then go your own way.*

When all else fails, lower your standards.

"I'll think about it, Lee," I said. "If I decide to work for you, there's a contract you'll need to sign. And a check, as a retainer."

"Ask around about Yancey," he said. "I'll be in touch."

He shook my hand before exiting via the ramp to the garage. I washed both glasses, left them in the wooden rack to drain. Turned off the raging waterfall. Didn't spot a single mike.

THREE

I hurried back to the garage, my head spinning. Who'd hung the microphone? Why? How long ago?

Everything had changed; nothing had changed. Fleckman was still haranguing "Not My Fault" Ralph, who seemed asleep on his feet, leaning against a wall. A beatific smile on Ralph's face made me wonder which drug he was presently abusing.

"You want to hear more about leases," I murmured, "the grapevine says that Ralphie here had a fling with another cab co., searching for greener pastures."

"Hey," Ralph said. "It wasn't my fault."

Jerome and I exchanged glances.

"It sounded friggin' great," Not My Fault went on. "You pay your money up front, then whatever you make's your own."

"Anybody here speak Hindi?" Gloria's voice

echoed off the cinder-block walls. I don't know how she gets that kind of volume without raising her pitch.

An excited murmur erupted from the mechanics' pit.

Gloria said, "Got a lost cabbie out in Waban. Need somebody to talk him in, but I'm not making it in English."

A grease-spattered man proudly took to the microphone, spoke for an eternity, and then informed us, in triumphantly halting English, that he'd advised his colleague to "head for the rising sun."

"Or the Citgo Sign," somebody chimed in.

"Tell him to stop when he hits the harbor," mumbled one of the Geezers in a rare show of concern.

This is the kind of conversation someone wants to record for posterity? I thought.

"I hear you had a great time leasing," I said to Ralph.

"Some deal," Ralph said. "No health, no bennies, no gas, no repairs. You bring your cab back to the garage three friggin' minutes late, they dock you. The medallion owners rake in their dough, no matter if you have the lousiest night on record. I couldn't make my nut. No way, no how."

"It's an immigrant-eating machine," Jerome said, scowling and crossing his arms over his narrow chest. "Nothing but a legal scam. Six months driving a leased cab, working eight hours before they put a buck in their own pocket, they're back to the shores of whatever godforsaken place they left, grateful to get out alive."

"So why do you drive, Jerry?" I asked with a smile.

"Why do you?"

"Oh," I said, "the lure of the open road. The incredible sense of adventure. My grocery bill."

"Yeah, me too," he said wryly. "And there's always the threat of violence. I really eat that up." Peering nearsightedly from behind wire-rimmed spectacles, he didn't look like an eager fighter.

"It's been crazy out there lately," I said. "On the crime front."

"Yeah," he said noncommitally.

"You know anybody who's been hit?" I asked quietly, hoping to steer the conversation to Lee's unreported assaults.

"Shhh," Jerome said. "You'll bring the evil eye."

"Keyn eyn-ore zol nit zayn!" I muttered automatically, spitting quickly over my left shoulder. Habits die hard.

"A *landsman*?" Jerome said, raising an eyebrow in surprise. "With that hair?"

"So you're not researching a scholarly article?" I asked as if there'd been no evil-eye interruption. I rarely respond to comments about religion, hair, or height: I'm half-Jewish; it's red; I'm tall.

"Think I could find a topic here at the garage?" Jerome asked.

"Hell, half a dozen," I said.

"Carlotta?"

Sam's voice, unmistakable. I was disturbed to discover that he'd approached without my sensing his presence, smelling his aftershave, feeling a jolt of electricity pulse through my veins.

"Be seeing you." Jerome backed off quickly. "Drive carefully."

"Gloria said I'd find you." Was it me, or did Sam's tone sound lazy and self-satisfied? The master's voice.

"And where've you been?" My words came out sharper than intended.

He was so close I could feel his breath on my hair. I didn't need to turn. I have Sam memorized from his unruly dark curls to the soles of his feet. All the good parts in between too.

He said, "You drove graveyard?" Resting his big hands on my shoulders, he started massaging the stiffness away with practiced fingers.

"That bother you?" I craned my neck, arching it slowly left and right. God, it felt good; the man knew where to rub.

He stayed silent for a beat. "Gloria wants to know if the fan belt's okay on three twenty-one."

"You've been demoted to errand boy?"

"Yeah," he said.

"That's a shame. You could make big bucks in massage. Work your way up to personal trainer."

"For you, anytime," he said.

I turned and faced him. Almost asked point-blank about the microphone. I couldn't see one from where we stood. Which didn't mean beans.

I'd call him tonight. Sure. If the garage was miked, his phone could be bugged.

Shit. I thought about taking his hand, pointing out the hanging mike. I considered the curious hordes who might observe us, decided against it.

Sam doesn't dress up for trips to the garage. Jeans and a navy sweatshirt, nothing fancier than cabbie garb. But you'd never mistake him for a cabbie. It's the little things: the shoes, the haircut, the posture.

You'd never peg him as Mafia, either. Honestly,

around here those guys wrap themselves in enough gold jewelry to sink a galleon. Like they've seen too many Hollywood movies. Sam didn't even wear a ring when he was married.

"Sam," I said, keeping my voice low, "Lee Cochran, from the Small Taxi Association, just tried to hire me. You have anything to do with that?"

"No."

"You didn't put him up to it, to keep me from driving nights?"

"Scout's honor."

"As if you were ever a Boy Scout. Does Lee have any history with Phil Yancey?"

"Just that they hate each other's guts," Sam said. "I was a Girl Scout."

"Cut it out. Do you know why they don't get along?"

"Carlotta, you could hold a Phil Yancey Admiration Day at Fenway Park and bring back Carl Yastrzemski to play left field and nobody would come."

"Nobody?"

"Nobody who knew Phil. That's how popular the man is. Why do you want to know?"

"Can't say."

"Well, if you ever consider going to work for Yancey, get the check in advance, and cash it before you lift a finger."

"Yancey's not hiring," I said. "I'm not sure I'm taking any case. So could you forget we had this little talk?"

"What talk?" Sam said obligingly. "Let's go tell Gloria I found you. She seemed to think you were pissed at me."

"Just because I never see you."

"You could stay home nights."

"If I had a reason, I might," I said. "I'm not staying home in case you decide to drop by for a quickie."

He wiped imaginary sweat from his brow. "I'm glad Gloria was wrong. Angry? You?"

"Sam," I said. "Grow up."

Gloria grinned when she saw us. She's convinced this "marriage" can be saved, and she's the one to do it.

"Fan belt?" she asked.

"Lousy, like the rest of them."

"Three twenty-one's got inspection next week. Don't you check the schedule?"

"It'll never pass."

"Leroy'll make it purr like a pussycat," she insisted.

"Only if he sticks one in the carburetor."

"Sam's gonna get me a computer," Gloria announced, deftly changing the subject. "He tell you? We're on our way to high-tech city."

"No kidding," I said, thinking about the microphones.

"Well, you don't have to get sarcastic," Sam said.

"No, really, I'm interested. Believe me. What kind? Where? I've been looking—"

Gloria interrupted, sotto voce. "He's got a friend, gonna give us the deal of a lifetime."

Sam leaped on the bandwagon. "It's ridiculous, running this place without a computer. Gloria can link up with my PC, and I won't have to keep racing around with trip sheets and insurance forms and medallion renewals. We can keep a client list on file. No more address mix-ups—"

"How about me?" I said. "Can your friend do something for me?"

"What?"

"I'm looking to get on-line."

"No," Sam said immediately.

"What do you mean 'no'?"

He pressed his lips together. "Let me think about it."

"What's to think about, Sam? Your friend deals in stolen merchandise?"

"No."

"Then why?"

"Let me get back to you."

"When?" I said. "Seriously, Sam, who's your friend?"

"Nobody you know."

"Sam, come on."

"Really, Carlotta, he's not somebody who can help you."

"You don't even know what I want, Sam."

"Carlotta, you *don't* want to do business with this guy."

"But I do?" Gloria said, her eyes narrowing.

Sam said, "How do I get into this shit? Why do you need a computer, Carlotta?"

"Business," I said. "Same as you. Maybe I could explain it better to your friend."

"Dammit," he muttered under his breath.

I sat in one of the uncomfortable plastic chairs, swinging my foot, waiting.

"Okay," he said finally. "When do you want to go?"

"Now would be nice."

"The guy sleeps in," Sam said.

"Tomorrow, then," I said. "I'm free tomorrow."

"Tomorrow night?" he asked. "That way, maybe we could—"

"Daytime," I said.

"You're busy Saturday night?"

"Maybe," I said.

"Daytime," he agreed angrily. And pivoted on the heel of one expensive loafer, and walked out.

Gloria sent two cabs to opposite sides of the city, glaring at me all the while.

"Carlotta," she scolded, "how come you're always making him so goddamn mad?"

"I don't know, Gloria. Why don't you ever ask how come he makes me so goddamn mad?"

Or why he doesn't invite me out to breakfast? Or back to his place for a quickie?

"Can somebody help me with this fan belt?" came a pitiful bleat from the grease pit.

"Sure," I said. "I'm in the mood."

Half an hour later I was back in the bathroom, using liquid Borax in an attempt to scour the oil and grit off my hands without removing skin. I'd located four hidden microphones without half trying.

Like mice and cockroaches, there's never just one.

FOUR

Saturday mornings, 8 A.M.—rain, shine, snow, sleet—I can be found at the Cambridge YWCA, playing killer volleyball for the Y-Birds on the old wooden gym floor.

Fourth game of the match, we were up eleven-ten on the Boston Y. Boston-Cambridge is a traditional rivalry, always taken seriously. The first two games, both close, had split evenly: one apiece. We'd stolen the third so easily I suspected our opponents were playing possum, taking a breather, preparing to mangle us.

So far, so good.

We took possession after a long volley when one of their setters mis-hit and sent the ball spinning out of bounds.

Rotate.

Loretta, who is far from my best friend on the team, leaned close as I bounced the ball on the service line.

" 'The score stood two to four,' " she recited, hand over heart, " 'with but one inning left to play—' "

"Shut up," I said firmly. I know I'm not the world's best server. Rarely an ace from me. Whenever I go for broke, I skim it low and whack the net.

Movement in the bleachers caught my eye. The ball cleared the net with two inches to spare. A short woman with a raggedy blond ponytail called for it and squatted into a terrific dig. Their middle blocker had half a foot on ours. No contest at the net. No point. Their ball.

Damn.

Net is where I live. I'm an outside hitter. Next rotation I could do what I do best: jump high and smash low.

For the moment I settled into the back-row game. The rhythm was pretty basic: dig, set, spike, over. Dig, set, spike, again. Some games have a funkier beat, a skyhigh setup or a floor dive breaking the tempo. During long volleys I tend to hear song lyrics in my head. Blues or driving rock. I'd been moving to "Have a Heart," with Bonnie Raitt doing that hoarse Janis Joplin moan on the high notes, for most of the match.

I must have shifted to "Ain't Gonna Be Your Sugar Momma No More" about the same time I realized the movement in the stands was Sam Gianelli, taking a seat next to my Little Sister, Paolina, my one-girl personal cheering squad.

Everybody knows where to find me Saturday mornings.

Paolina grinned up at Sam, and I felt tension melt between my shoulder blades. Paolina's not a blood relation. She's my Little Sister from the Big Sisters organization, my chosen sister, my meant-to-be sister.

I wondered if Sam knew how rare Paolina's once-plentiful smiles had become. I hoped so, hoped he fully appreciated it.

Up till fifteen months ago, Paolina considered herself one of four kids fathered by Jimmy Fuentes, a lively Puerto Rican rover. The truth, uncovered by accident, hit her hard. She's a half sister to her small brothers, sired by a different father, a Colombian, like her mother. A member of one of Bogotá's finest old families, a leftist guerrilla by some accounts, a drug lord by most. A man I'd dealt with over the phone. A man currently sending bundles of dubiously earned cash to my home.

My very own chance to do time in a federal pen for income-tax evasion. Maybe they'd have a good volleyball squad.

I wondered if I'd subconsciously noticed Sam while still at the service line, switched tunes to suit him. Not that I'm anybody's sugar momma in the financial sense. Sam would be more of a sugar daddy if I let him, but I'm not happy about where his money comes from. Most of the time we go dutch.

Hypocrite, I scolded myself, almost missing an easy setup. You accept money from Paolina's father, tons of money, and balk at letting Sam foot the bill for Chinese food!

His head was bent low, close to Paolina's. They spoke softly, using hand gestures for emphasis. It seemed an animated discussion, almost a heated one.

I tried to focus on the game, but once the topic rears its ugly head, it's hard to stop thinking about thirty-five thousand in cash. Thirty-five with three zeroes. And more to come. And what the hell to do with it.

When I'd promised Paolina's father I'd use the money for her education, I hadn't expected so much so soon.

The Boston Y's server, thinking I might be napping, fired one at me. I dug it out, gave her a look.

Maybe with the shooting death—call it legalized murder, assassination, fair fight, what you will—of the legendary Pablo Escobar, Señor Carlos Roldan Gonzales, the new alleged number-one gun in the Medellín cartel, now felt a certain urgency to provide for the daughter he'd never acknowledged, except to me, her Big Sister.

The stacked and banded greenbacks, currently stuffed inside the tumbling mats in my tenant's third-floor digs, haunted me. What was I going to do with all that cash? Roz knew about it. She's honest. Say what you will about her—and you can say plenty, starting with her raunchy wardrobe and working your way toward her postpunk artwork—she's honest.

Sam, with his Mafia-underboss father, had probably learned money laundering at Papa's knee. Sam would know!

The ball came whizzing by my left elbow and hit the floor. A clean kill.

"Can't play while the boyfriend's here?" Loretta snapped. "Get with it, Carlyle!"

Goddammit, I felt like responding, it's not sex. It's money.

I sucked in a deep breath and let the outside worries

fly: Paolina, Sam, the cash, the bugs, the future. Concentrated on playing the point, playing each point as it came. Glued my eyes to that white sphere. Rotate. Front line. Up against the giant middle blocker.

We made guarded eye contact across the net. Her towering hair, an arrangement of braided and beaded tails, made her seem exotic and enormous. Minus the do, she was still three inches taller than I, and I'm six one. I pushed damp hair off my forehead.

She thought she could tip it over me. I read it in her eyes, in her stance. If I'd realized it was game point, I might have let it sail. I trust my back line. Damn good diggers and setters all. I'd lost count. I thought we were midgame, that a rush might put the Bostons off guard the way a net-charging tennis player spooks a baseline opponent. So I leaped with everything I had, movement before thought, my arm swinging, circling 360°, gathering speed, my fist tightening all the way. I caught the ball on the flat of my knuckles, reversed the arch of my back in midair. The ball crossed the net, angling straight down, crushed the floor, and bounced so high it almost took out a lightbulb.

Pandemonium. Game and match!

"Show-off!" Kristy, our captain, screamed in my ear.

"Shit, Carlyle, I thought you were asleep," Loretta sang.

It was good-natured, so I let it ride, along with the glare from the woman across the net. We slapped hands and retreated to the locker room, where we kept our crowing to a minimum. The Y doesn't run to separate quarters for winners and losers. It barely runs to hot showers.

"Dunkin' Donuts," Kristy announced. "Carlotta's treat."

"If I'd known it was game point, I'd have let you take it," I protested.

"Sure," she said, lifting a thumb to her nose. "Nyah-nyah. Show-off always pays."

I felt a tug at my waistband.

"Hey," I said, looking down at one of my favorite faces. Paolina's chocolate eyes sparkled with excitement.

"*Felicitaciónes*," my Little Sister said. "*Muy bueno.*"

"*Gracias,*" I answered, leaning down to give her a hug. We'd agreed to speak Spanish as much as possible, given my lousy command of the language, ever since her mom declared Paolina in danger of losing her Colombian heritage due to my gringa influence.

"Can you come outside?" Paolina whispered.

"Soon as I'm dressed, hon."

"*Ahora mismo.*"

"*¿Por qué?*"

"Sam," she said, forgetting to whisper. "He's really gotta talk to you."

Catcalls all around.

"He can't wait for it, babe," Loretta shouted. "Sweat turns the man on."

Paolina looked uncomfortable. At twelve years old, she's streetwise in some ways, painfully shy in others. Sam wouldn't have sent her to fetch me unless he had good reason. Our computer appointment wasn't for hours. He wouldn't sit through a game to admire my spiking prowess.

Shorts, kneepads, elbow pads still on, I hauled my soaked T-shirt back over my head, wrapped a towel around my dripping hair. Barefoot, I stepped toward the door.

"She comes when he calls," somebody hooted.

"Does she call when he comes?" came the inevitable response.

"Mind shutting up?" I replied, placing a firm hand on Paolina's shoulder and guiding her back to the gym.

"What's in the bag?" I asked to break the silence. I already knew; the Brighams logo was a giveaway.

"Jelly beans," she answered with a conspiratorial grin. "Half a pound. No licorice."

"Sam likes you," I said.

"Want some?"

"Maybe later."

She gazed at me with solemn eyes. "Should I have told him to wait? Did I do something wrong?"

Paolina sniffs out disapproval like a bloodhound. Gets so much at home she expects it everywhere else.

"You did exactly right," I said. "Is that what you and Sam were talking about? Whether you should come and get me?"

"No." She clamped her mouth into a thin line and turned away. Demanding the substance of the conversation would have been futile. She didn't intend to tell me, and if she doesn't want to reveal information, she'll refuse outright or lie convincingly.

She's twelve; she's not a baby, I reminded myself. Somewhere along the path, recently, she'd lost the gift of openness. Part of growing up, part of separating herself from me.

"Can I stay?" she asked tentatively.

"Practice your serve, okay?" There's a mother-daughter volleyball squad at Paolina's school. I'm allowed to play in exchange for a little coaching and a written permission slip from Paolina's mother.

Sam was seated on a bench, hands clasped, staring straight ahead, feet eighteen inches apart, weight evenly distributed. Relaxed, at first glance; tense, ready to move, on close inspection.

In full business regalia, he seemed out of place. Crisp white shirt, yellow power tie. Vested pin-striped navy suit. His black wing tips had the soft deep shine cheap cop shoes never acquire. A squat lawyerly briefcase occupied the floor beside him. I'd never seen him carry a briefcase.

"Go get the ball," I said to Paolina, ruffling her dark hair.

"What's so important it can't wait till I shower?" I asked.

Sam emerged from his reverie. "Good game. Good point."

"Thanks."

"Sorry," he said. "I just dropped by to tell you: no computer today."

"Why not?"

"I have to take a quick trip."

"I could go by myself," I suggested. "Give me the address—"

"No," he said.

"When'll you be back?"

"Tomorrow."

"Can't postpone one lousy day?"

"Nope."

"Family stuff?"

"No way. Not family." It came out vehemently, like the answer to the wrong question.

"Okay. No big deal."

"Can we make another date?"

"To pick out a computer?" I said. "Soon as possible." I peeled off my right kneepad, started on the left.

"For a *date*," he said.

"Sure. I'm easy." Most of our evenings do not involve "dates." They involve take-out food and bed.

"Could you do me a favor while I'm gone?" Sam stared at his wing tips.

I plunked both kneepads down on the bench, removed my left elbow pad.

"What?" I had a vision of him pulling wads of cash from the briefcase, asking me to hide them. Long as I was in the business.

"Don't drive the night shift," he said.

I sat on the bench, towel-drying my hair, leaning over and rubbing vigorously so Sam couldn't see my face.

Don't go computer shopping till I get back. Don't drive while I'm gone. The man was starting to sound like my mother, not my lover.

"I'm gonna die of sweat, I don't get in the shower," I said. "Probably nothing but ice water left by now."

He stood.

"Be careful," he said.

"Sam, things happen. Plane crashes. Hurricanes. Kids get hit by ice-cream trucks."

"So throw yourself in the path and avoid the uncertainty."

"If I want to drive, I'll drive," I said.

"Great," Sam said. "And a special thanks for mentioning plane crashes."

He started to walk away.

"Sam," I said. "I need to ask you something."

He turned. "Sounds serious."

"It is. There are bugs at G and W. And I don't mean the crawly kind."

"Jesus, you didn't touch any of the mikes, did you?" Of all the things he could have said, that was the one I'd least expected.

"*You know about them?* What the hell kind of a way is that to run a business? Does Gloria know?"

"Carlotta, you don't understand," he said. "Promise me you won't say anything to anybody. I'll explain when I get back."

"I don't see how."

"I'm late, Carlotta. I don't have two minutes for this, let alone an hour."

He stalked off without a farewell, much less a kiss.

I watched Paolina toss and serve, a frown line creasing her smooth forehead. She's got a decent underhand, but she wants to serve the way I do. Even though I've told her I'm no role model in the service department. No role model in the man-woman relationship department either.

I showered quickly, spent eleven bucks and change on doughnuts for hungry teammates, vowing to keep better track of the score from now on.

When I got home, Phil Yancey was waiting on my front porch.

FIVE

The old man gripped a walking stick. His crinkled, long-nosed face was familiar from photos in the *Hackney Carriage News*, a publication I subscribe to in order to learn what conventions are currently invading which Boston hotels. Conventioneers make good tippers.

"About time. I've been waiting long enough," he said. The accent was pure Brooklyn, jarring.

A black Lincoln Town Car lingered at the curb. If he'd chosen to loiter on my porch, that was his business.

"Most of my clients make appointments," I said pointedly.

In defiance of Massachusetts law, the car's windows were so deeply tinted I couldn't tell if it held any passengers.

"Would you happen to be the lady investigator Lee Cochran's been shooting his mouth off to?"

"No comment," I said, digging in my handbag for keys.

"You don't have to ask me in," he said.

"I wasn't planning on it."

"It might not look right to your neighbors, old coot like me and a sweet young thing like you, huh?" He was making a labored noise, his thin shoulders shaking underneath his dark jacket. *Sniggering* is the only word I can use to describe it. He found the situation so humorous that his dyed-pink carnation— my least favorite blossom—almost shook right off his lapel. I was surprised it hadn't wilted from his cigar breath.

"You must be the original trust-fund kid, huh, living this close to Harvard?" he said. "Cambridge, what a wimp of a town."

"Feel free to leave," I said.

"First, I want to talk about Lee Cochran."

"Lee Cochran," I repeated.

"Small Taxi Association."

"Oh," I said.

"See, it all comes back. You know who I mean."

"I've met him," I confessed.

"Somebody phoned, said he's been spreading lies about me—"

"Did you recognize the voice?" I asked. "The person who called?"

"Man tells me—"

"You sure it was a man?" I asked.

"Quit with the interrupting! I said a man, a low voice, hell, these days who knows? Some guy tells me this rumormonger's been wagging his tongue in your direction. I figured I might as well drop by and set you straight."

"Don't think I don't appreciate it, but I have things to do."

"They'll wait till I've had my say." Phil Yancey banged his walking stick on the granite. It missed my toe by half an inch. He didn't walk or stand like he needed a cane. Probably used it to whack dogs that crossed his path. Or old ladies.

"Lee's a small-timer, and he always will be," Yancey sneered. His glance said he numbered me among the small-timers of the world as well.

"Since you're here," I said, "maybe you *can* clear the air."

"What did he tell you?" Phil Yancey insisted. "I'll get the bastard for slander."

"Not on my say-so, Mr. Yancey . . . isn't it? My name is Carlyle. Ms. Carlyle."

"What did he say about me?"

"Ask him," I suggested.

"Lee's got a bee in his bonnet about medallions, gets hot under the collar. I don't need his rabble-rousing when the Hackney Bureau's finally getting off its ass. Ever since the Hynes Auditorium got itself built, and with the new Prudential Center linking the four big hotels, this city's got life in the convention market. They're not going to blow it with no cabs to pick up convention goers. You'll see. New medallions within the year!"

"Are you interested in acquiring more medallions?" I asked.

"You got one to sell?"

"Hypothetically?"

"What, you're a lawyer, you get to use words like that? Let's say I might do you a favor at a price. *If* you had a medallion for sale. I think they're good investments."

"Even if new ones come out within the year?"

Yancey sniggered again. "You never know, do you?"

I said, "Now, if you'd get off my porch—"

"I know a lot of important people, young lady. It would be wise to listen when I talk."

"Make an appointment," I said.

One of the big Lincoln's doors yawned. I had my key in hand. Quickly I worked it into the lock, yanked open my door, slipped inside, and flipped the bolt behind me.

I stood for a moment with my back against the door, listening to the old man's retreating footsteps. So that was the famous Phil Yancey. I felt like taking another shower.

SIX

"So," I said to Sam, who'd finally turned up after four days instead of the promised one. "How'd you like to hire me to find out who's bugging Green and White? I'm available, but it could be a limited-time offer."

Lee Cochran hadn't gotten in touch; I was starting to wonder if he would.

"Carlotta, listen carefully, I *know* who's bugging Green and White."

"You do," I said.

"I do. Same folks who bugged the Angiulo brothers in the North End. Same folks who've been trying to listen in on my family for generations. The Organized Crime Task Force."

"But you're not involved with—"

"My name's Gianelli; that's all they need. Look, Carlotta, I've known about the mikes for a month. I had them checked out. By experts. Organized Crime's the only outfit who uses ten-year-old FBI-issue equipment. I know the score; I don't mess with it. If I did, they'd think I had action going down at the garage. Or worse, they'd get up-to-date bugs, and I wouldn't know where the hell they were hidden."

"What about your constitutional right to privacy?" I said.

"What about it?"

"Your cabbies talk."

"Carlotta, you didn't touch any of the mikes, did you? I have your word on that?"

"Absolutely," I said. I hadn't touched a single one. I'd photographed them, sent the film to a woman I know who works at the FBI lab in Quantico, Virginia.

Sam said, "The Organized Crime Task Force is not interested in what my cabbies have to say, Carlotta."

"Okay," I said. "I concede your point."

"Can I get that on tape?"

"What I oppose is this togetherness routine on the computer deal. Since the salesman's a buddy of yours, I think it will definitely put a crimp in my bargaining style."

"Great," Sam said. "Then we won't go."

"I *want* to go," I said. "Alone."

"My friend lives in a slime pit. Lone females are prey."

"When I drive, I don't pick and choose neighborhoods," I said curtly, lifting a handful of hair off the nape of my neck and wondering how long it had been since I'd had it trimmed.

"But this time you'll be carrying cash," Sam said.

I bit my lip, brought up short by such a reasonable protest. I glowered out the bow window. My hostile gaze didn't alter the weather. November in Cambridge. Bleak as Melville. Whoever decided winter didn't begin till the December solstice must have lived to the south. Chill gray drizzle smacked the windowpanes.

"Sam," I said, clapping my hand to my mouth in consternation. "Your apartment. Your bedroom! Are they bugged?"

"Relax," he said. "I have my place swept once a month."

"Good for you," I said fervently.

"Of course, I videotape everything," he said.

"Dammit, Sam. This computer stuff, I'd do better by myself."

"Sure you would," Sam agreed, his voice infuriatingly cheerful. "Read about you in tomorrow's papers."

"I guess that's how you learn about a lot of your pals," I snapped. The second I said it, I wished I hadn't.

As the son of a ranking mafioso, Sam might actually need to check the news each morning to stay up-to-date on his infamous family, if not his friends. Who'd gotten shot, who'd been imprisoned, who was up before a grand jury, who'd taken the Fifth . . .

Sam's surname guarantees instant restaurant reservations in the North End. I understand other perks are available. I understand that Sam has chosen not to exercise them.

The Organized Crime Task Force evidently doesn't agree with me.

"You sure three hundred will be enough?" I asked into the dropped-brick silence.

"He may not take it," Sam said after a long pause. "He's a little offbeat. Eccentric. He might not answer the door unless I'm with you."

"Scared of women?"

"Just . . . a little weird," Sam said, easing up from behind and wrapping his arms around me. I leaned into his sweater, its texture rough against my cheek. "Look, here's how I see the situation," he murmured in my ear. "You want a computer. I can introduce you to a friend who has computers for sale. The deal is you have to let me come along. If that's too much to ask, then go retail. Spend a thousand bucks on your hot new toy."

"I don't need the latest thing," I protested. "I could put an ad in the paper—"

"Why'd you ask me to set this up? Why do you hate it so much when I can do you a favor?" He paused for a minute, then continued slowly, "Maybe you should ask your shrink friend."

Aha, I thought. Oh-ho.

"It's not like I've seen you that much lately, Sam," I said carefully, staring out the window like I could see something other than our wavery reflections.

"I've been out of town."

I breathed on the window and traced a five-pointed star in the fog. "Out of town. I like it. It's so specific."

"Washington. And I made a detour on the way back. My uncle's sick. In Providence."

"A sick uncle," I said, hand to heart. "I don't think I've heard that one before."

"Come on," he said impatiently.

"My shrink friend do anything to bother you?" I asked.

"Guy's always hanging around the house."

"He lives two doors down. He brought me a client a while back."

"Excuse me. I thought he lived closer."

I wondered if Sam had seen Keith Donovan departing in the wee hours, or maybe in full morning light.

"I don't believe this," I murmured, resting my forehead against the icy windowpane. "The guy happens to be 'seeing'—as in 'screwing'—Roz, my femme-fatale tenant."

Roz is, in her fashion, a femme fatale. She is undoubtably my tenant. She is also my housekeeper, my sometime assistant, my unlikeliest friend, and the owner of the most complete and bizarre T-shirt collection on planet Earth. She has the body for it.

"Oh" was all Sam said, his unblinking eyes widening with disbelief. And instead of swelling with righteous indignation, I felt guilty, not because I'd slept with Keith Donovan but because I kept considering it. Entertaining the possibility. Fantasizing, if you will.

Things keep up like this, I might as well marry Sam. Get it over with. Then I can commit proper infidelity, and we can have the whole business legally cancelled. Sam's father would absolutely insist on an annulment this time. Signed by the Pope, no less.

"You having my house watched, Sam?" I asked.

"I keep running into him, is all."

"Nervous" is not a word I usually associate with Sam. He's broad shouldered, six four, a big man. I'm attracted to tall men, since I like to argue nose to nose, but most of my attachments have been to skinny, wiry guys. Sam's the mesomorph exception to the rule. I watched him pace my living room restlessly, cracking his knuckles, straightening the cushion on my late aunt's rocking chair, staring at his watch every ten seconds, and generally behaving like my ex-husband coming down from a three-day cocaine binge.

"Sam," I said, "you know you don't need to come along to translate computer talk for me. I've done my homework. I'm not dumb."

"And dumb was what attracted me in the first place," he said, staring at me earnestly. "That, and your tiny little feet."

"Okay, okay," I said grumpily. "How much do you know about this guy we're going to visit?"

"Frank," he said.

"Frank who?"

"Just Frank," Sam said.

"This Frank with no last name, how do you know he'll have what I need?"

Sam shrugged. "He will."

I sucked in a deep breath and grabbed my handbag, locking up carefully, taking time to find the big Medeco key and turn the dead bolt. My thoroughness seemed to increase Sam's irritation, and I found myself slowing to a near crawl.

When I was a kid, I couldn't understand why my parents kept the air jangling with their disagreements. Now, seems like I'm in proximity to a man long enough, I feel that old electric current in the breeze.

I used to wonder why my parents got divorced, why they couldn't make the damn marriage work for my sake, because they loved me. Now I wonder how anyone sticks it. The years of grating on each other wear you down or drive you nuts. Marriage. What a choice, what a bargain.

My mother worried I'd never wed. Too uncompromising. Too hard to get along with. Too tall. She'd have been shocked when I strolled the aisle at a tender nineteen.

I think I married Cal to provide my dad the opportunity to give the bride away. God knows I didn't grant him many other causes for rejoicing.

Mom wouldn't have been shocked when we split. By then Dad was dead too. I guess I didn't need to impress him anymore.

I sneaked a sideways glance at Sam. So hard to make your father proud of you. And I wasn't a son. And my dad was no Gianelli, just a Detroit cop.

Each of the Gianelli boys had taken a run at making Papa proud: Gil "making his bones" by murdering a rival mobster at an age when most kids are working up the nerve to ask a cheerleader to the prom; Mitchell, unfit for the armed-services career chosen for him in the cradle—weak eyes, I'd heard—had studied accounting at Papa's request, so there'd be a family watch on the money, even though Mitch wasn't particularly interested, said it made his vision worse; Anthony, aka Tony Playboy, had made the leap effortlessly—named for, looking, sounding, and acting just like the old man.

Sam, the youngest by far, had tried his hand at killing, too, cloaking it in the legality of Vietnam, returning with a Purple Heart and a sour taste in his mouth. Gave up on pleasing Papa, sent the Purple

Heart back to D.C. as an alternative to flushing it down the toilet.

The two of us waded into the mush. My size-eleven boots had fended off last winter's glop triumphantly waterproof. The guarantee must have read "one year only." I wriggled my toes into tight balls inside squishy socks.

"New car?" I asked Sam, lifting an eyebrow.

Sam likes cars. Usually owns two or three, and I don't ask questions, since any one of them could be a gift from Papa and I have a thing about loan-sharking and prostitution, activities in which Papa Gianelli has long reigned supreme. During the past year I've driven with Sam in his Lincoln Continental, his Acura Legend, his aging, elegant Porsche. . . .

He stood beside a rusted-out Chevy Nova, dangling the keys. Wrenching the passenger door open, he beckoned me inside.

"It's a loaner," he said.

"And you must be the garage's most valued customer," I replied, deadpan. "Let's take my car instead."

"This car's what we want," he said.

"Is it hot?"

"Stolen?"

"As in borrowed without consent of the owner."

"You have a vivid imagination, Carlotta."

"And tiny feet."

The Nova's interior smelled of stale beer and cigar butts. I cranked open a balky window. Just a slit at the top, big enough to admit fresh air and mush flakes.

I hate to be chauffeured. I never relax with someone

else at the wheel. My body automatically assumes brake-pedal access. I struggled to keep my right foot still.

"What, no blindfold?" I asked sarcastically.

"Frank would have liked that," Sam admitted. "A midnight visit. A blindfold. Late-night e-mail bounced off a chain of anonymous remailers."

"Will I be able to call this Frank guy later, if I have questions?"

"Unlisted phone. You can call me."

I stared at the dashboard. AM radio only. I flipped the dial to 1120, WADN, raised static and Les Sampou, singing "Chinatown."

"Sam, have you heard of anything odd going down in the medallion market?"

"Odd?" he said.

"Could you just answer the question?"

"Business as usual," he said. "Far as I know. Which means bad, but not as bad as New York. Tense. It'll get worse here if everybody changes over to leasing."

"Explain," I said.

"Me and Gloria, we run a small business. The drivers earn a percentage of their daily receipts. We cover partial health, gas, repairs. Vacations. Leasing's a whole other animal. Management companies rent medallions from small investors—you know, doctors, the guys with extra cash who used to put their dough into fancy boutiques and restaurants that failed in two months—and then they lease 'em to drivers."

"How?"

"Through the big garages."

Like Phil Yancey's, I thought.

"Driver pays in advance," Sam went on, "maybe a hundred bucks for a decent shift. No unemployment. No Social Security. The cabbie has a bad shift, does under a hundred, tough. The medallion owner's got his. The management company's got theirs."

"So a shift to leasing would drive up the cost of medallions," I said slowly.

"Right. Because the medallion owner's income is guaranteed, a sure thing."

"You think this is a good time to buy medallions?" I asked.

Sam shrugged. "It's like the stock market, Carlotta. Maybe it'll go one way, maybe another. Hackney Carriage Bureau could outlaw leasing tomorrow, or they could put another two hundred medallions on the street, drive the price down."

"Sounds more like roulette," I said. Possibly a game with a fixed wheel, so Yancey'd win either way. If he was planning to take a big plunge into leasing, every medallion he got his hands on might turn to gold.

Maybe I'd been wrong. Maybe Yancey could be the bogeyman in both of Cochran's scenarios. What could I do about it with no client? *Why hadn't I heard from Cochran?* Had Yancey threatened him? Scared him off?

"Keep your money in your mattress," Sam advised, blissfully unaware that his remark was close to the truth.

"Thanks," I said.

"You're welcome."

I tried to wiggle myself comfortable in the passenger seat. No deal. It was worse than one of Gloria's old Fords.

"So who the hell is Frank?" I asked.

"An old friend."

"All the years I've known you, Sam, you never mention any Frank till five, six days ago. It's late to spring an old buddy on me."

"Frank and I go way back."

"Yeah?"

"Grammar school."

"Catholic?"

"Yes, ma'am. Except we said 'Yes, Sister Xavier Marie.' And she whacked us with a yardstick if we gave her any lip. Right across the butt."

"Turning you into the pervert you are today," I said sweetly.

"Yeah, old Sister Xavier Marie. Thank God for her."

While we spoke, he was driving a twisty, turning path, but he couldn't fool me. Ever since Sam gave me my first cabbie job, I've been navigating Boston's back roads. Few areas of the city retain their secrets.

Mattapan holds more than most.

Mattapan used to be quiet, peaceful, almost like a suburb, I've heard, before 1968, when, so the story goes, the Boston City Council decided on the quiet to integrate it, and the realty agents colluded to drive down prices. Between redlining and blockbusting, parts of Mattapan are now what people mean when they lock the doors, shudder, and invoke the term *inner city*.

The closest most whites get to Mattapan is the Franklin Park Zoo, a mile or so away, and most suburbanites are scared to go there.

Cabbies go everyplace, by law. You can refuse a fare and risk getting suspended by the Hackney Bureau, or you can beg your dispatcher to send a more fearless cabbie to pilot your fare into Roxbury or Mattapan or Dorchester or Southie. But if you do it often, you get a bad rep, and you don't get enough radio calls to make your weekly nut. So, with my hair tucked up under a cap, no makeup, a no-nonsense attitude, and a length of lead pipe beneath my seat, I drive where the fare wants to go. I'm cautious in passenger selection: I won't take groups of teenage boys anywhere. The teenybop girls are less than trustworthy fare-wise, but they rarely try to beat you up.

Sam turned onto Altamont Street, across from the New Calvary Cemetery. The way the street looks— garbage-dump vacant lots interspersed with ramshackle tenements and sag-porched triple-deckers—you might argue that the folks buried in the ground have a better situation.

At first I thought Sam had slowed due to potholes. I was startled when I realized he was looking for a parking place.

I was glad I hadn't come alone.

SEVEN

Sam wedged the car across from a gray triple-decker that should have sported a CONDEMNED sign. By mutual agreement we left the battered Nova unlocked. That kind of neighborhood, locking a car is an unspoken challenge, street shorthand signifying that something inside might be worth stealing.

I peered at the three closest dwellings; two were boarded up.

"Coming?" Sam was heading briskly up the walkway toward the deserted triple, skirting puddles. I stared at the house again, shielding my eyes with a gloved hand. No curtains. No mailbox. I could smell rotten wood through the peeling paint. Boards gave as I climbed three warped steps to the spongy porch.

Ignoring four doorbells—the house evidently included a basement flat—Sam rapped on the left-hand door, three long, two short, two long, a pause, and then a single rap.

"Your friend sells crack? This a crack house?" I asked.

"Shhh."

We waited while the wind whipped my hair into a knotted tangle. I'd already decided that the mysterious Frank wasn't home when Sam knocked two more times.

The door creaked.

"In," ordered a low-pitched voice. "Come on. Move it."

"Take it easy," Sam said soothingly.

"Get up the stairs. I don't want the door open too long."

A nutcase, I thought. The stairs were steep and narrow, the stairwell smelly and dark.

Frank's second-floor digs featured cardboard-covered windows and overhead fluorescents, one of which was at the drive-you-crazy blinking stage just before burnout. Bolts turned and chains rattled into place. Then Frank scurried upstairs and proceeded to pace like a caged animal. If Sam had a case of the nerves, he'd caught it from Frank.

I was torn between staring at Frank—as tall and skinny a specimen as I've encountered—and examining his dwelling. Since he seemed to be gawking at me, I concentrated on the surroundings, a cross between a computer warehouse and a junk shop. It didn't take long to catalog the furniture: two tables, two metal folding chairs, four gunmetal-gray bookcases jammed with technical manuals and unbound printouts. Everything else was machinery, cable, or cardboard box. Of the eight or nine visible monitors, none was a TV.

While I gazed, Frank jabbered nonstop. Sam's contribution to the mostly incomprehensible monologue was to toss in an occasional "slow down."

Since they'd terrorized Sister Xavier Marie together, I figured Frank must be the same age as Sam, pushing forty. I'd have guessed him younger or older. Younger due to his sheer nervous energy. Older since his hairline was receding, his long, dark hair graying at the temples, with flickers of silver throughout. His beard was shot with silver, too, shaggy and unkempt. His face was thin, his cheeks hollow, his temples sheer, bony plates.

He wore brown leather pants and an open-necked white shirt, clothes with a decidedly foreign air. His accent was the same as Sam's, pure Boston. Affected by education and travel, yes, but definitely more Revere than Riviera.

Frank grabbed Sam by the shoulders. Staring at each other, they grinned hugely, then clinched in a bear hug, patting each other on the back, speaking rapid Italian. I tried to follow, becoming more and more aware of the limitations of my sole Romance language. I'd seen Sam with his four older siblings, three brothers and one sister, only a few times. They'd never embraced or kissed; they'd hardly smiled.

This, I thought, is how I picture brothers from a big Italian family reuniting after a long separation.

Frank, both delighted and frightened, exhilarated by

our arrival, extended a grimy hand in my direction. I shook it. He held on too long, pressed too hard.

"Miss Carlyle." His voice was pleasantly deep, but he spoke quickly, with a jerky rhythm. "Miss Carlyle, I'm happy to meet you, so very glad. Heard about you, uh, heard about you so very much." He swallowed the beginning and ending of each sentence. I had to watch his mouth to catch the words, practically lip-read.

"I don't know your last name," I said.

He glanced approvingly at Sam. "She doesn't . . . uh, Frank. Just Frank. Frank will do."

"So will Carlotta."

Frank drew in a deep breath and crossed his arms over his chest. "You haven't married this one, Sam. How come?" He seemed to realize that his question wasn't exactly tactful, and sped on quickly. Nothing about the man stayed put, his arms were in constant motion, he jigged and jogged even when he wasn't pacing. If I stayed in the same room with him long enough, I thought, I'd develop a tic.

"How's the blessed family?" he asked Sam. "How's the holy trinity?"

"My older brothers," Sam explained to me with a grin.

"Gilbert, Mitchell, and Anthony," Frank sang in a pseudo-operatic falsetto.

Sam laughed.

"Which one's the fattest?"

"Mitch. Can't keep away from Mexican food. Drives Papa crazy."

" 'Old Mitch the Mooch,' we called him," Frank

said. "He'd steal your lunch money so fast you didn't know it was gone."

"He wasn't so fast; you were slow."

"And Tony, can't keep away from the girls?"

"Right," Sam said.

Frank folded his arms and walked stiff-legged around the room. I realized it was an imitation of Papa Gianelli even before the voice came out, and the voice was superb, mimicry worthy of applause. "It's a good thing I hava da one boy screwed together straight. Gilberto, son of my heart."

"Gil's carrying on the family tradition," Sam said. He'd heard the routine once too often, or else he didn't like the way Frank was trying to impress me.

"Your heavenly sister's married?" Frank inquired, standing very still.

"Separated."

"That bum, Carlo?"

"No, she married Irish. Papa had fits."

"Good for her. They have kids?"

"Three girls. Boy died."

Sam bit his lip to keep from saying more, and I wanted to blurt out that the boy's—the man's—death was not my fault. It wasn't. It was past history. Sam and I had managed to come to terms with the disaster. Far as I was concerned it was none of Frank's business.

"Papa still keep a shrine to your sainted mama?" Frank asked.

"It stayed up a long time," Sam said. "Flowers and candles and pictures. I almost feel like I remember her. Pop's working on wife number four now."

I decided to turn the Q and A on our host.

"And your family?" I said to him. "They live close by?" It was the only way I could see him choosing this house. An elderly mom, dad, or aunt who refused to leave the downstairs flat.

"Sit," he said. "Please, sit." He glanced at the room as if he'd never seen it before. "Uh, sorry. I'll get another chair." He disappeared and returned instantly with a third metal folding job, banged it into a semiconversational grouping. "I've got cold beer. Potato chips."

"You were telling me about your family," I said, amused by his attempt at kid-in-a-dorm hospitality.

"Dead," he said bluntly. "I'm an orphan."

"Married?"

"No."

"Never?"

"Not now," he said, his mouth twitching into what could have been a smile. He didn't look at me when I questioned him. If I'd been a cop and he'd been a suspect in the interrogation room, I'd have read him his rights and dialed a public defender. He had to be a perp. Jumpy, nervous as a cat, afraid to make eye contact.

I checked out his pallor and his clothes again. Maybe not a foreign country. Maybe prison. Solitary confinement, a place where he hadn't needed to communicate with humans.

Maybe a speech impediment or a hearing deficiency. I wished Sam had told me more about the man.

"You have kids?" I asked.

"You?" he responded.

Sam rocked back in his metal chair, uncomfortable with the exchange. "Look," he said. "Let's forget the small talk and do business."

Frank frowned. "That's no way to treat an old buddy, Sam. You look terrific. Life's been treating you pretty damned good."

Sam stayed silent. What could he have said: "You look like hell"?

"We can't stay long, Frank."

Frank stretched his lips over his teeth in an attempt at a grin. "Uh, okay. That's okay, I guess. I won't need to know much. How will she treat the equipment? I mean basics, is she okay? You sure about her? Positively, I mean?"

Sam replied solemnly, "She's good with machines. A good driver."

"Stick shift?"

"I change my own oil," I said. "What the hell is this?"

"You're the first woman who's been in this apartment," Frank said, so softly I almost missed it.

Now, that surprised me. If Frank reminded me of an animal pacing his lair, the beast was wolf-like.

"You move in recently?" I asked.

He laughed, stood, and slapped Sam on the shoulder. "I like her," he murmured to Sam. "It's a deal."

What had Frank looked like as a child, what manner of blood-brother oaths had the two little boys exchanged? I've met a few of Sam's male friends over the years, although he tends to keep me away from his family since cops and robbers don't mix. They aren't all handsome, but they all share a certain level of polish.

Not this one.

Frank's flat smelled greasy. Burger King wrappers were strewn in the corners. God knows what else.

To hurry things up, I said, "Sam tells me you've got some extra computer equipment."

His chest swelled. "Whatever you need."

"A basic PC and a modem."

"That's all?" He seemed disappointed.

"That's all."

"You into reading BBSs?"

"I want to link into an information database, a major one."

"An infomart like PC Profile or—"

"I was thinking U.S. Datalink."

"They're all available," he said. "But as far as a PC goes, you'll need something decent or you're gonna work up a hell of a phone bill. Something where you can program a macro search strategy off-line. Datalink has good front-end software. Very compatible. I could fix you up with ProComm, maybe, or CrossTalk, or there might be something pirated. I'll scan the BBSs. The bulletin boards. BBSs is short for bulletin boards."

"Pirated?" I repeated. It was one of the few words I'd picked out of his rushed babble. "I'm not interested in merchandise that fell off the back of a truck."

"No, no, no," he said quickly. "I'm talking software. The hardware's bought and paid for; it's obsolete for what I do, that's all. I'd like to give it a good home. Software's different; it belongs to everyone. Information belongs to everyone. You think we should padlock libraries, give the librarians the keys? Give the keys to

AT&T and the goddamn technocracy, so the masses can be worker bees for the rest of their lives?"

"Frank," Sam said firmly, "we'll take the equipment, not the sermon."

"An old PC/XT," Frank mumbled, as if he were talking to himself. "That's the ticket, that's what you need. With a modem card."

"How much would a PC/XT set me back? With this modem card?"

"You plug it into any phone jack."

"How much?" I asked.

"Good home?" He looked at Sam.

"Excellent. Highest recommendation."

"A gift, then."

"No," I said.

"She's got a cat," Sam amended.

"A cat." Frank looked horrified. "Is she going to get rid of it?"

"What are we talking about here?" I asked. "I have a bird too. The world's oldest, nastiest parakeet."

"Cat hair's bad for computers," Frank said hurriedly. "So is dust. And you have to get a static protector if you're working on carpet. And . . ."

I glanced at Sam, eyebrows raised.

"It's a good home," Sam said earnestly. "She'll do right by your PC, Frank."

"Since there's a cat, fifty bucks," he said, crossing his arms. "Fifty firm."

I felt like I was slipping through the looking glass with a skinny version of Tweedledee holding out a helping hand.

"Done," I said. I'd never envisioned paying less than three hundred to get myself on-line. I'd feared the price tag might go higher.

And much as I hated to admit it, on-line was the future. If I was going to keep cutting it as a private eye in this town—a less sexist place than some, but still not a utopia where many seek the help of a female P.I.—I was going to have to keep up-to-date.

Computers have arrived. There it is. Pretty soon there'll be a different kind of cop show on TV. Uniforms'll sit around and punch keyboards and discover—gasp—who checked out porno tapes from Videosmith today. I wish I could get *into* computers, but they have a level of abstraction that doesn't make me tingle. Cars are truly the only machines I enjoy tinkering with, probably because I grew up in Detroit when cars were sacred chariots.

Things change. I drive a Toyota. I need a computer.

"You want a Coke?" Frank asked, as if suddenly remembering that he ought to inquire. He couldn't seem to decide whether to rush us out the door or hold us hostage. "I mean, if you're not into beer?"

"I'm not real happy about leaving a car on the street," Sam said.

"You brought your own car?"

"I borrowed something."

"And you parked in front? What are you trying to do to me? Jesus. You better get going."

"Let's get the stuff first. You know where this PC happens to be?"

"Of course I do. Original carton. I'll help you load it."

"I can carry it, Frank."

"I could use the air."

I could see his point. I wanted out and I'd only been there fifteen minutes.

It took another twenty for the three of us to locate the correct equipment plus manuals, and for Frank to swear that he'd run a search for whatever software could get me the best bang per buck on Datalink. He spoke in initials and put his phrases together so oddly, with no apparent punctuation, that I didn't understand half of what he said. I kept looking to Sam to translate as if Frank were speaking Italian, and then I'd realize that the words were English, just double-timed and oddly used. Verbs for nouns. Nouns for verbs. Acronyms sprinkled throughout.

"Getting dark" was one phrase I caught.

"We'll be going," Sam said. I tried not to nod agreement too vigorously.

"You can't stick this baby in the trunk, Sam. You want to rest it on the floor of the backseat, on a blanket, or better, she could hold it, maybe."

"Yeah, 'she' could hold it," I said. I counted two twenties and a ten into his hand and decided not to give advice about what to do with the cash. A moving van sprang to mind.

"You could pay me later," he said. His dark eyes had short, bristly lashes. His eyebrows almost met, knitting themselves into an angry slash across his face.

"I like to settle up as I go along," I said.

Sam carried the computer. Frank grabbed the manuals away from me. Also a carton of diskettes he'd insisted on tossing in as a last-minute bonus. I had to promise not to let the cat shed on them.

The deepening twilight hadn't improved the block's appearance. It obscured the mush puddles. My feet were soaked in an instant. Sam had parked close to a streetlamp. Its feeble bulb provided little light. The borrowed car appeared unmolested, but it could have had an additional dent or five. I wouldn't have noticed.

Frank fiddled and fussed and decided the computer carton was too large for me to hold on my lap. He took his time arguing about safe stowage, then set off on a lengthy cautionary tale about surge suppressors.

I was starting to follow his accelerated speech, but it took concentration.

I didn't see the black van turn the corner. I heard the screech of tires. It should have had its headlights on. It shouldn't have been going so fast, I thought as Sam crashed into me, shoving me to the ground, yelling at Frank to get down, get down. I was falling by the time I heard shots. Instinctively I turned my head, too late to keep my gaping mouth from filling with slush. I spat and felt Sam's weight on top of me. I saw the flash, coming from the passenger side of the black van. Flash and flash again. Automatic fire lit the sky like lightning.

I could feel Sam's heart beating furiously. I tried to shift him off me, but he raised his hand, covering my mouth. With both hands trapped underneath me there wasn't much I could do about the imposed hush. I breathed deeply, flexed my arms and legs, found them in working order.

What struck me was the silence. If I could have, I would have screamed, just to release tension. Nobody cracked a window, nobody yelled.

I couldn't expect much from the graveyard residents, but one of the living neighbors might have roused himself from TV-induced stupor or drug-dealer-bred fear, inquired if we were living or dead.

Mush fell.

EIGHT

The first noise, other than my rasping breath, was cop cars, sirens pulsing.

Sam's bulk shifted and moved. "Get in the car!" His voice seemed too loud.

"We've gotta wait—"

"Get in, Carlotta."

"Dammit, how's Frank? Are you okay? Am I okay?"

"Frank's gone. We're gone." He yanked me to my feet and pushed me toward the Nova.

I found myself unceremoniously shoved inside. "What the hell?" I could have invited a broken shoulder by butting against the slamming door. Instead I wriggled closer to the steering wheel, my teeth chattering.

Sam gunned the motor before he shut the door. He didn't burn rubber taking off; neither did he imitate a Sunday driver heading to church.

I kept my voice under control with effort. "What do you mean, Frank's gone? Dead?"

"He can take care of himself. He's . . . resourceful."

. I breathed. In and out. In and out. Counted to twenty twice. My left hand was shaking and I stuck it between my thighs to steady it.

"What was that about, Sam?" My breathing was screwed up. It took me three tries to get the words out.

"A drive-by. What's the matter? Don't you read the papers anymore?"

"A drive-by," I repeated. "And what else?"

"Nothing else. You hear them?"

"I heard you yell and I got tackled."

"Fuckers. Leaning out the windows, screaming that 'kill honky' bullshit. We are not exactly in an integrated area. One of the neighbors is probably chief whitey watcher for some street gang."

"And they never spotted Frank before?"

"He doesn't go out."

"Did you get a look at them? Were they wearing colors?"

"What?"

"Gang colors, Sam. Could you pick 'em out? Bromley-Heath? Academy Homes? Goyas?"

"No, Carlotta. I did not concentrate on what the fuck they were wearing."

"Sam, where are you going?"

It took him a while to admit that he didn't exactly know.

"Pull over. Let me drive."

He squealed the brakes and yanked the wheel. We

came to a stop under an ailanthus tree. "You know where we are?"

"Get out and do a fast runaround. I'll slide over, get us into Franklin Park and back to the Arboretum and we can—"

"Don't drive to a police station," he warned as soon as he hit the passenger seat.

"I'll park someplace in J.P.," I promised. Jamaica Plain is a residential neighborhood where they allow on-street overnight parking. The Nova wouldn't stick out.

"Abandon the car," Sam agreed eagerly.

"At least check to see if it's wearing bullet holes. We could be leaking gas or transmission fluid—"

"Somebody may have seen it. We need to ditch it."

"Sam, what the hell is going on?"

"Carlotta, I am not getting involved in this. It was a racial thing. That's it. But the minute my name comes into it, it will be a Mafia thing, and you damn well know it."

"Sam, it wasn't your fault. You're a victim here. You should call the cops."

"Listen to you," he said, shaking his head. "You talk like a child. *Fault*. My family, everything's been my fault since I was born."

The steering wheel felt warm against my icy hands.

"After my mother died," he went on, "when I was a baby—a toddler, I guess—my brothers took me to church and left me there, like they thought God would accept me as an offering, a kind of exchange, and give Mama back."

"The priest must have been happy to see you," I

said. Sam doesn't speak of his childhood often. The gunfire seemed to have loosened his tongue.

"Oh, they didn't take me to the local parish. Not that dumb. They wrapped me in rags, stuck me in a stroller they'd pinched from a garbage dump. Not the fancy Gianelli carriage all the mamas in the North End could identify. I was just a baby dumped on a doorstep, well on my way to a wonderful life in foster care."

"Who found you?"

"I only know this from stories, the way it was told to me. Papa jumped to the conclusion that I'd been kidnapped, the biggest crime since the Lindbergh baby. Fired the nanny on the spot. She didn't have her papers, had to go back to Italy. He wanted her arrested, but he settled for deported."

"It wasn't her fault."

"There you go again," Sam said.

"How did your father find you?"

"He heard my brothers praying in the nursery, asking God to take me instead of Mama. Beat the crap out of them till they talked. I remember he said by the time he got me back, I was sick. A cold, but he thought I was really going to die."

"Do you believe it?" I asked. "The story? I mean, your brothers were adolescents, teenagers. Old enough to know God doesn't play *Let's Make a Deal*."

Sam shrugged. "My father could have made the whole thing up. Any of the boys could have invented it, as a way to let me know they didn't want me around. That's the most likely explanation, but hell, I suppose I could have been kidnapped by the Winter Hill Gang. It doesn't matter."

I licked my lips. My hands weren't shaking anymore. They felt numb.

"When Gina's son died, they blamed me," Sam went on.

"Did Gina blame you?"

"No," he said with a trace of a smile. "She blamed you. Whatever, what I'm trying to say is, I'm not getting my family involved in this."

"Even if it was a Mafia thing," I said.

"I don't know any Italians who hang in that neighborhood," Sam said.

"Frank looks Italian. Could it be somebody after Frank?" I asked.

"The housing inspector, I suppose. Code violations."

"What if it was an Organized Crime Task Force thing?" I said. "Considering they're so interested in you."

"Not their style, Carlotta. They're the good guys."

"Sam, I think you should let me inspect the bugs."

"Don't start, Carlotta. I know what I know. When I said I had experts check them out, I meant *experts*!"

I drove slowly, stopping at each yellow light. If I piloted a cab like that, I'd get picked up on suspicion.

"What about you?" Sam asked suddenly. "Is somebody gunning for you?"

"Who'd you have in mind?"

"You were a cop."

"A while ago."

"Are you into something I don't know about?"

"Such as?"

"You working for any crazies?"

I ran through my almost nonexistent caseload. Two

skip-traces that would be speeded up by the acquisition of the computer. One inconclusive store surveillance, possible clerk theft.

Phil Yancey.

"Maybe Roz is jealous," Sam suggested.

"You think she's got the hots for you?"

"The shrink next door. I think *he's* got the hots for you."

"When Roz wants me dead, she'll poison leftovers in the fridge. Did you see the guns sticking out of that van? Like Prohibition photos."

I turned onto a dark lane off Centre Street.

"Gas station with a pay phone three blocks from here," I said, pulling over and parking behind a gray Nissan Stanza.

"Good. Let's go," Sam said.

"First, you tell me whose car this is. Chances are the cops will get the plate number. And somebody's gonna talk, and we're both gonna get roasted. I've got my P.I. license at stake. I'm supposed to report crimes, not assist cover-ups."

"You've never kept anything from the cops before, Carlotta?"

I didn't bother with a denial. "The best thing we can do is call the police—"

"The car's expendable."

"'Expendable.'" I bet Papa Gianelli used that word a lot. "Frank's the most likely target, Sam. Why's he living in a slum like that?"

"Let's get to the gas station," Sam said impatiently. "I'll carry the computer stuff. We'll call Gloria and she'll send a cab."

"For chrissakes," I said. "You're hopeless. Good thing you didn't go into the family business. If we're not gonna report this, at least we gotta wipe our finger- prints off the goddamn steering wheel."

If you're going to break the law, do it right.

NINE

"Theater is life.
Film is art.
Television is furniture."

Roz, my delightful tenant, has taken to adding words to her artwork, black graffiti surrounded by swirling orange, green, and fuchsia acrylics. She field-tests her paintings by hanging them near my bed, the idea being that if I don't puke when I see them, she might be able to sell them. Possibly she considers them more saleable if I vomit.

She snitches most of her slogans from daytime TV soaps: "Can Catherine prove she's Dominic's ill-fated half sister?" "Luke and Laura ponder home decoration." She uses TV commercials, too, did a whole series based on "It's not your father's Oldsmobile." She despairs of Reebok, insists they parody themselves too perfectly for commentary.

The theater, film, and television poster is what I saw when I came out of a sweaty nightmare. I liked it enough to wonder if she'd give me a discount.

I could lie and say that yesterday's shooting was like a dream. It wasn't. It was for sure the hell real. I had achy knees and a black-and-blue spot the size of a silver dollar where Sam's elbow had caught me between the ribs. And a king-size case of the guilts, worse than any hangover.

A hangover, you drink a quart of O.J., step under a cold shower, hit the Y, play volleyball, swim twenty laps. If you don't die, you're cured. The guilts are worse. They require confession, particularly if you grew up in a Jewish-Catholic family. Probably the only thing my mom and dad agreed on was the vital importance of guilt.

O.J. and a cold shower had no effect.

As soon as I went downstairs I spied last night's spoils, the hardware—keyboard, computer, and screen—on my desk. I mentally tagged them Exhibit A.

I snagged the plastic-bagged morning *Globe* off the snow-covered stoop and spread it across my desk. I drank more orange juice, from a glass this time.

The cat, T.C., rubbed against my ankles. I didn't respond with food, so he stalked off in a huff.

The drive-by hadn't made the front page. Slaughter in Bosnia, the umpteenth series of Senate hearings on organized crime, remembrances of the Warsaw Ghetto. It took two runs through the Metro section to find mention of my crime. It rated barely two inches of column space on page 26, under the fold. Frank must have escaped unscathed. Injuries would make for more drama, greater detail.

I found my hand wandering to the phone, caught it and brought it back.

Dammit, I wanted to call Mooney.

Mooney is my main contact with the Boston PD. He used to be my boss. He's achieved his dream job: lieutenant in charge of homicide. My fingers inched toward the phone buttons, hesitated. It wasn't like I could provide blinding insight. I'd never seen the shooters, wouldn't be able to ID the vehicle. I could point the police at Frank, but the cops would have done a routine door-to-door.

It came down to personal loyalty to Sam, compounded by a question of law and order. A question, also, of getting in trouble. I felt like a gawky adolescent, deciding whether or not to tattle on a schoolmate: Judy's smoking in the girls' room.

Where was Sister Xavier Marie when you needed moral guidance?

I telephoned area hospitals and inquired about gunshot wounds. The paper hadn't mentioned injuries, but half of what they print is filler and the other half is dubious. That's what cops tell me.

Most gunshots are admitted to Boston City Hospital. It's got location, location, location, as the realtors say. I used my social engineering skills to determine that none of their bullet-ridden patients was a tall, gaunt white man. It galled me that I didn't know Frank's last name.

When the phone rang I jumped, expecting Mooney. Our knack for reading each other's thoughts helped when I was on the force. Now that I'm off, it scares me.

Sam's deep baritone sounds soothing even when his words don't.

"Just checking," he said.

"On what?"

"You know."

"I don't know."

"Your line's been busy."

"Is this the loyalty oath part, Sam?" I said icily. "My mother once told me the great grief of my grandmother's life was that she never got to testify before the House Committee on Un-American Activities. She used to rehearse her speech in front of the mirror, telling HUAC how they ought to be ashamed of themselves, hounding good Communists when they could sink their teeth into J. Edgar Hoover without half trying."

"What are you trying to tell me, Carlotta?"

"I have a bad attitude about loyalty oaths."

"You feeling okay?" Sam asked. "Otherwise?"

"Bruises. Do you know if our, uh, companion is also in good health?"

"He's fine," Sam said.

"You want to hire me now? To find out who wanted to waste your friend—or you?"

"What I want to do is forget it. It had nothing to do with us. It wasn't personal, Carlotta."

"When I get shot at, I take it personally."

"Well, do it on your own dime. If you're dying to find out which gang we ticked off, waste your own time and money. Leave me out of it."

"Suppose I need to find Frank," I said. "Suppose his junk doesn't do squat when I plug it in?"

"He'll find you," Sam said. "He'll want to know that the computer's okay. That it didn't get hit by a stray round."

"What about me?"

"He asked after your health."

"Should I be flattered?"

"Are you?"

"What's Frank's last name?"

"He doesn't use it."

"He serve with you in Vietnam?"

"Why?"

"Something about the way you both hit the ground together. Like teamwork. Like you both knew the ropes."

"Carlotta, neighborhood we grew up in, we didn't have to visit Southeast Asia."

I waited. He'd called me, not the other way around.

"I have some advice," he said finally.

"Yeah?" I thought he was going to issue a dire warning about the consequences of calling the cops.

"Leave Frank out of it. I know it's a good story, but leave Frank out. If you can't live with your goddamn conscience, make it you and me, but leave him out completely."

"That could be part of the deal," I said.

"What deal?"

"I don't go to the cops, and I won't mention Frank, on one condition."

"What?"

"You tell Gloria that G and W's bugged."

"Why?" he said. "You think she runs numbers out of there in her spare time?"

"She deserves to know," I said.

"Her room isn't bugged. I had it swept. It's sound-proof. The G and W bugs can't touch it."

"Tell her or I call the cops. Simple as that."

I could hear him breathing over the line.

"Okay," he said finally. "Deal."

"Tell her if she doesn't like it, she can start playing loud music. Lots of garages play music."

"That wasn't part of the deal," he said.

I waited.

"I'll mention it," he said. "You want me to recommend any tunes?"

"Depends," I said. "If Gloria's tired of the Geezers, I'd go with rap. If she enjoys inhaling stogie smoke, she should find some Irish stuff. The Chieftains."

"I'm sure the task force would prefer The Chieftains," Sam said.

"Now, why the big hush-hush about Frank?"

"I don't ask a lot of favors, Carlotta. I'm asking. Don't do anything to hurt him."

I drummed my fingers on the desk top.

"Please," he said quietly. "It's important to me."

Maybe he sensed I was about to argue.

He hung up. I held the receiver to my ear until the phone company beep drove me off the line.

TEN

Life sputtered on. Newspaper recipes for turkey leftovers gave way to instructions for homemade Christmas stocking stuffers. All roads leading to shopping malls were impassable. I dumped the summer clothes out of my closet and into one of the empty rooms I could rent to a Harvard student if I got truly cash poor.

With manuals in hand, cursing whoever had laboriously translated them from the Taiwanese, I managed to hook up my computer, only to find it utterly useless without Frank's promised software. I wound up locating my skip-traces the old-fashioned way, using guile and fast talk.

I did not hear from Frank.

Lee Cochran did not return my calls. I went to his office. He was out. I shoved a note under his door: Please call.

I cleaned the birdcage and the litter box. After re-caulking my bedroom windows for the forty-seventh time, I started reading the replacement-window ads in the *Globe*. I was developing a craving for heat, a phe-nomenon enhanced by too many nights at Sam Gi-anelli's cozy apartment.

When the phone rang in the middle of the night, it took me a minute to realize I was sleeping at my place. The socks nailed it; I never wear socks when I sleep with Sam.

"How much you charge an hour?"

"Gloria?" I could hardly make out her voice over the relentless beat of a rap tune.

"You asleep?"

I groped for the light. "It's what? Four in the morn-ing? You're calling about food, you're a dead woman."

"I asked a question." Impatience underlined her mellow voice. "Two questions: Are you available? And what do you charge?"

"I can barely hear you," I said.

"What do you charge?"

"Depends who I'm working for."

"Working for me."

"Call it a favor."

"Straight rates."

"Two fifty a day," I said, giving her a quick half-price deal. "Less if it waits till morning."

"Get in your car and come over. Now. You'll need a cab for this, a radio."

"For what?"

"Don't shout at me."

"Gloria, should I wear my ball gown?"

"Dress for driving."

"You don't need a cabbie bad enough to pay P.I. rates."

"Marvin's in trouble."

Marvin is Gloria's largest and oldest brother. He *is* trouble, but I didn't say that to Gloria.

"I can't raise him on the radio," she said. Either she'd turned the music down a notch or I was getting used to its roar.

"Marvin's piloting a cab?" Far as I knew, Marvin's cabbie license had expired for good during his last stint on the state. No convicted felons driving cabs in the Commonwealth.

Unconvicted ones, yeah.

"I wouldn't have let him drive," Gloria explained, "except two more guys quit on me today. There wasn't anybody else."

"What about me?"

Silence.

"Gloria—"

"Sam told me to keep you off the graveyard shift."

"Since when—"

"Listen up, Carlotta. I just got a call here, anonymous, saying eight twenty-one's in trouble, somewhere in Franklin Park."

"Eight twenty-one probably broke down. You send your own brother out in that clunker?" I wondered whose tag Marvin was hacking on. Probably one of his brothers', both of whom have failed to score in the courts, for undefined reasons. God knows, it's not that they haven't done anything illegal.

"I mean real trouble," Gloria insisted.

"Get the cops."

"Last call I sent Marvin on was Franklin Hills," she said, naming a Dorchester housing project I wouldn't go near on a bet.

"Pay phone or apartment?" I asked.

"Corner."

"Great."

"Marvin can handle himself."

"Sure he can. Call the cops."

"They'll shut me down, Carlotta, using an ex-con for a jockey. I'm hiring you instead. As of right now."

"To do exactly what?"

"Check out Franklin Park."

"It's one hell of a big place."

"Find Marvin."

"Did Mr. Anonymous sound familiar? Friend of Marvin's?"

"No."

"Would Marvin try to scam you?"

"Carlotta, please. Get over here."

"Go trolling through Franklin Park at four in the morning. That's what you want me to do." Sam will be ecstatic, I thought, and the idea of his anger made the job more attractive. The nerve, ordering Gloria to keep me safe.

"I wouldn't ask except for my brother," she said. "You bring your gun, hear?"

I hung up and got dressed. No jeans when I drive; there's a dress code. I stepped into loose elastic-waist sweats, a matching long-tailed shirt. If it doesn't need ironing and it's cheap, I can put up with anything the fashion industry dishes out.

I sped downstairs, unlocked the lower left-hand drawer of my desk, unwound my Smith & Wesson .38 from its undershirt wrapping, and loaded it with slugs kept in separate quarters. I shoved it into the waist of my slacks, icy against my back. When I threw on my wool car coat, the gun became unreachable, so I relocated it deep in my right-hand pocket. I ponytailed my hair with my hands and managed to subdue it under a black watch cap. Headed out the door.

In the weeks since the drive-by, Gloria had never once mentioned sending a cab to J.P. in the middle of the night to collect me and Sam and the computer equipment. I'd have thought that would pique her curiosity, and once Gloria's curiosity is piqued, you're better off just telling her what she wants to know.

Maybe she'd tackled Sam about it; maybe he'd manufactured a successful lie. It must have been a good one; Gloria keeps her ear to the ground.

If she thought the Hackney Bureau would close her down for using an ex-con driver, the Hackney Bureau would do just that.

I made it from my house to the bumpy street fronting the Mass. Pike in seventeen minutes, which is damn good time.

Gloria's wheelchair loomed in G&W's doorway. She was holding out keys, shaking them like Christmas bells. "Take the Ford in the shop. Seven sixteen."

"Location?"

"Got the police scanner going and a couple good drivers out lookin'. Guy's who'll keep their mouths shut. I'll send specifics soon as I can."

"Sure you don't want cops?"

"This stays in the company, Carlotta."

If the music jams the bugs, I thought.

I said, "See you."

"Be careful."

Go find a convicted felon in a missing cab somewhere in Franklin Park in the wee hours. Take your gun.

And be careful.

ELEVEN

I snapped on the radio as soon as I slammed the cab's door, before Gloria could possibly have wheeled into position behind the phone console. I set it on full-band, then backed off to two-way. If Gloria wanted to risk sharing our conversation with others, that would be her call.

"Carlotta?"

"Heading up Harvard Ave., squeezing the yellows. Almost to Comm." While I drove I wrestled with my coat buttons. There's a period of adjustment to getting long-haul comfy in a cab. I punched buttons and moved levers; if I remembered correctly, 716 didn't offer much in the way of heat.

"Good girl. Keep it movin'," Gloria said. I could hear the music over the box. I wondered what the cabbies thought about Gloria's sudden conversion to rap and rock.

"Look," I said, "you call any of the places Marvin might've stopped?"

"Carlotta, my brother is not pumping iron at Gold's Gym. He didn't stop for a nightcap. I have dialed every bar he hangs his sorry ass in, and those bartenders know that if they want any cabs picking up their drunks, they'd better tell me the truth."

Traffic eased after the Purity Supreme. I raced through Coolidge Corner and Brookline Village, one eye peeled for traffic patrols.

A burst of static ushered in Gloria's voice: "I got something. Woodsy area past the old clubhouse. Man thinks he saw tire tracks leaving the road, possibly the shadow of a car, all topsy-turvy. Guy sounds like he might be drunk. Not sure if he should call the cops. Didn't even get out of his car. Just split, damn him."

I didn't blame him. Why ask for trouble?

"I'm on it," I sang out. As I spoke, I flipped off the radio, convincing myself I'd need total concentration on the upcoming stretch of road. The Jamaicaway's speed limit is thirty. Most drivers start having qualms at twenty, that's how bad the street is, curving like an imitation mountain trail around Jamaica Pond. The mush storm and subsequent freeze had opened fissures in the pavement the size of craters. I braked from fifty to forty-five, nursing the accelerator. No good bottoming out in a pothole and losing the back axle.

Road conditions were my excuse for radio silence. I didn't want to speculate on Marvin's fate, didn't want to hear what Gloria was fielding on her scanner. Car overturned in Franklin Park, close to the Franklin Hills Project. Gloria would blame herself forever if something awful happened to Marvin.

The road branched left, then straightened for a short run after the pond. I swung left at the rotary. No traffic, no cops, so I blasted over the bridge into the park.

No approaching sirens shrieked. The streetlamps in the park get vandalized so often they're no longer routinely replaced. No moonlight to aid my search. I flipped on my high beams along with the radio.

"Anything else?" I asked.

"Keep your radio on, dammit, girl. Nothin'. Guy took off before he could be sure what he saw was a cab."

"Did he call it in?"

"Yeah." Gloria did not sound comforted. "Finally did a nine one one, and cops are what I'm trying to avoid here. Good news is that Area B's swamped. Break-ins in progress, two assaults, a gang bust-up. A 'maybe, maybe not' accident sighting's not gonna be any number one priority tonight."

I passed the left turn leading to the zoo and slowed to a crawl. Tire tracks leaving the road on my right. The ground looked muddy enough to hold prints, layers of rotting leaf mulch keeping it warm. It would take good eyesight to catch tracks on a dark street. You had to wonder. Luck. Or possibly the perp himself had called it in. Maybe Marvin, if he was drunk and had totaled the cab.

"Hang on, Gloria. I'm gonna park and walk some, then come back, drive on, and try it by foot again. Too easy to miss something this way."

"Okay. Leave the radio on."

"Will do. Flashlight in the trunk?"

"New batteries."

"Thanks."

I pulled to the side of the road, killed the lights, locked the doors as I exited, keys in hand. Just my luck to run into a car thief.

I walked ten feet, decided the car's headlights would help, went back and flicked them on. Gloria was singing an unsteady hymn on the radio.

Fifty feet. Nothing. I went back for the car, drove it slowly along the verge.

"Hold it. I think I see something," I said, squealing the brakes.

Gloria's singing stopped. Her voice turned cautious. "Babe, maybe you ought to wait for the cops."

"I thought you didn't want them."

"Should I send another cabbie? Two's better than one."

"Who's on?"

She mentioned a couple names I didn't recognize. Unknown backup is worse than no backup, I decided.

"Gloria, I'm going to leave the radio on. You hear anything that sounds wrong—like gunshots, for instance—dial nine one one, and don't take no for an answer." I cranked down the windows and abandoned the cab on the grass, its warning lights flashing. As an afterthought, I grabbed the chunk of lead pipe from under the seat. I like to have options other than my revolver.

On close inspection I could decipher twin tracks, clear, fresh, with textbook tread. The incline was far

steeper than I'd estimated from a quick flashlit sweep.
I started down too fast, following a muddy rut, and fell.
Sat, cursing silently.

My next attempt was more cautious. Oblique. I hung
close to a scraggly line of trees, trying to dig my heels
into the mud. The undergrowth snared my feet. My
boots kept slipping in the mire. The second time I fell,
twisting my ankle sharply on a hidden root, I made a
desperate grab for a sapling, missed, and slid the entire
length of the grade. My forehead smacked hard against
a thick branch, momentarily stunning me. My nose hit
as well. I bit back a scream; a low moan escaped. I
seemed to have landed in some sort of prickly shrub.

I counted to twenty twice, blinking teary eyes, panting. The fallen flashlight shone in my face like a search
beacon. I moved, scraping skin against brambles. I inhaled deeply, slowly. No sudden pain. Probably no broken ribs. Good.

I touched my forehead, winced. Lowered my hand
to inspect my nose, probing the soft cartilage with
practiced fingers. My nose has been broken three
times.

Not again, I thought. Dammit, not again!

It hurt like hell, but retained its familiar shape, a
lone bump and a slight bend below the bridge. I tasted
blood. And me with no handkerchief in my pocket, just
a gun.

I rolled and crawled out of the prickly stuff, inching
along, disoriented. When I realized I'd have to stick
my arm back into the thorns to grab the flashlight, I almost wept.

Once in possession of the flashlight, I sucked in a

quick breath, snatched a handful of soggy leaves from a branch, and smeared blood off my face.

Middle of the night, you'd never guess Franklin Park's the heart of a huge city. Designed by Frederick Law Olmsted as the crown jewel of his Emerald Necklace of Boston parks, its silence is so deep you can imagine yourself in the wilderness, in some far-off wolf-inhabited woods. When I lifted my face, trying to stanch the flow of blood with gravity's aid, I could see stars invisible in neon-lit Back Bay.

The cab rested on its side, passenger door up. No gasoline smell. Engine off. I used the lead pipe to swipe at branches obscuring my view, then stuck it under my arm and hopped to a nearby tree. My ankle wasn't functioning. I tested my weight on it, leaning against the trunk for support. The pain made me break into a sweat. I hopped and limped and lurched and held on to convenient tree limbs to get closer to the cab. The pipe was too damn short for a crutch. Useless.

I shined light in the cab's back window. Side window. Nothing. Aimed the flash full on the front visor. The plastic slot where the cabbie's ID card, mug shot and license, should have been, was empty.

I checked the colors, the logo, the medallion. G&W 821.

I didn't hear any noise that didn't belong to the woods. No breaking branches, no crunch and crackle of leaves. I strained for the whoosh of wheels on the road above, but either no one passed or the road was too distant. I was contemplating the ascent, whether I could hop it on one foot, whether I'd need to crawl, when a hand closed on my shoulder. I yelped, jumped a good six inches, forgetting my ankle, raising the pipe over my head.

"Don't yell!" Marvin ordered.

"It's me," I said, at the same time. "Carlotta. Remember?"

"Carlotta," he repeated.

"Marvin? Marvin. Shit. What happened? What did—"

"Get that light outta my eyes, goddammit, and don't be scared what you see. I been hurt worse."

I bit down on my lower lip. He was breathing heavily, but then so was I. He was standing. If I'd found him prone, I'd have screamed. Blood must have gushed from his scalp to soak his torn and crumpled shirt so completely. His face bulged, the nose mashed to one side.

"Maybe you ought to lie down," I said, holding out a hand. "You hit the windshield?" Amazing it hadn't spider-webbed, I thought.

Marvin stared at me, touched my cheek. "I remember you," he said. "Gloria's friend. The ex-cop. They hit you too?"

"I fell."

"They busted up my radio, or I'd be gone. Hell, if the car wasn't flipped, I'd drive outta here. I was gonna give myself another half hour to rest up, and walk it. How'd you find me so quick?"

"Gloria's half crazy. She started checking the police band."

"Goddamn," he whispered. "Cops comin'?"

"They'll get you to a hospital," I said. "You could—"

"I don't want a hospital. I need to get away from here, so nobody knows I was driving."

"Marvin, why don't you sit down?"

"Shit, if you were anybody else drivin' a G and W, I'd pound your head, grab your license, and steal your cab."

"You ought to be in a hospital, Marvin, talking like that." As I spoke, I limped back a few steps and got a better grip on the pipe. Marvin's the biggest of Gloria's brothers; he used to be a prizefighter.

"Goddammit, listen to me. This thing needs quiet handlin'. Cops have to report this shit to the Hackney Bureau. And you know what they'll do to Gloria? Using a jock with a record? I don't need no hospital. I need to get outta here. Don't give me no argument."

"You drunk?"

"No. Wish I was."

"You didn't drive over the edge?"

"I was goddamned hijacked. Beaten."

"By whom? Why? Personal business?"

"You gonna help me get outta here?"

"Marvin, honest, I don't think I can walk up the hill. Twisted my ankle. Damn near broke my nose." My head was pounding. I closed my eyes tight, opened them wide. The hammering seemed dull and far away.

The two of us were whispering instinctively. Talk too loud, somebody might come by and mug you. The idea that anybody lingering in the Franklin Park bushes would qualify as a Good Samaritan was ludicrous.

"Shine that light your way. Lemme see you better," Marvin said.

I held the light under my chin so I'd look like a Halloween spook. From Marvin's tight-lipped reaction, I realized the eerie lighting was merely gilding the lily.

"And you got a hack up there, right?" he said slowly.

"You thinking about a switch?" I asked. "I look that bad? Like I got beat up?"

"You'll do."

I listened. No sirens.

"Carlotta, I'm hirin' you. As of right now. My credit good?"

"Gloria already hired me." I made up my mind quickly. "Top of the hill. Shut the flashers on the cab. The radio's on, but only Gloria can hear."

"I ain't trustin' no radio. Scanners, you ever hear of them?"

"Okay, don't bother with the radio. Think you can yank my license, get back down here, and stick it in eight twenty-one?"

"Give me the flashlight and I can." His face changed and I realized his bloated features were attempting a smile. The stuff of nightmares.

Then he was gone, up the hill. I could hear him crashing through the brush like a grizzly bear. Five long minutes later, he leaned into the damaged cab with a groan and jammed my license into the visor, almost upsetting the cab's teetery balance.

"How you gonna play it?" he asked. "I could tell you what they looked like—"

"No time. I'm gonna go unconscious. I won't remember a thing," I said.

"Good," Marvin said.

"Money in the cab?"

"Not much."

"They know you?"

"Nope."

"Why you staring at me?" I asked.

"You could maybe use more blood," he said judiciously. "Three guys beat you."

"Three? You better see a doctor."

"I know boxin' folks'll fix me up, no police report."

I listened again for the wail of sirens. Nothing.

"Black guys, white guys?" I asked.

"Salt and pepper. Third one maybe Latino."

"How come they left you in such good shape, Marvin?"

"Because I started out in terrific shape—and mostly I played dead. They had serious guns. They wanted me dead, I'd be meat. Look, babe, I gotta little penknife . . . you know, one flick, your nose'll bleed a little more and—"

"Marvin, stay away from my nose! You cut me, fucker, even a scratch, the deal's off. I wake up in the hospital, I'll remember, and Gloria'll have your ass in a frying pan."

The threat of his not-so-little sister stopped him cold. I could almost see the tension leave his body. Maybe he wouldn't have done me serious damage. On the other hand, he wanted to mess with somebody.

A faint wailing siren split the air like a steam whistle from an old forgotten train.

"Get going, Marvin," I said, "before I come to my senses."

"Lie down. They'll tape your ankle. Get crutches. And you got memory loss."

"Move," I ordered. "If they find you, they'll think

you beat me up, jerk. Take the pipe. And my gun, dammit. They'll never believe me if I have a gun."

Please, I thought, don't let Marvin commit a felony with my piece. Please, God, let it come home to its drawer unfired.

I heard him scramble up the hill as I artfully arranged myself in the grass and closed my eyes.

"Call Gloria," I said. "First thing."

I couldn't make out his reply.

Things I do for Gloria, I ought to get my head examined. Picked up three guys. Forced me off the road. Nope. Nobody'd buy that one . . . I'd never pick up three guys, not in my right mind. Temporary amnesia, only way to go.

At least I didn't have liquor on my breath.

I lifted my leg and massaged my ankle, gritting my teeth. It occurred to me that here I was, remaining at the scene like a righteous citizen, the way I hadn't waited when I'd actually been a victim. Maybe that's why I'd volunteered—not for love of Gloria and Sam and G&W, but as an act of crazed atonement.

I envisioned myself explaining it: See, Mooney, I was shot at from this black van, and I didn't report it, so then a few weeks later I pretend to be a crime stat.

I ought to schedule an appointment with the shrink almost next door.

I wished I'd caught a glimpse of the drive-by shooters. I could describe them to the cops as the guys who beat me up and dumped me in the prickle bush. The prickle bush . . . Would the cops trace my descent, catch me in a lie?

My ankle throbbed. Liquid, presumably blood, continued to trickle from my nose. I recited multiplication tables slowly, made it well into the nines before I heard the slam of a car door, unrecognizable voices. Cherry lights flashed.

I closed my eyes. Amnesia was my savior. Let the cops figure it out. With my eyes shut I muttered a silent prayer for Marvin. Drive carefully. Don't pass out on the road. Don't use or lose my gun. Find a good, quiet disbarred physician.

Do doctors get disbarred? Why do people think prayers are more likely to be answered when they scrunch their eyes shut?

The dark night was my friend. So were the cops and paramedics churning the ground, calling out to one another.

"This way," a voice shouted. "Down here!"

I wondered if Marvin and I shared the same blood type. Would the cops see anything beyond a simple auto accident? I willed my body limp, tried to stop my mind from exploring every possible avenue of discovery and failure.

I cheered myself with the thought that what had really happened was too unlikely for the cops to guess.

TWELVE

I played possum while cautious paramedics immobilized my neck and lifted me onto a backboard, then a gurney, for the slow uphill march. I made a brief return to "consciousness" in the ambulance, lingering long enough to demand Beth Israel over Boston City. Beth Israel's nurses are the best. Besides, nobody comes to visit at Boston City Hospital; they're scared of getting shot en route. I also vetoed blood transfusion. Not that I needed it, but you can't be too careful.

I listened to the paramedics chatter about which fast-food joint they'd patronize on their next break—and tried not to curse out loud when they jostled my ankle. Swaying in the overheated ambulance, I started sweating till my shirt was soaked, molded to my body underneath my coat. Blood and mud and perspiration and prickles everywhere. I couldn't breathe through my nose, which worried me.

When the police officer bouncing along in the jump seat asked what happened, I wearily closed my eyes.

I'd decided to stay knocked out for admission. My wallet was in my hip pocket; they could locate the appropriate ID and insurance cards without my help. I spent the travel time visualizing the contents of my wallet, so I'd know if any of the staff suffered light-finger syndrome, whether or not to stop credit on my Visa.

I attempted to salve my conscience. First I told myself that my ankle would have required orthopedic attention anyway—probably not in such dramatic circumstances, but definitely not during regular office hours. An emergency-room visit is an emergency-room visit.

Then I tried reminding myself that if not for my intervention the hospital would have been stuck with Marvin. Marvin's more serious injuries would assuredly bill higher. I tried not to think about my insurance deductible.

Wham. The doors opened and the show began.

My headache escalated from simple pounding to full bass drum. I was indoors. Lights burned down on me. Voices surrounded me.

"Get her vital signs."

"Accident! Full level-one trauma protocol!"

"Find the surgical resident!"

"Okay, let's go. Type her blood and cross-match for six units."

"She's out." A deep voice cut across the rest. "Have to establish an airway."

Someone stuck a cold metal scope into my mouth and I came up spluttering. "Quit that!" I said.

"I think we've got an airway," the man with the deep voice said. He was a little past middle age, cocoa-colored and silver-haired. Handsome. "Can you hear me?"

"Yes."

"Can you move your right hand?"

I did.

"Good. Your left?"

"It's my ankle," I said. "Left."

He ignored me. I repeated myself, but he was occupied with my forehead and my nose. Evidently head wounds took top priority.

"Get her to X-ray," he said. "Whole body. Skull films. She was unconscious for some period of time. After X-ray, move her right to the CAT scan."

Bright white lights and machinery everywhere. My stomach felt queasy. Had I fallen into poisoned brambles? I heard more sirens approaching and closed my eyes in case they were police units, not ambulances.

Gloria was at my side when I woke, massive, dark, and silent in her wheelchair. As soon as I opened my eyes and allowed them to focus, she held a warning finger to her lips. I blinked and shook my head. Some anesthesiologist must have wiped me out. I had no idea what time it was.

The room had two beds. The second was vacant, blank and sterile as a clean sheet of paper. The wallpaper was sky blue. A pattern of tiny yellow-and-white buds crawled up toward the gleaming white ceiling. The curtains echoed the cheery yellow. Yuck. A sink was tucked into a tiny alcove, a paper-towel dispenser overhead. Two wall-mounted tissue boxes held latex gloves.

I could smell again. I sniffed deeply and wished I hadn't. Even the best hospitals smell of rubbing alcohol and tidied-up death.

I lifted a hand to my head. Gauze and tape covered a two-inch patch above my right eye.

Following Gloria's pointed gaze, I glanced at the doorway. A stolid cop on duty. Thanks, Mooney, I thought, less than gratefully.

"How's he doing?" I murmured to Gloria.

"She awake?" The cop demanded at the same time.

"Hush," Gloria said, ostensibly to the cop, but I could tell she was worried I'd blurt out the real story. Maybe she thought the anesthesiologist dealt in truth serum as well as morphine.

"You fooled them, told them you were my sister, right?" I asked in a low voice.

"Your momma," she answered dryly. "Sam's away again or he'd be here. Paolina, now . . . she's been haunting the waiting room."

Paolina! I used the guardrail of the bed to haul myself into a sitting position.

"Where is she?" My head spun. Too late, I remembered that hospital beds came equipped with controls to gently raise and lower the patient.

"Carlotta, calm down! I told her you'd be fine. Told her you'd visit as soon as you could. She's gone home."

"Thanks," I said, easing myself back onto the pillow. My stomach felt like somebody was mixing a vodka collins within.

"I'm the one to say thanks," Gloria murmured.

"Miss?" The door cop had managed to locate a pencil and flip open his notebook. "Can you describe the men who attacked you?"

So. I hadn't passed muster as an accident victim. Some forensic digging had been done. I can't say I was astonished, not with a cop at the door.

Gloria stared at me. Hard.

I said, "Where am I?"

I've always wanted to say that: "Where am I?" like in an old black-and-white film. I suspect I may have fluttered my eyelashes. Who-eee. Whatever did that anesthesiologist stick me full of? I felt fine as long as I was lying down. Just fine.

Out of the corner of my eye I could see Gloria choking back laughter. She recovered nicely, said, "Officer, maybe you ought to tell the nurse she's awake."

"I'm supposed to write down everything she says."

"You get the part about 'Where am I?'?" Gloria inquired.

"Maybe you could fetch the nurse," the cop said huffily.

"Maybe," I said brightly, "I could press the call button."

"I need to talk to the lady alone," the cop said to Gloria, stressing *alone*. "If you could locate her doctor, please . . ."

"And call Paolina," I whispered.

"She might be in school."

"Leave a message with Marta. Phone the school."

"Sure thing," Gloria said. She gave me another searching once-over.

I returned her gaze steadily. One thing I learned from my years on the force: Stick to the Big Lie. "I don't remember anything." That was my story, and it was a good one. Strong alibis are simple alibis. You start messing with little bits and pieces here and there, like the phase of the moon, or who you picked up last, and you've got a whole stack of lies to memorize. Stick to basics. I don't remember. The end.

Gloria wheeled herself out.

"Uh, what's your name?" the cop asked. A waste-of-time question, I thought. Not a cop question, a doctor question. Right up there with shining lights in my eyes and checking to see that my pupils matched. Mooney must have assigned my case a low priority.

"Carlotta," I said. "Carlyle. Like the nineteenth-century British essayist." I wound up spelling it.

"Now, Carlotta," the cop said. That's why he wanted my name, so he could get chummy with me. "I want you to think back and tell me the last thing you remember."

I wrinkled my brow in utter concentration. "You asked me my name," I said triumphantly.

"Before that," he said. "Before the hospital."

"So that's where I am," I said, eyes wide with phony relief.

"Do you know why you're in the hospital?"

"Uh, am I sick?"

"Think back."

"I can't seem to recall . . ."

"Let's try this. You were driving . . ."

"Did I have an accident? Hey, something's wrong with my leg."

He was writing it down, his tongue clamped between his teeth. You'd think they'd have sprung for a tape recorder.

"You hurt your ankle," he said. "It might have happened when you tried to run for help."

"I tried to run for help?" No way Mooney had trained this bozo. What kind of rookies were they getting these days? Maybe if I let him prompt me enough, he'd tell me the whole story. Then I could ID some suspects. He probably had handy mug shots available.

"We have reason to believe you may have been assaulted," he said firmly.

"Not an accident?" I murmured.

"Were your assailants black?"

A probable racist to boot. I wished Gloria would come back. "My what?" I asked.

He lowered his voice to a more confidential level. "Guys try to rape you? It's okay, you can tell me. I'm a cop. You can talk to me about anything."

Why me? I wondered. Why do I rate the jerk who missed the sensitivity-training class?

"I don't know what you're talking about," I said. "I don't even think you're a policeman. You get any closer, I'm gonna start screaming."

"Lady—"

"Carlotta, remember? I mean it. One more step—"

"Look, I just want to know what happened."

"Who do you work for?"

"I'm asking the questions here."

"You are?"

"Yeah."

"Well, go ahead."

He glanced down at his notebook, flustered. "Uh, do you have any recollection of the events of the night of December fourteenth?"

Dear Lord, a graduate of the Agatha Christie Police Academy and Charm School.

"What's today?" I asked.

"The fifteenth."

"What time is it?" I was having fun. I was asking the questions again. The doctor and Gloria interrupted.

The handsome cocoa-colored gentleman was still on duty.

"You're going to be using crutches for a while, young lady," he said.

Crusty, I bet that's how his patients described him.

"Doctor," I said. "My name is Ms. Carlyle. How do you do?"

Those little backless johnnies make me revert to the strictest formality. I didn't remember changing into any goddamn johnnie. Where were my clothes? It's not that I'm immoderately modest. It's that I dislike being inspected like a lamb chop. I'd rather be treated like a sex object than a chunk of damaged meat.

"Broken?" I asked, indicating my ankle.

"Severe sprain. You were lucky."

"I feel okay. I can handle crutches. When do I leave?"

"We'll have to decide that."

"*We?*" I said, my voice taking on the edge it reserves for the royal pronoun. "My vote's for right now. What time is it anyway?"

"A little past noon. You were brought in this morning at five."

He did the light-shining bit and asked me where I was born and tricky stuff like my mother's maiden name. Probably in cahoots with my imagined wallet-ransacking admissions clerk. Wanted the information to fake out a jewelry store with my credit card.

With my line of credit, he'd have to shop Kmart sales.

"Where's my stuff?" I asked.

"The police have it," the cop said.

"All of it? They've got my underwear?"

"Possible evidence." The cop smirked. "I've got a receipt you can sign."

"Terrific."

"With head injuries we prefer to keep the patient overnight for observation," Doctor Crusty said after testing the reflexes in my good leg. "I don't believe there's any residual trauma or interior bleeding, but since you were unconscious when you were brought in, it would be unwise to release you until tomorrow."

"What if I had a friend spend the night?"

He smiled as if I'd told a particularly funny joke. "A friend who'd wake you every two hours and take your blood pressure? A lawyer, I presume?"

No way was I getting out with Doc Crusty on call. He departed to flirt with other patients, and I resigned myself to my fate. I strongly suggested that the door cop call in the amnesia report and return to meaningful work in his chosen profession.

He stayed put. Gloria and I conversed in quiet verbal shorthand.

"M?" I asked.

"Okay. Take it."

"What's this?"

"Dollar. You once told me you needed a dollar to—"

My fingers closed on the bill. "Where am I gonna put it, client? Hang on to it for me."

"Babe, what it is, I think, somebody might be trying to close me down."

"Close down G and W?"

The cop approached and we segued into meaningless chatter. Gloria stayed and I was grateful for her reassuring presence. She gossiped about weather and friends. I drifted in and out. The day started to take on a rhythm. When my ankle throbbed, I'd press the call button. A nurse would appear with a tiny paper cup of pills. Just ibuprofen, but they worked.

Paolina came by at three, which meant she'd cut her last class. I didn't mention it. I didn't have a chance.

With a contemptuous glance at the cop, she started rattling away in Spanish.

"Whoa," I said. "I can't keep up. *Despacio, por favor*. And please, before you yell at me, give me a chance to apologize. I'm sorry I scared you. I'm hardly hurt at all, and I was careful. Sometimes you can be careful and still get messed up."

Her words spilled out in an angry rush, English this time.

"Look at your leg. What about volleyball? There's a game tomorrow. At school. I was counting on you. You promised," she said furiously. "I thought that now you weren't a cop, I wouldn't have to worry like I used to. Sam's right. You're crazy to drive a cab."

"That what you and Sam were chatting about at the Y? Deciding my future for me?"

"The way you try to do for me? No. We said nothing about you. *Nada*."

"What did you talk about?"

"What difference does it make?"

"Sit down, baby. Please. I don't want to fight."

"Don't call me 'baby.' I always tell you that."

Gloria said, "Girl, I still call *her* 'baby,' and she's bigger than most."

I was grateful for the interruption. It took some of the wind out of Paolina's sails. She was geared for battle, eyes flashing. Storing her fear and anger since early morning, letting them simmer and come to a boil. She'd dressed for confrontation, in her most grown-up outfit, a dark sweater and matching skirt. I preferred her in bright colors.

She was right. I wanted her to stay a baby. If not a baby, young. Very young for a very long time.

The hell of it was, I understood her fury. As a child, she'd been too often abandoned, dumped with one relative or another so her mother could try out a new live-in boyfriend without the added burden of kids. She'd see my hospitalization as another in a series of betrayals. As a horrid reminder that I could die, become another transient "aunt" in her life.

"Paolina," I said. "I'm sorry. There'll be other games. I promise. My ankle's not so bad. I'm not out for the season—"

"I hate you," she said, her low voice charged with emotion.

And stomped out of the room.

I swallowed. Twelve years old, I probably said that to people. To my mother. And I wasn't Paolina's mom, just her adopted Big Sister.

I shook my head, stirring the rumbling ache under the bandage. She didn't mean it. I knew she didn't mean it, but the cold fist that closed around my heart made me want to apologize to my long-dead mother all the same.

THIRTEEN

Bureaucracy ruled and I squirmed the night away in my mechanical bed, unable to punch the pillow into a comfortable shape, awakened by nurses bearing blood-pressure cuffs, annoyed and annoying to all. I toyed with conspiracy theories: Mooney knew all about the switcheroo with Marvin, was holding me prisoner pending an arrest warrant.

A warrant for what? Impersonating a victim? Obstruction of justice?

Mooney himself paid a visit before my release. He brought flowers, which made me feel terrible. Wicked. Evil. Better he should have brought a warrant.

The Big Lie, I reminded myself: Don't remember a thing.

I never lie to Mooney when I can help it. And when I absolutely have to prevaricate, I try to do it via telephone. He has one of the best bullshit meters in the business. I've heard hardened perps discuss crimes with him in a way they wouldn't talk to their priest during confession. I don't know why. It's a gift, like music. Some have the ear, some have the instrumental skill, some have the voice.

Mooney's got something extra in the lie-detector field.

He also has a linebacker's body, wide shoulders, narrow hips, and dresses like he never saw a cop uniform. Sneakers, faded jeans, button-down shirts, tweedy sweaters: a Harvard prof who spends his free time working out. I like the way he looks. Tell the truth, if we hadn't worked together so long, we might have had a fling. Maybe more.

But I'd committed the cardinal sin of sleeping with my boss before I'd ever met Mooney. My first boss, Sam Gianelli. And in spite of everything—Sam's brief matrimonial venture, my own semiretaliatory wedding vows—the two of us still manage to generate electricity at combustion levels.

I never—well, almost never—get that melted-chocolate feeling when Mooney's around. Maybe he's right when he says I prefer outlaws to cops.

Mooney looks like he expects the best from you, like you'd disappoint him with a lie, like he's always known you and he can see inside your head. A deadly blend of teacher, priest, and your father when he was at his most understanding, and you felt you could tell him all about the way your stomach tingled when that boy in your math class kissed you for the first time.

And wasn't that a big mistake! I steeled myself.

Mooney nodded the guard out of the room.

I was glad I didn't have to face Mooney and his posy of gift-shop flowers in my johnnie. Anticipating departure, I'd changed into old navy pants—one leg ripped to accommodate my ankle—and a white cotton sweatshirt. I'd told Roz the exact items to bring, plain, serviceable, reliable. Without instruction, she might have turned up with anything from a satin teddy to gym shorts.

Mooney smiled down at me.

If a nurse came in to take my blood pressure right now, they'd keep me an extra day. Maybe more. I purposely slowed my breathing. You can outwit the machines, the lie detectors and the blood-pressure cuffs.

Can you beat Mooney?

He surprised me. Totally. First he bent down and awkwardly kissed me on the cheek. Then he dumped the flowers in the sink like he didn't want to mention them.

Instead of saying "Hello" or "How are you?" or asking a single question, he simply unsnapped his service holster and took out his gun.

"Mooney?" I said.

"You see what I'm holding, Carlotta?"

"I know what a gun looks like."

"Here."

"You keep it for me, Moon," I said, wondering if I should buzz for the nurse. "I'll feel safer."

"Tell me, what's your carry-gun these days, Carlotta?"

"My old Chiefs Special thirty-eight. You know that." Except I didn't have it. Marvin had it.

Mooney said, "Your hardware's out of date. Cops

don't carry six-shot thirty-eights anymore. See what we're issuing now?" He handed it to me, butt first. I wouldn't touch it till he removed the magazine and showed me the empty chamber. "Glock Seventeen Auto Pistol. Nine-millimeter. Seventeen rounds and one ready."

"Ugly too," I said.

"Stopping power. You need to upgrade your hardware, Carlotta."

"What kind of hospital visit is this? You shill for the NRA on your time off?"

His voice grew noticeably cooler. He sat in the chrome-and-vinyl visitor's chair. "Three weeks ago, I catch a report on a drive-by. They zip across my desk like roaches. This one's a zero. Nothing. Nobody killed. Nobody down. Garbage paperwork. No witnesses willing to say much beyond 'screw you.' You know the kind?"

I kept an expression of polite interest glued to my face.

"Except there's this seven-year-old boy says he saw a white lady, real tall with real red hair."

"When you're seven, everybody seems tall," I offered.

"That's how we're gonna play this?" he asked.

"I don't know the game," I said.

"I think you do. And I think you know who knocked you out of your cab too."

"Mooney—"

"How about hypnosis?" he said. "You willing to try hypnosis? The department has a good person."

"It's inadmissable evidence. Waste of time." I

clamped my mouth shut. A simple no would have been enough.

"Why did I know you were going to refuse, Carlotta? And I bet you still can't remember a thing. Temporary amnesia. Right. But I can't keep a guard on you forever. I don't have that kind of manpower. So when you get out, we're gonna visit a gun shop, and maybe you'll make a little investment in staying alive."

I said, "You ever think of doing volunteer work in your spare time?"

"The Glock's fine when it's fully loaded. Light touch. You should try one. The balance isn't that great after you fire. Metal top, plastic stock, fewer bullets you have in the magazine, the more top-heavy it gets. I hear S and W makes a good nine."

"That's enough, Mooney." If he was trying to scare me, he wasn't doing a half-bad job.

"It's not enough, Carlotta. You get shot at, you get mugged. You're having a bad stretch, and you're not telling your friends why. You may think you've got good reason, okay. But I'm not satisfied. I'm going after your client list. I already questioned Roz—"

"Bet you got an earful. Look, Moon, I understand your curiosity, but don't give me any rot about how you're so damned concerned for my safety. If I were a cop, you'd have my ass riding decoy in a cab."

"I might," he admitted.

"What rips you is you can't order me around. So, please, don't try."

"What rips me is I see a lot of pieces and none of them fit." He paused for a moment, lowered his voice, and composed himself. "So, you wanna make a bet?"

In the squad room, Mooney and I bet on everything, from how long it would take to close a particular case to how many pimps we could ID in a single night patrolling the bus station.

"Terms?" I said.

"If you're telling the truth, I'll let Roz cut my hair. That's how sure I am you're lying."

What a lost opportunity.

"If I'm not telling the truth?"

He gave me a look. "Buy a gun or take a vacation. If you want to talk, you know my number." He shoved his chair back with a scrape that sent shivers up my spine. "Bye."

After he'd been gone thirty seconds, I grabbed my crutches and hobbled to the door. "Thanks for the goddamn flowers," I yelled down the empty corridor.

A cheery nurse poked her head around the corner and shook her head reproachfully.

At 2 P.M. I was formally released. At 2:05 Gloria sent a Green & White to take me home.

FOURTEEN

I sat on a lobby bench until Leroy, Gloria's youngest and most polished brother, the one who reputedly bit the ear off a fellow NFL player, squealed the cab's tires against the curb, jumped out, and attempted to carry me from the hospital portico to the backseat.

"Front seat," I protested. "I'll smack you with a crutch."

He glared at me. He had his orders.

"Leroy," I murmured, with a touch of flirtatious guile. "Come on. How can we talk if I'm in back?" Gloria doesn't realize how vulnerable her brother is to feminine wiles. If I could con him, with my raccoon-bruised eyes and heavily bandaged leg, he was way too easy.

I had no intention of screaming my demands through a bulletproof, practically soundproof shield.

"Where's Marvin?" I inquired as soon as the cab was under way, bumping along Brookline Avenue. City workers had strung skimpy greenery studded with the occasional Christmas light between streetlamps. The half-hearted attempt at festivity made the afternoon gloom more intense. I opened the passenger window a chilly crack and breathed deeply. After a day and a half of canned hospital air, exhaust fumes smelled sweet. "How is he?"

"Fine," was the cryptic reply, which I found hard to credit.

"Takes a lot to bust up Marvin," Leroy continued. "Me and my brother, Geoffrey, tried it all the time when we was kids. That's why prizefightin' came so natural to him."

"I want to see him."

"Gloria says he needs to rest up first."

"Now."

"No way. Gloria says—"

"Get her on the horn."

"Don't give me no sass."

"Take me to Marvin," I said. "I can feel my memory returning. If I don't see him today, I'm going to the police, or maybe the Hackney Carriage Bureau."

"Gloria warned me," Leroy said dourly.

"What did she say?"

"Said you're the only other woman she knows stubborn as she is."

"So?"

He pulled a sudden U-turn that left openmouthed commuters aghast, their horns bleating. "So we go visit Marvin. You relax now."

He crossed Huntington Avenue and headed south-east toward Roxbury, the heart of black Boston, increasingly known as "the 'bury," pronounced like a fruit, neither luscious nor sweet. After we crossed Melnea Cass Boulevard, Leroy started making a slew of turns, some so unnecessary we circled the block.

"Lost?" I inquired.

He eyeballed the rearview mirror.

"White Chevrolet Caprice. You know who that might be?"

"You sure he's following?"

"Look for yourself."

"Unmarked unit," I said disgustedly. Ah, Mooney, trusting Mooney. "The cops didn't buy the amnesia thing."

"I'll lose 'em," Leroy said calmly. "Check and see if they're doin' a two-car box. One car I can shake easy."

"It's a single," I said after a couple blocks of clear sailing. "Unless they're playing fancy with radios. Remember, if they flash their cherry, stop. Gloria'll get in trouble if one of her cabs breaks the law."

"Breaks the law?" Leroy feigned innocence. Then he floored the accelerator and two-wheeled a turn through a crowded Purity Supreme parking lot. A battle-scarred Pontiac Bonneville backed out of a space. Leroy swerved, a paint scrape away. The driver slammed on his brakes, his horn, and raised one finger in a derisive salute. Heads craned, and other horns joined in the song. More brakes screeched. Leroy gunned the car out of the lot, turned right and right again, then stopped dead in an alleyway, concealed behind an overfed Dumpster.

He turned to me, brown eyes aglow. "Hope that didn't mess your foot up."

I swallowed. "No sweat. But if our tail's a cop, he'll radio our plate."

Leroy said, "Keep your eyes open. Anybody else takes an interest in us, we'll head back to your place and try again tonight."

"You didn't arrange this little show for my benefit, did you, Leroy? You and Gloria. To discourage me from seeing Marvin?"

"Girl, you don't trust anybody."

"Occupational hazard," I said.

"Keep an eye out, okay?"

I rolled down the window and aimed the side mirror so I'd get a better view of the street. I didn't see the white Chevy.

"Good," Leroy said, hanging another horn-blasting U-turn.

The bar, on a cross street off Columbus Avenue, was not a familiar one. Hardly looked like a bar; a lone flickering Bud Light sign differentiated it from residential dwellings on either side. We parked in a back alley and headed for what appeared to be a solid slat-boarded wall. Leroy kept a protective hand on my arm.

"Gloria said it'd be better to wait till Marvin could come to you," Leroy remarked as we picked our way through discarded trash and broken bottles.

"I hate waiting," I said.

"Huh," he muttered disparagingly. "Lot you're gonna do hoppin' on crutches."

He banged on a section of wall twice in quick succession. A beautiful caramel-skinned woman wearing floral-print bike shorts, a black bra, and earrings that dangled past her shoulders, opened a well-camouflaged door. Her hair was braided and piled regally high, twined into a coronet.

"Leroy, you're crazy," she whispered, staring at me and shaking her head.

"Yvonne," he said, "this woman gets it into her head to do something, takes more than me to stop her. Carlotta, meet Yvonne."

I held out my hand. She regarded me with disfavor bordering on disgust. When confronted with glares directed at my light skin and red hair, I feel a dread compulsion to defend my political beliefs, announce my racial awareness—which isn't perfect by a long shot, but what outsider's can be?

Yvonne didn't look like she cared about my voting record.

"Marvin feel up to talking?" I asked into hostile silence.

His gravelly voice came from a distance. "'Vonne, this gal's okay. You don't have to kiss her, but please, invite her in."

Wordlessly, Yvonne swung the door open. She walked away with graceful dignity, head high.

Leroy locked the door behind us with the snick of a massive bolt.

Marvin's sickroom suggested a hastily converted warehouse, with liquor cases stacked so high around the brick walls they almost made walls themselves. The place smelled musty, with a sharp undercurrent of spilled whiskey. Light from one overhead bulb, partially shaded by a tattered paper party lantern, revealed a linoleum floor, its seams buckled with age.

I half swung, half walked toward a corner partially blocked by cartons. I'd forgotten how hard it is to use crutches, how much space the damn things take, how much upper-body strength.

"You're lookin' good," Marvin lied, blinking his eyes and inching up on one elbow.

"You too," I lied in return. "Sorry if I woke you."

He made it to a sitting position, gritting his teeth so he wouldn't groan with the effort, shook my hand with a firm, dry grip, then lay back. A bloodstained sheet covered the narrow cot. Marvin's bare feet hung about eight inches over the edge. He wore a stained T-shirt and boxer shorts. His swollen face had purpled around the eyes and nose. A gauze bandage wrapped his forehead. Unlike the clothes and bed linens, it looked fresh.

"Yvonne a nurse?" I asked.

"She knows about nursin'. Knows more about runnin' a joint."

I became aware of background noises: the faint rumble of conversation, hand slapping, cash register. Somebody called out numbers with precise regularity. Bar noises. Gambling noises.

"Leroy," Marvin said, "fetch the lady a chair, don't just stand there. Get her a drink. Me too. Something cold."

Cold? The room was frigid. I wasn't tempted to remove my coat. I unbuttoned it, so he wouldn't think I was eager to leave. I noticed a blanket heaped on the floor at the end of the bed, asked Marvin if he'd like help retrieving it.

"Nope," he said. Probably didn't have a fever, I thought.

We chatted about his injuries till Leroy returned. Marvin seemed proud of the fact that only two of his ribs had been broken. With no X-ray setup I didn't see how he could be so sure.

"Okay," I said, seated on a wooden bar stool, the neck of a frosty beer bottle numbing my hand. "Tell me."

"Temporary amnesia?" Marvin said.

"Don't even try it."

"Just a joke."

"You're allowed one joke. Okay? I just spent the night with nurses poking needles in my butt, my Little Sister says she hates me, and I lied to the only cop I like. Make me feel righteous about it, Marvin."

"It's not like I've been out havin' a high time, Carlotta."

"Sorry," I said. "Really, I apologize. Can I start over?"

"I'm not goin' anyplace special," he said. "I've got time."

I said, "Gloria thinks somebody might be out to shut down G and W. Did you tell anybody you were driving?"

"No."

"Mention it on the radio?"

"Just used my cab number. I'm no fool."

"A girlfriend?" I asked, thinking of Yvonne.

He swallowed a good third of the amber-colored liquid in his tall glass.

"It was a radio call," he said slowly. "Pickup on the corner of Shandon and Harvard."

"Near Franklin Field," I said.

"Gloria gave me a name. She's got it written down. Stevens, maybe."

A useless alias unless we were dealing with truly stupid crooks.

"Go on," I said.

"I see a brother on the corner, looks okay to me. He's standin' under a streetlamp, so I see he's wearin' a cap and a raincoat, and I think it's one hell of a long coat, and right away I wonder does he have somethin' under it. But it's just one guy and mostly, people take a good look, size of my neck and shoulders, nobody bothers me. I check, though, to see if anything's stickin' out of that coat,'cause I heard a baseball bat'll take out a partition. Or a shotgun. Less than a shotgun or a bat, I'll drive him, I figure. Not much worries me."

Marvin lifted a hand to scratch his forehead. The bandage interfered. He rubbed it hard and scowled.

"Well, my fare's already got the door open right back of me when two men come outta no place. Runnin', and they ain't dumb. Don't waste time tryin' the other doors, like they know I would've had 'em locked. Before I can hit the accelerator, one's got his piece, big as a cannon, pressed against my side window. Guy gettin' in the backseat says, 'Roll your window down.' That's the first I know my fare's in on it. I figure *he's* the one gonna get robbed until he talks."

"You recognize his voice?"

"Nope. I roll down the window. Man reaches in and flips off my top lights and shuts off my radio."

"He ask you how to do it?"

"Nope. So I say, easy as I can, 'This is your lucky day, boys. You just earned yourselves some money.' I always carry a hundred on me, five twenties, on account of robberies. You don't give 'em somethin', they kill you."

"They weren't interested?"

"Oh, they took it. But the man by my open window hits the door-lock string, and a second guy with another cannon slides in front, right next to me. That makes two in the back, and the front guy says nothin' but 'Keep your hands where I can see 'em' and 'Turn right here,' 'Turn left here.' Don't ask for more money. Don't seem to hear nothin' I say."

"What did you say?"

"What would you be saying, honey,'sides your prayers? The one up front is white, and I ain't seen the third one good, but I know there's a brother in back. I try bluffin' that I got a tracer on the cab, and this white guy laughs real evil. Says then he'll have to kill me quicker. I figure it's just talk; wants me to sweat, so I act cocky, like I would if somebody's trying to psych me out in the ring."

"What did the white man look like?"

"Young and mean. Evil face. Skinny and sharp, like he ain't never had enough to eat."

"Hair, eyes, height?"

"Light brown. Buzz cut. Pale eyes. Medium height."

"Five ten?"

"No taller than that."

Marvin ran out of booze and signaled his brother for a refill. While Leroy was gone, Marvin asked me to help him get more comfortable. I stuffed pillows behind his back. He didn't quite muffle his groans this time. Had to keep up the bravado for baby brother, I guess.

"We could do this another time if you're hurting," I said.

"Your leg don't hurt none?"

"It hurts," I admitted.

"Let's get back to business. You know, I'm tryin' to be cool and sweat's pourin' off me like I'm gettin' ready to go fifteen rounds. I got an adrenaline high so bad I can hardly sit still, and I figure, hey, if they're gonna waste me, they're gonna have to bleed first. I follow directions till I know where I am. I figure the two guys in back are mostly out of it, 'cause they're behind the shield, and what I need to do is get outta the car and mess with these fuckers. I'm gettin' angry."

I nodded.

"I know the park real good. I know those brambles. Got tossed in 'em plenty when I was a kid. Guys in back tryin' to talk to whitey, and he reaches back to open the partition. Gives me a chance, so I hit the brake hard, then floor it, twist the steering wheel, and jump the curb where I know it's steep. I'm hopin' whitey's gonna whack his head on the ride down. Soon as we stop, I'm out. But the guy behind me's out quicker, and he slaps me down with his gun. That's how I got this lump on the head. Then they're all over me. And I figure I'm dead, them kickin' me and all. And I'm startin' to think it might be better if they shot me."

Leroy brought Marvin's glass, full, and another beer for me. I declined, so little brother sipped it.

"Then?" I said.

Marvin shrugged. "I lie there like I'm dead. They kick me a couple more times, but I don't move. I can take a body punch."

I nodded. I'd never seen him fight, but I'd heard.

"White guy, I think, comes real close, sticks his cannon in my ear. All I can do not to cry out. Then somebody says 'Stop.' Same voice says 'We ain't gettin' paid enough to kill.'"

"Hold it," I said. "Exact words?"

Cabbies are getting beaten for a reason, Lee Cochran had said. Finally, confirmation, a legitimate reason to investigate!

"I'm tellin' it as close as I can," Marvin said defensively.

I touched a hand to my forehead. The headache was revving up.

"This is something the police ought to know, Marvin," I said.

"It's not something I can tell them, Carlotta. That cannon don't move from my ear. White boy's pissed, says 'This guy's different; he tried to kill us.' Other guy says 'Wouldn't you?' and kinda laughs and the gun comes outta my ear. I'm tryin' to keep still, like when you throw a fight."

"Marvin!"

"You so naive, babe. I forget."

"Marvin, they say anything else? They use names?"

He started to shake his massive head, thought better of it, and said, "Don't remember any names."

"Phil Yancey?"

"No. Sorry."

"Descriptions of the other two? ID marks? Anybody got something useful like a tattoo, a scar?"

"I saw the black dude best, under the lamppost. Hat and raincoat, medium height, medium weight, nobody who'd stand out in a crowd. White guy I told you about."

"Third man?"

"Nothin' but a voice."

"You thought Hispanic?"

"I'm not sure on that."

"You know why you thought that? Accent?"

"I dunno."

I wondered if Marvin was holding back, keeping quiet about some detail he could use to wreak a more personal revenge once he'd regained his formidable strength.

Yvonne's staccato heels announced her. "Leroy, your brother's tired to death." She scolded Leroy but her eyes drilled into me. "Look at him. How much you give him to drink? You tryin' to kill him?"

"Vonnie," said Leroy.

"Don't 'Vonnie' me. Get out of here and take the trash with you."

"I'm Marvin's friend," I said. "I came to help."

"Sure. We get lots of help from your kind."

"I'm not here to represent white people. I'm a friend of the family's. You can apologize anytime. Break right in."

"Carlotta," Leroy murmured, "she ain't gonna do no apology."

I said, "I'm out of here. Take care of yourself, Marvin. And change the damn sheets once in a while, okay, nurse?"

"Change 'em yourself," Yvonne said.

I sucked in a deep breath. If I stayed any longer I'd have to apologize to her, and I wasn't in the mood.

"Marvin," I said. "You've got something belongs to me."

"Yeah?"

"Come on."

He reached a hand under the pillow, came out with my .38. Unfired. Or recently cleaned and reloaded.

"Thanks for the loan," he said.

"Leroy," I said, suddenly exhausted. "Take me home."

FIFTEEN

Leroy insisted on helping me up the walkway and onto the porch of my three-story Victorian, inherited from my late aunt Bea and located in an area of Cambridge where I couldn't afford to rent, much less buy. He kept his muscled arm tight around my shoulders. I wondered whether anyone in the People's Republic of Cambridge could be scandalized at the idea of a white woman with a black boyfriend. On the whole, I thought not.

"Gotta go," he said, before I could invite him in for coffee, far more wary of racial hostility than I was. "Gloria's gonna be mad. I shoulda checked in."

If there are such things as mama's boys, I thought, there are certainly sister's boys; Gloria owned three.

I entered the hall and negotiated the single step down to the living room, my concentration riveted by

the lurching, swinging motion required to advance via
crutches. As soon as I stopped moving, sinking gratefully into my aunt's rocking chair, I knew something
was wrong. I couldn't spot anything out of place. A
slightly different smell. Had Roz, in a burst of frenetic
energy, polished the furniture? I ran my finger across a
mahogany end table, left a streak in the dust. No. Had
something spoiled in the refrigerator and managed to
send its pungent fumes this far?

"Roz," I yelled. She lives on the third floor, within
hollering range.

No reply.

My desk had changed.

Even from the back, I could see that the cables and
wires from the useless computer had been arranged in
a different configuration. I hopped over and sat in my
desk chair. The computer setup was alien. It wasn't the
one I'd bought for fifty bucks, and at considerable bod-
ily risk, during my outing with Sam.

"What?" Roz demanded from the doorway. No
"Welcome home." No "How are you?" Just "What?"

I'd interrupted her at some vital task, that was obvious from the attitude. Possibly painting, which would
account for the crooked orange smears across her forehead and cheek. Aside from the vivid Day-Glo high-
lights, she was a vision in black. Skinny black tights
disappeared into high-heeled ankle boots. A loosely
crocheted black sweater, its open pattern revealing a
lack of underwear, completed the ensemble. Except for
the black turban. And the multiple earrings. And the
ring for each finger.

She looked like I'd caught her in the middle of whipping up a cauldron of witch's brew.

"Whoa," she said. "Neat eye makeup." I trusted she was kidding. "But the crutches are retro."

Having no idea how to respond to that, I said, "Roz, something's different."

"Do you like it?"

"I can't tell," I said.

"I wasn't sure you could see it from there."

"What are we talking about, Roz?"

She yanked down the neck of her sweater, came closer. "Incredible, huh?"

Between her assertive breasts was a tattoo any dishonorably discharged Marine would have been proud to call his own. Two screaming eagles engaged in a perverse sexual act is probably the best way to describe it.

"You designed it yourself," I guessed.

"Yep."

"But it comes off?"

"Forever. Like a diamond."

I sucked air. I do not comment on Roz's fashion statements.

"I'm gonna get more. I have incredible sketches," she said.

I envisioned the tattooed lady at an X-rated circus.

"Oooh," she said suddenly. "You got another package."

"Huh?"

"From Miami Sleaze."

Thurman W. Vandenburg is the lawyer who handles

Carlos Roldan Gonzales's many entanglements in the States. I've never met him. We've talked on the phone. Miami Sleaze sums him up nicely.

"I figured I ought to open it," Roz said, "considering the other ones. You were in the hospital."

"More cash?"

"Seven large. My tumbling mats are stuffed, so I put it in the cat box."

She's honest, I recited to myself. Weird, weirder, weirdest, but honest.

"So, I've got dough stashed in my gym mats. You've got major bucks in the Kitty Litter. If I start smurfing it, I could sleep better nights."

Smurfing is drug lingo. Smurfers—the bottom feeders of the business—make bank deposits, each no more than $9,900 because cash deposits of ten thou or more have to be reported to Uncle. Typically the smurf gets the extra hundred for his time. Big dealers need lots of smurfs.

"What's your problem?" I asked. "The money's lumpy? You don't have to sleep on it, Roz."

"It's just I don't like it when I bring new guys over. One of them might have a nose for cash."

"I'll take care of the money," I promised. I didn't like the idea of smurfing. Local banks have been on the lookout lately for repeat nine-thousand-buck depositors. I didn't want a collection of accounts all over town. If the cash kept Roz from sleeping with strangers, I thought, maybe I ought to leave it where it was.

"Soon," Roz said.

"This is not my computer," I said, trying to get the discussion back on track.

"So?" Roz observed.

I stayed mute, raised one eyebrow.

"Man from the store brought you an update," she said. "No big deal. He sold you the wrong model, or they came out with a new model right after you bought the old one. Something like that. Your warranty covered it. No charge."

"Tell me about the guy from the store, Roz."

"He taught me how to use it. Neat."

"He gave you lessons? That must have taken a while."

"Well, he stayed maybe four, five hours.

"What did he look like?"

Roz stared at the floor. She never blushes, but when her eyes start searching for dust bunnies, you know she's up to something. Such as concocting a likely story.

No way would Roz let a strange woman into my house, much less near my desk and files. A man, however, a remotely fuckable man, and security precautions fly out the window.

"The man who sold you the computer," she said. "Old friend of Sam's and all. Frank. Seemed like a friend of yours too."

"Tall; skinny; beard; long, greasy, graying hair?"

"Tall. Thin. No beard, no gray, and a damned fine haircut," she said. "Good-looking. You know, one of those boney, artsy faces—so ugly it crosses the line and turns handsome."

Sounded like Frank had made an effort to impress. Seemed like he'd succeeded.

I surveyed my desk. The new equipment looked about twenty years newer and a hundred times costlier

than my previous stuff. It included an extra telephone.
A red one. The hot line.

Roz continued, "Frank said you'd need a hard disk
if you're going to use Kermit or XMODEM, like to
download—"

"Kermit?" I said. "As in frog?"

"It's an FTP, a file transfer program," Roz said,
smirking. "Frank explained. He said I'm a natural, a
potential 'cyberpunk.' Cyberpunk is very cool."

Great. I couldn't fire her. She understood the new
computer. The new printer. I hadn't even bought a
printer. I knew somebody with an extra who'd promised
to donate it. Frank had tossed one into the grab bag.

"Did you establish a lasting relationship with
Frank, Roz?"

"Huh?"

"You know."

"He's not a salesman, right?"

"Right, Roz."

"Something funny going on."

"You're on a streak."

"He seemed interested in you."

"What did you tell him?"

"I lied a lot, for the hell of it, to string him along. I
thought he was cute."

"Cute?" Maybe we weren't talking about the same
guy. "Intense?" I asked. "Talks fast?"

"Yeah, that too. Kinda old, but very experienced,
you know?"

I kept quiet. I was afraid she'd tell me, in graphic
detail.

"I got the license number of his repair van."

"Good for you," I said. Me, I like to minimally trust a guy before I go to bed with him. Roz regards sex as exercise, on a par with a good karate workout. If the CIA held an audition for the next Mata Hari, Roz would make the cut.

They'd never take her. Too subversive.

"What made you suspicious?" I asked.

"He was too focused on you. Asked questions."

"Maybe he thinks I'm 'cute,'" I said.

"Van plate didn't pan out." She sighed. "Stolen. Later recovered. No leads. No damage."

"Guy's a little old for joyriding, Roz."

"Not so old," she said.

Roz likes her men young, old, married, divorced, black, white. She's equal opportunity, all the way.

She went on, "When the license didn't work, I was really pissed. Good thing I'd searched his wallet. You always say go for the Social Security number. His was right on his driver's license. Dumb. Even I know enough not to put my SSN on my Mass. license."

"Bingo." I didn't want to ask how she'd managed the details. Probably picked the man's pocket during a post-orgasmic snooze. You have to admire Roz.

"And get this. It's a total phony," she said.

"What?"

"His SSN. Francis Tallifiero—that's the name on the card—died at the age of two. In some hick town near Bangor, Maine."

"You didn't copy the wrong number?"

"Carlotta."

"Go finish whatever you were doing," I said. "And don't let the bastard in here again."

"Shit. My hair," she said, grabbing at her turban and charging upstairs.

No wonder the house smelled odd. The orange streaks were hair dye, not paint.

And Frank was not Frank.

Who knew? Sam knew.

I dialed his number. His message machine answered. I started to hang up, decided to wait. I know the recording by heart. Five steady rings, then the pickup, the mechanical hum of spooling tape, the deep, sexy voice: "You've reached five five five, eight two five four. Sorry I can't talk now. Leave your name and number after the beep and I'll be in touch."

I listened to Sam's bass-baritone, his phrasing. The pattern was as familiar as breathing, automatic, beyond thought.

Abruptly, a new sentence: "In case of emergency, you can reach me at two oh two, five five five, oh three two three." I recognized the Washington, D.C., area code.

I picked up the receiver and pressed eleven buttons. A woman answered energetically. A pleasant voice. Youthful. Soprano. No discernible accent. Her simple, repeated "hello" threw me. I'd absolutely expected a hotel operator, an institutional response.

On the subject of men, my *bubbe* liked to say, *Me ken im getryen vi a kats smetene.* "You can trust him like you can trust a cat with sour cream." I clamped my tongue between my teeth.

"Hello? Is anyone there?" she said. Then she must have turned away from the mouthpiece. I heard her mutter faintly, "Just a sec, honey, I'll be right with you."

I said, "Excuse me, I think I may have the wrong number."

"What number are you trying to reach?" she asked politely.

"Two oh two, five five five, oh three two three."

"Right. To whom did you wish to speak?"

I heard his voice in the background. A rumble, off mike, but recognizable. I pressed the plunger gently. The click sounded loud and final.

Honey.

SIXTEEN

I'm not sure how long I sat at my desk. I replaced my .38 in its locked haven, unloading it and sniffing the barrel for telltale signs of use. My nose told me nothing. Maybe I was coming down with a cold. Mooney's threatened gun-shop excursion filled me with apprehension. I'm not bonded to my .38; I have no weapons nostalgia. I just never dreamed I'd need a machine gun to stay in business. Maybe, I thought idly, I should consider using some of Paolina's father's dough to invest in an armored car.

If my ankle hadn't started throbbing, I might have brooded all night, yanking my hair out strand by strand. Driven by pain, I belatedly followed doctor's orders, hobbling to the kitchen, where I discovered, to my dismay, that both ice-cube trays had disappeared from the freezer. Despite my threats, Roz continues to perform chemical experiments in her sideline as a photographer, absconding with any kitchen utensil that strikes her fancy. The missing ice-cube trays might be lurking in the basement darkroom, rendered unusable by the residue of one of her chemical cocktails.

There are advantages to having a lousy housekeeper and an old refrigerator with a defrost mechanism that quit functioning in the fifties. I attacked the caked ice on the sides of the freezer compartment with a carving fork. No dice. I don't own an ice pick; a screwdriver did the trick.

I piled ice chips on a dish towel, folded it in three lengthwise, hopped back to the living room.

Underneath a sock and layers of bandage, my ankle was a multihued, puffy distortion. I wound the makeshift ice pack around it, haphazardly securing the ends of the towel with paper clips. Then I propped the whole shebang on my desktop blotter and leaned back in my chair.

Elevation and ice. The wonders of medical progress: exactly the same treatment my mother would have advised. The doctor hadn't offered her other fail-safe prescription, chicken soup, but I would have cheerfully downed a bowlful had the homemade variety been available. Campbell's lacks the healing touch.

This woman in Washington, who the hell was she? I knew enough about Sam's family to rule out his sister, his cousins, even distant relations. "Honey," she'd called him. The casual endearment grated. Sam's mistress? His intended bride? How had I gotten mixed up with a man who didn't have the nerve to tell me?

Maybe *nerve* was not the right word. Maybe he had a hell of a nerve.

A sick uncle in Providence? Or a lady in Washington?

Now, now. There, there. I cautioned myself against jumping to conclusions. But it seemed to me that the message on Sam's machine meant that he was spending a great deal of time at the 202 exchange.

Stop it! I scolded myself.

I reviewed my meeting with Marvin, scribbling notes to record his exact words. I stopped mid-sentence and reached for the phone. No reason I couldn't dial Mooney, tell him I'd recalled that one of my attackers had said he'd been paid to beat up cabbies.

No reason except that Mooney wouldn't believe my selective memory. He'd insist on hypnosis.

Hypnosis. Maybe that wasn't such a bad idea. Maybe Keith Donovan, the shrink almost next door, could do the trick.

Bad idea. I knew it as soon as it crossed my mind. Despite his thing with Roz, I had more than a mild yen for Donovan myself. I suspected it was mutual. Donovan had said as much, admitting that he found himself intrigued by women who seemed comfortable with violence. Specifically by me. Except for Sam, matters might have developed. And now . . .

Stop it!

I had a client, even if she'd only paid me a dollar thus far, and that on account. I concentrated on details relating to the evening of Marvin's beating: the chill, damp air, the moonless sky, the piney tang of greenery.

Maybe Mooney was right. Maybe a hint, a clue, lay dormant in my unconscious.

I leaned back and closed my eyes. The icy cloth felt fine against my ankle. Conversations replayed themselves like faint taped messages. Gloria, her voice as close to panic as I've ever heard it: *"I wouldn't have let him drive, except two more guys quit on me today. . . ."*

I sat bolt upright, jarring my foot. I'd forgotten her words in my anger over her next admission: Sam had ordered her to keep me off the late-night shift.

Two drivers quitting on the same day? It wasn't as if the economy had done a quick one-eighty, with jobs for ex-cabbies plentiful. I grabbed the phone and dialed.

"Green and White," she answered.

"Gloria," I said, speaking loudly over the pounding background music, knowing I wouldn't have to identify myself. Call her more than once and you're in Gloria's memory bank for good. "I need names and addresses for the two who quit right before the Wednesday night graveyard shift."

"Hang on. Phones're hot."

I got slammed into telephone limbo before I could protest. I checked my wristwatch. Five-o'clock rush. Gloria works phone lines like a keyboard artist plays the organ. With her great pipes and reassuring manner, she's as soothing as a minister. When she says she's gonna send a cab within ten minutes during an ice storm, you believe her.

"Why?" was all she said when the phone clicked back to life. The master manipulator had no need to check whether she'd reconnected to the right party.

"I talked to Marvin—" I began.

"Leroy said."

"I need to follow up on something."

"Those guys who left me didn't beat on Marvin, babe. Little shrimpy men, both of 'em."

"Gloria, I want to talk to them."

"Both Haitians, different last names, livin' at the same address. Flophouse, phone in the hall."

"Give me the address."

"And don't ask questions? With me your client and all and payin' for your precious time?"

"You'll miss cab calls, staying on this line," I said.

"You're looking for Jean Halle and Louis Vertigne. Twenty-eight forty Vinson. Dorchester."

"Phone?"

"Five five five, seven eight oh six. Now, what did Marvin say? He blame me? Is that woman looking after him right? I want him in a hospital, but he says he's fine. He don't look fine."

"I'm hanging up, Glory."

"No wonder you attract so many clients," she said. "It's your phone manners."

"And I'll need a list of all the cabbies who've quit on you lately," I said. "Say, in the past year."

"You're kidding."

"No."

"I'm supposed to give you everything you want, and you won't answer a single question."

"How's your diet going?"

She hung up. I knew that would get her off the line.

I let the phone ring seventeen times. Eighteen. Nineteen. I don't usually hang on that long, but a rooming house is not a home. A blaring phone is nobody's true responsibility. You need to wallop somebody over the head with the idea that they'll get no peace until they answer.

Twenty-five, twenty-six.

The voice was female and ill-tempered. A little hazy, like I'd woken her from a deep sleep.

Sweetness and sincerity seemed worth a try. "Sorry to disturb you," I said, wishing I had a voice as compelling as Gloria's. "I wouldn't unless it was urgent."

"Sure," the woman responded dryly, unimpressed.

"I'm trying to reach Mr. Jean Halle or Mr. Louis Vertigne," I ventured, taking a stab at pronunciations I'd heard only once.

"So?"

"It's extremely urgent that I speak with one of them." Was I laying it on too thick? Can something be more urgent than urgent?

"They live on the third floor," the woman admitted grudgingly.

"Are they home?"

"How would I know?"

"Is there some way you might be able to find out?"

"Well, it's like this: I could hustle up three flights of stairs in my fuckin' bathrobe and bang on the door. The question is, why should I?"

"Hello?" I said.

Silence.

Undaunted, I dialed again. Busy signal. No doubt she'd left the receiver dangling in a gesture of neighborly goodwill.

Shit. Face-to-face is the way to go. I wouldn't have bothered with the phone except for my ankle.

As I leaned over to examine its yellow-green bruising, the doorbell rang three times. Three times means Roz, which is a good thing since I had no intention of hopping to the door like a wounded bunny.

Roz raced down, high heels pock-pocking the steps. Her hair was fully exposed. I shuddered involuntarily.

The orange streak across her forehead was the tip of a bizarre iceberg. Orange, purple, and blue were the colors: orange on the stubbly third of her head she'd shaved to a glossy shine two weeks earlier. Purple faded to blue on the other side. Trimmed short in back and dramatically longer in front, it resembled a flying wedge and was tastefully bisected by a single cornrow of neon purple.

Just when I think she's hit the edge, Roz breaks new ground. She's her own best canvas.

Keith Donovan—between patients, no doubt—had removed his tie and suit jacket, revealing a crisp white shirt trisected by red suspenders. Had he considered their acquisition long and hard before purchasing? Had he analyzed what they might communicate about his personality? Had he thought half as much about his choice of bedmates?

He looked great as usual, slim and fit, but the suspenders made him seem younger than he was—and he must have been a whiz kid to speed through med school and hang his own shingle while in his late twenties. I bet none of his patients ever glimpsed the fireman suspenders. Perhaps they were a special treat for

Roz. Maybe she used them to tie him up in some original and erotic fashion.

"Carlotta," he said, breaking stride when he saw me. "You okay?"

Roz tapped her toe on a step, annoyed at the delay. Keith has a well-established practice, probably can't take more than an hour off to fool around. I felt cranky at the very thought. All I needed was to spend time with my foot on ice listening to Roz in ecstasy. Roz is noisy. It's not an item I thought about covering in our initial tenant-landlord interview: Do you shriek when you make love?

"I am not okay," I said. "I need help. You're an M.D., right?"

I watched him notice the crutches and absorb the reason for the ice pack.

"I need to walk," I said.

"Let's take a look." Solemnly, he unwrapped my foot. If I'd known I was going to have a gentleman caller, I'd have used a clean dish towel.

"Keith," Roz protested from the staircase.

He probed my ankle with gentle fingers. "Place your hands on the television screen," he intoned, "and repeat after me: I believe in the Lord, I believe in His healing powers."

"Keith," I said, "I keep my TV in the closet and this is not what I had in mind." He had a faint dimple in his left cheek. I'd never noticed it before.

"Bruises on your face hurt?" he asked, crouching down and lightly tapping his fingertips against my cheek, over the bridge of my nose.

"Not much," I said. "Careful."

"I have an air splint," he said, "left over from a ski-ing sprain. I don't know if it'll work, but it might. You inflate it. Conforms to the contours of the ankle. Size shouldn't be a problem."

"Why didn't my doctor give me one?" I asked, aware that I'd been staring into his eyes with far more intensity than the situation required.

"You in an HMO?" he asked.

"Yeah."

"Crutches are good enough for the likes of you."

"Thanks a heap."

"I'll be right back."

The door slammed. Roz shot me the evil eye.

It didn't take him more than five minutes. When he returned, he cradled a Gap bag.

"Roz," he said, "could you bring me a clean towel?"

"There's one in the bathroom," she snapped. "Right through the kitchen, Mother Teresa."

"Roz, you're an angel," I said. She stayed resentfully put while Keith ran his own errand.

He brought back two towels, one of which he knelt on after carefully hitching his trouser leg to preserve its perfect crease. With the other he dried my foot, wriggling it this way and that. His hands felt hot against my skin.

The air splint was a plastic contraption fitted with a beach-ball-type valve. Keith raised the gizmo to his lips and blew. After rolling up his shirtsleeves, he disappeared into the kitchen. I could hear water running in the sink.

"Checking for leaks," he called.

"Good idea," I said.

He came back, fastened the splint loosely around my ankle, puffed up his cheeks, and added more air.

"How's that?"

"Weird."

"Wear a loose shoe, an unlaced sneaker or something. You should be able to walk, but don't overdo it," he said.

I placed my foot on the floor and applied pressure. "Feels great."

"It won't if you spend the night standing on it. If your ankle's badly swollen when you take it off, call me. Anytime."

"I didn't realize psychiatrists made so many house calls."

"Jeez, Keith," Roz said, doing an about-face and flouncing upstairs. "If you're planning a long chat, don't let me keep you."

He blushed to the roots of his blond hair. God, he looked young.

Lowering his voice, he murmured in my ear, "This Roz business, it, um, got a little out of control. Sort of *totally* out of control."

I approved of his aftershave, cologne, possibly his shampoo. He smelled faintly of lemon—tangy, spicy. "She's intense, huh?" I said.

"And you're unavailable."

"I was," I said.

"Past tense," he said.

I bit my lip, twined a strand of hair around my finger, and yanked. "I'm not entirely sure it's past," I said.

"Who's ever sure?" he asked lightly. "Things hap-

pen. Like Roz, for instance. There I was, panting at
your feet, fascinated, eager to learn more about you—"

"Odd methodology, Doctor," I said. "These intimate
research sessions with my assistant." It was easy to
whisper, our lips were so close.

"It's not permanent, me and her."

"Glad you realize it," I said. "The lady in black
breaks many hearts."

"And you?" he inquired.

"Keith," came Roz's plaintive wail. She sounded
like a cat in heat. "Either make it fast or don't bother."

"I could come by and massage your foot later," he
murmured.

"You won't have the energy," I replied unkindly.

After a moment's hesitation, he called upstairs.
"Roz," he said, staring me straight in the eye. "I can't
make it tonight. Sorry and all, but something else has
come up."

I concentrated on keeping a straight face till he
closed the door behind him. Far overhead, I thought I
heard one of Roz's shoes bang the wall. I hoped she'd
removed it from her foot first. The lath and plaster in
these old houses isn't that strong.

SEVENTEEN

I gulped a breath and stumbled to the foyer, abandoning the makeshift ice pack to melt in a wastebasket. As I buttoned my coat, my ankle muttered: *Why not wait till morning?* Because by morning the Haitians might be on the run. Might be driving to New York, might be flying home. When I was a cop, I waited till morning once and found my potential witness hanging from a meat hook in a restaurant kitchen. It left an indelible impression.

On the way to Dorchester I learned that you should never drive with a splint on one ankle. Even if it's your left leg, and you lay off the clutch as much as possible. Potholes don't play favorites.

I'd wedged my crutches across the backseat, but once I'd scoped the area around the target address, I knew I couldn't use them. Neighborhood like that, crutches attract muggers; I remember when crutches earned you a seat on the subway.

Louis and Jean's dwelling was basically awful—a tumbledown shell of maimed Victoriana—but someone had made an effort with the trimmings. A gallant stand of rosebushes was staked behind a barbed wire fence. The clipped hedge threatened to give the term *flophouse* a good name. Near the curbside, two scraggy holly bushes poked through the hard dirt.

A foil-wrapped poinsettia plant decorated the front stoop. No one had gotten around to stealing it yet.

Security was not included in the rent. I entered the foyer past a row of metal mailboxes so small that all the marketing circulars lay strewn on the floor.

Guided by a faded label, I marched upstairs to Room 35 and banged the door. "Marched" is a bit vigorous, but I tried not to put all my weight on the handrail. I'd have liked to—my ankle alternately flamed and ached—but the flimsy railing might have cracked. After waiting a twenty count in front of Room 35, balancing on my right leg, I pressed my ear to the door, heard the blare of a television or radio, and knocked louder.

"Qui est là?"

All my rotten Spanish, useless again! Haitians spoke French, some kind of French patois. Creole. Still, these gentlemen had passed the cabbie exam. Either they'd bribed somebody, or they had rudimentary English.

Awkwardly I bent and stuck a business card under the door. People tend to find embossed print reassuring. I also sang out a friendly *hello*, so they'd realize I was female. A woman at the door isn't so bad. She's probably not the local loan shark's muscle, for example.

A chain rattled and the door opened a crack. A cautious eye appeared in the darkened slit. "Po-lice?" a voice whispered, separating the word into two distinct syllables.

"Gloria sent me. From the cab company. I work for her. *¿Entiende usted?*"

"*Parlez français?*"

"*Solamente español,*" I replied. "*¿No inglés?*"

"*Un moment, s'il vous plaît. Louis parle l'anglais mieux que moi.*"

I understood enough to realize I must be talking to Jean.

"Could you open the door?" I asked.

It slammed before I could stick a foot in it. Not that I would have, what with the splint.

I leaned against the wall. If I'd brought one crutch, I could have used it as a battering ram.

"Good evening, Miss Carlyle," said a light tenor voice. "You would please to come in?"

"*Merci,*" I replied, exhausting one third of my French vocabulary.

"*Je m'appelle* Louis Vertigne. You may call me Louis. My last name, it is difficult, *non*? This is Jean. As you say, John."

I was welcomed in both English and what I took to be French, a lilting melody that rose and fell like water trickling through a rocky brook.

Scrawny little fellows they were. Gloria's been known to exaggerate, but the two of them, soaking wet, probably weighed far less than she did. They were short as well as stringy. I towered over them, which they seemed to find amusing. Less amusing was the mottled bruising on the first man's face. And the circle of burned, shredded flesh encircling his neck. I wondered if his clothing covered other wounds. Louis's face was unmarred.

They had to be close relatives, brothers I'd have said, except for the different last names. Both had similar features, skin the color of shriveled walnuts, and close, kinky hair, dark with a white sugar frosting. Both wore khaki slacks, too cool for the season, and gray hooded sweatshirts. I'd have had trouble telling them apart except for Jean's injuries.

Louis, noticing my bruises and my splint, quickly invited me to "Sit, please, sit, mademoiselle, eh? Madame, perhaps?"

In the sparsely furnished room, there weren't many choices. I got the pick of the litter, a folding card-table number whose glory was that all four legs touched the ground simultaneously. The other two, a mismatched set of wooden uprights, required balancing acts. The TV was the only visible item of any value, and it was a twelve-inch black-and-white a self-respecting thief would reject out of hand. Neither man made an effort to turn it off.

I ignored it, although I can't imagine background music less tolerable than TV whine, especially commercial crescendos. I wanted to make nice, gather information, not aggravate the tenants.

A table shrouded in a plastic cloth nestled beside the TV. On it rested a collection of small religious figures made of porcelain or some kind of paintable clay. I recognized a crucified and gory Christ, a kneeling Mary Magdalene. Mary and Joseph and the whole crèche were there too. Before and after. A vase of scrawny mums shared the surface, perhaps an offering.

Three other suffering Christs decorated the room: two painted crucifixions, one wood carving with a particularly vicious crown of thorns jammed down over His bleeding forehead.

"Your leg? The stairs were *difficile*?" Louis inquired politely.

I spoke slowly and distinctly. "Difficult. Yes. There is no elevator and I need to speak with you."

"From Gloria?"

"No trouble," I said as they exchanged worried glances. "I'm not here to make trouble."

"This is good," Louis said. He mumbled a few words to Jean, who visibly relaxed.

"I also drive for Green and White," I said.

Louis studied my card. It's simple: name, address, phone. A gap, then PRIVATE INVESTIGATIONS.

"You work for the cab company?" he asked.

"As a driver, like you."

"You should not do this 'investigations' business," Louis counseled in his gentle way. "Your *papa*, your *maman*, *votre mari*—do not they object? Is *dangereux*."

I ignored his observation. "Why did you stop driving?"

"Look at my brother, my half brother," he said. "Regard his face and his neck."

"I see."

"You do not see. He could have lost his eye. He could have lost his life. He is now much improved."

I said, "Did you call the police?"

The word *police* was enough to bring a surge of sound from the injured Jean. The word for *immigration* sounds pretty much the same in French as it does in English.

"An accident," Louis declared, staring at the floor. He was not a gifted liar.

"I wondered if Jean might have been attacked. Threatened. Like me." I pointed at the splint. "By three men."

Jean let out another torrent, accompanied by gestures and curses.

"Please," I said to Louis, wishing I spoke his language, "I won't make trouble. I don't have anything to do with Immigration. Jean got hurt and I got hurt and somebody should pay. That's all. Not with money, but with time and pain."

Louis exchanged heated words with his brother. I couldn't keep up with the rapid-fire delivery. "Time and pain," Louis repeated finally. "We would like that. But we make no talk to the police. *Comprenez-vous?*"

I said, "May I record what you say? If you slip into French I could have a friend translate for me. It would help."

"No machine," Jean said flatly. I wondered if he understood everything I said.

"Then tell me. I'll remember."

Louis hesitated. "Evil men beat my brother. They do more than hurt him. How should I say, they embarrass him. They break his spirit. He wants now only to go away. We come, we work, we send money home. Gloria is good to us and we regret to leave her rudely."

"I'm sure she understands."

"My brother says it is whites hating blacks, hating especially Haitian peoples."

"Can he describe the men?"

There was a quick exchange. *"Les trois,"* I decided, must be the same as *"Los tres."* The three.

I asked if this was so.

"Yes, there were three, but they blindfold him and he gives his word he will not speak about them. *Jamais.*"

Like *jamás.* Spanish for "never."

"Did *you* give *your* word?" I asked Louis.

"I found him. And no, I did not give my word."

Abruptly Jean rose and left the room, a torrent of sound trailing behind him.

"He is full of hate," Louis said. "But not so angry as I am when I see him, when I smell him. My brother is a man of culture and refinement. In my country he is a teacher of botany, a man who makes flowers grow from concrete."

"Did he plant the rosebushes?"

"He makes flowers everywhere, even here."

"What did they do to him?"

"He is truly afraid it comes from our country, from the Tontons Macoutes. You know of them?"

"Secret police?"

"Secret torturers."

"You speak English very well."

"I work for Americans in Haiti. Long ago. It comes back to me. When you are young, you learn."

"What did they do to Jean? To make you quit."

"He has not told me all. He is like a child now. He screams in the night."

"You found him?"

"We work always the same shift. We are partners with our own radios. Like they call walkie-talkies. We speak with each other every half hour, because something terrible may happen. You know how many of my countrymen are wounded driving cabs this year, this city? Four good men, and one shot and he lives, but with a bullet so near his spine, he may yet die. And no one is caught, no one punished."

"I know," I said.

"Jean and I thought this country would be different."

"I'm sorry."

I waited for him to speak.

"Wednesday afternoon, three-thirty, I do not hear from Jean. I know from his last call where he was to go and I also go there. I drive up and down each street until I find his cab."

"No police?"

"Our papers are not so good."

Gloria's lax on the Immigration Act of '86. I am too. Start hollering about America for Americans, I figure we'll all have to pack. I have no desire to reside in the slice of Poland my grandmother called home.

"His cab is empty, on a street in Dorchester. I wait a bit. Maybe he has gone to help an old one up the stairs. I hear sounds, but it takes time to know, to realize they come from the trunk. And then I have not the keys and I forget about the thing you can push inside to open the trunk and even when I remember, the doors are locked. So I smash the driver's window with a brick.

"I reach in, with my jacket wrapped around my arm

so the glass does not cut me, and open the door. I release the lock and I find Jean."

From the other room I could hear faint noises, as if Jean was pacing, listening.

"He is without clothing, naked, so cold he shakes. He is tied with harsh rope, rough like you would use to bind an animal. The rope is wound around his legs and around his neck so that when he kicks to make the noise to save himself the rope tightens around his neck. His neck is all blood, covered with blood. If I do not come, he would be dead. He would struggle, keep on struggling. Jean would never lie still like that, in a pool of stink."

"Was he gagged?"

"Gagged?"

"Was something covering his mouth, so he couldn't scream for help?"

"Nothing. He had yelled for some time, till he was—how you say?—hoarse, given up. He decide to kick. Why?"

"Never mind." If Jean's attackers meant to ensure his death, they'd have taped his mouth. I wondered who knew about the twosome's walkie-talkie connection.

"Please, go on," I said.

"I cut the ropes and cover him with a blanket. . . . He tells me, a very long time later, after he bathes and bathes, he tells me the three men jump in the cab, they take him to a park, they beat him and threaten him, order him not to drive again or they will kill him for sure. They piss on him while he lies naked in the trunk of the cab, tied like a calf they will butcher. They park the cab on the street."

"Did they rob him?"

"He had only a few dollars. We are cautious; often we bring money here and hide it. They take his clothes and his shoes, but they are worth less than nothing. They take them for sport."

"Who?"

"Americans."

"Black Americans, white Americans?"

"Jean does not talk about them."

"Is it possible he knew one of them?"

"Why do you ask this?"

"One of the men who hurt me was a cabdriver, or knew something about cabs." I hadn't said anything to Marvin at the time, but a guy who could reach in an open window and disable rooflights and radio with no direction from the driver had to have some experience with cabs.

Louis's dark face puckered in concentration as he considered the possibility that a fellow driver might be involved.

"The walkie-talkies," I said, "the half-hour check-ins. Were you always so careful?"

"No. But with so much hurting going on—"

"Do you know anyone else who's been beaten? Threatened?"

"Not one, but many."

Jean came back into the room. From the few understandable bits of the ensuing argument, I got the feeling he'd followed most of what we'd said.

I decided to test my theory.

"Jean, would you agree to hypnosis? To identify your attackers?"

He stopped and faced me, fingering the noose mark around his neck. "I would not."

"You understand what I say."

"Louis is the older brother. It is better we speak with one voice."

Louis continued to do so. "Jean believes this violence is directed against Haitians only."

"I'm not Haitian. I'm not on any Tontons Macoutes hit list."

"Then Jean believes you were unlucky."

"Does he know of others who were unlucky? Any other non-Haitian victims?"

Another round of impassioned French passed between the brothers. Incomprehensible.

Louis said firmly, "We may know of others, but Jean does not wish me to speak of them. He believes they are only—how you say, the red fish? The red herrings. He says if you are an investigator—which he greatly doubts—you should investigate these hate crimes against the Haitian peoples. He says Americans believe the Haitians come here to spread AIDS, and someone must tell the world otherwise—"

"I'm not a politician."

"I only translate for you what my brother says. I do not think he is right, although there is much hatred."

"Were most of the victims Haitian?" I asked.

"Many. And they do not go to the police. Not without immigration papers."

"Did all the victims work for G and W?" I addressed my question to Jean. He remained maddeningly silent, merely shaking his head in his brother's direction, ignoring me.

"No," Louis said.

"Did any own their own medallions?" I asked.

"A medallion costs the earth," Louis said. "We work for the company. The company owns the medallions."

"I understand," I said. "But there are independent owners. People who own their own cabs, or who share a medallion. Have any of them been beaten, threatened like Jean?"

Louis stared hard at Jean. Jean gave no sign.

"Perhaps," Louis said. "I do not know."

"Do you belong to the Small Taxi Association?"

"No."

"Then you don't know Lee Cochran?"

"The name is not familiar. Jean, *tu le connais?*"

"*Non.*"

"Did you or your brother ever drive for a large company, a company owned by Phil Yancey?"

"Yet another name I do not know."

"The big three: Yellow, Town, Checker?"

"When we arrive, our countrymen recommend Green and White. Because, they say, the owner, she is not so hard on drivers with bad papers. Also she is a woman of color. Jean, he would rather work for a man. But once he meets the lady, he, too, is charmed."

My ankle throbbed with a dull ache.

I stared at Jean, spoke slowly, addressing my words to Louis. "If your brother changes his mind, Louis, or if you change your mind, call me. I could use a list of names. Haitians and non-Haitians. I guarantee no one will get in trouble with Immigration."

I sensed that Louis was on my side. Unmoved by my plea, Jean fingered the damaged flesh on his neck.

I'd gotten nothing. Not a single victim's name. Not from Jean or Louis, who admitted they knew many. Not from Lee Cochran, who'd sworn he knew of three.

Nothing.

EIGHTEEN

Louis wished, please, to escort me to my car. His offer provoked agonized wails from Jean. Louis gravely apologized: he so regretted that his formerly brave brother was now afraid to be left alone after dark. I insisted I could make it to my car solo. Louis insisted I could not.

At a stalemate, we trooped downstairs, the two little men and I, one preceding me, one lagging behind, only to find my car secure and the desolate street empty. I admired the rosebushes, in a vain attempt to buck up the visibly trembling Jean. It didn't work, for him or me. I saw the carefully tended stalks differently now, in harsh counterpoint to the surrounding blight.

Decent gestures; they get driven off the six-o'clock news by constant calamities.

"*Merci*," I said as I left. "*Au revoir*." There. My entire French vocabulary. Except for *escargot*, which is harder to work into conversation.

I drove slowly, the stereo on full blast, Rory Block soothing my spirit, singing "Faith Can Lift Me Up on Silver Wings." I didn't buy the Haitian hate thing, not with Marvin involved. Marvin's absolutely African American; aside from skin pigmentation he had nothing in common with the brothers I'd just interviewed.

He'd fought back; seized the initiative. Was there anything the three assailants could have done to scare Marvin the way they'd terrified Jean?

I considered simple racial hatred. A white supremacist thing. Except, according to Marvin, one of the perps was black. I couldn't see a black man fronting for a reborn KKK.

A cab is always risky. I've heard them described as automated teller machines on wheels. All the advantages of your local bank's ATM, no armed guards in the lobby. But these particular guys, the ones who'd hurt Marvin, spooked Jean, were not after money. They were salaried. Or paid for piecework. What was the goal? Scaring cabbies? Why? To get them off the street? Why?

Why hadn't Lee Cochran hired me? Because I'd refused to take his orders? Had Phil Yancey paid him a warning visit?

Who benefits when cabs disappear?

The question repeated itself over and over, keeping time to the music's insistent beat and the throbbing in my ankle. I drove faster, hoping Dr. Keith might make a late-night call to check on my foot.

Leaning heavily on the crutches, inching up the front walk, I thought seriously about ringing the bell three times, making Roz bolt downstairs. I was actually happy to hear the click of welcoming tumblers.

Until I realized who was opening my front door.

"Frank" had certainly spruced up his act since the drive-by. Gone were the leather pants and the cheap white shirt, replaced by Gap jeans and a light blue cotton chambray number. He was clean shaven, revealing a blunt chin that altered his appearance for the better. His hair had been cut short, shampooed shiny. The gray streaks had vanished.

I could see why Roz had succumbed.

"Welcome home," he said. There was a florist's arrangement on my hall table. Exotic blooms laced with bear grass.

I listened for footsteps, for another voice: Sam's.

"Sam loaned me his key," Frank said quickly, as if to forestall my question.

"Liar," I said. I shrugged off his attempt to help, hung up my coat. My ankle felt like it was on fire.

"Ah." He seemed pleased at my response.

"Ah?" I repeated.

He folded his arms smugly. "Either Sam doesn't have a key, which I like, or you don't trust me."

"Roz," I guessed.

"Your charming tenant."

"Roz!" I hollered upstairs.

"She didn't let me in. Not this time."

"No?"

"She graciously accepted the flowers on your behalf, but she was most hard-hearted concerning entry. I waited till she left."

"You broke into my house."

"You should have your security parameters checked."

"I think I just did," I said. "They're not up to par."

"Don't get upset," he said. "You're very well protected from the average thief."

"Makes me feel all warm and fuzzy," I said, "knowing the above-average can break and enter at will."

"Your foot. Did that happen when we were shot at? I saw Sam tackle you."

"It happened later. I lead an exciting life."

"Please. Let me help you."

"Leave me alone, okay?"

"Perhaps I should go."

"Perhaps you should tell me how you got in first," I said, "so I can make sure it won't happen again."

"You're angry."

"No kidding."

"I thought I might be able to help—with your work."

"Yeah, you've already done so much. I can't tell what the hell's on my desktop,much less what I should do with it."

"That's why I'm here. To straighten things out about the computer."

This Frank not only had clean hair, he had different mannerisms, a new body language. He'd acquired a nontechnical vocabulary, a slower, more relaxed speech pattern. Which was the real man? The one I'd met in Mattapan or this guy? Was he an accomplished actor as well as a computer nut?

Don't look a gift horse in the mouth, my mother used to say. I wondered if she knew a similar saying about wolves. Don't look a gift wolf in the eye.

"I'm not paying more money," I said. "If this is some kind of scam, some new con game, count me out."

"You don't understand," he said.

"No," I admitted. "I don't."

"You're Sam's friend, I'm Sam's friend. He's my *family*, for chrissakes, more than a friend. Anything I can do for *his* friends, it's like settling an old debt. A debt of honor."

"So you honorably broke into my house."

"Do you want to see how I did it?"

"Sure. Just let me get this splint off, and pack my foot in ice, and you can tell me the whole damn story."

"Can I help?"

"Talk. I'll listen."

I'd known the kitchen window was ripe for a burglar. I just hadn't expected one so soon, or one so determinedly friendly. Sam's buddy foraged for ice slivers in the freezer. He stuck them in Saran Wrap so that the ends of the ice pack adhered to each other, no paper clips required. We sat at the kitchen table while he described his B&E technique.

"Great neighbors I've got," I commented when he'd finished. "You'd think one of them would have called the cops."

"Don't blame them," he said earnestly. "I wasn't furtive. I came in broad daylight. Just went up a ladder. I was a repairman, a phone lineman, a painter. Come on, tell the truth, haven't you ever forgotten your key and used the kitchen window?"

"To be honest, I haven't."

"I'll bet Roz has," he said. "It's a breeze."

"Why do I get the idea you've done this sort of work before?"

"Your foot's swollen," he said.

"I can see that."

The silence in the kitchen stretched till I broke it, uneasy under his scrutiny.

"Why did you suddenly decide I needed a better computer?"

"I like your house," he said.

We were having one of the least responsive conversations I'd had in a while, two kids in a sandbox each constructing a separate castle.

"Sam has good taste," he said finally.

"In what?" I asked.

"Women."

"Why don't you give me my computer lesson and save the shit? I'm tired. My dance card's full. I'm not in a flirting mood. Get it?"

"Are you ever in a flirting mood?"

"Are you Sam's friend?"

"Where is Sam?" he asked.

"I don't keep tabs on him."

"He's spending a lot of time in Washington. You ever think about what he's doing there?"

I kept the memory of my recent phone call off my face. "I don't brood about it excessively."

"Maybe he ought to keep closer tabs on you."

"I don't need a keeper. Back off."

"Computer lesson. Then I leave."

"The way you've got the new stuff hooked up, could

you find something for me, something the cops might have on-line?"

His eyes glittered. "What?"

"A list of recent cab robberies. I need the name of the cab company each driver worked for. I'd like to know if any independent drivers have been attacked, whether or not they're affiliated with radio associations. Whether more cabbies have been attacked after radio calls or flag downs."

"Hold it. Robberies. You're trying to track someone who robbed you? Who injured your foot?"

"Yeah."

He considered it. "I can get you the past few months of the *Globe* or the *Herald*."

"I doubt these robberies made the news. What about police files?"

"The Boston system's too primitive."

"Too bad. Have to rely on my old sources."

I didn't feel bad about it. I felt good. Better. Superior. Smug. I was glad he couldn't just press some damn buttons and ace all the answers.

"I can get you other things," he volunteered eagerly. "Library access anywhere in the world. Credit access. Terrific for missing persons."

"Show me."

"You want to start with somebody famous? Pick a movie star. You want to know Nancy Reagan's dress bill at Neiman-Marcus?"

We moved into the living room, settled behind the desk.

I said, "Let's start with you, Frank. Why not enter your Social Security number?"

No hesitation. "Okay."

I took notes as he typed the magic passwords, sequences of letters, numbers, and punctuation marks.

"It's not too interesting," he muttered apologetically as he punched in his nine-digit code.

Francis Tallifiero's credit history zipped across the screen. Visa. MasterCard. AmEx. Most of the major purchases came from unsurprising sources: CompuAdd, Dell Computer, Radio Shack.

"I don't consider it boring, Frank," I said. "I find it fascinating."

"Yeah?" He edged his chair a little closer to mine.

"I'll bet there aren't many dead little kids with credit records like this."

His eyes panicked seconds before the rest of him pushed back his chair in such a rush that it fell over, smacking against the hardwood floor.

Hammering at the front door echoed the crash. I hobbled to answer it. Before I could get there, Frank yanked open the door, shouldering Keith Donovan out of the way. Frank's steps raced down the walk, growing fainter, distant, disappearing into silence.

"You shouldn't be walking on that foot," the psychiatrist commented.

"I agree completely," I said.

NINETEEN

A powerful act of betrayal, sex. A simple consummation of desire, it seemed at the time.

I'm not looking for absolution, but maybe I was searching for guilt. Blame it on pain medication. Blame it on anger—at Roz for allowing Frank's invasion of privacy; at Frank for his broad hint at Sam's infidelity. At Sam, somewhere in Washington.

Or accept responsibility. I wanted Keith; he wanted me. Bonnie Raitt sings it, over a thumping bass: "When I hear that siren call, just can't help myself."

It started with an innocent foot massage. He lingered at a pressure point on my instep. I gave a brief moan and closed my eyes. So simple, a thumb pressed against the arch of my foot. So sensual it drew a sound that belonged in the bedroom. After that, I let his hands stray. I kept quiet when I could have said stop, maybe should have said stop. I didn't want to. I didn't choose to. The warm feeling in my stomach spread through my body and the dark ache of wanting him, wanting his touch and taste and smell, made the responsible adult in me mute before the eager animal.

Something to it, this business about doctors knowing their anatomy . . .

Cold morning light filtered through the bedroom curtains. Keith stirred and murmured in his sleep. Too young, I scolded myself, inwardly grinning ear to ear. The man was easily five years my junior. Hell with that. Wasn't I years younger than Sam? Ouch, a subject to avoid.

Either my ankle was much improved or the rest of my body, raw with the rhythm of lovemaking, had silenced my ankle to a whimper. I felt good. Physically alert. Healthy, almost sated.

I ruffled Donovan's stubbly, too-short hair. I couldn't say with dead certainty that I'd never had a more fair-haired lover. There'd been a time, right after my divorce, when I'd specialized in self-punitive one-night stands. But Keith's astonishing blondness, his almost hairless chest, seemed both erotic and endearing.

Different. Not better, not worse, I admitted, but gloriously different. I'd been with one man too long; routine had set in, confining as a straitjacket. I don't mean that Sam and I had bad sex. We had easy sex, comfy sex. We'd quit stretching borders, exploring boundaries.

I moved against Keith and he opened his eyes. Blue eyes, with a hint of gray. He smiled, and closed them again.

"If you say anything about 'the psychological moment,'" I murmured softly, "anything at all 'psychological,' I'll strangle you."

"No analysis," he agreed, stretching his arms wide. "I'm off duty."

Just pleasure, I thought. That's it. Now. This moment. Desire. Uncomplicated coupling. Two adults. One bed. One groan. A tight gasp of delight. The expected and the unexpected, and the joy of forgetfulness in release.

The jangling phone had the courtesy to wait till we lay back exhausted and giggling, billowing the sheets over our sweaty bodies. I held a stern warning finger to my lips.

Gloria.

I sat, tucking the top sheet under my arms, across my breasts. Keith yanked it down. I batted my eyelashes in his direction and tried to keep an office-crisp voice for my client.

"You sound good," she said suspiciously.

"I'm fine. And you?"

"Okay. You see the Haitians?"

"Yeah."

"Just yeah?"

"One of them got beaten up. Could have been the same perps."

"Time to call the police?"

"Only if you want your former drivers visiting illegal-immigrant detention camps in Florida."

"Don't like the sound of that," she said.

"What I need to know is this: Why would a person want fewer cabs on the road?"

"Honey, I want every one of my cabs on the road every minute of the day. You know that. Soon as your foot's okay, you haul your ass over here and take a shift—"

"No, Gloria. Why would someone, some hypothetical person, want cabbies off the road?"

"Wait up, got to take a call."

"I love you," Keith Donovan breathed into my left ear.

That was news I did not want to hear.

I listened to dead air with feigned attention till Gloria got back on the line. "Some psycho," she suggested. "Got a thing about cabdrivers."

"Give me better than 'psycho,' Gloria. 'Psycho,' and we wait for the cops to catch him in the act."

"Hmmmph," she snorted. "If it was cops gettin' beat up, we'd see some action."

"It's not cops," I said. "You make that list for me?"

"Ready and waitin'."

"You fire anybody for cause lately?"

"How lately? You didn't tell me to put that on the list."

"Last few months. This year."

"Why?"

"I'm not a cop, Gloria. I'm working for you. Answer the question."

"Answer mine."

"One of the perps might be a cabbie. Or an ex-cabbie."

She considered it. "Okay, that's reasonable. I'll go through my files. Nobody sticks out, but that's 'cause I deal with so much riffraff. Guy woulda had to be some kind of special before he'd stand out from the run of losers come through here."

"Anybody have a grudge against you personally, Gloria?"

"Honey, I'm sweetness personified."

"Grudge against the company?"

"Well, that would either be 'cause I fired somebody or Sam ticked 'em off."

"Nothing else?"

"Hold on. Phones're ringing."

"Don't do that!" I said to Keith Donovan. "Christ, wait till I'm off the phone."

"Then can I?"

"What about medallions?" I asked Gloria when she returned.

"What about 'em?"

"The number's fixed by law, right?"

"Yeah."

"Lee Cochran thinks somebody's trying to corner the market."

"Possible," Gloria agreed. She didn't sound enthusiastic. "I mean, say some guys wanted to buy medallions and couldn't, they might start attacking independent owners, encouraging 'em to get out of the business and sell their medallions to the highest bidder."

"But Marvin's not a medallion owner. Your Haitians aren't owners," I objected.

"No, but they were all drivin' for me, and if I can't keep eight cabs on the road, I might have to sell medallions to keep the company afloat."

"You thinking about it?"

"I'm thinking 'bout a lot of things. I got to get going."

"Gloria—"

"You sure you're okay, Carlotta?"

"Fine," I said.

If the roughed-up cabbies who didn't personally own medallions all drove for small companies, I wondered, and if they suddenly quit, would that be enough to shut down the mom-and-pop operations? Would the moms and pops sell their businesses to Phil Yancey? Would he buy? At what price?

Keith eased his hands back under the covers.

"Carlotta," Gloria said. "Is Sam with you?"

I swear she's got radar.

"I don't know where the hell he is," I said, sounding exactly like I was lying.

"You see him, have him call me," she said dryly.

"Sure. And, on the list, put a star by the name of anybody you fired. Anybody who quit mad." I hung up before she could protest. Or think up more questions about Sam.

Keith said, "If I can't talk about anything psychological, what can I talk about?"

"Bed stuff," I said firmly.

"Like who was your first, were you a virgin when you got married?"

"No, no, no," I protested. "That's psych stuff. Talk about baseball. Try to name the Seven Dwarfs."

He was momentarily silent. Maybe he was too young to have seen the movie.

"Music is also good," I suggested.

"Mostly I listen to New Age stuff. Soothing. Enya. I like her."

I sighed. "No Robert Johnson, no Son House?"

"Don't know who they are."

"Were," I corrected. An old blues junkie, I'm a sucker for Mississippi Delta guitar. I keep my National steel under the bed, practice less than I should.

"Do you play sports?" I asked.

"I fence."

"You sell stolen goods?"

"Like in the movies. Like the Three Musketeers."

"You must have grown up rich," I said.

"Is that a psychological probe?" he responded.

"Seen any good movies lately?" I asked after a long first-date pause.

We both burst out laughing.

"Why do you fence?" I asked.

"I'm good at it. Why do you play volleyball?"

He knew about that. Must have questioned Roz.

"I'm good at it," I said.

"Something in common," he observed with satisfaction.

"I like pillow fights," I said. "Then we can try to name the eight reindeer."

"Happy, Dopey, Sneezy—"

I said, "You're getting the hang of it."

"How about a shower?" he said. "A bubble bath?"

"Long as it's foreplay," I said.

TWENTY

I kept glancing over my shoulder while we foraged for breakfast, wondering why in hell we'd wound up in my bed rather than moving two houses down to the relative privacy of the doctor's digs. Had the heat of passion made me careless? Was I really that angry at Roz? Did Keith want her to get the picture as soon as possible?

Roz does the weekly shopping and cleaning in exchange for greatly reduced rent. I doubt she could do a lousier job at either task, but she might try.

I opened another cupboard. Can after can of fruit cocktail. Why? Who eats this candy-colored stuff? I make a shopping list, I honestly do, but Roz, using Stop & Shop coupons as her bible, buys whatever's on sale.

What would I say if she waltzed in and discovered us *in flagrante* munching stale toast and jam, smiling across the table, holding hands, basking in the shiny afterglow? Roz has studied karate for years. She's barely five feet tall, but I don't underestimate her. I don't understand her, either, which made me increasingly nervous. She might blitz through the door, grin, and bellow "Hi! Have fun screwing?" Or take one look and kick me in the teeth and Keith in the balls.

It's not like she's monogamous. Her karate instructor is far more than her karate instructor. When they work out on the third-floor gym mats—the same mats currently substituting for a bank vault—they make noises I've never considered remotely martial.

"How's the ankle?" Keith asked. I liked the fact that he hadn't criticized the meager fare, hadn't sat like a stone and watched me fetch and carry. He could put dishes on the table, find the butter in the fridge, make coffee.

"Better," I said. A testimonial in favor of a steamy tub and a professionally wrapped Ace bandage. "Do you hypnotize people?"

"You saying that's how I got you into bed?"

"Professionally," I said. "In the line of therapy."

"I've done it, but I'd generally defer to a specialist. It would depend."

"On?"

"I don't do behavioral hypnosis: stop smoking, stop drinking, stop overeating. I do crisis intervention, occasionally deeper analysis. If a long-term psychoanalytical patient felt that a greater understanding of a key event in his or her childhood, a traumatic event, might help him or her to work out issues as an adult, I might regress that person to the earlier time. I'd discuss the matter with colleagues first."

I took a bite of toast. Jam dripped on the table.

"Why do you ask?" Keith said. "About hypnosis?"

"You ever try hypnosis with police witnesses, get them to recall specific details, license plate numbers, that kind of thing?"

"No."

"Would you?"

"I don't know."

"Maybe you could discuss it with your colleagues."

"Maybe."

I gulped coffee. I needed caffeine to clear my head.

Lee Cochran. Phil Yancey. Beatings. Medallions. Green & White.

I chased Keith out as soon as I could, sidestepping his efforts to set up a date for the evening. Do you call it a "date" once you've gone ahead and consummated the relationship? Did this relationship have a future?

I hate the word *relationship*. I'd enjoyed the night. Enough. I'm not a clinging vine. I didn't even ask if he'd call.

Part of me whispered, secretly smug, "Because you know he will."

TWENTY-ONE

I sat in my desk chair and swigged the last of the orange juice. I hoped it was Roz's day to go grocery shopping.

Time to go back to the beginning, I thought, propping my foot on my desk. Lee Cochran.

I'd never before had a potential client accuse a person of wrongdoing, and then, abracadabra, had the good fortune to have said wrongdoer appear on my front porch for a chat.

Who knew about my appointment with Cochran?

Answer: everyone Cochran'd mentioned it to. He'd checked me out with his lawyer, somebody Gold. Must be twenty lawyers named Gold in Boston. Or Gould. Lawyers tend toward closemouthedness as a rule. Cops talk. Cochran had discussed hiring me with cops. He'd asked Gloria if I was any good.

Sam knew; I'd told him. I'd revealed it outside of

Gloria's soundproofed bug-free room. Did Yancey have an in with the Organized Crime Task Force?

Sunlight glinted off my new computer screen.

Following the instructions of "Frank," I logged on, using the password he'd given me: KLPT5ZMX. Whose password it actually was, mine or "Frank's" or someone else's, I had no idea. Did the rapidly multiplying number of computer services have a clue about security? Or did they cheerfully disclose secrets to anyone who happened to type in an eight-digit code that clicked?Just one big happy family, eager to share the info that makes the world go 'round.

With crib sheet in hand, I used a local gateway called Mellon to hook into a major credit bureau. Let's get this straight: I knew what I was doing was not strictly kosher. Private investigators are not allowed to roam through TRW, CBI, or Trans Union at will. Even if I were paying their exorbitant rates, which somehow, thanks to "Frank," I was sure I wasn't, there is the Fair Credit Reporting Act. There is a difference between Full Credit Bureau Files and Header Files.

As soon as I'd seen what "Frank" yanked up for his credit history, I knew we were deep in computer shadowland. He should have been able to gain access only to so-called header info: name, date of birth, Social Security number, and such. Not the actual credit file.

But then, he was such a good burglar. Such a talented programmer. It seemed a shame not to use what good fortune had dumped in my lap.

I typed in *Yancey, Philip*, and his last known address, which I got from that useful source, the telephone directory.

Bingo.

The screen lit up, and I had SSN, DOB, employment, and full credit. I hoped "Frank" was billing the cost directly to the FBI, nonetheless I did a quick download to transfer the file. No reason to run up the phone charges.

Yancey was rich. Major rich. And the rich are different. They have more and higher mortgages, for instance, because mortgage interest is tax deductible and only suckers pay now and enjoy later. Phil owned property on the Vineyard, in Yarmouth, Falmouth, Plymouth, all over Cape Cod. I wondered when he'd bought, if he'd paid a little in the seventies or a lot in the eighties. What were the properties worth now? I scribbled addresses and banks into my notebook. It would be interesting to find out.

Why was I bothering to scrawl notes when I could print out the whole report with a couple of keystrokes? I sighed; it was going to take a while for my brain to catch up to my technology.

Yancey's credit rating was good. Very good. No bad paper, no bankruptcies.

I went for Lee Cochran's vital stats. He was paying off a modest mortgage on a three-family in J.P. His Cutlass Ciera dealer had nothing nasty to say about him.

I typed in my own name and SSN. Downloaded. Interesting reading for later.

I used Mellon to hook into the *Globe* index, yanked all stories dealing with cab robberies. Downloaded. Printed.

Matters had come to such an ugly head that a recent *Globe* had neatly summarized matters under the heading BOSTON'S CABDRIVERS HAVE THEIR WORST YEAR YET. A black-boxed article listed the attacks.

I could see why Jean Halle was alarmed. Most of the injured drivers had Haitian surnames. I read quickly. No mention of three attackers. No arrests.

I turned back to the keyboard, typed *Cab Medallions*. Drew a blank, which seemed odd, since Lee Cochran had insisted that the medallion wars were heating up again. Tried *Taxi Medallions*.

Nothing. The big zip. It was incredibly frustrating, all this information at my disposal, and no way to get at it. I felt like a rotten speller confronted with a full set of the *Oxford English Dictionary*.

The phone rescued me. Seldom have I welcomed its jarring ring with such enthusiasm.

"Hello?"

"Well, hi there!"

"Lucinda," I said, leaning back in my chair with a grin. "How y'all doin'? Feds treating you right?"

"Don't y'all mimic my accent; it's rude."

"I apologize. I can't help myself, it's so—"

"Temptin'?" Lucinda said.

"Charming, I was going to say. Pervasive. *There*."

"Hon, those photos you sent, that's why I called. Mail, honest to God! Don't you Yankees know what a fax machine is?"

"Don't start, Lucinda," I said. "What are they?"

"The microphones? Our own little birdies returning to the nest. Oldies, but moldies."

"So if you saw these things in person, Lucinda, you'd definitely say they were FBI mikes."

"They *are* FBI mikes, hon. Our celebrities. Same

kind brought down the whole Patriarcha family in your neck of the woods."

"Lucinda, have some been stolen, say, in the past few months? Have you heard of any of that breed that have gone missing?"

"Stolen?" she echoed. "I dunno. More to the point, I don't know why. They're out-of-date crap. Anybody wants 'em is probably a few sandwiches shy of a picnic. If you're interested in good stuff, I got some babies down here'll knock your socks off."

I smothered a laugh. Lucinda spreads her accent thicker than jam when she knows I'm listening, laces her sentences with extra down-home phrases for my amusement. She can't help it any more than I can help imitating her dialect.

"I'm not in the market," I said. "But thanks for the help, Lucinda."

"Come on down and visit," she said. "Weather must stink up there."

"Thanks. It sure does." I eased the receiver back into the cradle.

Sam's bugging expert agreed with my bugging expert.

With a sigh, I returned to the monitor, immersed myself in the general index: taxi drivers: rate hikes; rules and regulations . . .

Damn. Exasperated, I logged out, made a call to the Hackney Carriage Bureau, part of the Boston Police. The BPD has the final say about cabs—they set rates, issue medallions, and better still, I know a guy there, a fixture, one Lieutenant Brennan, assigned to taxi because he used to violate Miranda six ways from Sunday. He liked taxi, took root there.

"How many cabs are there in the city?" I asked.

"Fifteen hundred and twenty-five," he told me.

"What about the forty wheelchair-accessibles?"

"Yeah. So it's up to fifteen sixty-five. A real growth industry. Up forty since 1945."

"What's a medallion go for these days?"

"This month, seventy-five thou. You hit the lottery?"

"Why'd the Department of Public Utilities back down in '91? They were going to issue hundreds of new medallions."

"Maybe the right question is, why'd they start up? Why mess with the status quo?"

"Things have changed since 1945," I said.

"Not the streets of Boston," Brennan maintained. "Still overcrowded cow paths."

"The hotel owners wanted more cabs, right?"

"Them and the Tourist Bureau. Convention Center. We even got a la-di-da Film Cooperation Bureau, like Hollywood's beating down the door. I mean, why'd anybody shoot their film in Palm Beach or Vegas when they could party in Boston?"

"Where they roll up the sidewalks at midnight," I said.

"Yep," he agreed.

"And there's winter," I said.

"Middle of blizzard gulch," he said. "Some people think the weather's a matter of fucking public relations."

"Brennan, why would somebody want to scare cabbies out of business?" I asked.

"Hell," he said. "Got me. Most of the cabbies in this town don't earn enough to eat at McDonald's. Guys live in their cars, sleep there. Divorced guys. Wife's got the house and kids, they get squat. Conk out over at the lot at Logan, shower at the L-Street bathhouse—"

"So why scare 'em off?"

"Ask me why so many convenience stores get robbed. Gas stations. Excuse me, Carlotta, but I could be napping at my desk."

"Sorry to bother you."

For a minute I thought he'd hung up on me. Then his world-weary voice came over the line. "I can't figure it, what with the economy like it is, but there's action."

"What kind of action?" I asked, trying not to sound too eager.

"Two things. Neither of 'em makes a nickel's worth of sense, far as I'm concerned."

I waited.

"You didn't hear this from me," he said, lowering his voice.

" 'Course not," I said.

"Rumor is, the hotel people, the restaurant people, the convention team, they're coming back. Hired themselves a fancy law firm, got a new stooge, some cabbie wants a medallion so bad he's got a hard-on, and they say this time they think they're gonna get maybe seven hundred new cabs on the street. You heard it here first."

No, I hadn't.

"You know which law firm?" I asked.

"What I know is with the economy like it is, they ain't got a snowball's chance in hell."

"So why?" I said, thinking out loud.

"Got me," he said. "Doesn't sound like the kind of case a lawyer would handle on contingency."

"Brennan, you said there were two things bothering you. What's the other?"

"Lots of medallion transfers lately."

"Phil Yancey," I muttered under my breath. "Brennan, this is important. Is Yancey buying?"

"Now, there's a thought," Brennan said.

"Is he?"

"You ever heard of 'straws'?"

I said, "In real estate, they're phony buyers."

"Right. Sometimes they're in on the action. Sometimes they're dummies, like folks in nursing homes, never know their names are used."

"I get it," I said.

"If Phil Yancey's buying medallions, he's using straws. Of course, anybody could be behind it, even your guy, Gianelli."

"Wouldn't it be dumb to buy now, with even the barest possibility of the department issuing new medallions?"

"It's not going to happen. No way."

"One more question and I'll let you go. Any rumors about big conversions to leasing?"

"Interesting," Brennan said. "If Yancey was planning to change even thirty percent of his cabs to leased vehicles, he'd make a pile."

"But you haven't heard any rumors?"

"Haven't heard shit about leases. Mind you, nothing Yancey tries would surprise me. Shit, Carlotta. Instead of spending the rest of the day asleep like an honest cop, I guess I'd better check out some of these new medallion owners, see if they're on the up-and-up."

"I owe you one," I said.

"You can buy me a drink," he said. "And give my regards to Mooney."

Half the police force thinks I'm sleeping with Mooney. And I never did. I swear.

TWENTY-TWO

"How's the foot?" Gloria asked when I showed up at Green & White at two that afternoon. I don't know when the woman sleeps.

"Okay," I said. Thanks to the air splint. A few more days of rest and rehab, with frequent foot and body massage administered by a qualified psychiatrist, I'd be back on the volleyball court.

Music blared: vintage Aretha Franklin.

"Good sound," I said approvingly. "How's Marvin?"

Worry creased her forehead. "Moved him here yesterday, into the back room. Didn't seem like that Yvonne knew much about nursing, just a lot about cuddling. I had to get one of my own drivers to take me down there, fetch him back. Like hauling a hungry tiger without a cage, but all Leroy and Geoffrey ever tell me is he's gonna be fine, gonna be fine. Protect your little sister, you know? Take over my life if I let 'em."

"Can I talk to him?"

"I had a doc come by, friend of mine. That bang on the head sure made Marvin cranky."

That or being forced to leave the lovely Yvonne, I thought.

"Doctor gave him some stuff to help him sleep," Gloria said. "Knocked him right out. You wanna talk, come by later."

I was hitting brick walls everywhere I went.

"Lee Cochran ever hire you?" Gloria asked.

"Funny you should ask," I said. "No."

"Look, Carlotta, all I did was tell him you were an okay P.I. when he asked. I'm sorry if I did something wrong. I won't do it again."

"Did you happen to spread the news of my upcoming meeting with Mr. Cochran?" I asked.

"Honey, I don't gossip unless I mean to gossip. Lee didn't exactly tell me the gruesome details, so I didn't have anything juicy to pass along."

I believed her.

"Now, if you want to tell me what it's all about," she continued, "if Lee's wife's leaving him, or he wants you to kidnap his kids and deprogram them from the Church of the Holy Nutritionist, I'll be happy to put it out over the radio."

"Diet getting on your nerves?" I asked.

"Huh," she said. "With Marvin living here, it's gonna be rough on me. I only get to eat when he sleeps."

She was taking advantage of the opportunity. Hostess Sno Ball wrappers covered her desk. An almost empty sack of M&M's drooped near the phone console. She opened a desk drawer, hauled out a jar of Planters peanuts, and twisted the lid.

"Want some?"

"No, thanks. You got that list of former employees who hate your guts?" I asked.

"Why's that important? You think somebody's beating on cabbies 'cause they hate me? Just as easy to come by and beat on me."

"People are devious."

"Most of 'em are plain stupid, Carlotta. Look how they're willin' to pay to lose weight. These diet places charge more than a fine restaurant would. That's crazy."

"Hackney Carriage Bureau says the hotel lobby's gearing up for a new push. Talking about adding seven hundred medallions."

"See," she said. "People are crazy."

"Gloria, would the cabbie organizations, like Cochran's STA, be telling the truth if they told the Hackney Bureau there aren't enough drivers to handle the cabs already on the road?"

She stopped eating for a moment. "There's heavy unemployment. Heavy unemployment usually means plenty of drivers."

"But you're having trouble staffing the night shift."

"Yeah. So?"

"So if a lot of cabbies got beaten up and stopped working . . ."

"Carlotta, what are you saying? That the small owners are rousting their own cabbies so they can tell the city there's no point issuing more medallions 'cause nobody's willin' to drive?"

Didn't sound likely, phrased that way. "Let me have the list, Gloria."

"Take the phones. I got it in the back room and I don't want you wakin' Marvin."

"I never mess with hungry tigers."

"Just pick up the calls. You know the routine. I could use a little movement."

Probably had a stash of potato chips in the back room along with Marvin.

I got busy on the console, plugging one ear with my index finger so Aretha's "Respect" wouldn't block out the callers. A man wanted a cab on Hemenway Street—right now, please—and a woman with a high, prissy voice needed one near Boston College. I took names, addresses, apartment numbers, and gave out the standard ten-minute spiel. Lots of cabstands near Symphony Hall. I wasn't sure who was out near B.C. I punched buttons.

"Who wants four fifty-eight Hemenway?" I asked.

"I do. Number forty-three. You ain't Gloria talking."

"I know. Can you take Hemenway?"

"Got it. That you, Carlotta?"

"Yeah, who's that?"

"Come on, you remember Al DiMag?"

"How you been, Al?"

"Thriving. You?"

"Okay."

"Haven't seen you. You riding dispatch?"

"Filling in."

"Take care."

"Al, hold it a minute. You, or anybody out there, you been robbed or threatened lately?"

"I heard some guys got their butts kicked real good," Al said.

"Names?"

"Just talk."

"Anybody else?"

Three minutes of jumbled free-for-all in several languages followed, with partial translations. Everybody'd heard rumors. Nobody mentioned Marvin. Details were few and sketchy. Street names. Bar talk. Drunk talk.

"Twenty bucks for anybody writes me up a report with a genuine name and an address to match," I said. "Leave it with Gloria at Green and White."

"And trust you for the money?"

I thought I recognized Al's skeptical voice.

"I'm putting two tens in an envelope even as we speak," I said.

Gloria wheeled her chair into position. "Bribin' my drivers?" she asked.

"That okay with you?"

"Anything makes 'em drive faster. Here. List goes back a year."

Two pages, double-sided. "You've got some turnover problems," I said.

"Average for the industry."

"If I check for prior arrests, how many you figure I'll net?"

"Hon, this is a cab company. They got a license, they can drive. They don't need to be perfect. You gonna have Mooney run 'em?"

"I can run 'em myself. I have access. Anybody you'd start with?"

"None of these boys gonna win the Nobel peace prize."

"Any real nasty little snots?"

"This one," she said, tapping the starred name of Zachary Robards with the eraser end of a yellow pencil. "But that probably ain't his real name,'cause he dropped right after I asked him for some papers, Social Security, stuff like that."

"What did he look like?"

"White kid. Local. No immigration problems; I cut more slack for immigrants. He just didn't seem to like the job. Didn't like answering to a black woman boss, maybe."

"Give you a reason when he quit?"

"Didn't show one day, didn't show the next. Little creep. I called the cops."

"'Cause he didn't show for work? You should have called his mother."

"He didn't bring a cab back. Cops found it someplace in Southie. No damage. Goddamn miracle."

"They find the guy?"

"Wrong name, wrong address; guess they gave it a look."

"He on a missing persons?"

"I didn't file on him. Ain't no dearly beloved of mine."

I underlined Zachary's name on the list.

"Marvin awake?"

"Sleepin' like a baby." Gloria hesitated, selected the

bag of M&M's, shook it over her desk till it was empty. The twenty or so candies must have looked lonely, so she added a handful of peanuts, blending her own trail mix. "Uh, you sure you haven't seen Sam?" she asked after downing a mouthful.

"Nope." I hoped I didn't sound as guilty as I felt.

"Must be in Washington."

"He got a lady there?"

"Not so he'd tell me."

"You get your computers?"

"Not yet."

"Did Sam mention a guy named Frank?"

She shook her head. "No. Is that the computer freak?"

"Maybe he brought him by." I described the man I knew as Frank, but even as I spoke I realized how useless the words were. Beard, no beard. Silvery hair, dark hair. The things people remember are the easiest things to change.

Gloria took two more calls on the console, urged a cabbie onward toward B.C. "Sam doesn't share this place much," she said. "It's not exactly snazzy reception desks with cute little secretaries. And Sam doesn't seem to have many men friends, you know what I mean? His brothers, he's not real close to."

"Let me know if Sam shows up with Frank," I said.

"You and Sam getting along?"

I said, "Can't get along with him when I don't see him."

"Look, would you please ride graveyard tonight? Otherwise I got a cab with no driver."

"It's time away from the investigation," I said.

She grinned. "You might get lucky. Beaten and robbed. ID the suspects."

"I thought Sam grounded me," I said.

She shrugged her massive shoulders. "He ain't around, he won't know," she said, placid as a huge Buddha, nodding and munching in her metal chair.

TWENTY-THREE

By eleven forty-five, a full moon hung lazily in the sky, surrounded by a corona, gleaming like scoured bone. Scudding clouds covered it, dimming the glow before I could slam the door against the biting wind. The motor groaned twice, turned over. I shivered in spite of two pairs of wool socks and a heavy cable-knit sweater worn over a cotton turtleneck. I'd tucked the shirt into houndstooth-checked men's slacks, thirty-four-inch inseam, elastic waist, a Filene's basement bargain too flamboyant to bring top dollar retail.

No gloves. They get between me and the feel of the wheel, interfere with the connection.

Midnight's my favorite driving time. The regular folks are home in bed, kiddies tucked under quilts, furnaces roaring. The impatient horn-honking commuters are gone, banished from sight and mind.

Night people are more relaxed in some ways, edgier in others. When I drive graveyard, my senses come alive; my whole body tingles on alert. Sometimes I feel like I'm back in a squad car, searching alleyways for the unexpected shadow, listening for the sound of running feet.

I felt a rush of anger at Sam Gianelli, at anyone who'd try to deprive me of this blustery star-pocked night, shelter me in some spun-sugar cocoon.

"Twelve seventy-eight," I sang into the radio. "What've you got for me?"

Gloria's voice came over the box, relaxed and easy, Aretha singing backup. "A good one. French Consulate clear to Sudbury."

"Giving me cushy jobs? Sam's orders?"

"You don't want it, I got other customers, babe."

"Thank you much," I said, goosing the accelerator, catching the yellow light. An upper Comm. Ave. to Sudbury is a cabbie's dream: forty bucks and a fat tip. Party for the Francophiles tonight, maybe. Charity shindig with too many free drinks. I sped up. Didn't want my party guest to tire of waiting and stumble over to the Ritz-Carlton's cabstand. Didn't want some cruising independent to steal my big tipper.

Wait inside the consulate, I willed him or her. Have another drink. Wait for the Green & White.

Bare elms and maples lined Comm. Ave.'s well-groomed strolling mall. In front of the multistoried brownstones, twisty-branched magnolia trees loomed like witches' broomsticks. I cut a close corner and my tires churned up spray from leaf-choked gutters, the leaves a brown and shapeless gunk, tattered remains of red-gold October.

G&W 1278 had a working heater, a luxury.

As I drove, I considered Gloria's list. Zachary Robards was a dead end, a phony name. One Gustave Fabian had a juvie record that was sealed for all eternity, as did two of Gloria's other former employees. Either G&W was fielding a lower class of applicant these days or general standards were down. Gustave had done time as an adult too. Arson. Favor for a friend in a failing Lowell furniture business. Short sentence. Good behavior. Record cleansed so he could get his hack license. How many second chances did someone with a record stretching back to childhood deserve?

Out of prison at twenty-two, had he paid his debt? I'd be the last to condemn a kid in his twenties to a life of unemployment. On the other hand, as someone who runs her own small business, I'd think twice about hiring a happy firebug.

"Psychologically well-adjusted," some shrink had written on Gustave's parole recommendation. "Responds well to penal regimentation." If he behaved so nicely in prison, became so "well-adjusted," I thought, maybe he should rot there.

I wondered what Keith Donovan would say to that, found it odd that I had no idea. We hadn't talked much. . . . It used to seem so important to me—talking, knowing you shared certain ideas and values before you hit the sheets. Instead of becoming more conservative with age, I seemed to be getting more reckless. Except about disease. Maybe it boils down to

AIDS fear. If the man seemed clean—smart enough to know the risks and take precautions—he became desirable. Not desirable enough to forgo a friendly condom, mind you.

Just chemistry, I thought. Just that old boy-girl positive-negative charge I don't understand and have quit trying to analyze. What I had with Sam. What I have with Donovan. What I can't quite spark with Mooney.

I pulled the cab to a halt in front of the consulate. It was not a honking neighborhood. Chandeliers blazed, and I strained to see if someone kept watch out the window. I counted to twenty, then mounted the stairs and pushed the bell.

A tiny woman, well over sixty, vigorous, opened the door. A stream of French issued from her heavily lipsticked mouth, a different brand of French from Louis and Jean's, but recognizably the same language. I was glad it was addressed to someone inside the consulate, not to me. She hesitated at the top of the steps, and I guided her down with a little elbow assistance. Tipsy or nearsighted. Maybe just having trouble adjusting her eyes to the dark after the glitter of so many jeweled necks.

She gave the address in accented English. Easy half-hour ride out. Turnpike to 128 to 20. I checked in with Gloria. I'd have to deadhead back. Boston cabs can't pick up in other towns, not even in friendly Cambridge right across the Charles. And who'd I pick up at midnight in respectable Sudbury, where everybody's fast asleep except the teenagers screwing on the family room rug?

The lady didn't speak; neither did I. I wanted to punch on an old blues tape, but the fare, in her twinkling jewelry, looked like classical music. I turned to WBUR and watched a smile flicker across her wrinkled cheeks. Good guess. Better tip. The psychological art of cab driving.

On the return trip, I played blues at top volume, shaking off the melancholy sonatas with a dose of Blind Lemon Jefferson:

> "Have you ever heard a coffin sound?
> Have you ever heard a coffin sound?
> Have you ever heard a coffin sound?
> And you know a good boy's in the ground."

Talk about melancholy.

"Twelve seventy-eight."

I turned down the music.

"Where you been?" Gloria demanded.

"Sudbury, where you think?"

"I been trying to get you."

"Out of range," I said.

"Hold on. Your bad penny's turned up."

Sam's voice came over the crackling box, so deep and smooth it stole my breath. I wasn't ready to deal with this. Why the hell couldn't he have stayed in Washington? A few more days. Till I'd at least *imagined* a way to tell him about Keith.

"Hey," he said. "I don't like being stood up."

"Me neither," I said.

"I brought flowers, but I already gave them to Gloria."

"I hope this isn't going out across the band."

"It's a private conversation."

"Sure, with every scanner freak in the area listening in."

"I'll wait till you come by."

"I'm working. I'm not planning any stop at G and W. I've only made a couple fares."

"Then why'd you send me mail?" His voice was indignant.

"What mail?"

"E-mail. Meet you at Green and White."

I swallowed and felt a chill climb the back of my neck. "I didn't send it."

"Come on. It's late for Halloween pranks."

"What did I happen to say? In this e-mail?"

"One A.M. Meet you here."

I glanced at my watch: 12:50. "Sam," I said, my mouth so dry I could barely spit words. "Do me a favor. Get outside."

"What?"

"Who else is there?"

"Me. Gloria. Marvin's in back. I heard about what you—"

"Please. Get out."

"Carlotta—"

"Sam, humor me. Wait across the street. Shit, you're gonna need help getting Marvin out. Call in the nearest cabbie. Wait at the restaurant. They've got phones. Soon as you're out, dial nine one one."

Growing up Mafia, he should be more suspicious, more careful. Dammit, hadn't the Gianellis ever been threatened?

"Will do," he said curtly.

Message received. I breathed for the first time in minutes.

The rumble filled the car like thunder, distant, growling, growing louder. It turned to a crackling hum and the radio hissed into silence.

"Sam!" I said. "Gloria!" I shouted. I pressed buttons. "All cabs! Call a nine one one to Green and White."

I floored the accelerator, held it there, screeching turns, ignoring red lights. Sweat beaded my forehead. I fumbled at the dash to turn off the heater, couldn't take my eyes off the road, the speed I was doing. Sweat poured down my face, trickled down my back. I cracked a window.

Greenough to Arsenal, the Charles River a black ribbon to my left, the wheels screaming the turns. Market Street, left at North Beacon, blessedly clear, using the opposing traffic lane to pass the few slow cars.

As I approached Cambridge Street, I could hear sirens. I never looked to see if they were chasing me.

TWENTY-FOUR

Lights blinded me. Cherry. Yellow. Blue. Harsh white spotlights trained on the blaze, illuminating towering ladders, powerful spurting hoses, black-and-yellow-slickered firemen. Engines from Ladder Company 19. District 7 pumpers. Boston Police. News vans, satellite dishes raised to the night sky.

I shoved my foot to the floor, bypassing emergency vehicles. Then I stood on the brakes, spinning the steering wheel full left at the same time. Rubber shrieked. Cars honked. The noises floated by—distant, unrelated—as I fishtailed into the restaurant parking lot. I couldn't yank my eyes from the surging smoke, spiraling gray against the blue-black sky like a lurid tornado.

I think I parked between yellow lines. I ran.

"Behind the tape. Get back. Keep back," yelled a voice in my ear.

I stuck out an elbow, connected with something that grunted, and kept running, head down. I ran till the heat forced a halt. The stink of burning rubber filled my nose. Acrid smoke seared my tongue. I was unable to go forward, unable to step back; my pulse raced, my heart pounded. I rubbed a sweater cuff across my wet cheeks and oozing nose.

A shattered chunk of cork lay at my feet. I knelt and touched it. A cup-hook protruded. The keyboard, a fragment of the board where Gloria hangs, hung, used to hang, the cab keys. Kneeling felt better. Hugging knees to chest, lowering my head, I turned myself into a round ball.

Gloria. Sam.

GLORIA. SAM. I don't know if I spoke the names aloud, don't know if I muttered them, screamed them, shrieked them to the indifferent air.

A small round ball, rocking back and forth, refusing to look, refusing to accept the evidence of sight, I coughed and choked on bitter fumes, willed my fingers to unclench, my hands to release their grip, my legs to straighten.

Standing, I could see the metal crisscross shield, guaranteed to protect G&W from outside invaders, hanging crookedly from the side of the stucco shell, resting against a blasted-out cab. Forked tongues of flame licked skyward, hissing at jets of water, steaming.

Hands grabbed me around the waist, yanked backward. I let them.

A policeman spoke; I couldn't hear him. His mouth moved, but I was deaf—from the noise of crackling flames and flooding waters, from the shouts of firefighters and the chattering herd of onlookers. From shock.

Ambulances.

Ambulances with whirling lights.

Survivors. Ambulances might mean survivors. I couldn't bear the hope. Hope was almost worse than loss. The fear of hope worse . . .

I stumbled over a hose, tripped, staggered through a puddle. The policeman, still hovering, clutched my elbow.

"Get the fuck away from me," I muttered, striding toward the ambulances.

Body bags lay on the ground. Flat, unzipped, waiting.

I saw the wheelchair before I heard the voice, her achingly beautiful voice. How they'd moved her massive weight from chair to stretcher I don't know.

"Gloria!"

"Carlotta?"

I shoved, melting through the crowd, seeing an inch as an opening, a hand span as a thoroughfare.

"Marvin" was all she said when I reached her, leaning over to stare into her eyes. She was swathed in a mound of shiny Mylar, covering her from the neck down. The gurney seemed fragile underneath her. Blood traced a pattern in her hair, trickled down her forehead. A raised welt started above her left eyebrow, slanted up. Soot smudged her cheeks. "Marvin," she repeated. That's all, but I knew from the way her voice broke, crackling like dry branches, that one body bag was reserved for his remains.

"Don't talk," an EMT ordered her.

"They already took Sam," she said.

"Where?"

"Move away. She needs to get some air in her lungs, for chrissakes."

"Where did they take Sam?" I persisted.

The EMT shoved me back, strong hands against my shoulders. I crossed my arms in front of me, made taut blades of my hands, the way I'd seen Roz do so many times.

It's just a move I've seen. Someday someone's going to call my bluff and kick the shit out of me. The EMT stared into my eyes and backed off.

"Mass. General," Gloria said. "Burns and trauma. Legs trapped . . . his legs caught under a beam . . . Marvin. Oh, Marvin." The way she spoke his name made me close my eyes and look away. Not a cry or a scream or a wail, but an almost unearthly keening, the vocalization of a grief so intense that it grabbed my intestines and wouldn't let go.

"Somebody fightin' with him," Gloria said. "Door to the back room bursts open. I hear two voices, cursin' each other. Marvin. Marvin says 'Stop!' or 'No!' I couldn't see; he's still in the other room. Sam started runnin' and that's when everything went—"

The EMT inserted a needle into one of her bulging veins.

"Did Marvin say a name? Did he know the person? Was the voice familiar?"

Gloria's head lolled, rolled slowly sideways.

"Will she—" I started to say before my voice was lost in the roar of the engine. If I hadn't moved, the ambulance would have run me down. I could have claimed my own body bag.

I turned and watched the blaze, transfixed by the whistling wind and water, soaked by the spray, unable to avert my face from the flames, a primitive ape staring at a magical lightning strike, reeling with the fear and fascination of fire.

Minutes later, hours later, a police officer in a yellow slicker tapped me repeatedly on the shoulder. He said, "Lieutenant Mooney wants you. His car. Now. He's waiting."

I couldn't find words, so I nodded. I followed.

TWENTY-FIVE

"Why Mass. General?" asked a flat, zombielike voice. My voice. I couldn't seem to raise or lower the pitch. My throat burned when I swallowed. Smoke inhalation . . . Something wrong with my ears . . . Maybe I'd always sound this way now—numb, affectless, dead.

Dead. Marvin dead.

Gloria injured. Sam injured . . .

I tried to stretch my legs, but there wasn't room in the backseat. Must be one of the new command cars. No steel-mesh screen to separate cops from perps. My hand rested on a working door handle.

Between the front seats—jump seats instead of the standard straight-across bench—a computer screen took up the usual radio space. Below it, a keyboard. Communications devices bristled. Mooney was nursing a handheld mike, advising someone of our destination.

"Call the Arson Squad," I said.

The uniformed driver wove through Storrow Drive traffic, blue lights flashing, siren screaming. Mooney yapped into the speaker. The unfamiliar officer beside me scribbled in a notebook for all he was worth.

"The Arson Squad," I repeated, placing a hand on Mooney's shoulder.

"What?" he said. I could hardly hear him.

I shook my head. I felt like I was underwater, drowning, observing through filmy mist. I covered an ear with my index finger, tried to swallow.

"You gonna faint?" Mooney asked.

I breathed in and out, counted to ten, breathed. Yawned. The ear popped. I could hear.

"What about the Arson Squad?" Mooney said.

The suit beside me stopped scratching with his pencil. "It's an idea," he said eagerly. "I can see it. The Gianelli kid tries to blow up the place. I'll get on to his broker, his bank, his insurance company, see if he needs cash. Boston Mob, Jesus, figures they'd screw up. Whole shit-canful should blow themselves to kingdom come."

Mooney's quick. Before I could move, he'd turned in his seat and fastened his hand around my right wrist.

"Oglesby's with the Organized Crime Task Force," Mooney explained hastily. "New. He doesn't know the, uh, situation."

"And I suppose *she* does?" Oglesby said, a smirk creasing his thin lips. He sat so stiffly his backbone didn't touch the upholstery. A self-righteous guy who didn't need starch in his shirts. "These goombahs, they're always so up-front with their, uh, what do I call you so as not to offend, huh? His main squeeze?"

"Sam's not Mafia," I said, my voice still flat. It wasn't my ears, it was my throat. Felt like a skeletal hand tugging my vocal cords. "You should know that if anybody does."

"Well, excuse me," Oglesby said sarcastically. "Anthony Gianelli's boy, you can understand my confusion. What do the Italians say? 'The acorn doesn't drop far from the tree'?"

I was going to hurt him. Now or later.

"Why Arson Squad, Carlotta?" Mooney asked, cautiously releasing my hand.

"Sam was supposed to be there when the place blew." I swallowed; it hurt. "Me too."

"Why?"

I shook my head. "I'm not sure."

"Speculate," Mooney ordered, like I'd suddenly returned to the force. How many times had I heard him say that word?

I swallowed again, trying to form thoughts into sentences. "Sam got e-mail telling him to meet me at G and W at one A.M."

"Fire department was called before then," Oglesby interrupted.

"I *know* that. I put out an emergency call. All cabs. At twelve fifty-two."

"Go on, Carlotta." Mooney gave Oglesby a warning glance.

"I was helping Gloria earlier today. Took over dispatch, asked for information about cabbie beatings. A lot have been reported, but more haven't been. Immigrants scared of cops. Cabbies who believe the threats. You know: You call the cops, we'll get your wife, we'll get your kid."

Mooney didn't say anything. Oglesby looked like he was dying to break in, but Mooney held his eye.

Mooney said, "So somebody who didn't want you poking your nose into the cab beatings might have assumed you'd be dispatching, and he sent Sam by to keep you company? That's a big assumption, considering the amount of time Gloria spends handling those phones."

"Doesn't make sense," I muttered.

"Sam know anything special about the beatings?"

"I don't know. I don't think so."

"Carlotta?" Mooney said softly. I don't know how long I'd sat motionless before he spoke.

"Is Sam dead, Mooney? Is he dying? If you know and you're not telling me—"

"I honest to God don't know. Only thing I heard was 'multiple trauma.' Let me get on the radio, send a team from Arson over to G and W."

Sam. Multiple trauma. Burns. Legs trapped under a beam.

I've seen burn victims. Auto accidents. Blackened skin hanging in shreds, exposed muscle, raw flesh . . .

"Bet he'll have great docs, a whole team of them," Oglesby said cheerfully. "Most of their last names'll end in vowels. And I wouldn't worry if I were you. He'll make it. You know what doctors say: Scumbags never die."

I hit him. A short right jab that snapped his neck

back. Mooney could have stopped me, but he didn't try. Maybe he wanted me in custody, and assaulting an officer was good enough.

I covered my face with cupped hands, tried to keep my shoulders steady. Goddamn Oglesby wasn't going to see them shake, wasn't going to get the treat of a single tear.

Mooney should have locked me in a cage car. I don't hit people; I was out of control. I glanced at Oglesby and was savagely glad to see blood dripping from his nose.

TWENTY-SIX

Mass. General is the big one, with the ether dome and the nurses capped in dome-shaped snowy white to commemorate the fact that anesthesia took a giant step in Boston. The one with the history and the rep that makes other teaching hospitals drool with envy. What it doesn't own outright, MGH "cooperates" with. What it can't own or cooperate with, it devours. When Massachusetts General Hospital desires a new department—say, high-risk pregnancy—it steals top personnel from other hospitals with a snap of its collective fingers. Along with a Harvard affiliation, a Mass. General credential brings great riches in the medical world.

Conventional wisdom holds that if you're really sick, your ailment both deadly and rare, you want the General. Routine disorder, you're in the wrong place.

If the docs at MGH don't find something worthy of their talents, they might be tempted to experiment.

That's what cops tell me. They also say don't mess with MGH Emergency. Too crowded.

Mooney's driver dropped us near the massive front entrance and sped away. As I marched up the granite steps, sandwiched between Mooney and Oglesby, I wiggled the fingers on my right hand. Nothing broken. I scanned the knuckle abrasions thoughtfully. Could I pretend they hurt worse than they did, get myself closeted with a doctor or nurse, escape?

"You buy a better gun yet?" Mooney asked.

I shook my head no. I'm not sure he noticed the response; it could have been a rhetorical question. Lot of good a new automatic would have done me; I could have shot Oglesby instead of smacking him.

Mooney led the way. We'd already traversed the main lobby, two endless hushed corridors, and ascended three flights via elevator in stony silence. Mooney's hand clasped my arm too tightly for politeness. I assumed he didn't want to cuff me in public, scare the elderly lady carrying the bouquet of wilted geraniums, the harassed father with the scraggly teddy bear in tow.

I tried to remember what I knew about burns. Are third-degree the worst and first-degree the best? Or the other way around?

The waiting room had the kind of fluorescent lights that make people look like they've been dead for days. Or else the patrons had all assumed a ghastly pallor as they wondered what the green-gowned priesthood were doing to their loved ones behind surgical steel doors.

"Gianelli."

I realized Mooney had flashed his badge and spoken. A receptionist stared at him with the gaze cops inspire, a mixture of curiosity, irritation, and fear. An appraising glance, as if she was sizing him up against some TV police hunk.

She rattled terminology. I caught the catchall "multiple trauma" again, interspersed with words that had yet to be translated from the Latin.

I leaned close. "Will Sam be okay?"

She ignored me, continuing her Latin chat with Mooney. Maybe he'd picked it up at Mass.

"Will he be okay?" I insisted, my voice dangerously low.

"Shut up," Oglesby said, trying to grab my arm and haul me back.

"Condition as yet undetermined," Mooney said over his shoulder. "Watch the mouth, Oglesby."

"Life threatening?" I demanded loudly.

The woman at the desk, attempting to size up the situation with seen-it-all-eyes, said, "I wouldn't know that," in as condescending a manner as she could manage.

"The lady's already punched out a cop," Mooney warned her.

She shuffled papers, hesitating to keep up appearances. "You'll need to speak to a doctor," she said primly.

"When can I see Sam?" I asked her.

"A surgical team is currently evaluating Mr. Gianelli." The response was perfectly automatic, as if I'd yanked a string on a talking doll.

"When can I see him?"

"I can't tell you. I don't know."

"Is there anything you *can* tell me?"

"There are other people in line." She turned away abruptly and addressed a tiny woman with tears in her eyes.

The other woman's tears threatened to trigger my own. Mooney took my hand.

"Let's find a doc," he said.

Mooney was a pit bull; he wouldn't give up or let go. He used his badge, threw its weight around.

Within twenty minutes, a gowned intern informed us that she "didn't believe Mr. Gianelli's condition would be termed life threatening at this time."

I hadn't realized I'd been holding my breath. It came out in such a rush I had to stiffen my knees to keep them from buckling. I gulped and bit the inside of my cheek. Hard. Sam's not going to die, he's not going to die.

Gloria's not going to die.

Marvin's dead.

And somebody else. Who else?

Mooney's hand gripped my arm. We were seated at some distance from the receptionist, side by side on a low beige couch. Oglesby was tucked into a nearby chair, one brown shoe waving back and forth, back and forth, rhythmically, hypnotically. My feet must have crossed the carpet. Oglesby held a steaming plastic foam cup in his right hand. I wondered if he'd offered me coffee. I'd have taken him up on it if I'd heard him.

"Okay, Carlotta," Mooney was saying, "it goes like this. I book you for assault unless I hear the whole she-bang, anything remotely relevant. That covers drive-by shootings, cabbie beatings—reported and unreported. Your stint as a mugging victim in Franklin Park, what Gloria hired you to do—"

"Sam's in good shape," I said. "His blood pressure's low. He exercises."

"He'll get good care," Mooney said. "Talk."

"Maybe they need blood," I said.

"They do, you can donate. No plasma shortage in this place."

Oglesby said, "If there were a blood shortage, believe me, they'd find juice for a Gianelli. Put out the word, get a dozen goombahs in here faster than pizza delivery."

I stared at the guy. He'd shifted the cup from his right hand to his left. His fist was balled. He wanted me to hit him again. He was orchestrating it.

"I'll talk to you, Mooney," I said slowly, "but not to this jerk. Get him the hell out of earshot."

"Oglesby," Mooney said pleasantly, "why not take a hike?"

He glared at both of us, but he finally stood and departed. He took his sweet time.

"Mooney, I hate to ask this, but are you wired? You planning to record me for posterity?"

"No."

"Is Oglesby a close personal friend?"

"No."

"Will you feel honor bound to tell him every word I say?"

"No."

"Is he going to press charges? He's not hurt, which I regret."

"He'll press if I tell him to. Or if you keep pissing him off. With Organized Crime, he spends a lot of time proving how tough he is. When I tell his boss he got sucker punched by a lady P.I., he'll hate it."

"Don't tell."

"I was looking forward to it," Mooney said wistfully.

"I want to talk to you as a friend, Mooney."

"A friend who's a cop," he said.

"Don't make this harder than it is."

"Carlotta, I'm sorry as hell about Sam and Gloria and Marvin. Marvin was something else, but he didn't deserve what he got. This is a homicide investigation, and you know what I've gotta do."

"You wouldn't know it was homicide without me. Not yet." I blinked my eyes. A TV set was suspended from the ceiling. People nearby were hunched in their seats, watching reruns of daytime talk shows in the middle of the night.

Mooney said, "Some favor. How long you think it'll take Gloria to talk, with her brother dead?"

"Depends on when she comes around. I saw a paramedic shoot her full of dope. Hypo the size of your arm. Is she here too?"

"Yeah."

The TV set had hypnotic power. I found my eyes drawn to it. A red-faced man with glasses was speaking to someone on the telephone. Napalm. I was sure he used the word *napalm* in the same sentence as the Bill of Rights. I folded my hands in my lap. I didn't realize how tightly the fingers were laced until I felt Mooney prying them loose, heard his low, comforting murmur.

"Moon, I don't know where to go. I don't know whether to stay near Sam or Gloria or—"

"Talk to me. Best thing you can do for either of them."

The message had come by e-mail. It hit me like a fist in the stomach. *Frank would use e-mail.*

I confessed to swapping places with Marvin. I talked about the Haitians, Jean and Louis. Mooney's got no more interest in helping the INS deport working people than I do. I mentioned Lee Cochran and Phil Yancey and what I'd heard about the hotel and restaurant lobby wanting more cabs on the road. I said I'd been checking a list of drivers who'd quit Green & White, drivers Gloria'd fired.

"Why?" Mooney pounced on the last item like a hungry cat on a canary.

"Why what?"

"Why ask Gloria for a list?"

I ran both hands through my hair. "Let me think. Let me think. . . . Because it seems like Green and White's suffering more damage than other companies. Lee Cochran said two of the drivers who got attacked and didn't report it to the cops were independents."

"You happen to get their names?"

"No."

"Go on."

"But Jean got hit, and Marvin. Gloria's having trouble finding new jockeys. Lee told me he *knew* Phil Yancey was at the bottom of everything, trying to corner the medallion market, but then Lee dropped the whole thing cold. Brennan, over at Hackney

Carriage—remember Brennan?—said Yancey wasn't buying medallions—"

"Brennan's so dumb, he probably doesn't have a clue."

"He sends his best to you, too, Mooney, and he promised he'd go over some recent medallion transfers, see if Yancey might be dealing under the table, using straws."

"Brennan's so lazy, he'll probably get around to that by the Fourth of July."

"So *you* check it, Moon. Anyway, nothing quite meshed; nothing made sense. And I'd already asked Gloria for the list, so—I don't know—I thought I might as well follow up on it. . . ."

"Let me make sure I've got this," Mooney said. "The target could have been you, because you were gabbing on the radio earlier today about cabbie beatings. It could have been Sam, because he got the e-mail. It could have been Gloria, for some kinda freakin' revenge, or because somebody's after Green and White's medallions. . . ."

I bit my lip, nodded.

"You think Marvin spotted the bomber?"

Frank could be dead, stashed in a body bag, I thought.

"Carlotta?" Mooney said. "What?"

I licked my lips, managed an answer. "Marvin wasn't supposed to be there. Gloria moved him in this afternoon. If Marvin saw a stranger fooling around in his sister's room, no matter what kind of pain he was in, he'd have tried to stop the guy."

Mooney said, "I hope we find enough parts to ID." I must have shuddered because he added, "Sorry. I'm not doing real well on tact."

"Mooney," I said, making up my mind. "There's another thing."

"Just one?"

"Maybe more. Let's start with the drive-by."

He said, "I thought we might get to that eventually."

I gave him the plate number of Sam's borrowed car. I gave him the block on Altamont, the house number. Told him I'd bought a used computer.

"Yellow Pages?" he asked sarcastically.

"Friend of Sam's."

"Name?"

"Joe somebody."

Keep Frank out of it, Sam had warned. Pleaded. Begged.

Mooney asked more questions. The attack vehicle? Gang colors? Racial slurs? Number of individuals involved? Question after question I couldn't answer to his satisfaction.

"Why is Oglesby here?" I said, trying to change the subject, divert him momentarily.

Mooney sighed. "You say his name and here he comes. Why don't you ask him?"

Oglesby didn't sit. He seemed strangely elated.

"You really think this is Mafia related?" I asked him.

"Yeah," Oglesby grunted, staring at the glass doors.

"I told you, Sam's not a player."

"Yeah?"

"That the only word you know?"

He opened his mouth to speak, but Mooney stopped him with a glance. I know that glance.

"What's going on?" I asked sharply.

Mooney stared at the rug, avoiding my eyes. "Oglesby's got a hard-on for anybody named Gianelli is all," he said so smoothly I knew he was lying. I was almost grateful for his treachery; I didn't feel guilty about keeping Frank a secret.

"Mooney," I said. "Did the Organized Crime Task Force clear it with the Boston Police before they bugged G and W?"

"Shit," Mooney murmured. "I don't believe I'm hearing this."

Interdepartmental rivalries in Boston's law enforcement circles are legendary.

"You heard the lady, Oglesby," Mooney said softly, a threat implicit in every word. "If you have tapes, they're material evidence in a homicide, and I want them. Now!"

"I don't know what she's talking about," Oglesby said. "Probably, she's hysterical."

"If there are tapes," Mooney said, biting off each word with the slow precision he uses when he wants to shout, "you might as well give them up. I'll find out, and when I do—"

Oglesby stiffened, practically saluted.

Papa Gianelli and entourage entered. A woman young enough to be his daughter clung to the old man's arm, trying to slow his pace. She wasn't his daughter; I'd met his only daughter, a dark-haired, sharp-featured replica of her mother. This woman was fair-haired with an expensive shimmer and plenty of cool allure. Sam's latest stepmother. Grouped behind were four men in well-cut suits, wearing heavy gold rings and flashy cuff links. I recognized two brothers, Gil and Mitch. Gil looked more like Sam, a squat older version. With Mitch it was harder to tell; he'd gained enough weight to blur his features. The other two men were strangers: uncles, capos, possibly bodyguards. Their eyes scanned the room.

Oglesby breathed faster. One hand trembled and he stuck it in a pocket. He looked like he felt the urgent need to grab a spiral notebook and scrawl license-plate numbers.

Papa G surveyed the room as well. His eyes froze when he saw me. He burst into voluble Italian. The only word I understood was *putta*. Whore.

Mooney picked up on it too. He took my arm firmly. "Time to go," he said.

"I'm staying."

"We'll come back when the troops leave."

"They won't leave."

Oglesby backed into a chair and tried to look inconspicuous as Papa G steamrolled his way to the front of the queue. Inconspicuous, hell. He couldn't tear his eyes away from Gianelli. The dumbest Mob soldier would pick up on Oglesby. He stuck out like a beacon. Might as well put him in uniform.

"Let's find Gloria," Mooney said. "Oglesby, I want an immediate update on any change in Gianelli's condition."

Oglesby gave me a long look and rubbed his jaw slowly.

"Oglesby," Mooney said carefully. "It was a punch. You've taken worse. You want to hear about it the rest of your life, fine with me. You go into a bar, cops'll stop talking and point at you. Laugh a little. Carlotta and me, we go way back. We tell a good story."

Oglesby grunted.

Mooney shrugged, looked at me.

"No charges," I said.

"No witnesses," Mooney said, "no charges."

It could have been a promise; it could have been a threat.

TWENTY-SEVEN

Time spent in hospital waiting rooms is measured differently. Like dog time: Every minute equals seven minutes; every hour, seven hours. I wasn't allowed to see Gloria; I wasn't allowed to see Sam. Doctors were "assessing their condition, please take a seat, ma'am." It was maddening. Without Mooney at my side, I might have lied my way in. Claimed kinship. Hell, stolen a lab coat and charged into the room.

If someone would kindly tell me which was the right room.

As news spread through the cabbie underground, a trickle of vaguely familiar faces became a stream. All asking the same questions. How is she? What can I do? How can I help?

Give blood, a passing nurse advised.

Knowing the blood we donated wouldn't necessarily go to Gloria, but would be credited to her account, unable to find another task to occupy the hours, we lined up at the blood bank. Cabbies and pols, street people, cops, society matrons, three-piece suits, all waiting patiently. It took me a minute to figure out what was wrong with the picture. Color, that's what it was: the full spectrum of flesh tones. In Boston, movie theaters cater to black crowds or white crowds. Restaurants rarely attract racially mixed gatherings, although there's a sprinkling of South End places that manage. At Red Sox games you can spot more blacks on the playing field than in the stands. Same thing at the Garden when the Bruins play. The Celts are marginally better.

Boston is two separate cities, one black, one white. Gloria had managed to cross the boundaries. People knew her by her voice.

Roz came and went, provoking raised eyebrows and shocked stares. I issued terse instructions, which she grudgingly accepted. I waited, overhearing tales of Gloria from generations of cabdrivers, from nurses and doctors who'd treated her long ago, helped her cope with her paralysis. I waited. I wished they would stop. The stories sounded elegiac, final. At one point, the line included seventeen nurses.

I waited.

When Lee Cochran joined the group, I immediately abandoned my place.

"Lee." He was unshaven and his clothes were wrinkled, as if he'd been sleeping in them.

"Carlotta."

"Two things, Lee: Who told you Phil Yancey was behind the beatings?"

"What?"

"You seemed certain. Dead sure. Why?"

He shifted his weight from one foot to the other. "In my job, you hear rumors," he said uneasily.

"Rumors?"

"Yeah. Gloria's going to make it okay, isn't she?"

"Yes," I said. "Yes. Now, the other question: Did you tell Yancey you were planning to hire me? *The truth, Lee.*"

"Jesus, Carlotta, why'd I do a thing like that?"

"Why didn't you return my calls? Too busy threatening Yancey?"

"I don't know what you're friggin' talking about," Lee said.

"How's this sound? *You* start the rumor that more medallions are going out on the street. Hackney Carriage says it'll never happen, by the way. But your pal Yancey asks you to talk it up, figures the rumor might scare a few small owners into selling."

"Why?" Lee asked.

"You're the one who said he was out to corner the market."

"Why the hell would I help him?"

"Money, Lee. Maybe a kickback on every medallion transfer. Yancey could afford it if he's planning to turn his garages into lease factories, couldn't he?"

"I wouldn't work for Yancey in a million years," Lee blustered.

"Not even for a million bucks?"

"Not for ten million."

"Really? Well, Lee, *somebody* told Yancey you'd talked to me. And I don't like being used. If you're working some medallion scam here, if you had anything to do with this thing at Green and White—"

"You're accusing me?" He puffed out his chest. "Because if you are, you'd better have the facts to back it up."

People were starting to stare at us, murmur uneasily.

"I mean it, Carlotta," Lee said. "I've worked hard in this town, and I don't have much to show for it. Just my reputation. You mess with that, I'll fight you every step of the way."

His fists were clenched; so were mine.

"Enough," I said, breaking the tension, holding up a hand in surrender, briefly closing my eyes against the merciless lights. "This isn't the place or the time. I'm sorry, Lee."

"We're all pretty upset," he mumbled gruffly.

The woman who'd stood behind me in line allowed my reentry. Time had stopped, after all. No rush.

If Mooney hadn't intervened I'd never have crashed hospital security and made it into Gloria's room. Immediate family only was the decree. Leroy and Geoffrey, the middle brother, dominated the tiny space like lions, massive in presence and threat. They scared *me* and I knew them; I felt ashamed of my gut reaction. No two imposing white men would have had the same effect.

I watched Mooney's police guards, one black, one

white, observe Gloria's brothers. Both kept their hands too close to their weapons for my taste.

It was easier to keep my eyes on Leroy and Geoffrey or on the police, than to watch Gloria. Gloria, who spent all her waking hours wheelchair-bound, yet never seemed helpless. God knows how she'd accomplished it, perfected it, how she maintained the illusion of self-reliance. It was her special grace.

The bombing had shattered it completely.

At first I was worried because she remained unconscious; then I was glad. She was hooked up to machinery that showed stable vital signs. Better oblivion than humiliation and pain. An IV line dripped solution into her veins. No breathing tube; she was managing that on her own, at least. No hospital gown. None could have fit. She was shrouded in gauze. Her forehead had been bandaged. After a few squirming minutes, I couldn't bear it. There was nothing I could do to help, nothing I could say. I squeezed Leroy's hand as I left. I don't think he felt it.

Mooney couldn't get me past the Gianelli watchdogs.

I cabbed home in daylight, my eyes tearing in unexpected sunshine. I shut them, leaned back, and tried to fall asleep despite honking traffic, jostling potholes. Images flooded my mind: the scowl on Papa Gianelli's face when he refused to let me see Sam; the Christmas decorations dotted like funeral wreaths along the hallways.

My ear bounced against the windowpane, jarring me awake. The cab halted and I dug in my handbag for the fare. I didn't know the cabbie, some independent

I'd flagged. He asked me whether Gloria was holding her own.

I couldn't find my keys. I fumbled with the lock.

Roz was seated in front of the computer, a pencil thrust through a braided fake-hair topknot, busily punching keys. I caught the scent of peanut butter. An open jar stood guard on the blotter. Sticky keyboard.

"I know what you told me at the hospital," she said, immediately seizing the defensive. "But I can't find Frank. Not a goddamn trace."

"Why?" I demanded.

"You ever heard the expression 'guy-go'?"

"What?"

"Garbage in-garbage out. GIGO. What do you expect me to feed this machine? Nothing old 'Frank' told me was real."

"He's *got* to be there," I insisted. "Run the phony SSN, see if it turns up any aliases."

"Get some sleep. I'll keep trying."

I peered at my wristwatch, blinked. The Roman numerals seemed to be jumping around. "Two hours," I said. "I'll set the alarm."

"You could use more than that."

"Be ready to go when I say."

"Where?"

"Out."

"Yeah, Ma, but where?"

"I'll let you know," I said.

"How are they?"

I told her I'd seen Gloria.

"Sam?"

Sam. Sam undergoing emergency surgery, legs trapped under a beam, the building blazing—

"Carlotta?"

"They wouldn't let me in."

"Go to bed," Roz said. "I'll call the hospital for updates. Every half hour."

"Thanks."

I didn't get any two hours' sleep. Mooney phoned.

"The address you gave, on Altamont," he said without wasting breath on hello. "Thought you might like to know the place is abandoned. No furniture. No fingerprints. No trash. Landlord lives down the street. Tenant paid three months in advance, plus security deposit. Cash. Guy didn't even know his tenant had scrammed. If we'd had the information earlier . . ."

Frank was gone. Why was I not surprised? What the hell kind of old buddy turns up out of the blue, makes a move on your girlfriend, sends you e-mail to get you to a garage, tries to blow you the hell to kingdom come . . . ?

Probably the dead kind, I thought.

"Mooney," I said. "Don't blame me. Your precious cops got called on a drive-by. According to the drill I remember, they do a careful door-to-door search—"

"If we'd had the address—"

" 'If my grandmother had wheels, she'd be a truck,' Mooney. You know what that means? You're spinning yours. How about 'All the king's horses and all the king's men'? You heard that one? Is that what they tell little Irish kids?"

"That's what they tell little Brit kids," he said.

"This missing tenant have a name?"

"Ben Franklin. Like on the hundred-dollar bills he gave the landlord."

"Mooney, is there any . . . anything new on Sam?"

"No. But there's a tentative ID on the second corpse."

I expected it to be Frank. No matter what the name.

"Zachariah Robertson. Ring bells?"

When I wake suddenly, usually I'm groggy and slow, but sometimes I'm still generating alpha waves, making quick connections.

"Wait a minute," I said.

I grabbed the list Gloria'd written, the names of drivers she'd fired.

No Zachariah Robertson, but certainly a Zachary Robards, the one who'd quit his job so theatrically, abandoning his cab in Southie.

"I know a lot about him," I said. "I think. The question is how do you?" Nobody does an autopsy that fast.

"Anonymous phone tip. Woman. Young. Lover boy didn't come home after taking off with a can of gasoline tucked under his arm. Worried about him."

"Touching," I said.

"Now give."

"He used a slightly different name."

Mooney listened. "Revenge," he said. His voice was cool, like he was ticking off an item on a grocery list. "Makes sense. Lately you fire somebody, they come back with an AK-47. Bastard."

"Very neat," I muttered, propping the phone on one

shoulder, swinging my legs out from under the quilt. "Positively tidy."

"Go back to bed," Mooney said. "Sorry I woke you."

TWENTY-EIGHT

Go back to bed. Sure. I punched, patted, and smoothed my pillow. It was burning hot on one side, icy on the other. No way could I sleep. I stripped off my clothes and let them lie where they fell as I marched to the bathroom and turned the shower taps on full. Would Roz hear if I shrieked over the pounding water? I wanted to scream. Shatter my grim reflection in the mirror. Smash someone in the face, feel the soft cartilage give. Feel blood.

I lowered the lid of the toilet seat, sat abruptly. Cold. I felt gooseflesh as I folded my arms, hugged them to my chest.

Zachary Robards. Zachariah Robertson. A name on a list, a list I hadn't bothered to pick up till yesterday. A phony name. But with the same initials. I should have checked with the cops, seen if they'd come up with any aliases when they'd run his name for Gloria. He should have been my first interview. Would have been . . . if my ankle hadn't hurt. If I hadn't taken time out to screw the shrink next door. If Gloria hadn't asked me to drive. If . . .

I stepped into the shower, adjusted the spray, needle sharp, hot. Soaped and rinsed, soaped and rinsed, washed my hair twice. I sniffed, swore I could still smell smoke. I scrubbed as if I were trying to scour away scenes seared on my eyeballs, images I was afraid I'd never forget.

Zachary Robards was dead. No medallion plot. No cab scam. Just a crazed ex-employee with access to explosives.

The e-mail message? A coincidence.

And at "Frank's"? A drive-by. A racial thing. A nothing.

I didn't believe it; I didn't want to believe it.

I dressed in jeans and a baggy blue sweater. High-top boots. I bent from the waist, shook out my hair, toweled it semidry.

Roz, computer bound, gamely plunked keys with one finger, as if she were seated at a piano, never having taken lessons.

"Find anything?" I asked.

"Phone wake you?"

"Guy who died with Marvin's been ID'd. Tentatively. A phone-in tip."

"Friend of Marvin's?" she asked.

"I figure the second corpse for the perp. Marvin surprised him. A bomb went off early, a match got lit too soon."

"Perp's idea to blow G and W? Or somebody else's?"

"Gloria may have fired this guy a few months back."

"Grudge?"

It was a rote response. Anyone would think that.

I shrugged. "Is there more peanut butter?"

"Help yourself."

In the kitchen, I rummaged for a clean spoon. Roz uses her finger. A utensil makes me feel more civilized.

One spoonful of peanut butter made me realize I was ravenous. I found a loaf of bread, blue with mold, and dumped it in the trash. The Ritz crackers were merely stale. I smeared some with cream cheese, some with peanut butter. I brought a carton of orange juice into the living room, swigged it from the container, watching Roz.

"What have you got?" I asked her.

"We're not exactly legal here. This setup, I mean."

"No kidding."

" 'Frank' doesn't want your hard-earned bucks going to the phone company or the National Credit Information Network. I bet he wants you to give me a raise instead."

"Roz."

She blew out a breath that shot her bangs, her longest remaining tuft of variegated hair, into the air. They stayed aloft, a triumph of mousse over gravity.

"From what I can tell, he set you up as a phony business, an employment agency based in the Cayman Islands. Where the fuck are they?"

"Caribbean Sea. The exotic world of thatched huts and tax havens," I said. "Check a map."

Employment agencies are routinely granted access to credit bureau information. Just have to pay the fee. A hefty fee.

"What's the name of my company and who owns it?" I asked.

"Siren Hiring. Say it fast, it rhymes: Siren Hirin'."

"Love it," I said flatly. "Owned by?"

"Getaway Ventures of Singapore. A holding company. It's gonna take me a while to get the names of the board of directors. And this phone—"

"Is registered to Elvis."

"One better. Doesn't exist. I do the phone company ring-back on it, it's got no number at all. NYNEX is gonna turn blue figuring out who to bill."

"Good."

"So I thought, why not take advantage?"

"And how have you done that?"

"Grab some printout and you'll see. I'm chasing a goddamn shadow."

She'd tried everything I'd asked and more, I'll say that for her. Public-records search: no judgments, no tax liens, no bankruptcy, no linkage with any corporations, no real property, no limited partnerships, no workers comp claims, no criminal record.

Of course, all we had to go on was a phony Social Security number, a phony name.

Roz said, "Don't get me wrong, this is loads of fun, kinda like a video game from hell, but it's strictly dead-end unless we can find out who he really is."

"Sam knows," I said.

"He's in fair condition," Roz said. "Whatever that means."

"It means we search his place," I said.

"Key?"

I nodded.

"I like doing things legal. Speaking of which," she said, "I want that cash out of my bedroom."

"Roz, I am up to my ears—"

"Yeah, well, you may have noticed that one of my regular dates, you know, the shrink man, he sorta dropped out of the race."

"Roz," I said, "honest, I meant to talk to you about that."

"What's to talk about?" she said.

"No, really, I want to apologize."

She seemed amused. "Why?"

"I don't do things like that," I said. "I don't see myself as somebody who snatches another woman's guy. It just happened."

"Lighten up," she said. "We weren't exactly married. Keith's too young for me anyway, kind of naive, you know? But there's this guy at the club. Very cute. I'd like to bring him by for a visit. Your money's hurting my social life."

"I'll take care of it," I promised.

"Soon," she said.

Too young, too naive. Ouch! I thought.

"Roz," I said, "before we go, why don't you change your clothes?"

She stared down at hot-pink leggings and a well-filled turquoise tee, which would have been an eye stopper even without its illustration of a hunky surfer. The saying IF IT SWELLS, RIDE IT printed below the graphic in Day-Glo orange was the coup de grâce.

"Why?" she asked.

"We ought to aim for unmemorable."

"Oh. Yeah, I can do that."

I refrained from comment, finished the orange juice while I listened to her feet marching upstairs.

The doorbell stopped at two rings. For me, not Roz.

Keith Donovan clutched the morning paper. His face looked pale above his neatly knotted tie.

"I called," he said.

"Roz didn't tell me."

"Anything I can do?" he asked.

"A hug would be welcome, I think," I said.

It started out fine, but I kept imagining he was Sam.

"Trouble?" he said.

"Lots. Do you remember Gloria?"

"The, um, enormous woman I met here at dinner?"

"She prefers 'fat.' You do crisis intervention?"

He licked his lips. "Sometimes."

"You affiliated with MGH?"

"Yes."

"I'll pay if her insurance won't."

He ignored the money angle. "What's the crisis?"

I explained. Hurriedly. In the foyer with the flats of my hands pressed against his shirt, my fingertips barely brushing his collarbone. His arms loosely circled my waist. At some point in the tale I reached behind, opened his hands, stepped back and away. I felt like I was suffocating. "She'll blame herself for his death. She blamed herself when he got beaten up, and that was bad enough. I don't know how she's gonna come out of this. Will you help her? Will you try?"

"Pro bono," he said.

"I thought that was lawyers."

"Lovers," he said. He stared directly into my eyes. No smile.

"I'm not sure," I said.

"About being lovers?"

"About owing you."

"We can talk about it," he said.

Roz cleared her throat before descending the stairs. An unprecedented tact attack.

"When we have time," I said.

TWENTY-NINE

Roz wore black tights teamed with an oversize white shirt and Doc Martens. Her broad-brimmed hat was black, with floppy roses on the crown. Conspicuous, yes, but compared to her surfer shirt, a positive camouflage job.

I circled the block three times, which, since Sam lives in the Charles River Park apartments, meant about a mile per revolution. We checked for marked and unmarked police units, found none. Either they'd already finished or they hadn't arrived yet. There were no parking spaces, legal or illegal.

I shouldn't have stopped for sleep. Caffeine and adrenaline have seen me through before. I tooted at a slow Ford Escort, passed its trembling silver-haired driver on the right.

A battered blue Volvo abruptly vacated a prime

spot. I braked, swerved, and fronted in. The van behind me honked. Roz shot the finger, saving me the trouble.

Sam has the penthouse in the southernmost structure. Health club, pool, sauna, concierge. Access by private elevator key. I twisted my copy into the keyhole above the elevator buttons.

We rode upward in rosewood-paneled elegance. Roz chattered about the computer. She'd found several fascinating bulletin boards. Her favorite was "alt.sex.bondage."

She let out a low whistle when the elevator doors parted. Sam's entryway's impressive, but I've been there so often that the artwork doesn't jump out at me anymore. I already know that the mobile is an original Miró, a minor classic.

At the end of the hall, his bedroom. Our bedroom. Suddenly I wished I'd come alone.

"We'll split it like I said."

"I get the boring stuff," Roz muttered as I passed her a pair of latex gloves, the kind docs use for surgery.

I couldn't get my mind off doctors and hospitals. Surgery on Sam's left leg today. Condition holding at fair. Second-degree burns, right leg only. Both legs badly broken. Shattered ankle. Surgery for eight hours today. Eight hours.

"You do the kitchen, the living room, and the guest room," I said firmly. "Take special care in the guest room. If Frank ever stayed there, I want to know it."

"I'll bring you one of his pubic hairs. We can get it DNA-typed."

"The answering machine's in the living room. Make a copy of all incoming calls. Leave everything exactly as you find it. The cops may come and I don't want to tamper."

"You don't want to get nailed tampering," Roz corrected.

"Whatever."

She followed me down the hallway, stood in the doorway a little too long, eyeing the king-size water bed.

"Start with the phone calls," I said.

As soon as her footsteps receded, I sat on the bed. Ripples fanned out beneath the quilt. I lay back and stared at the familiar ceiling. Maybe I should let Roz work solo. It felt wrong, being in Sam's bedroom without him. Too much like searching the victim's place after death.

I'd done enough of that as a cop.

I reached under the quilt on Sam's side of the bed, ran a hand over his pillow, hugged it to my face, breathing in the familiar smell of aftershave.

I sat and stared at the bookshelves. Belongings turn into so much junk once the caretaker's gone. Who would someday own Sam's collection of autographed baseballs? Why did he keep old birthday cards in the bedside table alongside a box of Trojans?

I swallowed. Did Sam have a will?

I didn't.

With Paolina, I needed one. With Paolina's abrupt influx of wealth, I needed a creative one.

Just do it, I scolded myself. Do it by the book, the way Mooney taught you. The way the cops will, if you don't hurry.

I yanked on my gloves.

Bureau drawers. Closet shelves. Jacket pockets.

Pants pockets. Nothing but loose change, movie stubs.

I felt between layers of sweaters, trying not to remember the last time I'd seen him wearing this shirt, that vest. Ran my fingertips over the undersides of drawers. Nothing behind the paintings. No wall safe.

"There are a hell of a lot of messages." Roz stood in the doorway.

"Any from 'Frank'?"

"Not so far, but I found an extra tape. I could substitute it. Just slip in the blank tape, take the used tape, and study it at home."

"Write every message down word for word, Roz. I'll help when I'm done."

"I'd rather look around. He's got some cool art stuff."

"Tell me if there are any messages from 'Frank,' Roz."

"I just thought you might be finding this hard to do, you knowing the guy so well."

"I'm going as fast as I can," I lied.

"No hurry," she lied back, retreating down the hall.

I needed a phone book, a Rolodex, a yearbook from whatever parochial school Sam had attended as a child. Did parochial grammar schools do yearbooks?

The bathroom off the master bedroom had dark green marbled walls. Big oval tub, separate shower. Once I'd written him passionate lipsticked messages on the steamy mirrored medicine chest. I checked the contents. Nothing stronger than Tylenol.

Why had I started with the bedroom instead of the study? That woman's voice in Washington. The tape.

"Roz," I yelled. "When you play Sam's outgoing

message, there's a Washington area code number.
Make sure you get it."

"Huh?"

I repeated myself.

What the hell was wrong with me? I should have
switched jobs with Roz. Had I expected to find another
woman's nightgown in Sam's closet? A stash of machine guns? A numbers runner's guide? Evidence that
Sam was heavily Mob involved. That Oglesby and his
task force were right.

Mob involved. Wasn't the Miró a gift from Papa?
Wasn't his Ivy League education a gift from Papa, paid
for with earnings from running prostitutes, demanding
protection money?

I thought of the cash-stuffed tumbling mats at my
place. What would Paolina think if—when—she knew
where that money came from?

Do the work, dammit.

I moved into the study. Computer, laser printer,
fax, copier. The sheer amount of hardware was
daunting. So streamlined, automated. Clean. Unre-
vealing.

I ignored the machinery and started with the desk, a
massive rosewood block with eight hefty drawers.
Slips of paper, business cards, some with handwritten
scribbled notes, were tucked into each corner of the
blotter. I found them reassuringly human. I copied
phone numbers, wrote down names. Any of them could
belong to "Frank."

No Rolodex entry for "Frank Tallifiero." What a
surprise.

Should I steal the whole damn Rolodex? I flipped through the cards, eliminating names I knew.

Sam didn't keep a diary. I grabbed his last two phone bills and an unopened bank statement. His business records must be on-line.

I studied the computer. Very much like mine, the new model "Frank" had donated. For the first time it occurred to me that Sam might have paid for the equipment, given me a gift he knew I'd never accept.

Hard disk. Sam would keep backup diskettes. He was methodical. I found two plastic packets of floppies, one still cellophaned shut. I stuck the opened pack in my purse.

The elevator hummed. No problem, I told myself. Other tenants used it routinely, people without the special penthouse passkey.

I kept rummaging through the desk, finding nothing. Returned to the bedroom. Photo albums would help. A nice clear shot of "Frank."

Roz appeared in the doorway. "The elevator's coming up here," she said. "Another way down?"

"Stairs. Kitchen."

Too many locks. A police bar. A deadbolt. I didn't have the keys.

Roz said, "We can jump whoever comes out of the elevator. You move right. I'll take the left."

"Stay," I ordered. "I'll talk us out."

Roz stared through the kitchen window as if measuring the multistory fall. "One elevator," she said. "Hit 'em first, talk later."

"Stay," I mouthed. Sometimes working with Roz is like working with a dog. Loyal, but lacking.

I expected cops. Possibly Organized Crime Task Force. Possibly Mooney. With good fortune, someone I knew, someone who knew me.

I got robbers. Two guys Oglesby would have labeled "goombahs" at a glance. Between them, enough gold chains to open a jewelry store.

"Hey," said the taller of the two, smirking. "What have we got here?" His teeth were yellowed, oddly spaced.

"How's Sam doing?" I asked as if I fully expected an answer and a good one.

I'd come on too strong; I could see it in their eyes.

I sighed, smoothing my hair with an uplifted hand, kept the hand moving till it rested between my breasts. "I mean, I'm really worried," I said softly. Their attention was riveted. I used a finger to trace the curve of my bra line. "Is he okay?"

"Girlfriend," the shorter one observed. "A babe."

Roz sauntered out of the kitchen. "Two babes," she said with a dangerous grin. She'd removed the hat and yanked her shirt off one shoulder, giving the guys plenty to stare at.

"Busy fucker," the taller man said. "Like his old man. Picking up your undies, gals?"

"You guessed it," Roz said, coming closer, walking slowly so the guys could appreciate the body under the shirt. "Girl's gotta keep track of her intimate apparel, right?"

The small man said appreciatively, "Maybe Sam took dirty pictures. You got any dirty pictures?"

"Maybe," Roz said. I've never seen anybody bat her eyelashes like that outside a Hollywood film.

The little guy was almost drooling. "What if we wanna make sure that's all you got? You could be hidin' practically anything, you know what I mean?"

Roz kicked her right leg out so fast, so far, I almost ducked reflexively. The shorter man went down in a heap, out cold, hand clamped to his jaw. She kicked the larger guy in the balls, executing a balletic leap over the smaller man. He howled, went to his knees, and I whacked him over the head with a bronze replica of a Degas dancer Sam keeps on the hall table.

Silence.

Then we were in the elevator, heading down.

I leaned against the paneling, shaking my head from side to side. "Sometimes you scare me, Roz."

"Like seriously, you wanted to talk to *them*?"

We broke into smiles that turned quickly to giggles. I laughed till I slid down the elevator wall, hugging my knees to my chest.

"Those guys," Roz said when she could speak again, "they watch TV a lot, you think?"

It worries me when smacking people around starts to feel good. But I hadn't laughed in so long I couldn't stop.

THIRTY

Roz and I split, exiting the lobby via different doors in case any other wiseguys were keeping watch. We met at the car.

"Did you finish the transcription?" I asked as soon as we slammed our doors. " 'Frank' leave any words of wisdom on the tape?"

"Nope. I got all the messages, barely. Your boyfriend gets a lot of calls."

I shot her a look, wheeled out of the space faster than I should have.

"You want me to call him your *former* boyfriend, or what?"

Unlike Roz, I tend toward serial monogamy.

"Roz," I said, "while you were diddling the computer, you pull any files on me?"

"Nope, but that doesn't mean there're not there. You were printed when you were a cop, right? You've got a credit card. Shit, your mom was a member of the Communist Party."

"And proud of it," I said. "Before the Nazi-Soviet pact."

"Print it all out, there'd be enough paper to wrap presents."

"Frank teach you how to erase it?"

"Bet he could."

"When we find him," I suggested, "let's ask."

"Where now?" Roz managed in between contemplating her reflection in the mirrored sun visor, fluffing her weird hair, and humming the theme from the old *Addams Family* TV show.

"Mass. General. Find me a space."

Twenty seconds later she said, "Brown Buick pulling out. Left side, halfway down."

I U-turned across four lanes of Cambridge Street traffic and nosed in ahead of an overconfident T-bird. Under other circumstances I might have ceded him the spot.

"Put your hat back on," I suggested.

Roz grumbled. But she did it, carefully tucking her bangs out of sight.

Sam was in surgery, his outlook "guarded."

Gloria was guarded as well. Leroy and Geoffrey bracketed her door like matching bookends. I wondered if they'd spent the night. Whatever the hospital rules, I wouldn't have asked either one to move.

"Can I see her?"

"Shrink in there," Leroy said, glowering. "Why'd you send over a headshrinker? You think Gloria's crazy?"

"Leroy, when you're crazy they send you to McLean's Hospital, out in Belmont."

"Just if you're rich, white, and crazy. Black and crazy, you do your time at Walpole State Prison."

I said, "I was worried Gloria might blame herself for what happened."

"She didn't set no bomb," Geoffrey said.

"She moved Marvin into the back room," I said.

Geoffrey, I thought, might not look so scary if he didn't shave and oil his skull.

"Yeah, well, she was only tryin' to help," Leroy said.

"I know that," I said. "You know that. The shrink—whose name is Keith Donovan, by the way—knows that."

"Gloria's gonna be fine," Geoffrey said, as if daring anyone to contradict him.

"You eat anything lately?" I asked after a brief silence.

Leroy said, "I don't remember."

"There's a cafeteria. You trust Roz to get you stuff?"

Geoffrey nodded immediately. Leroy eyed Roz; he knows her better.

"Stick to sandwiches and cookies," I advised her. "Don't get fancy."

"That shrink is makin' her cry," Geoffrey said. His mouth barely moved.

"I need to check on Sam," I said. "Geoffrey, maybe crying's the best thing Gloria can do right now. Don't smack the guy if he comes out, okay? I like him."

"You like him so that means he's a good doc?"

It was a legitimate question and deserved a better answer than I had. I escaped to the waiting room on the surgical floor.

Oglesby, wearing the same cheap navy suit, lurked by the watercooler. A web of wrinkles starting at the backs of both knees and spreading down his calves told me he'd spent the night in a chair. His jacket had fared better; he must have hung it up. I hadn't awarded him more than a glance last night. His sandy-haired plainness surprised me; he was hardly the devil incarnate. His lower lip, swollen and cracked by two vertical gashes, gave me pause. When he opened his mouth to speak, I noticed dark blood trapped under his gum, rimming an upper incisor.

Maybe I owed the guy an apology. Maybe not. I said, "Oglesby, who's here from the family?"

"The Mob?"

"The Gianelli family," I said. "The *family*."

"One of the brothers. Mitch."

I grimaced. Mitch would have to do.

"What are you gonna—?"

I didn't hear the end of Oglesby's query. I was on my way to confront Mitchell, seated in one of a row of chairs bolted to the floor to maintain orderly aisles. Massive in his dark suit and tie, he almost overflowed the chair. His tie had been loosened; its dark silk was stained. Belly folded over his belt, head canted to one side, he could have been asleep.

The Gianelli constellation of sons began with Gil, leader, eldest, and heir apparent. Tony, the third son, Papa Anthony's namesake—movie-star handsome, a bit of a rake—was the apple of Papa's eye. Mitch, the middle boy, was just Mitch, a little too obedient, a little too eager to please. None too bright, not too quick. Most likely to be sent out for coffee.

I got the feeling Sam felt sorry for Mitch, when he thought of him at all.

Sam, born twelve years later than Tony, raised by nannies and stepmothers, had always seen himself as separate, an afterthought, a member of a different generation.

Figured the family'd leave Mitch on duty. Old reliable Mitch.

"Wake up," I said.

He stirred, snorted, sat up. "Huh? Something happen?"

I stuck out my hand, offered a smile. "When Sam was growing up, who were his best friends?"

"Huh?"

"Mitch, you remember me, right?"

He yanked his hand back. "Oh, yeah, I remember you, okay. Maybe you're bad luck for the Gianellis, ever think of that?"

"I'm going to find out who did this to Sam."

Mitch rolled his eyes at a soldier across the aisle. A dismissive gesture. An I've-got-the-situation-in-control kiss-off. "You can leave that to guys who know how," he said. "Cops already know who did it. Creep's dead. Blown to hell."

"Maybe."

"You don't buy it?" Something moved behind his eyes. I wondered if he was as dim as his family seemed to think. Maybe just slow.

"I'd like to make sure," I said.

"Sam said . . . Wait a fucking minute. You think I might pay you for this? Private heat, whatever the hell you call yourself, you think anybody's gonna pay you?"

"Forget about money. What did Sam say?"

"Shit. Nothing . . . Just that he might be selling the cabs. Too bad he didn't get out before this shit went down. That crazy bitch he works with fires some geek and then this happens."

"Sam wanted to sell? You sure?"

Mitch shook his head wearily, shrugged. "He had other irons in the fire, I guess."

"A new business?"

"I don't know."

I wondered if the new venture might have included a move to the nation's capital. A clean break. I blinked, refocused.

I was going to need sleep soon. Lots of sleep.

I went back to the beginning, to "Frank."

"What about the kids Sam hung out with, Mitch? When he was young? You remember any names?"

"Childhood pals? That's how you investigate?"

"Names, Mitch."

"I'm about a hundred years older than the kid. I don't know who the fuck he played with."

"He go to the same grammar school as you?"

"I guess. We lived in the same house after Mama died. No big difference. She was sick all the time anyway, barely moved out of bed."

"What school?"

"St. Cecilia's Star of the Sea."

"You have a teacher named Sister Xavier Marie?"

"Christ, they were all named Sister Something Mary or Marie or the other way around. I don't remember any Mary Xavier or Xavier Marie. They closed the old school years ago. Not enough white kids left in town."

Damn.

"The church is still there, right?" I asked. "St. Cecilia's?"

"Where's it gonna go? It can't move to the 'burbs like everybody else. Cardinal Law, he'd kinda miss it, you know."

I paused. "Sam holding his own?"

"What's it to you?"

"A lot," I said.

"I was with him a couple hours. What with the drugs, he's out of it. But, hey, I could share this with you. You'd appreciate it. He keeps calling a woman's name: Lauren or Laura. Not you, babe."

He aimed to hurt, so I smiled sweetly and said, "Thanks, Mitch."

"Hey," he muttered, "if I helped you any, I'm sorry."

Oglesby tried to corner me on the way out. "What did you get?" he demanded.

"You haven't got a mike planted in Mitch's lapel? What kind of crummy task force are you on?"

"I'm going to tell you something in confidence. We never bugged the cab company. Seeing what went down, looks like we should have, but we didn't."

"I'm supposed to believe you, right?" I said. "Maybe you should cross your heart and hope to die."

"I didn't file charges. Don't you think you owe me one?"

I said, "Maybe I'll feel like reciprocating if you answer a question."

"Shoot," he said in a resigned tone.

"If the cops have it wrapped, why are you here?"

" 'Cause it stinks."

"What? Why?"

"A Gianelli doesn't get blown up 'cause some—pardon me, is it *African American* or *black* this week?—some darkie broad fires a cabbie. It's gotta be somebody hates Papa and can't kill him. He's like Fort Knox, you know, you can't get next to him. Lotta thugs would like to take him down. Can't nail him, so nail his kid. Didn't used to be like that. The old-style Eye-ties kept kids out of it. Jamaicans, Colombians, it's fun for the whole family."

I thought about informing him that *broad* had gone out the same year as *Eye-tie*.

"So what did Mitch say?" he asked, leaning close.

Speak up for the microphone, Carlotta.

I said, "Told me to fuck off. Advised you to do likewise."

His face burned red. I didn't care. I'd noticed the top of her head peeking over the back of a chair, dark hair fastened with a white barrette, thin legs dangling an inch off the floor.

Paolina. My Little Sister. Who should have been in school.

THIRTY-ONE

I spun around, abandoning Oglesby with his mouth mid-flap, dodged through a row of seats, tripping over extended legs. I didn't speak until I had a grip on her shoulder. I've spent too much time chasing slippery preteens down hallways.

"Hi," I said. Hardly revolutionary, but an opening. Better than a question. Paolina hates questions. That is, she hates questions she's expected to answer. She doesn't mind dishing them out.

"Where've you been?" she demanded, standing because it was too late to flee. She must have remembered that she was angry at me. She clamped her lips shut in silent-treatment mode.

"¿Dónde estás?" I translated hesitantly, wanting to grab her and squeeze, the way I used to when she was seven and smelled of cherry Life Savers. Holding the impulse in check because Paolina's twelve-year-old hugs are grudging gifts at best.

"*¿Dónde usted a estado?*" she corrected. "You never get it right."

"I try," I said. "*Yo trato.* Past tense kills me."

Her eyes were a window on a private war. Should she speak to the enemy? Her defiant glare wavered. The enemy might have a vital battlefront update.

"We're meeting at too many hospitals," I said gently.

"They won't let me see him," she said, trying not to sound frantic. "I've been waiting and waiting, ever since I heard on the news. . . ."

"They won't let me see him either."

Oglesby hovered, so I grasped her firmly by the hand and led her into the broad corridor. He shot an agonized glance through the glass doors, but I knew he wouldn't abandon a genuine Gianelli brother to follow me.

"How long have you been waiting, Paolina?" Dammit. When I question her, I sound like a cop. Worse. An inquisitor. A fourteenth-century Spanish monk.

At least I hadn't demanded to know why she was skipping school.

"I didn't know where you were," she said. "I didn't have any idea. You weren't home. You weren't here. You could have been at G and W too. You could have been killed. Burned alive. Did you call me? Did you even try to call? You're not my sister. No way. Sisters don't behave like you. All you do is make promises. That's all. Dumb, stupid promises."

I tried to hold her, but she broke my grip with a downward slash of her hands, and kept talking. "You're walking fine. You don't even limp. You could have played volleyball with me. You just didn't want to."

A hundred responses flashed through my brain: Yeah, my foot is better now, but it wasn't okay for your game. I was going to call. We can play next week. A hundred excuses: I've been thinking about you. I've been trying to find a way to make you financially secure without winding up in jail. I've been busy, so goddamned busy. . . .

"I'm sorry," I said. "Honest-to-God sorry."

She stared at the floor, refusing to meet my eyes.

"How long have you been waiting, Paolina?" Interrogation time again.

She ignored my words, as if their tone rendered them inaudible. "I told him I wished he was my father," she blurted instead. "I wish Sam was my father."

It's unlike her to mention fathers. They never come up in conversation.

"When was that?" I carefully made my voice less inquisitorial. *Why* was what I wanted to know, but I'd settle for *when* as an opener.

"At the gym. He sat down next to me. You know, the time I went to get you in the locker room. Will he walk again? He's not going to—you know—die or anything, is he?"

"He's not going to die," I said. She stared up at me, seeking further assurances. With none to give, I waited while she scuffed the toe of her sneaker across the gray carpet.

"The last time I saw him, at the gym, he talked to me a long time. It was . . . I don't know. Strange."

"How?" I urged, to keep her talking.

"I don't know. . . . He said . . . he asked me, like, if I thought I could ever forgive my, uh, my father. For, you know, leaving me."

Casual courtside repartee.

"Had he ever asked about Carlos before?" On the rare occasions when Paolina and I spoke about the absentee Colombian, we called him Carlos, not "father."

"Never."

I was hoping she'd ramble on so I could avoid the inevitable question. She didn't.

"What did you say?" I asked.

She shrugged, perplexed. "I guess, that I didn't really have a father. Not like a father I grew up with, who spent time with me, or played with me and stuff. So how could I forgive him when I never even met him? And then Sam said . . ."

"What?"

Her voice was very low. I had to lean forward to catch the words. "He said something like: 'Well, what if your father came back?' "

I hadn't told Sam about the money. I never would have told him. Had Roz said anything?

Paolina squirmed uncomfortably, which meant she hadn't finished unburdening herself. I reached over and tucked a strand of silky hair behind her ear. My touch broke the dam.

"Sam said it was different with me, because I hadn't ever known my father. But that families should always forgive each other. Even if it's been years and years. They're family, so they should forgive. Carlotta?"

"I'm here."

"Did Sam have a fight with his father?"

A running war. A twenty-year battle. Had Papa won? Was the new business Mitch had hinted at Mob business?

Paolina averted her eyes. There wasn't much to see in the empty hallway, so she fixed them on a framed poster extolling the virtues of donating blood. She hates to cry in front of me.

"It's okay," I murmured. "It's gonna be okay."

"What if he never gets to tell his father the stuff he told me? About forgiving and everything?"

"Sam's not going to die."

"You're no doctor," she said defiantly. "What do you know?"

"Come on," I said softly, taking her hand. "I know Sam's going to be in surgery for hours. Maybe we can see Gloria. Have you seen Gloria yet?"

She started guiltily. "No," she said. "I wanted to be there when Sam woke up."

"They won't let you, Paolina. You're not family."

Her mouth worked. "I guess I wanted to pretend I was—that I was his kid."

Her words felt like stones pressing against my rib cage. A grim and terrible burden. Married women in rotten marriages must feel this way every time they hear the classic bromide: Stay together for the sake of the children.

Was I required to stick with a lover because my Little Sister adored him? Hell, couldn't we all be friends?

Talk about bromides.

We walked down silent corridors. Carpeting gave way to linoleum and the squeak of rubber soles.

A congregation had gathered outside Gloria's room.

Keith Donovan looked pasty and fragile next to Geoffrey and Leroy. Roz resembled a dwarf. An odd dwarf. She'd removed her hat. What the hell, with Leroy and Geoffrey keeping her company, nobody was going to criticize her hairdo. They chewed sandwiches, except for Donovan, who was talking desperately, as if he might be next on the menu. His look of relief when we came down the hall was almost comical.

I returned his glance searchingly, swallowing a sudden ache, wondering why I continually expect the opening of some extrasensory channel of communication with a new lover, the ability to read thoughts. I always think I'll grow out of it, but I don't. I can't read minds. I've known Paolina since she was a child, and I can't read hers. On the whole I accept that others are others. Separate. That we are each in the business of living alone.

But sometimes, despite reason, despite my insistence on the unromantic nitty-gritty here and now, between rumpled sheets, when a man moves inside me, I think he might be able to hear my soul.

"Your sister," Keith was saying, "has remarkable coping skills. She is not, in any sense of the word, 'crazy.' But nothing in her experience seems useful to her now. Her paralysis was accidental. She saw no reason to wrestle with issues of fault or blame. She's having trouble accepting that a person did this deliberately, that in trying to destroy her business, someone wound up destroying her brother."

"We don't like it much either," Geoffrey said vehemently. "If it turns out it wasn't that punk the cops say, the one got killed, we'll nail whoever did it."

"I don't think revenge has crossed your sister's mind. She's having a hard time wrapping herself around the idea that Marvin won't be walking through the door."

"Me too," Leroy admitted. "That make me crazy?"

"Human," Donovan said. "That's all."

I let out my breath. He was doing fine.

THIRTY-TWO

Dr. Donovan, his manner briskly professional, granted Paolina and me a brief visit with Gloria. I couldn't tell if he'd donned a bit of arrogance along with his hospital badge or if he was playing tough-guy-in-charge to counter a gut fear of Geoffrey and Leroy. At any rate, he didn't welcome me with a kiss, which, considering Paolina and her feelings for Sam, was a good thing.

No time to think about it.

No time.

Gloria's eyes were teary and bloodshot. She looked—hell, *wan* is as good a word as any, and it's tricky, describing a three-hundred-pound black woman as wan. Her thoughts elsewhere, she tried to summon a smile and a quip for Paolina.

"Can't feel much," she said. "Part that's burned.

Guess I found the positive side of paralysis."

Her massive legs hung in midair. Suspended by pulleys, swathed in white gauze, they glittered with a petrochemical glaze.

"Can't go to any more 'Eat Right' seminars," she went on. "My brothers'll definitely get a refund from that diet dump now."

Her heart wasn't in the banter. It fell flat.

"My brothers Geoffrey and Leroy," she said softly.

Paolina squeezed Gloria's right hand, the one unencumbered by IV lines, and we were silent.

The knock at the door was a welcome interruption. Until Mooney marched in.

"Hi, Glory. How're you doing?" His greeting was so perfunctory she didn't even try to answer. "Doctors gave me permission to snatch one of your visitors. Carlotta? Paolina, you can stay two more minutes and don't tire the lady out." He pecked Gloria quickly on the cheek.

"Wait a minute, Moon," I said. "How's Paolina supposed to get home? I'm not leaving her here."

"Roz can drive her."

"Hey . . ." I said as he seized my hand and tugged me toward the door. I didn't want to make a scene in front of Paolina. He must have counted on that.

"Roz." I regained my voice as soon as we were out in the hall.

"Keep walking," Mooney warned.

"I need to give her the damn car keys, Mooney, or she'll be stuck here with Paolina."

I thought I'd slip Roz the computer diskettes I'd lifted from Sam's place, but I couldn't bring it off.

Mooney never took his eyes off me even as he commiserated with the brothers. Donovan had done a disappearing act, which was just as well. Mooney'd met him once, on a recent case. Donovan had dared to offer a possible psychiatric defense. They'd clashed immediately. Mooney hates shrinks.

"Roz," I said quickly, handing over the keys. "When you take Paolina home, make sure her mother's actually in the apartment. If she's hungry, stop at McDonald's first. And tell her I'll call the minute I hear any news about Sam."

"Let's go," Mooney said.

"Is this a kidnapping?" I murmured on our way past the nurses' station. "If I yell, Leroy will—"

"Leroy will do squat unless he wants a traffic ticket every time he forgets to fasten his seat belt."

"Am I under arrest?"

"It can be arranged."

"Moon, if you're going to hold this assault shit over me for the rest of my life, I'd rather fight it now. I'll call my lawyer while you soak your head."

A unit, with driver, was poised at the front door. Mooney dismissed the chauffeur, stared at me dourly while I worked the passenger-door handle. He made sure my door was locked before he slid behind the wheel.

As if I couldn't unlock a door and run.

Run where?

"Oh, Mooney." I sighed, shaking my head.

"What?" His voice was sharp, defensive.

"You have that look about you."

"What look?"

"Righteous renegade. That's what the department brass called it. I prefer Caped Crusader."

"Dammit to hell."

Mooney rarely swears in the presence of women. Good Catholic upbringing.

"Did you happen to notice that Gloria didn't ask you a thing, Mooney?" I said.

"I know."

"Is that because you already filled her in?"

"Partially," Mooney said. "She knows we identified Zachariah Robertson's body."

"She didn't ask how Zach got ahold of whatever he used to blow the place? Dynamite? Plastic?"

"Not a peep."

"She didn't yell? Demand that you find out who's behind it? Didn't point out that the police would be out chasing down leads if it was a white man who got killed?"

"Didn't say a single word, Carlotta," Mooney stated with deliberate emphasis. "You saw how she is."

I'd seen. It scared me silly, Gloria's passive acceptance.

"Where are we going?" I demanded.

"Do you have money?"

Did I ever. Mattresses of money. Litter boxes of money.

"On me?" I asked.

"Credit card?"

"One."

"Visa? Master?"

"Visa."

"Fine."

He wasn't driving in the direction of the airport. I'd be spared that Western sheriff classic: "Catch the next stagecoach out of Dodge."

"I had to close the case," he said, changing lanes abruptly, provoking a VW into an outraged honk.

My sympathies were with the VW's driver. I said nothing.

"It sucks, this case," he went on. "It's got teeny little bows on it, it's so neat."

"We think alike, Moon."

"First off," he said, "the drive-by stinks."

"Why?"

"Nobody's bragging," he said. "Bragging follows gunfire like night follows day. After a drive-by, the next few weeks, every punk we pick up on a felony rap wants to talk, trade what he knows for a lesser charge. Nobody's chatting about that drive-by."

"You arrested the wrong punks. Big deal."

"You were there. Sam was there. Sam's been hit. Are you listening to me, Carlotta?"

"I hear you."

"Then there's the crap about paying off hit men to beat cabbies. I talked to your duo, by the way."

Jean and Louis. "I'm sure you made their day."

"The one who got beaten, Jean, yanked Robertson's photo from a six-pack. No hesitation."

"You happened to have a photo? Don't tell me, the girlfriend dropped off an eight-by-ten glossy."

"Mug shot," he said.

"Arson?"

"Possession, arson, car theft."

"You showed Jean other pictures, I assume. Robertson's pals. Known accomplices. Associates. Family members. Former cell mates. Anybody else seem familiar?" I could hear my voice growing increasingly sharp.

"Nope. So listen up. Gloria doesn't need a guard. She's got her brothers. Sam's got the whole god-damned Mafia. You, I'm worried about."

"I'll keep busy," I promised, glaring at my watch for Mooney's benefit.

We were heading outbound on Storrow Drive. Mooney didn't have his emergency flasher stuck on the roof, but he was racing well over the limit. If I jumped out, I'd have to join the party at MGH.

I settled back in my seat. "Wake me when the fun starts," I said. "I'm fuckin' tired."

Mooney seethes when I swear. For a while, when I was a cop, I foulmouthed deliberately, to rile him.

"You carrying?" he asked quietly.

"No," I said.

"Firearms card?"

"In my wallet. And my license to carry."

"We'll stop at your place, pick up your thirty-eight. You might be able to get a deal on a trade-in."

"This is not a good time to go shopping, Mooney."

"Dammit, aren't you hearing anything I say? *I had to close the case*. I've got other things on my plate. This is it. This is all I can do for you."

I opened my mouth to protest further, closed it without a word. Home, I could dump Sam's computer diskettes. Maybe scrawl a note to Roz.

"Mooney," I said, "what about the Organized Crime Task Force? Did you get the tapes?"

"Officially, there are no tapes. Officially, they weren't bugging G and W."

"Do you have any reason to believe them, Moon? Do you know anybody on the squad?"

"Nobody who wouldn't look me straight in the eye, swear on his mother's grave, and lie, Carlotta."

"Did you talk to Brennan at Hackney Carriage?" I asked.

"Something wrong with your hearing? I'm off the case."

"Mooney."

"Brennan doesn't know shit. I went to see Yancey. He's up to something. Or maybe just full of himself. Hard to tell."

"I wonder if he has any buddies on the task force," I said.

"I doubt that creep has any buddies at all."

"Could you nose around? Find out?"

"To repeat: I don't have any pals on Organized Crime."

"Moon, could you?"

"Yeah," he said gruffly. "Sure."

"Yancey has money," I said.

"What?"

"Just musing aloud, Mooney. Money can buy you friends."

"Can't buy you love," Mooney said, his voice harsh and unforgiving. I spent the rest of the journey staring out the window.

THIRTY-THREE

Big city turns to small town fast in New England. Sometimes I forget how compressed the Northeast is, a tiny corner of the map weighed down by its vast population.

Arlington, to the north and west of Cambridge, isn't small compared to some tiny burg in upstate Maine. The town has flavors all its own: upscale Arlington near the golf courses; downscale Arlington, its public schools in continual crisis; the town within a town called Arlington Heights. Up the hill past the water tower lurks Classic Main Street, Any Town, USA, lined with small grocery stores, a musty hardware emporium, a soda fountain, a pharmacy that's not linked to a major franchise, and a gun shop.

WE BUY, WE SELL shouted letters blazoned across the display window. If you live nearby, you know

who owns it. If you don't, well, we don't coddle outsiders.

Many cops prefer to buy their personal artillery outside the Boston–Cambridge axis. Mooney was probably not an outsider.

"I don't like this," I told Mooney as he parked
across the street.

"Your ankle okay?"

"Let's talk."

"Lock your door."

"Talk."

"Carlotta, I can't assign you a bodyguard; your
gun's a relic. It's that simple."

"You're overreacting, Moon."

"Save the psychological insights for the new
beau."

I blew out an exasperated breath. "You have a mole
in my house? A videocam?"

"Saw him at the hospital."

"He works there. Doctor, hospital, get it?"

"Uh-huh."

I tried another tack. "Mooney, this may not be the
best timing."

"Agreed. You should have done it sooner."

"Within the past forty-eight hours, I slugged a cop, I
hit a . . ."

"Yeah?"

If he didn't know about the goons at Sam's apartment, I wasn't going to enlighten him. "Never mind."

"It's time to ditch the thirty-eight and get real."

"I like the thirty-eight."

"For sentimental reasons?"

"You keep lobbing 'em back, don't you, Mooney?" I muttered as I reluctantly left the car. I'm not fond of guns. They're necessary; that's it.

A chain of bells tinkled when Mooney opened the metal door. So much for security. Your average mall jewelry shop boasts better protection against theft, a uniformed rent-a-cop at least.

Guns. Racks of rifles and shotguns. Display cabinets lined with light gray velveteen, packed with revolvers and pistols. New and used. Antiques. Signs advertising Colts, Berettas, Winchester rifles.

I liked the mounted ten-point deer's head over the doorway, enjoyed its casual juxtaposition to the semi-automatics. Gotta have a semi to take down Bambi's mom.

A man in his fifties, wearing a baggy sweatshirt over jeans, emerged from a back room, smiling. He smelled of gun oil and rubbed his hands on his pants.

"Hey," he said by way of greeting.

Mooney nodded in response. Noncommittal. Possibly a browser.

"For you or her?" the man asked.

Mooney nodded at me.

"Rifle?"

"Handgun."

"Protection?"

Another curt nod.

"Twenty-two?"

"Mister," I said, tired of being talked around. "I shoot a thirty-eight. I'm taller than you are." Stronger, I almost said, but I didn't want to wind up with a defective weapon.

Mooney interrupted before I challenged the clerk to arm wrestle. "The lady wants to move to a stopper."

"What's she using now?"

"Chiefs Special," I said.

"Trade?"

"Depends on the price."

"She got the card?" he asked Mooney, more comfortable talking to a man. I should have gone over to Collector's in Stoneham, I thought. The guys there always talk to me.

"Yep," Mooney said.

"S and W makes a nice nine. The Nine Fifteen DA Auto. Fifteen in the magazine," the clerk said.

"How much?" I asked.

"Four sixty-seven's list price."

"Let's go cheaper," I said. "A lot cheaper."

"When's your birthday, Carlotta?" Mooney asked. "I might kick in a few bucks."

"I'd prefer flowers," I said.

He grabbed me by the shoulder and spun me around to face him. The movement stunned me into silence.

"I'm not planning to lay them on your grave," he said. A muscle in his chin clenched and relaxed. "Understand?"

The clerk scuttled into the back room, quick as a cockroach exposed to sudden light. I wondered if he might call the cops or if he just wanted to take cover in case we started shooting.

He scurried back again with three black cases, the size of the Sanders candy boxes my dad used to bring home every Valentine's Day. No chocolates. Shiny, deadly toys.

"If you're really after stopping power," he suggested, "you might consider a ten. FBI's going to tens."

As I touched each gun, hefting and sighting it, I started to get into the game, recalling trips to gun shops with my cop dad, trips that had made me the talk and envy of eighth-grade pimple-faced boys. The satin-finished metal felt smooth beneath my fingers. A SIG—Sauer P228 fit my hand like it had been made for me. Eight hundred bucks. S&W's compact 9 wasn't bad. If it's life and death, I want to side with the winning team. I want the best toy on the market. We talked price. I started to waver.

A gun's an investment, the clerk insisted. A collectible.

I'd rather collect spiders, I thought. Brown recluses.

I displayed my .38. The clerk disassembled it with practiced fingers, quoted a price. Mooney called a conference at the other end of the store.

He'd reconsidered; I shouldn't trade the .38. He could arrange a sale to a police buff. There were guys who'd pay top dollar for a gun used in the line of duty. A killer gun.

I'd drawn it once. Killed a man. Quit the force.

"Look at some tens," Mooney urged.

"The S and W forties are nice," the clerk said.

Twenty-five minutes later, I owned a slightly used S&W 4053, with a single-stack seven-shot magazine, and two boxes of Glaser Safety Slugs. The gun was on sale, and Mooney'd talked the guy down another fifty bucks, but it was still pricey. I was tempted to buy a fanny-pack holster with a string pull, decided to keep my reputation as a cheapskate and stick to my waist-band clip.

"I'll have to put in hours at the range," I complained when we got back in the car. "The weight's different, the sight's different."

Mooney said, "Time at the range'll be good. Keep you off the street. You wanna shoot with me?"

"At the department range? Fuel the rumor mill? No, thanks."

"What rumors?"

I filed the question under disingenuous, ignored it. "That was easier than cashing a check," I said.

"What?"

"Buying a deadly weapon."

"You were with a cop."

"Clerk know that?"

"I've bought there before."

"You could have been fired. He didn't run any kind of check. Guy's computer terminal had dust on the keys."

"You have a valid firearms card, Carlotta. He asked to see it."

"I could have stolen it."

"Well, you didn't."

"I've had more trouble using my credit card to buy underwear."

"'If guns are outlawed, only outlaws will have guns,'" Mooney quoted cheerfully. The slogan had been cross-stitched into a sampler over the cash register.

"Wrong, Mooney. If guns are outlawed, only *cops* and outlaws will have guns. Then the good guys and the bad guys can play cowboys, and let the civilians live in peace."

"Tell me, who are the civilians?"

I shrugged.

We were silent. I wanted music, but Mooney's unit had nothing to offer but police band and AM. A new Chris Smither tune danced in my head: "The devil's not a legend, the devil's real."

"Kids," I said. "They're civilians."

Mooney said, "I see ten-year-olds, twelve-year-olds packing all the time."

"There have to be civilians, or who the hell are you sworn to protect and defend, Mooney?"

We turned onto Route 2. From Arlington Heights you can see all of Boston, a city in miniature. Just needs a model train running through it, over the bridges and the rivers, steaming and belching. Fourth of July, couples park along the verge of the highway, fool around till the fireworks start on the Esplanade. Tune the radio in and listen to the Pops play the "1812" one more time.

Mooney coasted down the hill, braking near the bowling alley. "Carry the forty, okay?" he said. "Keep it with you. No desk-drawer crap till this blows over."

"And when will that be?"

"You know that better than I do, Carlotta."

All I knew was the name of an old nun who might or might not be alive, who might or might not remember a kid named Sam Gianelli and his best friend, "Frank."

At the Concord Avenue rotary Mooney said, "Has Sam ever mentioned any trips to Providence?"

"As in Rhode Island?" I asked.

"As in the Mafia capital of New England," he responded.

"What if he has?" I said, thinking of Sam's "sick uncle."

"Federal penitentiary there. Sam's name's on the guest list, visiting old man Frascatti, former, and some say future, crime boss."

That was it, the secret Oglesby and Mooney had shared in the MGH waiting room, the information Mooney'd withheld from me.

"So?" I said, keeping my tone level, casual. Frascatti could be Sam's uncle, for all I knew. "Seeing an old guy, maybe bringing him a basket of fruit, doesn't mean Sam's involved in the Mob. Or does Oglesby think otherwise?"

"Try this one," Mooney said. "When Sam travels to Washington, does he get dressed up?"

"Huh?"

"Suit and tie?"

"You looking to change tailors?"

"I'm looking for a simple yes or no."

"Why?"

"Do I look like a lawyer?"

"You don't dress well enough," I said.

"How about this: Does Sam outfit himself like a man who might be testifying before a Senate subcommittee?"

"Interesting idea," I said after a long pause.

"That's all? Just interesting?"

I chewed my lower lip. I had more than Sister Xavier Marie. I had a phone number in the District of Columbia.

THIRTY-FOUR

It was dark by the time Mooney dropped me at my driveway, shadowy with the threat of snow, cold as a blue-steel grip.

I didn't invite him in. Exhausted, I worried I might relate the tale of "Frank," the computer whiz, over a can of Rolling Rock. I needed time to think. And why would I need company when I had a new S&W .40?

In the foyer I spread my hands near the radiator, reveling in the heat. As I hung my coat I took inventory.

A new semiautomatic. An old revolver. I wrapped my .38 in its T-shirt shroud, shoved it in the bottom left-hand drawer of the desk, locked the drawer.

The name of a nun. Sam's computer diskettes. The Washington, D.C., phone number.

Unanswered questions.

I sat at my desk, threaded my way through the on-hold operator shuffle at MGH to find Sam out of surgery, stable. He could not speak on the telephone. Could not be seen by anyone outside his immediate family.

Gloria, in satisfactory condition, must have been chatting on her phone. Thirty minutes later, the line was still busy. Maybe she'd landed a job dispatching cabs from her hospital bed.

More likely making arrangements for Marvin's closed-casket funeral.

I flipped on the computer, considered feeding one of Sam's diskettes into its maw. What I didn't know about computer compatibility could fill volumes. Would I be able to bring up his files on my screen? What were my chances of destroying them in the process?

Maybe Keith Donovan would like to hit a Chinese restaurant for dinner. For all his professed fascination with women and violence, I wondered if he'd be at ease with the new piece tucked into my waistband.

I hollered for Roz.

"What?" she responded, sounding more than mildly annoyed.

"Could you come down?"

"A sec, okay?"

While waiting, I slipped my new gun out of its hiding place, practiced jamming the magazine into the slot, and sighting down the barrel.

"I give up," Roz said. "Don't shoot."

"Busy?"

"Painting. I'm totally inspired."

"Want to earn money?"

"I'm painting. You got something against art?"

"I'm talking money, Roz."

"What do you want?"

I indicated the computer, started to babble about Sam's diskettes. Mid-sentence I had a brainstorm.

"Roz," I said, "stay inspired. Do a sketch of 'Frank.' A quick one."

She pursed her lips, considering. "Style?"

"Hell with style. No auras. No cubist shit. Make like a camera."

"Boring," she said.

"Lucrative," I said.

The tip of her tongue protruded through her sharp teeth. "Black-and-white sketch? Pencil?"

"Fine."

"Ten minutes," she said.

"Sam's phone calls? The transcriptions?"

"Here." She yanked crumpled notes from her pocket. I smoothed them on the desktop, wondering if they'd require translation, but what I wanted was printed clearly. A single number with a 202 area code.

I took a deep breath and dialed. Punched. I've got a touch-tone phone. One of the keys says *redial*. All those years, I thought *dial* had something to do with *round,* with rotary phones. Another language lag, a failure to keep step with technology. I stared down the blank computer screen while the phone rang five times. A mechanical click, then the cheery message began: "So sorry I can't take your call . . ."

I hung up. Couldn't bring off the phrasing without a dress rehearsal: Sam Gianelli's been wounded in a bombing. Who am I? Oh, someone who thought you might want to know.

I tapped my heels, twisted my hair into an untidy topknot, and discarded half a dozen equally inane opening lines. Finally I left my name, number, and a simple request to return my call day or night, collect. A promise to foot the bill impresses people with the urgent nature of the call.

Roz bounced downstairs, offered up her drawing without comment. She's a precise, well-schooled illustrator, although you'd never guess it from her artwork. If anything, she'd romanticized the man. His eyes had a vitality, a spark.

The picture made me certain she'd slept with him.

"Thanks," I said.

"You like it?"

"I'm not planning to hang it over my pillow," I said. "It's for ID."

"Gonna show it to a police artist?"

"Somebody better, I hope."

"Now?"

"Yeah."

"Want company?"

"No. Paint while the muse is with you," I said.

I knew a place I could go where they'd have to let me in, no matter the hour. A place I'd be reasonably safe, even without Roz. Definitely without Roz.

St. Cecilia's.

I wriggled my ankle. It was holding up better than the rest of me.

I glanced in the phone book under churches, Catholic. St. Cecilia's was on Hanover Street, the North End's main drag. Only problem would be parking. No Green & White to call. I wondered how soon

Gloria would be up and running again. I wondered about insurance. It would be somewhere on one of the computer diskettes.

The cab medallions were the major company asset. If Sam had planned to sell, he certainly hadn't told Gloria. Who'd buy? Phil Yancey? Brennan, at Hackney Carriage, hadn't called back. Mooney was right: Brennan was lazy, didn't like to shake things up.

I hadn't dressed for church since my dad used to haul me to Easter services over my mom's protests. The best way for a Jew to celebrate Easter, she had maintained, was to hide in the cellar, safe from pogroms. Dad would reply that I was only half Jewish. She'd retort that "half" wouldn't have stopped the Poles or the Nazis.

One of the many charming rituals of my childhood.

I didn't intend to pray, although it wouldn't hurt to light a candle for Marvin. I changed out of jeans into black wool slacks and a cream silk shirt. A long black vest hid the .40. I considered wearing a skirt, surely more appropriate, but the wind was chill and my legs needed a shave, so I went with the slacks. A red-and-gold scarf completed the outfit, a bit jarring with my hair, but I liked it. I could even pull it over my head if some throwback from the good old days gave my hat-lessness a condemning glare.

I like churches. I don't know the apse from a hole in the wall, but I enjoy the echoing silence, the sense of space, and the motion the architects always seem to manage, leading your eyes up, up.

St. Cecilia's was no cathedral. No storefront either. A reassuringly warm, well-lighted place. A sanctuary.

An elderly woman, face obscured by a black lace scarf, entered before me, genuflected, and padded to a pew as if she'd made the identical journey fifty thousand times. I echoed her movements, inhaling the odor of rain-sogged wool and pressed-linen sanctity.

The confessional was to the left of the altar. A man exited, mumbling under his breath, getting a running start on his Hail Marys. A woman slipped into the cubicle, head lowered. The thought of confession brought a rising panic to my chest.

I left and went in search of the parish office. In search of civilians. Outdoors, the air was brisk and damp. People walked the streets, carried on laughing conversations, loitered at intersections, under streetlamps. The North End stays alive and vibrant after the safest suburbs have tucked themselves in for the night. The residents feel protected, *are* protected, by their own. By reputation as much as reality.

I wondered if the parish office, a jutting brick addition on the right, had once housed the Star of the Sea grammar school. Up three granite steps to an imposing front door with a brass knocker. The sketch of "Frank" seemed suddenly futile, silly. After all these years to expect to stroll in and locate a nun who'd be able to provide a true name . . .

When they'd closed the school they'd probably shipped the teaching sisters to Zimbabwe.

So what? Dead end. I'd faced them before. Most roads lead to the same sign. It would be one more avenue explored, a byway crossed off the street map.

A woman answered the door. A nun, I guessed, although without regalia. Gray hair, no makeup, wire-rimmed glasses. On the street, an aging Cambridge radical. In these surroundings, a nun.

"Yes?" she said politely, smiling a gap-toothed welcome.

"Hello. I'm trying to locate someone who can tell me about the grammar school that used to be here. At St. Cecilia's."

Her eyes glowed.

"Are you a reporter?" she asked eagerly.

It's too easy. Honestly, it's as if people sit at home and invent scripts and wait for someone, some TV talk-show host, to waltz in the door and question them about their fascinating lives. I mean, everybody's life is thrilling fodder for a docudrama, right?

"Not exactly," I said gently.

"I miss the school," she said. "I know it's important to do what I do now, to liaise with the community, as they put it, but teaching was very special. Gratifying. I miss the children's voices."

I wondered how many current grammar school teachers characterized their work as gratifying.

"You taught there?" I asked.

"At the end. They closed the school in '78. Too few students."

"Did you know a Sister Xavier Marie?"

"No."

"The Gianelli children went to school at St. Cecilia's."

Her face altered subtly. The smile was on her lips but no longer in her eyes. "I know the name, of course," she said cautiously. "The children were grown by the time I started teaching."

"Are there yearbooks? Class photos?"

"All records have been sent to the central office. Near the cardinal's residence on Lake Street. You'd need to put your request in writing. I can give you the address."

"Are any of the teachers from the old days still alive? Still at this parish?"

She hesitated.

"It's a shame about the older teaching nuns," I went on quickly. "They gave so much and now they seem to get so little."

"Sister Claveria's here," she said. She'd made up her mind about me. I was concerned about the old nuns. I was okay.

"May I speak to her?"

"She's very old."

"I won't upset her. It's important."

"I don't know," she said.

"What's your name?"

"My name in God is Sister Mary Agnes."

"Sister Mary Agnes, if Sister Claveria had a chance to help an old student, would she leave him standing in the cold?"

"I'm sorry," she said, clearly flustered. "I'm sorry. Things are different these days, even here."

"It's okay, Sister."

She swung the door wide, without bothering to ask if I was armed or dangerous. Good thing.

"Sister Claveria might be asleep."

"Don't wake her," I forced myself to say. Sister Mary Agnes seemed inclined to help. I wouldn't push it. I could come back.

The foyer was filled with twice the furniture it should have held. Dark carved wooden benches. Overstuffed armchairs upholstered in deep green. The contents of a large house compressed into a single room. The furnishings seemed to suck up all the air. The heat was turned too high. I unbuttoned my coat.

Sister Mary Agnes reappeared at the door and nodded encouragingly. "I don't know your name," she said apologetically.

I handed her one of my cards.

"Follow me," she said.

Up one carpeted flight, then two more, steeper, bare. "Sister Claveria was reading," she offered.

I concentrated on my footing. "It's very kind of her to see me."

"Sister loves to talk about the old times. She's like the rest of us, only more so. Can't remember what she had for breakfast, but don't let that fool you. Get her going about the forties, about the time before she entered the convent, and she'll talk your ear off."

"Thanks for the warning."

"Oh, I didn't mean it like that. Not to warn you so much as to let you know what to expect. She's not foolish or senile; she's old. Some can't tell the difference."

There was no television in the room. That's what I noticed first, with relief. I felt the itch of the S&W at the base of my spine. Constantly blaring screens are starting to seriously annoy me. If I ever lose it completely, I'll shoot as many TV sets as I can find before they lock me up. In bars and restaurants and waiting rooms.

"Sister, this is Miss Carlyle."

With that, Sister Mary Agnes left me on the threshold. Had to liaise with the community, I suppose.

"Welcome." Sister Claveria's voice rasped like dry paper. I entered. In contrast to the overfurnished foyer, the room seemed cell-like in its plainness. Small, it gave the illusion of space. There was only the single bed, a table. One chair.

Sister Claveria's hair was yellowy gray, a far cry from Clairol silver. Her nose was long and bony, her chin sharp, her eyes hidden behind Coke-bottle lenses. I wondered if she'd be able to make out Roz's drawing. She closed a heavy book, the movement slow and deliberate. Maybe those were her reading lenses. They magnified her eyes.

"Sister Mary Agnes says you want to know about the school." She must have been a formidable classroom presence. When she spoke I stood straighter. Command voice, they called it at the academy.

"About a particular student," I said.

"A boy or a girl?"

"A boy."

"Is he in trouble?"

"Would that make a difference?"

"I don't know."

"Why don't you let me ask and if you feel comfortable answering, go ahead. You may not know my friend."

"Are you truly his friend?" she asked.

I thought of Sam, not "Frank."

"Yes," I said.

"Go ahead."

"Do you remember the Gianelli family?"

"Them."

"You do?"

"Like asking the Sisters in Brookline if they remember the Kennedys," she said scornfully. "You won't stump me on that one."

"The youngest boy."

"Quite a bright child. Mischievous, like all of them. We used to call him 'full of the devil,' but he was not the devil's child. It was a figure of speech. We shouldn't have used it, not here."

The devil's not a legend, the devil's real. I couldn't shake Smither's song out of my mind.

"You have a good memory," I said.

"For some."

"I'm interested in a friend of the youngest Gianelli boy, a close friend, his best friend."

She closed her eyes. Nodded her head. Her nose seemed enormously long. "Boys come and go. The years get mixed up. Who played together . . ." She'd lost her command voice; it had turned into a whimper.

"Did you know a Sister Xavier Marie?"

"In the bosom of her Maker. A finer woman never lived."

I unfolded Roz's sketch, the last forlorn hope. "This is the man I'm looking for."

She studied the drawing for some time, holding it close to her face, adjusting the glasses on the bridge of her nose, finally removing them entirely.

"This is not the Gianelli boy," she said.

"No."

"It's very like him," she said.

"Like who? You know him?"

"Like the father, not the child. But so many of the children came to look like the old man."

"Who?" I repeated.

"If he was at school with the littlest Gianelli boy it would have been Joey Junior. Joseph Frascatti."

"Frascatti," I repeated.

"You can see how it might have been," the sister said. "*F* and *G*. Alphabetical order. They would have been required to sit near each other, and though their fathers would have hated it, I'm sure, they were fast friends from the start. The little Gianelli boy, the little Frascatti boy. Yes. Yes."

The two rival families.

"Is there anything in particular you remember about Joey Frascatti?"

"What sort of thing?"

"Was he good at math, good with numbers? Interested in theater?"

"What does it matter now?" Sister Claveria said fretfully. "He could have been a fine student, but he was full of rebellion. He had a brilliant mind, a defiant mind. He caused mischief." The old woman stopped, seemingly lost in thought.

"What kind of mischief?" I prompted gently.

"I'll tell you the one thing in particular I remember about Joey Frascatti," she said. "I remember his funeral."

"His funeral."

"I'm sorry if you didn't know," the old nun said in her dry voice. "He was killed in that dreadful war."

"The war." I wanted to tell her she was mistaken. I wanted to stop parroting her words.

"Vietnam." She drew in a shallow breath, coughed, held up a hand to stop me from coming closer, trying to help her sit more comfortably amid the pillows.

"So many lovely boys, gone," she said. "Sometimes I think I've lived too long . . ." She searched for my name, settled for "my dear." "Too long," she repeated. "I pray each night that God will take this old soul."

She seemed to be sleeping when I left. Her breathing was regular. I didn't close her door or extinguish her light.

THIRTY-FIVE

Good thing the North End is safe nights. I wouldn't have noticed a band of roving muggers till they'd reached in my waistband and stolen my gun. I drove home with the extraordinary care of the drunkard.

Joseph Frascatti.

Joey Fresh.

So this was progress. I knew who "Frank" was. I could find his last known address, his real Social Security number, his true credit history. Track him right up till the time he died.

When? Vietnam. Vietnam. I'd been in grade school throughout most of the turmoil, shielded by spelling bees and Friday-night pizza parties. My mother had railed against the Imperialist War. My mother had railed against everything. This was another capitalist plot, another excuse to march, march, march. I'd probably tagged along, doggedly apolitical. I remembered snatches of songs, chants. "And it's one, two, three, what are we fighting for?" And for Lyndon Johnson: "Waist-deep in the Big Muddy and the big fool says to push on." I marched. I sang. I got to spend time with my mother. A little time.

Joey Fresh was Joseph Frascatti's street name. Joseph Frascatti, Sr. The only one I'd ever heard of. He'd been outmaneuvering organized-crime task forces since before I was born.

"Frank's" papa.

What now?

I could fly to Washington, meet the elusive woman of Sam's dreams. Run my fingers over the black granite memorial till they rested on the name of Joseph Frascatti, Jr.

I needed to talk to Sam. Sam, with a best friend in a rival Mafia camp. Had his father and brothers known about little Joey Fresh?

I blinked my eyes and yawned, forgot to signal a left turn. What I needed was sleep, a long dreamless solo interlude. A snack; I couldn't remember dinner or lunch.

Roz was out, but she'd scrawled a note. It was highlighted with arrows and stars and hung on the fridge so I'd have no chance to miss it.

I read as I swallowed orange juice. "Went through the G and W files. Seem okay. Please remove the you-know-what."

The you-know-what being the cash in the tumbling mats. I glanced at the clock. Sure, plenty of time to sew it into homemade pillows with a little fancy embroidery on top so no one would suspect. Maybe I could piece together a patchwork quilt while I was at it.

I found cold cuts, sniffed them suspiciously, wedged them between slices of Swiss cheese. No bread.

I thought I'd try the computer. If Roz hadn't erased Sam's files, they must work with my machinery.

The message light blipped steadily. I punched the button, scrabbled for note paper. I ought to do it the other way around.

"Hello," said a woman's voice, faintly familiar. "My name is Lauren Heffernan. I'm calling from the District of Columbia. Two oh two, five five five, oh three two three. Sam spoke to me from the hospital. I'll be arriving on the morning shuttle as soon as I can find an available seat. I'll take a cab to your house. If that's a problem, please call."

I was dialing 202 before she finished, my mind spinning with questions. Coming here? Early? When did the first Washington shuttle arrive? Probably around eight, in time for the government suits to put in a full day's work.

Come on, Lauren. Answer your damn phone.

Five rings. Answering machine.

I hung up.

I slept badly. The alarm buzzed at 7:15. Up early, but I didn't think I'd make volleyball practice.

THIRTY-SIX

By the time a cab disgorged a woman, at 9:31 A.M., I was wired. Three cups of coffee sloshed around the two blueberry muffins I'd downed for breakfast. I flung the door wide as Lauren Heffernan mounted the steps.

She's stocky, I thought. *She's plain*. With her feet on the same level as mine, she was easily eight inches shorter. She extended a determined hand, flashed a warm and knowing grin. Her blue eyes, clear as a child's, were set in a nest of tiny wrinkles. Sam's age. Older. Comfortably in her forties, with no pretense at anything younger.

Not the siren I'd visualized from her come-hither voice.

"Ms. Heffernan," I said.

"Call me Lauren, okay? We got stuck in a holding

pattern over Logan," she said. "I thought we'd never land. Carlotta. Good to meet you."

Please, I begged silently, don't say you've heard so much about me.

"Coffee?" I asked.

"I'm already floating. Bathroom?"

"Through the kitchen. Let me take your coat."

It was navy wool, serviceable, one button missing, neatly folded Kleenex in the pockets. She'd dumped her large handbag, more briefcase than purse, on a chair. If she'd taken it with her I'd have been curious. Since she left it in full view I was only mildly tempted to rifle it.

The toilet flushed. Water ran. She came back smiling.

"Have you talked to Sam?" she asked.

"They won't put my calls through. He hasn't called me."

"He bribed somebody to get around hospital rules when he phoned me."

Could have tried the same with me, I thought.

"He sounded exhausted, but he wanted me to arrange a few things that could only be done through Washington," she said, as if she'd read my mind.

Have to work on the poker face. She was disarming, this woman. Through Washington, she'd said, not in Washington. Using *Washington* as a synonym for government.

"Who are you?" I asked.

She sucked in a breath. "Can we sit down?"

"No problem," I said.

Just then Roz staggered down the steps, dressed in something gold and gaudy. Could have been a nightgown. God knows what time she got in last night. I hadn't heard her yowling. Must have taken her mate elsewhere.

"Carlotta," she said, acknowledging my presence. Her eye makeup was smearier than usual, her lips almost black.

"Roz, this is Lauren. Lauren, okay with you if we talk in the kitchen?"

She didn't stare at Roz, which must have taken a major-league effort.

"If I can change my mind about the coffee," she said cheerfully.

"Mind waiting for me there? I need to discuss something with my, uh, associate."

I waited until Lauren was out of sight, lowered my voice.

"Okay," I said to Roz. "I know you didn't find anything on the diskettes, but that's because you were looking for the wrong things."

"You know the right ones?"

"I think so."

She flexed her fingers like a pianist warming up for a Liszt concerto.

"First," I said, "get me whatever you can on Lauren Heffernan. Eighty-one eighty-two Warren Street Northwest. Washington, D.C."

She shot a glance toward the kitchen. "I see."

"I doubt it. Let me have hard copy on Heffernan. Then bring up Sam's G and W files and compare them with the bank statement in the top drawer of the desk."

"You have Sam's bank statement?"

"I lifted it from his place."

"Tricky you."

"Roz?"

"Yeah?"

"Why are you up so early?"

"I got home about half an hour ago," she said. "I haven't been to sleep yet."

When I entered the kitchen, Lauren seemed to be pacing the dimensions of the room. While she tucked herself into a cane-back chair and kicked off her low-heeled pumps, I put the kettle on to boil, and found two clean mugs in the drainer. I settled in across the wooden table and waited.

"Who am I?" Lauren Heffernan repeated. "That's what you asked, isn't it? You want to see my driver's license?"

"Not particularly."

"In this context, I'm Sam's friend. We were together in Vietnam. I was in the army."

There was an emphasis on "together." They were "together" during the war. "Honey," she'd called him. Maybe that was left over from the war as well.

"Joey too?" I asked.

She whistled a low note. "You know more than you're supposed to know."

"Tell me something I don't know."

"Like?"

"Start with how Joey died in Vietnam."

She rested her elbows on the table and lowered her head into her hands. Her chestnut hair was cropped short; it showed streaks of gray. Her index fingers traced circles at her temples. She wore no jewelry, no rings.

Staring at the tabletop, she said, "Why he died makes a better story."

"Why will do fine. By the way, is your name really Lauren Heffernan? The Veterans' Administration have records on you?"

"Laura McCarthy," she said, giving me the candid-blue-eye treatment. "Women change their names all the time. Lauren's my given name, but it wasn't popular then, so I used Laura. I've been married twice. Didn't take either time."

"Men don't change their names that often."

"You'd be surprised."

"Surprise me."

"Coffee?" she asked.

"Almost ready."

She stared at the kettle as if willing it to boil. It hissed like a steam engine.

Nothing to do but start talking. No distractions.

"Sam didn't have to go to Vietnam," she said. "Neither did Joey. They were volunteers near the end, when the draft was a true lottery. Didn't wait for their numbers, just enlisted. They saw themselves as a team. That's what I thought at first. I didn't realize what was going on till later."

"What do you mean, going on?"

A smile crinkled the fine lines around her eyes. "I'm not going to tell you Sam's gay."

"Well, that would have been a surprise," I admitted.

"He and Joey were eighteen-year-olds having an adventure, escaping. That's what they thought it was about. They didn't fit in back home, didn't want to become cogs in their fathers' machines. That's why they were such close allies, because they were both sons of big-time crooks. Neither one felt he'd ever be allowed to exist outside his father's shadow."

She said, "I'm Irish, but not from any fancy neighborhood. My town, they called them gangs, not Mafia or anything. Just gangs."

"The boys saw the army as a way out," I prompted.

"Water's boiling," she said with relief.

"Instant okay?"

"Milk and sugar."

I fussed with mugs and silverware for two minutes. She didn't start talking again until she'd tasted her drink, spooned in extra sugar.

She said, "I don't know whose idea it was to die. To rig a death. I know they'd both talked about disappearing, going AWOL. Deserting would have been a way to thumb their noses at their families."

"The Mob sees itself as patriotic," I said.

"Invade Cuba for you any day," she responded wryly. "I don't think they had a plan for what happened. It worked out of . . . serendipity, out of where they found themselves, and the chaos that marked the end of the war, the Vietnamization of the war, the withdrawal, their assignments. My job. I was an army nurse. Mobile unit. In a war zone, but not a fighting job. Support for our men in uniform."

"In a position to alter records?" I asked.

"Joey was a grunt. Sam had been temporarily assigned as company clerk. Typing skills. He wanted to get back to the front line, pound ground again, and he did before the end."

"Unit?" I asked.

"One ninety-sixth Light Infantry. Provisionals. One of the last brigades to leave."

I'd run that through my computerized lie detector. "Go on," I said.

"Joey had troubles. And he got into more. Troubles at home, with his family." Lauren rocked her chair so it rested on its two back legs. She drank coffee.

"Yeah?" I said. "So?"

"He got into drugs in Vietnam. I mean, we all did drugs, if you call marijuana 'drugs.' But Joey . . . When he wasn't toking, he was snorting. I think he was shooting up too. Anyway—what with his family screaming that they were going to pull strings with their congressman and drag him back home, and him messed up on dope and owing money in the black market—at some point, Joey decided to die. For real. Maybe it seemed like the easiest way out. Sam and I, it got so we just wanted to save him if we could. I once promised Sam that if Joey was injured, I'd make sure the injury got bad enough to send him home. I was a nurse. I can't imagine myself saying that today, but it was different then. Joey kept volunteering for more and more dangerous assignments. Volunteer Joe, G.I. Joe, the man who couldn't get killed, was starting to self-destruct.

"Friends were scarce," she said. "I don't condone what we did, but friends were scarce."

"What exactly did you do?" I'd drunk half my coffee without tasting it. I could feel caffeine thrumming through my bloodstream.

Lauren stirred her coffee, stared into its milky depths as if she were watching a blurred film of her past. "Joey crawled into camp one night, into my tent. Camouflage gear covered with blood and mud. Mud and blood. The hills were numbered then. No names. No Porkchop Hill. No Little Round Top. Just numbered hills a grunt was expected to give up his life for. And they knew by now that each hill was nothing more than a bargaining chip. Land that would be given back after they'd bled and died for it. The sky was so blue . . . every day there would be boys who'd never see the sky again, never see a white bird fly across a blue sky. . . ."

She shook her head and sighed, deliberately firmed her voice, went on. "Joey kept charging up the hills. Nothing could stop him. He was prime Section Eight material by then, absolutely psycho, but I couldn't get anyone to agree. He was doing heroin, black market, you name it. When I saw him that night, that morning, I thought he was a ghost. He was clutching his dog tags, holding them so tight I had to pry them out of his hands. It was only then that I realized they weren't his."

"Whose were they?"

She looked up at me then, a clear-eyed, steady gaze. "I don't believe—Sam doesn't believe—that Joey killed him. The dead boy wasn't popular, but he was just another ground pounder, not an officer, and fragging wasn't common in units near our position. And there was enemy action that night, on point. Where Joey was, always near the front of the column, waiting to die. Instead another kid got blown apart. The dog tags landed at Joey's feet. Like a gift, Joey said. Like a gift from Mary, Mother of God, he said. He had his own tags over his head and on the ground before he consciously thought about it, he said."

The "Frank" I'd met was a good talker, too, I thought. I didn't say it. I didn't want to break her concentration. She stirred her cold coffee with a spoon and the sound blended with the clack of computer keys from the living room.

She sighed. "So my friend Joey Frascatti was killed in hostile action. KHA. And then Sam and I made arrangements for him, for our buddy Joey, who had a different name now—Floyd Markham, the name on the dog tags, the name of a boy from Traverse City who was beyond help. It was easier for 'Floyd Markham' to disappear. MIA." She frowned. "We should have made him KHA, but that would have been trickier. We'd have needed a body. It would have been more merciful to the boy's family though. MIA, all these years . . ."

"Hard," I said.

"Sam and Joey bought and backdated a life insurance policy in the dead boy's name. And that's why Sam's been spending so much time in Washington lately. We've been trying to track what's left of the boy's family, through unofficial channels, to make sure they absolutely know their boy is dead, to eliminate any hope or fear. Fear that he deserted, that he was somehow abandoned, that he was tortured or kept alive. You imagine things when you don't know, when you never get to see a coffin and bury a body."

"Joey didn't keep the boy's name?"

She replaced her coffee mug on the table. "Joey was never going to come back to the States. That was part of the plan, the deal. No USA. No Italy. No place where somebody might see him and say 'Hey, that's Joey Fresh's kid.' There was no harm in it. The other boy, Floyd Markham, was blown to blazes. The Frascattis got to hold their big funeral. The Markhams didn't. Now that I'm older, I appreciate the ritual of committing a body to the earth. I was young. I never thought about it then. I don't believe any of us ever thought about it. . . ."

"Why did Joey come back?"

Her voice sank to a whisper. "He got in touch with Sam via e-mail. From Australia, then New Zealand. It was a shock. Sam and I had . . . woven a fantasy around Joey, the boy who got to start over again, the boy who'd promised to get clean and stay clean, if only we'd give him the chance. We'd all sworn secrecy; but more than that, we'd all sworn aid. If one of us was in need or in trouble, the others would try to help."

She stopped talking, looked at me. I might have been wrong but I thought she was searching for my approval.

"Three Musketeers is just a candy bar to me," I said. I kept thinking about Floyd Markham's mom and dad, his sisters or brothers, waiting, waiting, waiting. Wearing those copper bracelets, keeping the flame alive.

Her eyes hardened. "Sam came to me when 'Frank' called from California, earlier this year."

"And what did 'Frank' want?"

"To come home. He made it sound simple. Just to come home. He missed the people he used to hate. He'd never made a new life for himself, although he'd earned a fortune in the electronics industry. Sam and I had fixed it for him to die, and now he wanted us to fix it so he could come back from the dead."

"Could you?"

"If he hadn't been so pig-headed, possibly. But he wanted to come home as himself! As Joseph Frascatti, Jr. How could he? Joseph Frascatti, Jr., was dead. What could he say? He woke up in some field in Indochina twenty years later, no idea what happened?"

"You sound angry."

"I am angry. Sam and I'd turned somersaults to give Joey what he wanted, a new chance. We'd envied him, especially Sam. Fighting the same battle over and over with his father, Sam could say 'Well, Joey's out there, free.' "

"Why did Joey come to Boston?"

"I don't know. Sam and I were concentrating on learning as much as we could about the Markham family."

"If they were all dead, Joey's reappearance would be easier."

"If they heard a peep about Joey's 'resurrection,' we were fried. It would have been a case of 'Who's buried in Joey's tomb?' We'd written the family a letter, one of those 'he-was-a-hero' things, saying how Floyd had gone missing trying to prevent Frascatti's death. We'd turned them both into heroes."

"The kind of letter you keep," I commented.

"The kind of letter you remember," she said. "We tried to convince Joey to go away, to accept an alias. He said he couldn't. He had to be a bona fide relative to visit his father in prison."

Sam. The visits to Providence.

"Did Sam tell Joey Senior that his kid was coming home?"

"No," Lauren said. "Sam sounded him out, that's all.

Joey wanted to break the good news in person. He wanted to see his father. Said he was scared his father would die, and they'd never have a chance to straighten out all the things between them."

I set my coffee on the table. The bottom was wet; it would leave a round stain.

"So what do you think?" I asked. "Did Joey try to kill Sam?"

"No. Absolutely not."

"Why not? Sounds to me like he was jealous of Sam. I think you used the word *psycho*, said he was on drugs. How's this for a scenario? When he got what he wanted, and it didn't make him a different person, he bided his time, earned some cash, and now he's turning on the people he blames. It was e-mail that lured Sam to Green and White. I'd watch my step if I were you."

"I do watch my step," she said. "Joey's very upset about Sam."

"Where is he?"

"I can reach him."

"He's in Boston?"

"Why should he run?" Lauren said. "He would never hurt Sam."

I have a kitchen extension. I don't use it much, but it keeps me from burning dinner on the rare occasions when I cook and the phone rings. I picked it up and dialed a number I know well.

Mooney didn't answer. I thought about trying to raise Oglesby. Dialed another number and persisted till I had Leroy on the phone.

"How's Gloria?"

He sounded uncertain. "Okay. Quiet. Not like her. Okay, I guess."

"You?"

"I dunno."

"Leroy, I need a favor and there's nobody else I can ask."

"I'm not leaving the hospital."

"I'm not asking you to."

"What are you askin'?"

"Go stand outside Sam's room till I can get there or till I can get somebody there."

"Just stand?"

"Make like a guard."

"Sam's got plenty of guards, believe me," Leroy said.

"Yeah, but I don't think they're watching for the right guy."

"Carlotta, you know I'd do 'most anything for you, but that's one family I don't wanna mess with."

"I'll be there as soon as I can. You might save Sam's life. He's your sister's friend. He's her partner."

"Okay," Leroy said reluctantly. "Make it fast."

I gave a brief physical rundown on "Frank" as I'd last seen him. No reason for Leroy to hassle the candy stripers.

"You're wrong about Joey," Lauren Heffernan said as I hung up.

"Did he handle explosives when he was in Vietnam?"

"Carlotta!" Roz shouted from the other room. "I don't care what you're doing in there, you need to see this."

"You mind waiting?" I asked Lauren.

"I'll make more coffee," she said.

"You want to help," I said. "Here's the phone. Get Joey here. Whatever the hell he's calling himself today."

THIRTY-SEVEN

I stormed into the living room and halted at the desk. Roz, probably chilly in her gauzy evening attire, had pulled one of her more modest T-shirts over her head. It was chrome yellow and announced: BEER—IT ISN'T JUST FOR BREAKFAST ANYMORE.

She wore last night's fake nails, spiky and black. No wonder the keyboard clacked so loudly.

"What?" I asked.

"Crabby today," she observed.

"Very," I agreed, tight-lipped. "Make this fast."

She sailed a folded sheet of printout paper airplane-like across the room. "You were right," she said. "Yesterday I was looking for the wrong stuff. Checking if Sam was planning to sell Green and White. No indication of that. So there goes my next question. Who's he gonna sell to? He isn't selling. Ergo, shit."

"I didn't realize you spoke Latin."

"Huh?"

"Roz, what in hell did you find?"

"Sit down, stop pacing, okay?"

"Talk!"

"It's about money," she said.

"Money," I repeated. A fascinating subject.

"Sam's records are clear as the driven snow."

"Pure," I said. "Pure as the driven snow."

"Whatever. Receipts. Deposits. Salaries. Plant. Up-keep. Taxes. Insurance. Nothing the IRS wouldn't applaud. Green and White's not making anybody rich, but it's keeping its head above water. Not much in the way of expenses. Low rent. Gloria works cheap because she's got a place there, no rent.

"Sam's own stuff, his personal cash, is in several accounts, three different banks, which is smart because he can take advantage of FDIC. Green and White keeps all its accounts at Bank of Commerce and Industry. Loyalty, maybe. They loaned Sam money when he started out."

I stared at my watch. "Fascinating, Roz. Fascinating."

"Sam doesn't update his files often enough. The bank statement you lifted—Bank of Commerce and Industry—was still sealed. It made such interesting reading, I figured I ought to find out more. Courtesy of 'Frank,' I accessed the bank, and since I've got all Sam's account numbers and shit, I brought him up to date."

"He'll appreciate it."

"Dammit, Carlotta. Look. The past few months,

money's been going in and money's been going out like you wouldn't believe. I'm surprised a bank officer hasn't questioned Sam about the activity on Green and White's accounts. I would have, knowing how they've behaved in the past. Suddenly it's like a whole new thing."

"Where's the money coming from? Can you find out?"

"Most of it's wire transfers, which gives me locations of the banks. I made a list."

I read them. "Providence. New York. Chicago. Las Vegas. Cayman Islands. Bahamas."

"You want to know where the money's going?" Roz asked. "After it takes its little detour through Green and White?"

"You want to tell me?"

"The same holding company that owns Siren Hiring, your very own phony employment agency. Getaway Ventures. In Singapore."

"Frank."

"Lauren," I called. "You know anything about computers?"

"Not much." She entered the room balancing a tray and three steaming cups. "I can do Lotus One-Two-Three." I didn't realize Roz and I counted a tray among our kitchen crap. It looked metallic. I hoped it wasn't one of Roz's developer pans.

"Joey's on his way over," Lauren said.

"Good. Run Joey Frascatti for me, Roz."

"SSN?"

"Don't know it."

"Well, I need something."

I grabbed the phone book. "Last known address: Four fifty-two Howser. Boston."

She punched buttons.

"Here."

"Must be the father, not the son," Lauren said.

"Frascatti hasn't done any credit purchases in six years," Roz said. "Think he's dead? Or maybe he went to one of those financial self-help gurus, cut up his credit cards."

"He's in prison," I said, remembering my conversation with Mooney. "Dammit. Try any other Frascattis at that address."

"Okay."

"Get me employment histories. Credit. Business loans."

"Right."

"Hard copy."

The printout was easier to read than the screen. The Frascattis owned restaurants. Dry cleaners. Bars. Hotels. They'd received loans from banks in the Cayman Islands. The Bahamas. Providence. Chicago. Las Vegas. I blinked and stared again. The same locales that had recently become so beneficent to Green & White.

"Now run Gianelli," I said quietly. "Anthony Gianelli, Sr. Hanover Street. Boston. Same thing."

"Okay," Roz said.

"Some electronics expert," I murmured. "Young Joey Frascatti."

"Yes," Lauren said. She seemed genuinely puzzled. Almost defiant.

"He may be in the running for computer hacker of the year," I said sharply, "but I'm willing to bet he never earned an honest dime off electronics, Lauren. He stole every penny. Skimmed it. From his family. From other families. From the Mob."

"No," Lauren said. "He's worked all over the world. A freelance contractor. He's brilliant. Brilliant."

"Save it," I said. "I'm out of here, Lauren. If Joey shows up, keep him here."

"You want to look at this screen or what?" Roz demanded.

"Later, Roz. Keep him here, Lauren. I mean it."

"I'll try," she said.

"Roz," I said. *"Keep him here."*

THIRTY-EIGHT

I longed for flashing cop lights on my Toyota. Without them, I couldn't force slower vehicles to the side of the road, barge through stop signs or red lights. I flicked my brights at a Volvo doing the sightseer gawk in the fast lane, passed on the right in frustration. Squeezing by jittery traffic on Memorial Drive, I glanced at the other side of the river to find Storrow Drive almost empty. I whipped across the B.U. Bridge, made two illegal lefts, and sped onto Storrow. Clear sailing. No place to park near the hospital. I slammed the car into a loading zone.

"How's Sam?" I asked Leroy after giving him a hug.

"I don't know. Maybe you can tell me why I'm here, in case anybody wants to know."

"The guy I described, I think he wants Sam dead."

"That's not what I meant, Carlotta. Why'm I the

only one here? Any of these citizens look like Mob grunts to you?"

I did a quick survey of the waiting room.

"Is Sam still here? Is he okay?" I tried to keep my voice low, but I could hear it rising.

"Calm down," Leroy said. "He's sleepin'. I stuck my head in, and he's breathing, that's all I know."

"You're a good man, Leroy," I said. "Thank you."

"Sam don't deserve this shit. My brother didn't deserve it, either."

"I know," I said.

"Is somebody gonna try to kill my sister, Carlotta?"

"No," I said. "This isn't about her."

"You want me to hang around?"

"Please. A little longer."

I scribbled a phone number on a scrap of paper, dug a quarter out of my pocket. "Use the pay phone. Don't identify yourself. Tell whoever answers to let Papa G know that there are no guards at the hospital. Tell him it's urgent."

"Will do."

"I'm going to visit Sam."

There was nobody to stop me. I inhaled deeply and deliberately, pushed open the door. No one had told me much concerning his condition; I was almost afraid to look.

He wasn't sleeping. He was lying motionless, fingers steepled on his chest. His skin tone was bad, grayish in the glaring light. I leaned over and kissed him on the forehead. Aside from a small bandage on his right cheek, his face seemed untouched. I ran my hand over his left cheek. He hadn't shaved..He breathed. I closed

my eyes and said a brief prayer of thanks to a God I
didn't believe in.

"Visions of sugarplums?" I asked.

"Nowhere near such pleasant thoughts," he said.
"Glad you interrupted."

"Do your legs hurt?" The words came out before I
could stop them. His eyes were weary and glazed.

He said, "Pretty numb. Lucky. I remember starting
to run, to help Marvin. If he hadn't wrestled that door
open, hadn't yelled, I'd have been sheltered by the
desk, like Gloria. But then, if he hadn't tried to stop the
guy, I'd be dead. I'm alive . . . Marvin's dead."

"Your legs?"

"There was a fireball. I tried not to breathe, to hug
the floor. My back, well, it's not much worse than a
bad sunburn. The beam cracked and fell. It's like I can
still hear it. I know my hair was on fire. Gloria put it
out."

"Can I get you anything?"

"Water."

To reach the empty cup, the sink, I had to negotiate
my way past an IV stand. Burn victims need fluids; I
remembered that.

I held the cup while he drank through a straw. I
could see a patch of his singed hair. Smell it.

"I've got this gizmo," he said. "Pain pump. I push
the button when it hurts too much. Instant anesthesia.
Great stuff."

His left leg had so much hardware sprouting from it
that it barely resembled a leg at all. There was a huge
metal device clamped around one knee with shiny
metal pins descending into the flesh. Another chunk of

machinery clamped his ankle. His right leg was draped in gauze.

"Who tried to kill you, Sam?"

"Don't treat me like a case, Carlotta."

"I need to know. I'd *want* to know even if I weren't working for Gloria."

"Some goon Gloria fired," he muttered. His room was filled with overblown floral tributes: red-and-white carnations arranged in crosses, stuff that would have looked more appropriate at a funeral.

I pulled up a chair, sat, and took Sam's hand in mine. "Or maybe Joey," I said.

"Ah, sweet Jesus," he said. "What a mistake that was."

"What mistake?"

"He told you his real name. Now you tell me, Carlotta. Is Joey your new flame?"

Startled, I said, "No. No way. I'm not saying things are the way they were, but it's not Joey."

"Small favors," he said. "I never should have introduced you. But you insisted. And he wanted to know everything, everything, to absorb my whole life. What worked and what didn't. He was always like that. So goddamn curious, like he'd eat information for breakfast, swallow it whole. But he was never jealous before. He saw you, I knew there'd be trouble."

"Wait a minute—"

"Look, I'm not trying to make like you're Helen of Troy or something."

"Thanks."

"Any woman I was with, I think."

"Thanks again."

"Carlotta, quit it."

"Sorry," I said. "It's not every day I get compared to Helen of Troy."

"You love me?" he asked.

I felt my shoulders tense. "Sam," I said softly. "You were the first guy."

"Now." His voice was hard, implacable.

"I love you; I'm not in love with you."

Silence.

I said, "It used to be easy. I'd just see you—God, Sam. . . ." He glanced down at his sheet-covered body. On the leg that wasn't suspended from the pulley, only the toes were visible, grayish.

"Look at me now, kid," he said.

"I do love you, Sam."

"But there's somebody else."

"I assumed you had somebody else, Sam. You were spending all your time at Lauren's."

"It was over between me and Lauren before I ever met you."

"Yeah, well, I found out a little late. And it wasn't just Lauren. We were drifting, Sam. Going no place."

"Why was that?" he asked.

I chose evasion. "Look, Sam, this new guy, it may not work. He flunks a basic test."

"Lousy in bed?"

"Worse. He's a doctor; my mother would have approved."

"That damned shrink, right?"

"Nothing happened until *after* you'd decided we were lovers."

"Don't tell me I put the idea in your head."

"I don't want to talk about this. I want to talk about Joey."

"Long as you're not screwing him."

"He's screwing *you*, Sam. He's moving money through Green and White. He's using you to launder cash."

"No. He wouldn't."

"You knew about the money?"

"No, but *if* he's using Green and White, it's gotta be some temporary thing. He must have gotten in some kind of bind. Or it's a surprise. He's gonna earn me a pile in two weeks and surprise me."

"Sure."

"Joey would never do anything to hurt me."

"Sam." He seemed remote, distant in a way I'd never experienced before. He could have been in another room, having a different conversation.

"Don't protect him," I said.

"I'll protect whoever the hell I want to, Carlotta! You can't fucking read my mind! I have a right to my own thoughts. Get out of here!"

He couldn't make me leave, not flat on his back, not drugged.

"You can't keep protecting Joey," I insisted.

"I wouldn't. Not if I believed he did this."

"Tell me about him."

"You talk to Lauren?"

"She's at my place now. Talk about Joey, Sam."

"I'm supposed to be resting. I could buzz for a nurse, have you tossed the hell out."

"She'd have to get past Leroy."

"Why's Leroy out there? My dad's guys—"

"Are gone," I said. "Leroy's there to keep Joey from finishing you off."

"You're so wrong, Carlotta."

"Convince me."

He closed his eyes. Briefly. Sighed. "Joey," he said. "He's a hell of a responsibility."

"Even if he didn't try to kill you, he set you up. Unless he's incredibly stupid."

"He's coming in from the cold. I guess it was real cold for him out there."

"Guy sets you up, you forgive him? You feel sorry for him?"

"There are people in your life you forgive. Joey's mine. He's the guy with the great future behind him, you know what I mean? Christ, he's smart. I was half as smart as Joey, I'd run the world. When we were still in high school, he nailed the phone system. Got all these manuals from the phone company, some legit, some he dug out of their Dumpsters, and pretty soon he's asking me, do I want to talk to a friend of his in Germany. Friend of his in Sweden, Denmark. Pay phone. No charge. He's got phones in his locker, phones in his car. When he, uh, went AWOL, he had so many buddies overseas, I figured it would work. He had a bunch of pals in West Germany—"

"Hackers," I said.

"Phone phreaks. Hackers came later. You should have seen him work a phone. He's so single-minded, so patient. He could sit for a whole night, a whole day, without eating. If he wanted access, he got access."

"You knew he was a crook."

"I don't know that," Sam said angrily. "Whatever he

was doing got away from him. That's all. I absolutely don't think he wants me dead."

"Who, then?"

"I don't know."

"Ah, God, Sam."

We held hands. There were raw patches on his arms, lightly covered with gauze. I wanted to ask for more details about the explosion, the blaze. I wanted to know how he'd escaped, how it felt to take a breath, to know he was alive.

He said, "It's not everybody gets a second chance. I've been thinking about that. Lauren and I gave Joey a second chance. Marvin didn't know it, but he gave me a second chance.

"When I get out of here, I'm not sure about Boston. It's early to think about this, and I'm pretty far under the table. This drug is a nice drunk—a couple six-packs, but you never feel full. There's probably gonna be another operation. At least one more. But after recuperation and physical therapy and all . . . I got so many pins in me, I'd probably stick to a magnet. I lie here and look out the window. I like green trees better than black trunks. It's warm in the South. I've been cold since I got here, no matter how many blankets they throw on me, and they're talking a long time before I walk and maybe"—he swallowed—"maybe I won't walk the same. I know I'm not going to feel like sliding down icy streets."

"You tell anybody you were interested in selling the cab company?" I asked.

"No."

"Tell anybody else about your southern fantasy?"

"Never had it till now. I don't think I'm going to be much good on the ski slopes this year."

"Sam. If Joey killed Marvin, he's going to pay."

"I have no problem with that."

"Good," I said.

"I mean, look, use your judgment and all, Carlotta, but remember this: Joey's my brother. I got three brothers, luck of the draw, but Joey's the one. If you can see your way to cutting him a break, do it."

I leaned down and kissed him full on the lips.

"Mmmmm," he said. "We could try again."

"Someday," I said lightly, "Paolina wants you to be her dad."

"What that really means is she wants you to be her mom, don't you think?"

Shit. I have psychiatrists coming out of my ears.

I dialed my Little Sister from a waiting-room pay phone. I told her that Sam was going to be fine. It would just take time.

Time.

THIRTY-NINE

My opinion of meter maids who ticket near hospitals is unprintable. I shredded the orange slip on the spot. That I didn't earn another one on my flight back to Cambridge proves my point: too many meter maids; not enough traffic cops.

I didn't notice any unfamiliar cars on my block. Maybe Joey had taken a cab, like Lauren Heffernan. Maybe he hadn't put in an appearance. Lauren's promise could have been a diversionary tactic. Maybe she sat in Joey's corner now, not Sam's.

An extra coat hung on the hat rack: a leather jacket, smelling of musk.

"Frank"—Joey—sat on the sofa, relaxed and smiling, a glass of O.J. in his left hand. His jeans were tucked into cowboy boots. Lizard-skin boots. Expensive. But not to him; he hadn't paid for them, worked for them. Why bother, when he could rip off legit credit-card holders? Or the Mob. His shirt was of Western cut with a design of flapping eagles. Buzzards would have been more appropriate.

I wondered whether Lauren or Roz had played hostess. I remembered the gray pallor of Sam's skin, the tremble in his hand, and I wanted to knock the glass out of Joey's grasp, slap his face hard.

"Mooney called," Roz said. Her voice seemed to bubble up from underwater; I could barely hear her through my anger.

"He wants you to call him back," Roz said.

I crossed to my desk, lifted the phone, but didn't dial the police. Maybe I should have. Instead I called Sam's ward at the hospital, asked Leroy whether the reserves had arrived. They had, so I gratefully freed Leroy to return to his sister's bedside.

"How's it going, Joey?" I said, after hanging up. "Or would you prefer some other name?"

"Joey's the best," Joseph Frascatti responded cheerfully. "Better than all the aliases I've used."

"And what were those?"

"Frank I liked. Frank sounds honest. Georgio. George was too Waspy for a guy looked like me. Roger. Like in roger, over and out. I was Yves in Cannes one year."

"In Germany?"

"Gerhardt. Yeah, Gerhardt."

"And the whole time you were skimming from the Mob?"

"Well," Joey said, smiling, "almost the whole time."

"You had ambitions," Lauren said quietly, her

mouth set in a bitter line. "Excuse my naïveté, but I think you called them 'dreams.'" Seated in my aunt Bea's rocker, she propelled herself rapidly back and forth. "Why?" she snapped angrily.

The smile shut off and Joey was instantly on the defensive. Mercurial, this man, as well as clever. "I never thought about being homeless, you know. Or if I did, it didn't mean jack shit to me, Laura. I never thought about being lonely. I never thought about being penniless."

"You never thought," I shot back. "Your German friends didn't like you when you didn't have unlimited money anymore?"

"Oh, they liked me fine. I learned a hell of a lot from them. Good thing I'm one lazy, apolitical son of a bitch. They were into heavy shit. Hackers from the dark side. Logging into army systems on MILNET, some deep spook stuff. Names, addresses, phone numbers for CIA personnel. Saleable goods, you know what I mean? There for the asking."

"You helped them ask?" I said.

"Why endanger myself when all I wanted was money? There was plenty of Mob money. They were begging people to take it off their hands, clean it for them. I scammed what I could. I set up phony holding companies. I 'invested' for them. I did 'drug deals' for them, only the product always wound up missing. Fortunes of war, you know, Laura. Fortunes of war."

"Call me Lauren."

He didn't seem to hear her.

"It got easier and easier, wires and electronic transfers and stuff. It was a breeze. I was always a couple steps ahead. And then one day I thought, why should I be on the run, holding multiple passports, planning for a new name, a new pair of shoes to jump into just in case the heat came down. It was simple. I could go home. I wanted to see my friends again—hell, I wanted to see my enemies again—live in a neighborhood where everybody knew me, where I knew everybody."

"You hated the North End. It was corrupt. You hated it," Lauren said.

"I was fucking nineteen. I didn't know shit. I'd heard all this crap about 'earning an honest buck' from my best buddy, Sam Gianelli. One day it came to me: I wanted to be who I was, who I was born to be, not who he thought I was. I wanted to see my dad before he died. Make him proud of me. That's such a horrible thing?"

He stared at Lauren as if he could look straight through her, said, "You cheated me out of so much."

"What the hell do you mean?" she said.

"Don't get cute. You wanted me out of the way as much as I wanted to leave, right? So you could have Sam all to yourself. You were jealous, Laura."

She glared back through narrowed eyes, clenched her fists. Maybe she wanted to hit him as badly as I did.

"You know," he continued offhandedly, "at some point, I started keeping tabs on my family. One brother, he owns power boats. I mean, lots of power boats. Another married some fucking heiress, some Italian shipping magnate's daughter. My sister's got a house in Gloucester, right on the shore, with an Olympic-size pool in case the ocean's a little rough that day. What do you figure the prodigal son should get when he comes home?"

"We helped you," Lauren insisted. "Sam and I could have wound up in jail."

"You don't get it, Lauren," I said. "Sam's the fatted calf. Right, Mr. Prodigal Son? You sent the message, Joey. E-mail. You got Sam to the garage in time for the explosion."

"I don't know what you're talking about, lady."

"I'm talking about this: No way could you come back from the dead without giving the family a fall guy."

He shrugged.

"It's total bullshit, you being two steps ahead. They're gaining on you," I said. "You needed somebody to give the Mob. An embezzler. You decided on your old pal, Sam. Dead, he couldn't mount much of a defense."

"No way," Joey said.

Lauren said, "I don't understand."

"Did you tell your family about Sam?" I asked Joey. "Write your old man a note? About how Gianelli's kid was stealing from all the families?"

"I didn't do squat," Joey said.

"Except move money through Green and White."

"Christ, I never thought anything like this would happen," Joey said. "Sam's father's got clout; I assumed he'd protect him, get him out of the country, maybe."

"You didn't care, did you, Joey?" I said quietly.

He smiled. "Well, let's say there are a lot of ways it might have gone down. I didn't think they'd whack him. But, hey, he lived a good life, huh? It's my turn."

"He's not the same person I knew," Lauren muttered, shaking her head. "The drugs, or something . . ." Her voice petered out.

"So, Joey," I said. "If Sam were here, what would he say?"

Joey grinned. "He wouldn't believe it."

"Would he want you dead, Joey?"

"Dead?" he echoed. His posture didn't change so much as freeze. Sprawled on the sofa, holding a half-filled glass of O.J., suddenly still, as if someone were about to take his photograph.

I took the .40 out of my waistband. "You're already dead, aren't you?"

"Hey," Joey said. "Wait."

I watched him carefully. No move toward a cowboy boot. No motion. I didn't think he was carrying.

Lauren stared at the gun like she'd never seen one before. "Sam would let him go," she said shakily.

You'd figure he'd jump on the wagon. Instead he heaped more scorn. "Oh, yeah. Angel of fucking mercy, Sam. I never understood that, Laura. Why'd you bother screwing a guy with no balls?"

I sighted down the barrel. I hadn't even taken the damn thing out on the firing range yet.

"Sam would let him go," Lauren insisted. "He'll go back to Europe, to Australia. He can still make a life for himself."

"Lauren, I'm fucking pushing forty."

"Life begins at forty, Joey," I said. "Or it can end."

"What do you want?" he said. "You're not going to shoot me, so what do you want?"

"I like your choice of words, Joey. I wish I were as confident as you are that I won't shoot you."

"Put it away."

"Tie him, Roz. Rope in the closet. My hands are

getting tired. If I'd bought the Glock, I'm sure I'd have killed him by now. Glock's got a light touch."

"Laura," Joey said. "She's crazy."

"Oh, Joey," I said, "you don't know the half of it. Would you be so kind as to move to this chair? Please."

"What the fuck you want?" Joey asked.

"That's what I like to hear," I said.

I motioned with the gun and he moved to the vacant chair at my desk.

Roz approached from the rear and bound him to it before he could struggle.

"Tie his elbows to the arms of the chair," I said. "Leave his hands free."

"Why?" Roz asked.

"It's time to have fun with computers."

FORTY

I did it for Sam, but I admit I took advantage. I've never been one to gaze longingly at gift horses.

Trojan horses came to mind more than once as I watched Joey work his keyboard wizardry. I stared at the screen. Roz stared at the screen. He could have slipped one past us. Easily. He may have been too vain to try. He'd been on his own so long, he lapped up admiration like a puppy laps milk.

"I gave you a damned good machine," he crowed. "Not that you can appreciate it. Amiga Two Thousand with an IBM card and Mac emulation. What more could you want?"

I shrugged and blinked, wondering how his eyes could stand the glare from the screen.

"I can do more than this," he kept offering. "I can

clean your credit. You got car payments you want made? Mortgage? Rent?"

"I'm not a crook," I said.

"You got a gun pointed at my head," he said. "Excuse my confusion."

"I'm not a cheap crook," I amended.

He excised the FBI's file on my mother. I watched my name disappear off mailing lists.

"Want to watch me crack a missile range?" Joey asked. "I can log in through Aiken at Harvard. They'll never do a trace-back."

"No, thanks," I said.

"How about ARPA? Advanced Research Projects Agency. Part of DOD. Don't you want to see where your tax dollars are going? Have you no curiosity?"

"Not about the Department of Defense," I said. "They keep their secrets, I keep mine."

"That's just it," he said. "They don't. Keep secrets. Not well. I have trapper programs planted in so many systems—"

"Trapper programs?" I said.

"To catch accepted passwords. Trap them. Trapper programs."

"Don't you ever get caught?" I asked.

"It's getting tougher," he admitted. "More of a challenge. The Internet's got CERT."

"CERT?"

"A Defense Department operation. Computer Emergency Response Team."

"Are they good?"

"Not as good as me. I could teach you to do this," he

said earnestly. "Do it for good or for bad or for kicks or for money. For power. Just because you *can* do it. Don't you see? This is it, what I do. This is my fuckin' skill, my art."

I'd seen locksmiths like him. Carried away by the ability to gain entry. In prison.

"You have an art for betrayal, Joey," I muttered to myself. "Roz, Lauren, you mind leaving me and Joey here alone for a little while?"

Roz lifted one eyebrow skeptically.

"Roz," Joey said. "I got an idea. You take the gun with you. Carlotta and me, we won't need it."

"Yes we will," I said. I didn't speak again until the women's footsteps trailed upstairs.

"Now, Joey," I said, "I have money I want deposited to a new account, no questions."

"We all have our little secrets, eh?"

"We do," I agreed.

"No questions from me, or no questions from the IRS?"

"Both," I said.

"Where's the money now?"

"In the house."

"Cash? You're talking *cash*?"

"About forty-two thousand."

"Sam know about this?"

"No questions."

"Five trips to the bank," he said, echoing Roz's smurfing advice. "Once it's in the system I can manipulate it. Here, it's toilet paper."

"Makes me feel good about banks," I said.

"What should I do?" he said. "It's hard to type like this. Stupid rope's rubbing my arms raw. Can I log out?"

I said, "Joey, move forty-two K of *your* funds into something I can access."

"Huh?"

"I'll give you the cash. On the lam, you'll need cash."

"I never said I was running away. . . ."

"Entirely up to you. Your choice. Lawyers like cash," I suggested. "Defense attorneys. That's one way to get the dough back into circulation."

Angrily, he punched keys. "Okay. I stashed it in two accounts," he said, lips tight. "Caymans. T and C. That's Turks and Caicos, a new island tax haven."

"I'll need signature cards."

"Phone and ask for them."

"I'll need passwords."

He wrote them down: JFresh. Joseph.

"So you'll remember me," he said.

"Show me how you did that," I said.

He went through it step by step. I took notes.

"Now I'm going to cut the ropes, Joey," I said, circling in front of him, snatching a knife-sharp letter-opener off the desk. "When I give you the okay—and not one second before—move away from the keyboard. Sit on the couch and keep both hands where I can see them. Okay. Move."

I tucked the letter-opener out of sight at the back of a drawer, held the pistol in my right hand and typed awkwardly with my left, changing the passwords to my own.

"You think I can't figure them out?" Joey said.

"Most people are so dumb, they use their names, their phone numbers for PINs. Personal identification numbers. Even pros. And they never change the passwords. I change my passwords every week."

"Good for you."

"Want some advice?"

"Why not?"

"Go to Wonderland, to the dog track, buy a few tickets, and look happy as hell when the races finish. Then move the forty-two K to the U.S. Do it by wire transfer. Declare the money as racetrack winnings, and pay Uncle his share. That way, you'll have easy access to the cash. Less on your conscience. Less chance of getting nailed on evasion."

I said, "Advice from experts is always welcome."

"So's gratitude," he said.

We changed places, like awkward square dancers attempting a cautious do-si-do. I felt more comfortable at a distance, gripping the S&W.

"You gonna tie me again?"

"Not yet," I said. "Sit back down and move every cent of Mob money out of Green and White."

"The Mob's gonna want somebody," he said.

"I'd love to give you up."

"My dad would shelter me."

"Too bad you didn't just steal from him. You had to hit the Gianellis, the New York families. Jesus."

I called for Roz and Lauren to come back downstairs. Joey hunched over the computer for fifteen minutes. I've never seen anyone type half that fast.

"Okay. That's it. You happy?" he said.

I said, "Sam's legs are gonna hurt for a long time. If somebody doesn't kill him first."

"Look at the screen," he said. "Is that beautiful or what?"

This time he hadn't asked if I wanted access.

It seemed to be an index:

BANKAMER.ZIP 6809 06-11-94 Hacking Bank America

TAOTRASH.DOC 7645 09-04-94 Trashing

CITIBANK.ZIP 43556 06-06-94 Hacking Citibank

It went on, screen after screen.

"Not as good as the old days," Joey said. "Not up to Legion of Doom standards."

"Legion of Doom?" Roz repeated.

"Used to be you could access hundreds of dark-side files. How to make your own weapons. How to kill somebody's credit rating. You want revenge, there's no better way."

"Wipe it off," I said.

"It's out there," he said.

"It'll always be out there."

"*I'll* always be out there," I said. "You take the cash and leave the country and consider yourself lucky to be alive. You try to fuck with me or Sam or Lauren, your photo will be distributed to every police force in the world. With fingerprints, aliases, the whole nine yards."

"Too bad somebody figured the cash flow so soon,"

he said. "Came down so hard. I really thought Sam's dad would pull his ass out of the fire. Honest."

"Sure. I believe every word you say, Joey. The thing is, making Sam's dad believe everything you say."

"You gonna give me to old man Gianelli?"

"Tear a clean sheet of paper off the printer."

"Why?"

"Do it! I want a handwritten confession, exonerating Sam. Now! You don't need to sign it."

"Who do I write it to? 'Dear Carlotta'?"

I raised the gun half an inch. " 'To whom it may concern,' " I said.

He tried to stare me down. No dice. He scribbled a few hasty lines. Roz fetched it, keeping out of the line of fire. It would do.

"If you count me out," Joey said, "do you know who tried to ice Sam?"

"I think so," I said. "Yeah. Definitely. A guy who knows money. A guy who lied to me."

"You gonna call the cops?" he asked.

"It's a little complicated. Roz, copy all the G and W files—before and after—on floppies."

"Duplicate disks, yeah. And a holographic confession. Bank vault," Joey said. "For insurance."

"I've got someplace better than a bank vault," I said. "Roz, when you're done, tie Mr. Frascatti again. Do a great job on his arms. Leave his legs till he climbs upstairs. The blue room, the one with the big closet that locks. Put him in with my prom dress. No phone calls."

Before I left, I made sure he was secure.

"Roz," I said, "since he's posing so nicely, holding

still and all, take some photos—mug shots, profile—
before you lock the door. Remember to bag the glass
he used for his O.J. We can print it later."

"What if he needs to take a leak?" she asked.

"Stick an empty Poland Springs bottle in there."

Nothing but the best for my houseguests.

FORTY-ONE

"Do you know, or are you bluffing?" Roz asked as soon as we'd reassembled, minus Joey, in the living room.

"Thanks for that show of confidence," I said. "Roz, remember our buddies at Sam's apartment?"

She smiled an evil smile. "Probably not as well as they remember me."

"You think they have police records?"

"Is there justice in the world?"

I shrugged. It was still worth a try.

"I have to pay a visit, Roz, show some respect. While I'm gone, I want you to give this your best shot. There's this creep cop named Oglesby," I said, thinking out loud. "Organized Crime Task Force. No, forget him. You'd have better luck doing this through Mooney. Tell Moon you want mug shots. Gianelli goons."

"And why do I want them?"

I closed my eyes. Mooney would certainly ask.

"Be creative, Roz. Tell him one of them followed you home, I don't care. If you recognize either of our friends from Sam's, keep a poker face, get as much info as you can, but say you're not sure."

"Okay," she said tentatively. "I follow."

I said, "Roz, this is urgent, so give me your undivided. Get a name for one of our goons. A name and a phone number. Call him, and do the bimbo routine."

"I don't think either of those guys is gonna want to talk to me," Roz said. "I kicked them where it hurts."

"Yeah," I said, "but you've got bargaining chips. You took home these little computer thingies by mistake, instead of your lace bikinis, and you wonder if maybe the computer junk is worth some bucks. Let him make an offer. He'll want to call back, find out who you are. Don't let him. Do it from phone booths. Different phone booths. Dicker over price. He'll want to meet. He'll want a private place, so he can do a little violent payback. You want public. Stall and stall and stall."

"Fun," she said. "You?"

"I'm gonna have fun, too," I said. "Don't worry about me."

Lauren, who'd been immobile and quiet almost to the point of catatonia till now, said, "Roz is leaving. You're leaving. You expect me to stay here alone? With Joey in the closet?"

I wanted to point out that she was either alone or with Joey in the closet. Instead, noting her pallor and the shakiness in her voice, I said, "Why not take some time and visit a historical site? If you're not into Paul Revere's house, the Museum of Fine Arts is nice."

"I could visit Sam," she said in a small voice.

I called a cab to fetch her. I didn't care if she went to the museum or the zoo, as long as she wasn't around to turn Joey loose. I made a point of asking Roz to lock up after Lauren left.

"Make sure you turn the dead bolt," I said.

"You're going to leave him in a closet?" Now Lauren sounded both confused and skeptical.

"Maybe you'd better visit Sam," I said harshly. "Pay particular attention to his legs, Lauren. I'd dump your precious Joey in places that make my closet look like a suite at the Ritz-Carlton."

They wouldn't shoot me on sight, I thought as I drove through the winding streets of the North End. Papa Gianelli might spit on the ground and cross himself, but he'd hardly have me executed.

I found a parking place near St. Cecilia's. God's will or good luck. I patted the .40, snug in my waistband.

I wondered which of the loiterers I passed on my way to the Gianelli house would mention my presence first, crooning softly into the walkie-talkie concealed in his wino's paper bag. My neck prickled the way it does when I feel I'm under surveillance. How many top-floor apartments did the Gianellis own on this block? How many soldiers held the fort? Ever since the Angiulo brothers took the big fall from their Prince Street boardroom, North End underbosses have been on full alert.

I put some extra swing into my hip action. Give the guys something to look at. It would have played better in L.A. Boston in December, life's hard. Alluring doesn't come in layers from the L. L. Bean catalog.

On the other hand, layers covered the package I was carrying.

Gianelli central is a grand five-story corner brick, laced with ornamental ironwork balconies. Could be apartments, but it's all Anthony's personal living space. First floor looks like a respectable commercial establishment. Marble foyer. Single narrow staircase partially blocked by a regulation wooden desk. The second floor is astonishing, an art deco hallway leading to a kitchen that would do credit to a five-star restaurant. Two elevators, front and rear, key access only, lead to the rest of the house. Sam brought me here once, long ago, when every other family member was safely out of town.

A uniformed guard from rent-a-cop manned the desk. He was window dressing; the Gianellis didn't need anybody who charged above minimum wage for the job. By the time you approached the building, you'd been photographed, "made" if you were a cop, urged along the road if you happened to be a misguided Jehovah's Witness or hapless Greenpeace volunteer.

No one accosted me on the steps. Go figure. Women seem to throw the wiseguys off step. They don't know how to call it, even now, after quite a few of the Angiulo strike force turned out to be female. I could be a call girl, right?

I didn't think Papa'd be on the prowl for an outcall "date," but maybe Tony Junior, handsome Hollywood Tony, had a taste for purchased flesh.

I flashed a grin at the guard, who glanced up hastily from a magazine.

There were TV cameras in the four corners of the

lobby. Circular mounts on either side of the stairway hinted at infrared beams. And those were just the visible devices.

"Miss Carlyle," I said sweetly. "For Mr. Gianelli, Senior."

"Appointment?" The guard was flustered, but he managed to scratch my name on a pad.

"He'll see me," I said.

"I, uh, don't believe he's in at the moment."

"I don't think he goes out much," I replied.

"His, uh, son—"

"His son's in the hospital. I know. I just came from there. With an update."

"You're a friend of his son's?"

I started to run out of patience. I can only do the breathy young thing for a limited run. It wasn't working, so I switched to brusque. "Phone. Tell him I'm here. It doesn't matter if I'm a district attorney. Just mention my name and tell him I have something to give him."

"Wait outside, please."

"It's cold."

"I can't call unless you wait outside. Policy."

A good soldier, for all his paunch. If this guy'd been on duty at the Isabella Stewart Gardner Museum, they'd still have the Vermeer.

"You have another name besides Carlyle?" he asked.

I offered him one of my cards. I should have known I'd never get through to the old man.

I waited on the stoop long enough to wish I'd worn earmuffs and gloves. I try not to scoop them out of mothballs till Christmas, but this season was shaping up killer cold.

The guard left his station and motioned me inside.

"Upstairs," he said.

I felt light-headed with disbelief. I started rehearsing my speech.

"Leave the gun," the guard said.

"Metal detector?" I asked.

He nodded pleasantly. At his behest, I stuck the .40 in a drawer that already contained a Taurus .22, two Glock 9s, and a .357 Magnum. No way my gun would get lonely.

"You want me to tag it?" I asked, amazed by the small arsenal.

"I'll remember," he said. "Nice piece."

I bounded up the steps. Made it all the way to the second floor.

The blond woman who'd clung to Papa's arm blocked the ornate hallway. The third wife, the fourth wife? Stacey? No. I remembered Sam's dismissive laughter. "Stella!" he'd called her, imitating Brando.

The blonde looked like she might be imitating a movie star too. A soap opera diva. I took in the tight white sweater with rhinestones, the second-skin black stirrup pants. She was probably drenched in scent, but all I could smell was the cigarette smoke trailing from a butt in her taloned hand. I breathed deeply, sucking down my ration of second-hand ecstasy.

"What do you want?" she said.

That's the Boston Mob for you. Send a woman to talk to a woman. I almost asked for a cigarette. Five years on the wagon and I'm ready to topple anytime.

"I'm sorry to trouble you," I said earnestly. "The guard must have made a mistake. I need to talk to your father."

"He's not my—"

"I know," I said with a smile. "But he could be."

"Get out."

"I have information—"

"So you're Sam's piece of the action, huh?" She looked me over from stem to stern. "He could sure do better, that boy." Her voice was pure southern syrup. I couldn't tell if the accent was real, any more than I could tell if blond was her natural color or double D her God-given chest size.

"We could all do better, Mrs. Gianelli," I said, trying to keep a straight face. "I'm sorry if I insulted you. I only meant that you look very young."

"Thank you," she said uncertainly.

"I know your husband has had a bad week. I know he's an old, uh, older man. I won't take much of his time."

"Maybe you could see Mitch or Tony."

I said, "I don't think you're hearing what I'm saying."

"I don't think you get it, hon. No is no. You can't see him."

"Life and death," I said.

"For who?"

I didn't bother correcting her grammar. "His son," I said.

"His sons are grown men. They handle their own lives."

"He cares about them," I said. "Grown men or not."

"He's not well; he can't be disturbed," she said.

"Let him make the decision himself. Don't you owe him that?"

"Wait here," she said coldly. She swayed to the end of the hall, stopped before a brass-and-glass table, opened a rosewood box, extracted a telephone receiver. Punched buttons.

"Life and death," I called after her.

She spoke for some time, then waved the instrument at me. I hastened to take it.

"Mr. Gianelli?"

The voice was raw and angry. "You'd think I could send one bitch to talk to another. Wouldn't you say that was a reasonable assumption?"

He's an old man, I reminded myself. My hand tightened on the receiver.

"We should do this face-to-face," I said.

"I'll have you thrown out," he countered.

"I think I know who tried to kill Sam."

"Think? You think? Tell me when you really know."

"Mr. Gianelli—"

"My son gets himself blown the hell up with colored people. How does that make me look? In the community?"

"You don't want to know, do you?" I said. "Or maybe you already know."

He spoke in Italian then, and I couldn't understand anything except the hatred. I waited for a pause in his invective. None came, just the click when he hung up.

When I'd visited the house two wives ago, a portrait of Sam's mother hung in the hallway. It was gone without a trace. Not a mark in the perfect white paint.

I left my package—diskettes and confession—with

the guard at the door, trading them for my automatic. He made me open the parcel. No exploding envelopes for Papa G.

"Seems okay," the guard said.

"Let me add a little something," I said.

"What?" He looked at me like he was expecting folding money to materialize in my hand.

I borrowed a pen, scrawled a single line on the back of Joey's confession.

Ask your accountant it said.

Then I reassembled the package and told the guard to deliver it to Anthony Senior. To no one but Anthony Gianelli, Senior. In person.

He seemed uncertain. I dropped a twenty on the floor; his foot covered it before the corner-mounted cameras could record the transaction. We had a deal.

He shook his head as I left, like a grandfather mourning a grandchild gone wrong.

FORTY-TWO

Roz got home a good three hours later than I did. She was cheerful for a woman who'd spent most of her day at the cop house, having successfully ID'd the taller goon, a man with an awesome rap sheet displaying a broad assortment of dismissed felonies. Often, the complainant changed his or her mind about preferring charges. Sometimes the complainant left town hurriedly or disappeared completely.

Roz can read between the lines. She'd expected to find an intimidator. Even on the phone, he was loud, obnoxious, and threatening. No sense of humor, she complained.

A meeting was set for tomorrow night at a crowded Faneuil Hall watering hole.

I'd notify Mooney beforehand. I'd already left the floppies and Joey's statement for Papa G. I went down a mental list, putting an invisible check against each item. In volleyball terms, the match was mine. Twelve-to-one in the deciding game, my turn at net, and a six-inch advantage over the opposing blocker. No contest.

Joey Fresh remained in the closet. Lauren was spending the night in the beige room, far down the hall. With so many in the house, I'd begged off when Keith proposed to add one more, even though the extra body would have been warm and welcome, and wouldn't have taken up much space.

Keith said he'd succeeded in provoking Gloria to anger; he saw that as progress.

Sam had a gaggle of undercover police guards.

Everything under control.

Except the timing.

When I heard footsteps in the middle of the night, my first thought was that goddamned Joey had Houdinied himself out of the closet.

I grabbed the pistol from under my pillow. When I hold captives, I sleep lightly. I keep loaded weapons in unsafe places. Another reason to disappoint Keith.

Too many voices, low and gutteral. Lauren's was the sole high note, and she sounded frantic. Lauren wouldn't be terrified by an escaped Joey Frascatti. She'd still see a nineteen-year-old boy, frightened out of his wits, covered with another kid's blood.

Roz slept upstairs alone. I didn't like the odds.

I keep my bedroom door closed at night. I slid the bolt home silently. It wouldn't stop anyone for long. I lifted the phone. Dead, which I expected.

A professional invasion.

I yanked on the jeans lying at the foot of my bed,

more to have a place to shove the pistol than for decency's sake. I'd freeze in my tank top, but risking the squeak of a drawer was out of the question.

I stuffed two pillows lengthwise in my bed, threw the quilt over them, and tucked them in like a baby.

I slid up the window sash, going for speed rather than silence. It banged like a shot in the night. Listen up, neighbors, I thought.

I've lived in this house since I was sixteen. Since my mother died in Detroit, and I got sent to live with her older sister because nobody else wanted me. For a while I wasn't sure Beatrice wanted me either. I always kept an escape hatch. A downspout to an elm tree, a five-foot drop.

I hadn't used it since I was eighteen. Lighter, scrappier, with fewer broken bones and scars and sprained ankles. At eighteen I never, *never*, thought about falling.

Didn't have that back-of-the-neck tingle to contend with either, the image of a gun barrel aimed at my heart or my head.

The downspout was less than firmly connected to the roof. Had it always had that sway, that slight bounce? I twined my legs and inched my way down in blackness. The tree. How far to its sheltering branches? As soon as I had the thought, one poked itself at my behind. A skinny branch. No help. I shinned farther down the spout, praying it would hold, testing the area around my feet for a good crotchlike branch. It ought to fucking be there. I hadn't pruned the damned tree.

I stepped into it and sank low. I could hear voices from my room. The bedroom light flashed on. Good.

Ruin their night vision. Suddenly it snapped off. I held on to the branch and extended my body full-length. If anybody was gazing out the living room window, he'd have an easy pickoff. Quick drop and roll, or protect the ankle? I heard a shout that made up my mind for me. Quick drop, forward roll, out of the crouch running.

Keith's seemed miles away.

"Nine one one," I hollered through the door as soon as I heard the jangle of chain.

"What?" he said.

"Yell. Life and death. Whatever the hell you can think of to make it as top priority as top priority gets."

"What? Where are you—?"

"I'll be back," I said.

"I'll be there."

"Don't you fucking dare," I screamed. "Just call the police."

Then I really ran.

FORTY-THREE

A spindly black ladder rested against the back of the house. Like "Frank," they must have slipped in through the kitchen window. Why hadn't I nailed it shut?

I had choices: I could enter the same way; I could wait for the cops. Turnaround time on the 911 depended on intangibles: who was riding dispatch; what else was going down in Cambridge tonight. Would Keith Donovan choose the right words? "In progress. Break-in. Shots fired." I should have told him the code. He knew hospital lingo, not cop talk. I wriggled my bare toes in the freezing grass, crossed my arms, and tucked my hands under my armpits to keep them warm.

They had Lauren. Lauren might give up Joey. Lauren, believing they wanted the actual culprit, would talk. I imagined Joey, locked in the big closet, hearing voices in the dark.

I dug my pistol deeper into the back of my jeans, made sure the tank top covered it. Then I rang the front doorbell. I didn't have my keys.

I kept ringing. Got a good rhythm going. Twenty-two times before Roz said, "Who's there?"

"Me."

"Run!" she yelled. "You don't wanna be here."

The door swung open and Mitch—Sam's brother, good old Mitch, the middle boy—grabbed my wrist and hauled me inside.

"Where'd you go?" he demanded. He was dressed in baggy black sweats. His face was ruddy and his breath came hard.

"Where do you think? You didn't cut the phone lines on the whole block."

He chewed his lower lip. You could practically see wheels turning in his head as he glanced at his watch. "Give me the computer disks and we're history. We can forget this."

"It's gone too far for a kiss-off," I said.

"She packing?" one of Mitch's associates asked. I recognized the big goon from Sam's apartment. He was gleefully dangling Roz by her hair, one meaty hand twined in the colored strands. A bizarre marionette, she barely managed to balance on the tips of her toes.

"Here's her piece," Mitch said scornfully, waving my old .38. The bottom left-hand drawer of my desk hung open. Must have busted the lock. "Some big-time investigator. Keeps her gun wrapped in her ex's undershirt. Sam told me all about it. She couldn't bronze her ex's balls, so she keeps the shirt for a trophy."

"It's just you, Mitch, right?" I asked, feeling the weight of the new .40 sag my waistband. "Solo. Gil and Tony don't know."

"About what?" he said with an innocent smirk.

I didn't like taking my eyes off Mitch, but I had to view the damage. Lauren, sprawled on a chair near the arch leading to the dining room, clasped a hand to a reddened cheek. An unfamiliar man loomed over her.

She caught my eye, inhaled; she was ready to speak.

"I can't believe Papa G knows," I said, jumping in before Lauren could open her mouth.

"Always yapping," Mitch complained.

"You're the mouth, Mitch," I continued, willing Lauren to shut up. "Volunteering that crap about Sam selling the company. I almost believed you. On the whole, you did a hell of a job."

"Shut up," Mitch said.

"I like a good story." The goon near Lauren had a surprisingly high voice.

"Harry," Mitch snapped, "shut it."

Harry didn't seem intimidated. I made sure my voice was loud enough to reach him.

"What I like best is the way you took advantage of an already existing situation. You played Cochran and Yancey like a pair of violins, Mitch. Really. You have my admiration."

"I don't need it. I've got your gun. I want Sam's disks."

"Then there's the long-range planning," I said. "You hire a nasty little shit like Zach, figure Gloria'll take the kid on as a driver, but he's only around long enough to check the lay of the land. He quits and all the pieces are in place. Small owners always feel paranoid about medallions; you stoke the paranoia with rumors, rumors spiced with truth. Yancey's probably gonna try to move to leases, right? Make major money. You provide the spark to ignite the blaze. Simple. Two anonymous phone calls: one to Cochran; a follow-up to Yancey. You dial 'em yourself? Or did one of your goons do that?"

"The disks," he said, idly aiming my .38 at various parts of my body. "You shouldn't have taken them."

"You pay Zach and a couple freelance punks, nobody with Mob connections, to beat up cabbies, folks from Green and White, other small companies, independents. Zach knows the routine, how to kill the lights, the safety flashers."

"Good for him," Mitch said scathingly. "Never met the guy. I understand he blew himself to kingdom come."

"Mitchell," I said. "You made mistakes. The drive-by was stupid. What? You got impatient? Things moving too slowly for you? Maybe you were hoping Sam might take a shift when drivers got scarce, get killed in one of your staged robberies? He never would, Mitch. You know why? He promised your dad; Sam never drives."

Mitchell licked his chapped lips, grunted.

I hurried on. "You were lucky; nobody identified the drive-by shooters. Were you one of them, by the way?"

"Shut up," he said.

"I'll take that as a yes. So Zach keeps the game going, spreading the beatings around. You want it clear that Green and White's *a* target, but not *the* target.

When it comes, you want the explosion to seem like cab business, not Mob business."

"You always talk this much?" Mitch asked.

"You ought to know," I said. "You bugged G and W. You nabbed the old FBI mikes. You're the 'expert' Sam trusted. He'd trust his big brother, wouldn't he?"

"You done?"

"No," I said. "Actually I'm not. I have a major question, the big one: *Would you need that kind of dog-and-pony show if your dad wanted Sam dead?* Papa wants it done, I hear it gets done."

"Some decisions an old man shouldn't have to make," Mitch said, with more dignity than I'd expected. "Sam took our money. He took Gotti money, Gambino money. Nobody takes my money."

"Is this about money, Mitch?" I asked. "Or is this about hate? Jealousy? You've known cash was leaking out of G and W for months. You hung the bugs hoping to catch Sam on tape, saying things so damning Papa would have backed you up, applauded your gumption."

"Sam's a friggin' traitor; he travels to Washington every other day. Rats on us to some Senate subcommittee. Talks to Joey Fresh, visits the old creep in jail."

"If he'd said one word about the Senate on tape, you'd have had him cold. He didn't. So you tried to work a scam that couldn't come back at you, so Papa'd never know that you'd had Sam killed. Lucky Zach blew himself up and died when he did. His type, he'd have bled you for years."

Lauren said, "Wait—"

My voice rolled over hers. "I guess you wouldn't

want to go to Papa, Mitch. With nothing but computer disks for evidence. I mean, he knows you're good with numbers, but how's he going to react, you figure? Sam's the baby boy. Papa loves Sammy. Papa always loved Sam. Wore out the knees on his pants praying when Sam was in Vietnam, right? Sure, the old man wishes Sam were in the business, but Papa's proud of Sam, proud that one of his sons is making it on his own. Maybe he's gonna decide Sam's more valuable than you, Mitch. What exactly is it do you do for the family? You the brains of the outfit?"

He slapped me across the face. I sucked in my breath. Lauren screamed.

The scream wasn't for me, wasn't for the welt raised when Mitch's heavy ring scratched my cheek. It was for the revolver that suddenly appeared in Harry's hand. Lauren must have thought he was going to fire at her. Then, when he strode across the living room, at me. I flinched, didn't turn away.

Harry with the tenor voice, Mitch's companion and accomplice, placed the barrel of the revolver in Mitch's right ear. It was a small gun, a .22. I thought I recognized it from the drawer on Hanover Street. Taurus. Nine-shot cylinder.

"Harry. What?" Mitch's voice cracked. He dropped my .38 to the floor with a clatter.

"From your father," the man said in his high-pitched voice. "He told me, wait till you admitted it, in front of witnesses, that you tried to kill your brother."

"Come on, Harry. Put the fucker down. Sam's fine. He's okay. Come on—"

Harry kept talking. "Your dad told me tell you this,

Mitch, at the end. The last thing you're gonna hear: he said tell you he only had three sons."

The .22 hardly made more than a pop, the sound of a champagne cork. Mitch slumped to the floor.

Up till then, I thought the rest of us had a chance. Now the game had changed. Harry had no incentive to leave live witnesses.

I yanked the .40 from my waistband, released the safety.

"Scatter!" I yelled, throwing myself to the ground. Roz chinned herself on the big goon's arm, bit, kicked, and dropped, rolled behind a chair, screaming at the top of her lungs. Lauren found the strength to propel herself into the dining room. Harry, staring sadly at the floor, like a guy who'd had to put down his favorite dog, didn't react quickly enough. I fired and kept firing to let them know this was not going to be some easy mop-up job.

A puff of hot air passed my left ear. It had a sobering effect.

Lying flat on the ground, arms propped on elbows, my left hand steadying the unfamiliar .40, I stopped fooling around, sighted and aimed. Harry went down.

I dived past him, rolled behind my desk, hitting the floor with elbows and knees, keeping the gun protected. Behind me, over my head, shots pounded the computer. The screen imploded with a boom, shattering into a hundred shards. The machinery sparked, hissing like a nest of snakes.

I heard sirens. Welcome, blessed sirens.

I stopped shooting. The remaining gunman staggered out the door.

"When they question you," I yelled at Lauren, my

voice too harsh, too loud. "Shut up. Just shut up. You're a friend who came to visit. You don't know anything except what you saw tonight and you're not clear on that. Nothing, *nothing* about Joey! Roz, you okay?"

Silence.

"Roz!"

"Fucker ripped some of my hair out," she whimpered softly.

I breathed again.

"Run upstairs and tell Joey to keep it zipped."

"Why? Shit. Yes."

"Hurry back down."

I refused to speak to a cop till Mooney came.

FORTY-FOUR

By the time we released him, Joey Frascatti was all too ready to leave his closet. After hours of police interrogation—separate, en masse, in Cambridge, in Boston—none of us smelled like a spring breeze, but Joey took the honors.

Blinking in bright light, he seemed most horrified by the destruction of the computer. Its smoldering ruins bothered him a lot more than the stinking closet or the taped outline on the dark floorboards where Mitch Gianelli had bled away his life. Joey didn't grieve over my smashed knickknacks and broken windows. The bullet holes that admitted gusts of icy wind didn't faze him.

He took the cash, stuffed in a knapsack and a pillowcase. He promised not to write.

"Fuck him," Lauren said after he'd left. Then she sat on the sofa and began a serious crying jag. As I tacked plywood, I recalled my first view of "Frank's" tripledecker, with cardboard taped over the windows to shut out the light.

"Lauren could have been in love with Joey all these years," Keith said later, in bed. "After things went sour between her and Sam, she could have fixated on Joey, imagined him as the unattainable Mr. Right."

My head rested on his shoulder. His arm encircled me, fingertips massaging the nape of my neck. We were at his place. Crime-scene tape blocked the door to my house.

"I hope not," I muttered. "A world-class jerk."

"Turned out to be a world-class jerk. Must have been different once, to make two people care enough to give him a new life. Not many people get that, a brand-new life."

"Fucked up twice," I said.

"Which is probably what we'd all do, screw up over again."

"You're full of cheer."

"More than I can say for you."

"I'm not looking forward to my next assignment," I said.

"Oh," Keith responded in his noncommittal way. I could see why patients would accept the gambit, reveal their secrets.

Not me, I thought. I don't need a shrink, thank you, just a warm body to help me through the night.

I have legit P.I. work. Leaving tomorrow, traveling to Traverse City, Michigan, to explain to a family how their son and brother died some twenty years ago.

Quickly. In the dark. On a muddy path leading to a numbered hill. I'm leaving my new gun at home; airport security doesn't like them. I shouldn't need one for this case.

Mooney says it's a good time to leave town.

I've warned Lauren and Sam that I'm planning to tell the truth, the unvarnished truth as I've heard it. I wasn't there. If Floyd Markham's family wants to kick up a fuss, so be it. Sam sets great store by their Catholicism, says they probably accept and believe that their boy is in the arms of the Lord. If your martyred son resides in eternal paradise, it won't matter where his earthly remains are buried. Sam's counting on that.

I visited Joey Frascatti's tomb. I can describe the grassy slope, the dogwood trees, the vault, the Carrara marble angel that stands guard over their son. I hope the Markham clan won't ask me to.

If they want proof, if the Markhams need the certainty of closure, if they demand to exhume the remains buried as Joseph Frascatti Junior, that's up to them. It's their call.

Sam and Lauren are paying me well to take this trip, to face the mistake they made long ago. Sam even offered to buy me a new computer. I accepted. Nothing fancy. This time I'm planning to go legit, link up to a specialized network for private eyes, Investigators' Online Network or the PI SIG on CompuServe, whichever's cheapest.

If there's going to be an information superhighway out there, I'll be the one tooling along in a rusting pickup truck.

FORTY-FIVE

Two and a half weeks after Marvin's funeral, I picked up Gloria at Mass. General. She wanted to go for a ride in her van. Her doctors didn't object; they thought it might do her good. She wasn't eating. Not that the docs were against a judicious diet, but she wasn't eating, period. The skin on her upper arms was starting to hang loose. Her cheeks looked like withered apples.

I wasn't surprised when she asked to stop at Green & White.

I wheeled her close to the wreckage. The ramp leading to the back room's entry was melted and twisted into a tortured metal sculpture. Signs declared the building unsafe for habitation. The doors were boarded shut.

"Not much to see," I hazarded.

"Miracle they saved the buildings on either side," she muttered.

"The fire department did a hell of a job," I said.

Gloria inhaled a deep breath of motor-exhaust-filled air. "I'm gonna rebuild," she said.

I closed my eyes and swallowed hard. It was the first positive thing I'd heard her say since the disaster, unless you counted the *amens* at Marvin's funeral. . . .

She'd arrived and departed by ambulance. Flat on a gurney during the service, flanked by Leroy and Geoffrey. Of all the mourners in the New Faith Baptist Church, hers was the voice that rang in my dreams, chiming the *amens* in the calm, majestic note of a believer.

"We still own the medallions," she said. "We have insurance."

"Enough?" I asked.

Gloria wheeled her chair forward, taking particular care to avoid a rut in the pavement.

"Someone sent me a check," she said. "It should cover costs. Take care of your fee."

"Someone?"

"Anthony Gianelli, Senior, is the name on the dotted line."

I didn't respond.

"So, what do you think?" she asked.

Most of the cinderblocks had crumbled or toppled; some were jet-black with ash-gray edges, like giant charcoal briquets.

"It's his way of apologizing," I said. "Acknowledging his family's responsibility. He's not big on apologies."

"Doesn't seem right," Gloria said.

"What?"

"It feels—shit, I don't know—like he's paying me

off for Marvin's death. Like there was anything money could do to replace my brother."

"The check's an apology," I said. "Only that."

"Would you have trouble taking that kind of money, Carlotta? From that kind of man?"

"Gloria," I said. "You never heard this. . . ."

"What?" she said, immediately keen, sensing gossip.

"Paolina's biological father has sent me over forty thousand dollars in the past six months."

The wheelchair did a quick half-circle so she could face me. "That bastard, Roldan Gonzales?" she said.

"Alleged bastard," I said. "I haven't sent it back. I haven't donated it to charity."

"So, do you have a problem with where that money comes from?" Gloria asked, eyes wide and intent.

"It's money; it can send Paolina to college."

"Yes, but—"

"Why encourage deadbeat dads?" I asked, kicking at a pebble-size chunk of blackened stucco. It skittered fifty feet, came to a rest under a chain link fence.

"Guess that means you don't object to me cashing Papa Gianelli's check."

I said, "It means I'm not exactly the best person to ask."

"I don't know about that," she said pensively. "Least you've had experience."

We surveyed the ruins. Someone had swept the broken glass into a heap.

"Will Sam still be your partner?" I asked.

Gloria said, "I'm not sure. Depends."

I waited for her to continue. She seemed to have more to say.

"I may change the name of the company."

I stared at chunks of grimy concrete. It was hard to imagine the outline of the garage doors.

"I was thinking, maybe, 'Marvin's,'" she said.

"I like that," I agreed. "Nice sound to it. I'll bring a bottle of champagne, christen the new garage when the time comes."

"Bottle of Bass ale," Gloria said. "More Marvin's style."

"Fine," I said.

"He had style," Gloria said. "He kept the family together when most guys would have run as far and as fast as they could. Promoters begged him to go to Las Vegas, box the circuit, travel the country. He was that good. But then I had my accident, and he said no."

"It's okay," I said.

"It's just, I feel like he gave up his life for me. Twice. And that's too much."

"Gloria," I said. "It was his choice."

"Right," she said. "That's what your shrink says. His choice. I never could tell Marvin anything."

"Remember that. He was stubborn as hell, and he loved you."

"Guess I've seen enough," she offered fifteen minutes later. I was glad. It was cold. Gloria didn't seem to feel it, but I did.

"Think Paolina's home?" she asked, once I'd managed the business with the hydraulic lift and strapped her wheelchair into the shotgun position. "We could visit."

I said, "We could take her over to Herrell's for ice cream. Mocha with M&M moosh-ins."

"Think they'd put whipped cream on that?" Gloria inquired wistfully.

I never thought I'd be glad to hear Gloria ask about whipped cream.

I said, "I think it's illegal unless you order hot fudge."

"Hot fudge," Gloria repeated, like it was a vaguely familiar phrase from a language she'd once spoken fluently.

"Paolina'd like that," I said.

Gloria waited for a red light to stick in the dart. "She'd like it better if you and Sam got back together."

A battered Pontiac Grand Prix sounded its horn, passed on my right in a lane clearly designated for parking only.

" 'You can't always get what you want,' " I quoted.

"Marvin liked that song," she said. "Stones, right? 'But if you try sometimes . . .' "

"I know the rest," I said.

As we crossed the River Street Bridge, I finished the lyric in my head: "You just might find you get what you need."

What did Paolina need?

Her biological father? Carlos Roldan Gonzales?

"What do you think he's like?" She'd asked after our last volleyball game, staring at her reflection in the makeup mirror on the car's visor, sweeping up her hair to make herself look older.

"I don't know," I'd said.

"Carlotta?"

"Honey, leave your hair down."

"Someday, maybe, will you go with me to find my father?"

"Maybe," I'd said. "Maybe."

From the flash of her sudden smile, I knew she'd taken that second, hesitant *maybe* as a *yes*.

She's young; maybe she'll forget about it.

"Marvin's Cabs," Gloria said. "What color do you think we should paint 'em?"

"If his word were a bridge, I'd be afraid to cross." Or, as my *bubbe*, my mother's mother, would have said, in Yiddish rather than English, *"Oyb zayn vort volt gedint als brik volt men moyre gehat aribertsugeyn."*

Trust me, it's funnier in Yiddish. I know, I know: Yiddish is the voice of exile, the tongue of ghettos, but I'll shed a tear when it joins ancient Greek and dead Latin. For gossip and insult, you can't beat Yiddish.

I imagined that shaky bridge the entire time I was talking on the phone. Caught another glimpse of it later, while interviewing my client. But that's getting ahead of the story, something my grandmother would never do. *"A gute haskhole iz shoyn a halbe arbet,"* she'd say: "A good beginning is the job half done."

* * *

The lawyer's voice oozed condescension over a long-distance connection so choppy, it made me wonder if Fidel Castro was personally eavesdropping.

"Excuse me," he said firmly, the words a polite substitution for "shut up." Enunciating as though he were attempting communication with a dull-witted four-year-old, he went on. "I believe this conversation would be better suited to a pay phone. I'll ring you in, say, half an hour."

I've never met Thurman W. Vandenburg, Esquire. My mind snapped an imaginary photo: the tanned, lined face of a man fighting middle age, a smile that showed off perfectly capped teeth, pointed like a barracuda's.

"The same phone we used before, *if* you can remember the location—" he continued.

I stopped him with "I'm sitting in that very booth, mister. And you're eating up my dwindling change pile. I don't want trouble. I want the shipments to stop. *¿Entiende usted?*"

There: I'd managed five sentences without interruption. I'd included the key words: *Trouble, shipments, stop.* I hadn't said *money*. He'd understand I meant money.

"I'll call back in ten minutes," he replied tersely.

"Wait! No! I have a client, an appointment—"

I white-knuckled the receiver. I hate it when sleazy lawyers hang up on me. Hell, I hate it when genteel lawyers hang up on me, not that I have much occasion to chat with any. It's not that classy lawyers with plush offices and desks the size of skating rinks are a dying breed. It's just that I don't come into contact with the cream of the crop in the normal run of my business.

I compared my Timex with the wall-mounted model over the pharmacist's counter. *If* he actually called back within ten minutes, and *if* my after-hours client ran on the late side, I might barely squeak in the door ahead of him.

I wish drugstores still had soda fountains. I could have relaxed on a red vinyl stool, spinning a salute to my childhood, sipping a cherry coke, and reviewing my potential client's plight, a situation distinguished more by his breathless, excited voice than its unique nature. Missing persons are a dime a dozen. Amazing, the number of people in this anonymous big-city world who think they can make a fresh start elsewhere, wipe their blotted slates clean.

There was no soda fountain. Instead of enjoying refreshment, I lurked in the aisles, for all the world a shoplifter, or a woman too chickenshit to buy a box of Trojans from a pimple-faced teenaged clerk. The newsrack provided momentary diversion, what with the *Star* trumpeting "Death Row Inmate Gives Birth to Alien Triplets!"

The *Herald* led with a local story: "Will Voters Go for Divorced Candidate Wed to Woman 18 Years Younger?" *Boston* magazine handled the same business more tastefully, focusing on the upcoming gubernatorial race with a simple, "Cameron: The Man Who Would Be King."

By the time the phone rang nine minutes and forty-five seconds later, I'd guiltily purchased a pack of spearmint TicTacs for eighty-nine cents. Thurman W. Vandenburg, aka Miami Sleaze, might not be my idea of an upstanding member of the bar, but he was prompt.

"Nothing I can do," he said, not waiting for me to speak.

"Well, I can do something," I replied quickly. "Expect a large package of cash in the mail. I'll bet you know dodges the IRS hasn't come across more than a million times."

"The situation is somewhat delicate."

"Sure it is, buddy, but I'm out. I've managed to invest Paolina's cash so far. Legit. It ends here. *No mas.*"

"I never approved of this," the lawyer snapped. "There's no evidence that she's his daughter."

"Except he sends money," I replied dryly. "What's your problem? Afraid he can't pay your fees?"

"He's missing," Vandenburg said softly.

It took a minute for the words to sink in.

"No names," Vandenburg insisted.

"Jesus Christ," I murmured slowly. "Ooops, that's a name. Sorry."

Total silence followed by a muffled eruption. Could have been Vandenburg chuckling. Could have been Castro swallowing his cigar.

"No names," I repeated.

"I've been out of touch with our mutual friend," Vandenburg said, "for a certain number of days. That sets off a chain of events, financial and otherwise. I don't think you'll be bothered."

"Is he dead?"

"I have no idea."

"Don't blow me off. I need to know. *Is he dead?*"

Thurman W. Vandenburg terminated the call. No doubt he'd been clocking it with a stopwatch. No doubt he knew exactly how long it would take the DEA to get a lock on the pay phone.

The drugstore on Huron Avenue boasts one of the last of the true phone booths, with a tiny seat and a bi-fold door, a poignant reminder that once upon a time phone calls were considered private conversations. Ma Bell installed it and NYNEX obviously hasn't found it yet. If they had, they'd have ripped it out, gone for the handy-dandy wall model.

I automatically scanned the aisles before exiting. I assumed the Drug Enforcement Agency would be all over Vandenburg's calls simply because word is out: If you get nailed on possession of a narcotic substance in the great state of Florida, who ya gonna call? Vandenburg.

So I wasn't surprised to see him. Dismayed, yes, but not surprised. He wasn't watching me, wasn't waiting like a total idiot, cuffs in hand. He was strolling the aisles and his mild-mannered-browser routine might have worked if not for the incredibly hot weather, which surely wasn't his fault. His Windbreaker drew my attention like a red flag. The bulge under his armpit riveted my glance. The outline of a holstered gun is unmistakable.

I had no desire to explain my Miami connection to the DEA. My fingertips touched 911 as I slid slowly to the floor of the booth, my T-shirt riding up in back. The cool wall tingled against my sweaty skin.

The Cambridge emergency dispatcher answered on a single ring. That-a-girl!

I pitched my voice deliberately high, lisped, and

paused in a childlike way. "Um, uh, there's a man with a gun," I said cheerfully.

I heard a muted thud, like the woman had set down a coffee cup in a hurry. "Where, honey? Now, don't you hang up, child," she said.

"In the drugstore," I replied in my singsong little voice. "Mark's Drugs, I think. On Huron Avenue. I'm with Mommy and the man has a gun, just like on TV."

"Good girl, honey. What's your name? Can you leave the phone off the hook—"

I didn't hear the rest of her advice because I was crawling toward the back door, situated behind the pharmacy counter. The front door sports a string of bells to signal customer entrances and exits. The back door doesn't. I wedged my behind through the opening and slithered from air-conditioned cool into the inverted air mass that had hovered over Boston for the best part of a late July week, holding temperatures above eighty, redlining the pollution index. A streetlamp cast a yellowish haze. The night air hung thick and noxious: recycled exhaust fumes, heavy and sticky as a steam bath.

Ouch. Somebody ought to sweep the damned alley occasionally, I thought. Clear away the busted beer bottles. I inched my way forward. Glass, or maybe a sharp pebble, pierced my right knee. I felt for cleaner pavement, glanced up.

No visible observers. Distant approaching sirens. I'd have loved to hang around, listened to the Cambridge cops dispute territorial rights with the DEA.

Instead, I stood, quickly brushing my kneecaps,

and walked home, thankful I'd dipped into my savings for Paolina's three-week stay at a YWCA-run camp on a perfect New Hampshire lake. No chance she'd see a newspaper in the backwoods. If anything dreadful had happened, or did happen to her dad, she wouldn't run across some gruesome death-scene photo unprepared. . . .

I'd never told Paolina, my Little Sister from the Big Sisters Association, that I'd been in touch with her biological father, the alleged drug baron Carlos Roldan Gonzales. It had never come up in conversation. I'd never mentioned his irregular cash shipments.

I found myself hoping Carlos Roldan Gonzales was dead, then trying to take back the thought as if it had some power to do the deed. His death would make my life easier, no doubt about that. I'd never have to explain. I could present Paolina with the money as a gift, me to her, no intermediary, no ugly stain on cash that must surely have come from the drug trade. It could be what I'd named it for the IRS's benefit: track winnings. Simple luck, passed on with love from Big Sister to Little Sister. College. Travel. An apartment of her own when she turned eighteen . . .

Except it would all be a lie without Carlos Roldan Gonzales's name attached.

Lies don't usually bother me much, but I try not to lie to Paolina. She means too much to me. And lies have a sneaky way of tiptoeing back to haunt you.

I glanced at my watch and doubled my pace, vaulting a fence, cutting diagonally through my backyard.

I wondered if the guy had really been DEA or just a

casual drugstore holdup man. The cops would go a hell of a lot tougher on him if he were DEA. I know; I used to be a cop. They hate federal poachers.

Safely in my kitchen, I downed an icy Pepsi straight from the can, standing in front of the open refrigerator to bring my temperature down from boil. Then I stuck my hair in a stretchy cloth band, bobby-pinning it haphazardly to the top of my head. I was dabbing my sweaty neck with a wadded paper towel when the doorbell rang.

A prompt sleazy lawyer followed by a prompt potential client. What more could a private investigator want?

As I marched toward the front door, I wondered what lies Vandenburg, the sleaze, had slipped by me, what half-truths he'd told. What lies would this client try? With a touch—hell, a wallop—of vanity, I consider myself an expert in the field of lies; a collector, if you will. I've seen liars as fresh and obvious as newborn babes; a quick twitch of the eye, a sudden glance at the floor immediately giving the game away. I've interviewed practiced, skilled liars, blessed with the impeccable timing of ace stand-up comics. I don't know why I recognize lies. Somebody will be shooting his mouth, and I'll feel or hear a change of tone, a shift of pace. Maybe it's instinct. Maybe I got so used to lies when I was a cop that I suspect everyone.

I'd rather trust people. Given the choice.

My potential client beamed a hundred-watt smile when I opened the door, bounded into the foyer like an overgrown puppy. Even if he'd been a much younger man I'd have found his outright enthusiasm strange.

The number of people pleased to visit a private investigator is noticeably fewer than the number eagerly anticipating gum surgery.

He'd seemed both agitated and exhilarated on the phone that afternoon, otherwise I wouldn't have agreed to an evening appointment. He'd mentioned a missing person, given his name with no hint of reluctance. I'd checked with the Boston police; there was no file currently open on anyone sharing a last name with Mr. Adam Mayhew. Which left a ton of possibilities. Different last name. Hadn't been absent the required twenty-four hours. The missing individual might be considered a voluntary—a walkaway or runaway adult.

Possibly my client-to-be knew exactly where the missing person could be found. Quick case; low fee.

Which would be too bad, because the sixtyish gentleman currently shifting his weight from one foot to the other as though testing my wooden floorboards looked like he could donate megabucks to the worthy cause of my upkeep and not miss a single dollar. His shoes were Bally or a damned good imitation, slip-on tassle loafers with neither a too-new nor too-used sheen. Well-maintained classics, indicating a man with more than one pair of shoes to his wardrobe. A man with a hard-working wife who pressed his trousers after each wearing, or a gent with access to a good dry cleaning establishment. A formal soul, rigged out in full business attire on a shirtsleeves, sweat-hot evening.

No wedding band. Inconclusive. A class ring, the Harvard Veritas, common enough around here, but worn with justifiable pride.

Hair silvering nicely, hairline receding. Height: five nine, which made it easy for me, from my six-one vantage, to note that his crown was not yet thinning.

Fingernails buffed and filed. Hands well cared for. Prosperous. My kind of client. A lawyer? A doctor? A respected businessman? The speed from the phone call to initial appointment had curtailed my research.

"Mr. Mayhew?"

"Yes," he agreed cheerfully. "And you're Miss Carlyle."

He'd been eyeing me as carefully as I'd been observing him. I wondered what conclusions he'd drawn from my disheveled appearance and casual attire.

If the unexpected, unwanted cash hadn't arrived, I'd have attempted to dress for success. Worn makeup to accent my green—well, hazel, really, almost green—eyes, and belittle my thrice-broken nose. I'd have done battle with my tangled red hair.

I opened my mouth to utter polite excuses, realized that Mr. Mayhew didn't seem to expect them. I liked the way his level glance concentrated on my eyes, as though the measure of a woman were not in her clothes or her curves, but hidden in a secret compartment beyond all external gifts and curses.

I nodded him down the single step to my living room cum office.

"You may call me Adam," he said.

"Carlotta," I replied. I liked his lived-in, good-humored face—lines, pouches, bags, and all. His eyes were blue behind bifocal lenses, and seemed shy and oddly defenseless, as though the glass barrier were necessary for protection as well as visual acuity.

He toted a battered mongrammed briefcase of caramel-colored leather. Forty years ago it might have been a college graduation gift.

"I've wanted to do this for so long," he said as he settled into the upright chair next to my desk.

"Excuse me," I said. "You've wanted to do what for so long? Visit a PI's office?"

If the guy was a flake, I wanted him out. He didn't seem like a thrill-seeker. He seemed genuine. Sympathetic. So sympathetic I was tempted to tell him my troubles with Paolina and the drug money. I shook myself out of it.

"On the phone—" I began.

"Do you remember Thea Janis?" he said at the same time, glancing at me expectantly. "The writer."

Writer jogged my memory.

"It was a long time ago," I said, struggling to recall a faint whisper of ancient scandal relegated to some distant storage locker in my mind like so much cast-off furniture. "I remember reading her book."

"Not when it was published," he said. "You're too young."

"When I was fifteen, maybe sixteen." Over half a lifetime ago. My mother had bought it for me three months before she died. Did I still have it? The title hovered tantalizingly out of reach, a ripe fruit on a high branch.

"Thea was younger than that when she wrote it," he said. He could have uttered the words dismissively. Or flippantly. But he spoke with longing, with fervency and desire. Triumph as he added, "She was fourteen. Imagine. Fourteen. The critics didn't know that at first.

Unqualified praise. When they learned the book had been penned by a child, a teenager, the bouquets turned a bit thorny, almost as if some critics felt they'd been duped, not given the real goods somehow. Jealousy. Nothing more than jealousy."

"Why do you say that?"

"She was the goods," he answered simply. "A prodigy. We find it acceptable in music. Mozart."

"Thea Janis was a literary Mozart?"

"See? You can't keep the skepticism out of your voice. It's automatic. Cinematic prodigies, okay. Visual arts, okay, with reservations. We treasure the paintings of Grandma Moses. We glorify poets and authors who begin careers in their fifties or later. I wonder if it's endemic to the beast," he continued softly, almost as though he were speaking to himself, "a way in which humans maintain belief in our potential: Someday I'll write a brilliant novel, paint a great picture . . . a way to keep the meaninglessness of life at bay."

"We seem to have wandered a bit from Thea Janis," I said.

"Excuse me. Please."

The thought washed over me like a wave of ice water.

"She's not the missing person you talked about on the phone, is she?" I asked.

"Yes," he said. "Of course it's Thea."

"But she's been missing for—"

"Twenty-four years," he said.

"Twenty-four years!" I echoed.

"Yes," he said quite calmly. *Twenty-four years*, as if it were the same as twenty-four hours.